RANDOM HOUSE
LARGE PRINT

# THE WOLF GIFT

# THE WOLF GIFT

**A novel**

## ANNE RICE

RANDOM HOUSE
LARGE PRINT

Published in the United States of America by Random House Large Print in association with Alfred A. Knopf, New York.
Distributed by Random House, Inc., New York.

Cover photograph: iStockphoto
Cover design by Carol Devine Carson

The Library of Congress has established a Cataloging-in-Publication record for this title.

ISBN: 978-0-307-99076-1

www.randomhouse.com/largeprint

FIRST LARGE PRINT EDITION

Printed in the United States of America

10  9  8  7  6  5  4  3  2  1

This Large Print edition published in accord with the standards of the N.A.V.H.

This novel is dedicated
to
Christopher Rice,
Becket Ghioto,
Jeff Eastin,
Peter and Matthias Scheer,
and the
People of the Page

Say what you will to the force that governs the universe. Perhaps we'll call it into being, and it will yet love us as we love it.

# THE WOLF GIFT

# 1

REUBEN WAS A TALL MAN, well over six feet, with brown curly hair and deep-set blue eyes. "Sunshine Boy" was his nickname and he hated it; so he tended to repress what the world called an irresistible smile. But he was a little too happy right now to put on his studious expression, and try to look older than his twenty-three years.

He was walking up a steep hill in the fierce ocean wind with an exotic and elegant older woman named Marchent Nideck and he really loved all she was saying about the big house on the cliff. She was lean with a narrow beautifully sculpted face, and that kind of yellow hair that never fades. She wore it straight back from her forehead in a soft wavy swinging bob that curled under just above her shoulders. He loved the picture she made in her long brown knit dress and high polished brown boots.

He was doing a story for the **San Francisco Observer** on the giant house and her hopes of selling it now that the estate had at last been settled, and her great-uncle Felix Nideck had been declared officially dead. The man had been gone for twenty years, but his will had only just been opened, and the house had been left to Marchent, his niece.

They'd been walking the forested slopes of the property since Reuben arrived, visiting a ramshackle old guesthouse and the ruin of a barn. They'd followed old roads and old paths lost in the brush, and now and then come out on a rocky ledge above the cold iron-colored Pacific, only to duck back quickly into the sheltered and damp world of gnarled oak and bracken.

Reuben wasn't dressed for this, really. He'd driven north in his usual "uniform" of worsted-wool blue blazer over a thin cashmere sweater, and gray slacks. But at least he had a scarf for his neck that he'd pulled from the glove compartment. And he really didn't mind the biting cold.

The huge old house was wintry with deep slate roofs and diamond-pane windows. It was built of rough-faced stone, and had countless chimneys rising from its steep gables, and a sprawling conservatory on the west side, all white iron and glass. Reuben loved it. He'd loved it in the photographs online but nothing had prepared him for its solemn grandeur.

He'd grown up in an old house on San Francisco's Russian Hill, and spent a lot of time in the impressive old homes of Presidio Heights, and the suburbs of San Francisco, including Berkeley, where he'd gone to school, and Hillsborough, where his late grandfather's half-timbered mansion had been the holiday gathering place for many a year. But nothing he had ever seen could compare to the Nideck family home.

The sheer scale of this place, stranded as it was in its own park, suggested another world.

"The real thing," he'd said under his breath the moment he'd seen it. "Look at those slate roofs, and those must be copper gutters." Lush green vines covered over half the immense structure, reaching all the way to the highest windows, and he'd sat in his car for a long moment, kind of pleasantly astonished and a little worshipful, dreaming of owning a place like this someday when he was a famous writer and the world beat too broad a path to his door.

This was turning out to be just a glorious afternoon.

It had hurt him to see the guesthouse dilapidated and unlivable. But Marchent assured him the big house was in good repair.

He could have listened to her talk forever. Her accent wasn't British exactly, or Boston or New York. But it was unique, the accent of a child of the world, and it gave her words a lovely preciseness and silvery ring.

"Oh, I know it's beautiful. I know it's like no place else on the California coast. I know. I know. But I have no choice but to get rid of all of it," she explained. "There comes a time when a house owns you and you know you have to get free of it, and go on with the rest of your life." Marchent wanted to travel again. She confessed she'd spent precious little time here since Uncle Felix disappeared. She was headed down to South America as soon as the property was sold.

"It breaks my heart," Reuben said. That was too damn personal for a reporter, wasn't it? But he couldn't stop himself. And who said he had to be a dispassionate witness? "This is irreplaceable, Marchent. But I'll write the best story I can on the place. I'll do my best to bring you a buyer, and I can't believe it will take that long."

What he didn't say was **I wish I could buy this place myself.** And he'd been thinking about that very possibility ever since he'd first glimpsed the gables through the trees.

"I'm so glad the paper sent you, of all people," she said. "You're passionate and I like that so very much."

For one moment, he thought, Yes, I'm passionate and I want this house, and why not, and when will an opportunity like this ever come again? But then he thought of his mother and of Celeste, his petite brown-eyed girlfriend, the rising star in the district attorney's office, and how they'd laugh at the idea, and the thought went cold.

"What's wrong with you, Reuben, what's the matter?" asked Marchent. "You had the strangest look in your eye."

"Thoughts," he said, tapping his temple. "I'm writing the piece in my head. 'Architectural jewel on the Mendocino coast, first time on the market since it was built.'"

"Sounds good," she said. There was that faint accent again, of a citizen of the world.

"I'd give the house a name if I bought it," said Reuben, "you know, something that captured the essence of it. Nideck Point."

"Aren't you the young poet," she said. "I knew it when I saw you. And I like the pieces you've written for your paper. They have a distinct character. But you're writing a novel, aren't you? Any young reporter your age should be writing a novel. I'd be ashamed of you if you weren't."

"Oh, that's music to my ears," he confessed. She was so beautiful when she smiled, all the fine lines of her face seemingly so eloquent and pretty. "My father told me last week that a man of my age has absolutely nothing to say. He's a professor, burnt out, I might add. He's been revising his 'Collected Poems' for ten years, since he retired." Talking too much, talking too much about himself, not good at all.

His father might actually love this place, he thought. Yes, Phil Golding was in fact a poet and he would surely love it, and he might even say so to Reuben's mother who would scoff at the whole idea. Dr. Grace Golding was the practical one and the architect of their lives. She was the one who'd gotten Reuben his job at the **San Francisco Observer,** when his only qualification was a master's in English literature and yearly world travel since birth.

Grace had been proud of his recent investigative pieces, but she'd cautioned that this "real estate story" was a waste of his time.

"There you go again, dreaming," Marchent said. She put her arm around him and actually kissed him on the cheek as she laughed. He was startled, caught unawares by the soft pressure of her breasts against him and the subtle scent of a rich perfume.

"Actually, I haven't accomplished one single thing in my life yet," he said with an ease that shocked him. "My mother's a brilliant surgeon; my big brother's a priest. My mother's father was an international real estate broker by the time he was my age. But I'm a nothing and a nobody, actually. I've only been with the paper six months. I should have come with a warning label. But believe me, I'll make this a story you'll love."

"Rubbish," she said. "Your editor told me your story on the Greenleaf murder led to the arrest of the killer. You are the most charming and self-effacing boy."

He struggled not to blush. Why was he admitting all these things to this woman? Seldom if ever did he make self-deprecating statements. Yet he felt some immediate connection with her he couldn't explain.

"That Greenleaf story took less than a day to write," he murmured. "Half of what I turned up on the suspect never saw print at all."

She had a twinkle in her eye. "Tell me—how old are you, Reuben? I'm thirty-eight. How is that for total honesty? Do you know many women who volunteer that they're thirty-eight?"

"You don't look it," he said. And he meant it. What he wanted to say was **You're rather perfect, if you ask me.** "I'm twenty-three," he confessed.

"Twenty-three? You're just a boy."

Of course. "Sunshine Boy," as his girlfriend Celeste always called him. "Little Boy," according to his big brother, Fr. Jim. And "Baby Boy," according to his mother, who still called him that in front of people. Only his dad consistently called him Reuben and saw only him when their eyes met. **Dad, you should see this house! Talk about a place for writing, talk about a getaway, talk about a landscape for a creative mind.**

He shoved his freezing hands in his pockets and tried to ignore the sting of the wind in his eyes. They were making their way back up to the promise of hot coffee and a fire.

"And so tall for that age," she said. "I think you're uncommonly sensitive, Reuben, to appreciate this rather cold and grim corner of the earth. When I was twenty-three I wanted to be in New York and Paris. I was in New York and Paris. I wanted the capitals of the world. What, have I insulted you?"

"No, certainly not," he said. He was reddening again. "I'm talking too much about myself, Marchent. My mind's on the story, never fear. Scrub oak, high grass, damp earth, ferns, I'm recording everything."

"Ah yes, the fresh young mind and memory, nothing like it," she said. "Darling, we're going to spend two days together, aren't we? Expect me to be personal. You're ashamed of being young, aren't you? Well, you needn't be. And you're distractingly handsome, you know, why you're just about the most adorable boy I've ever seen in my entire life. No, I mean it. With looks like yours, you don't have to be much of anything, you know."

He shook his head. If she only knew. He hated it when people called him handsome, adorable, cute, to die for. "And how will you feel if they ever stop?" his girlfriend Celeste had asked him. "Ever think about that? Look, Sunshine Boy, with me, it's strictly your looks." She had a way of teasing with an edge, Celeste did. Maybe all teasing had an edge.

"Now, I really have insulted you, haven't I?" asked Marchent. "Forgive me. I think all of us ordinary mortals tend to mythologize people as good-looking as you. But of course what makes you so remarkable is that you have a poet's soul."

They had reached the edge of the flagstone terrace.

Something had changed in the air. The wind was even more cutting. The sun was indeed dying behind the silver clouds and headed for the darkening sea.

She stopped for a moment, as if to catch her breath, but he couldn't tell. The wind whipped the tendrils of her hair around her face, and she put a hand up to shelter her eyes. She looked at the high windows of the house as if searching for something, and there came over Reuben the most forlorn feeling. The loneliness of the place pressed in.

They were miles from the little town of Nideck and Nideck had, what, two hundred real inhabitants? He'd stopped there on the way in and found most of the shops on the little main street were closed. The bed-and-breakfast had been for sale "forever," said the clerk at the gas station, but yes, you have cell phone and Internet connections everywhere in the county, no need to worry about that.

Right now, the world beyond this windswept terrace seemed unreal.

"Does it have ghosts, Marchent?" he asked, following her gaze to the windows.

"It doesn't need them," she declared. "The recent history is grim enough."

"Well, I love it," he said. "The Nidecks were people of remarkable vision. Something tells me you'll get a very romantic buyer, one who can transform it into a unique and unforgettable hotel."

"Now that's a thought," she said. "But why would anyone come here, in particular, Reuben? The beach is narrow and hard to reach. The redwoods are glorious but you don't have to drive four hours from San Francisco to reach glorious redwoods in California. And you saw the town. There is nothing here really except Nideck Point, as you call it. I have a suffocating feeling sometimes that this house won't be standing much longer."

"Oh, no! Let's not even think of that. Why, no one would dare——."

She took his arm again and they moved on over

the sandy flags, past his car, and towards the distant front door. "I'd fall in love with you if you were my age," she said. "If I'd met anyone quite as charming as you, I wouldn't be alone now, would I?"

"Why would a woman like you ever have to be alone?" he asked. He had seldom met someone so confident and graceful. Even now after the trek in the woods, she looked as collected and groomed as a woman shopping on Rodeo Drive. There was a thin little bracelet around her left wrist, a pearl chain, he believed they called it, and it gave her easy gestures an added glamour. He couldn't quite tell why.

There were no trees to the west of them. The view was open for all the obvious reasons. But the wind was positively howling off the ocean now, and the gray mist was descending on the last sparkle of the sea. I'll get the mood of all this, he thought. I'll get this strange darkening moment. And a little shadow fell deliciously over his soul.

He wanted this place. Maybe it would have been better if they'd sent someone else to do this story, but they'd sent him. What remarkable luck.

"Good Lord, it's getting colder by the second," she said as they hurried. "I forget the way the temperature drops on the coast here. I grew up with it, but I'm always taken by surprise." Yet she stopped once more and looked up at the towering façade of the house as though she was searching for someone, and then she shaded her eyes and looked out into the advancing mist.

Yes, she may come to regret selling this place terribly, he thought. But then again, she may have to. And who was he to make her feel the pain of that if she didn't want to address it herself?

For a moment, he was keenly ashamed that he himself had the money to buy the property and he felt he should make some disclaimer, but that would have been unspeakably rude. Nevertheless, he was calculating and dreaming.

The clouds were darkening, lowering. And the air was very damp. He followed her gaze again to the great shadowy façade of the house, with those diamond-pane windows twinkling dimly, and at the masses of redwood trees that rose behind it and to the east, a monstrous soaring forest of coastal sequoia out of proportion with all else.

"Tell me," she said. "What are your thoughts right now?"

"Oh, nothing, really. I was thinking about the redwoods and the way they always make me feel. They're so out of proportion to everything around them. It's as if they're always saying, 'We were here before your kind ever visited these shores, and we will be here when you and your houses are no more.'"

There was something unmistakably tragic in her eyes as she smiled at him. "That's so true. How my uncle Felix loved them," she said. "They're protected, you know, those trees. They can't be logged. Uncle Felix saw to that."

"Thank heavens," he whispered. "I shudder when

I see all those old photographs of the loggers up here in the old days, chopping down redwoods that had been alive for a thousand years. Think of it, a thousand years."

"That's precisely what Uncle Felix said once, damn near word for word."

"He wouldn't want to see this house torn down, would he?" He was immediately ashamed. "I'm sorry. I shouldn't have said that."

"Oh, but you're absolutely right. He wouldn't have wanted it, no, never. He loved this house. He was in the process of restoring it when he disappeared."

She looked off again, wistfully, longingly.

"And we'll never know, I don't suppose," she said, sighing.

"What is that, Marchent?"

"Oh, you know, how my great-uncle actually disappeared." She made a soft derisive sound. "We are all such superstitious creatures, really. Disappeared! Well, I suppose he is as dead in real life as he is legally. But it seems I'm giving up on him now in selling the old place, that I'm saying, 'Well, we will never know and he will never come through that door there again.'"

"I understand," he whispered. The fact was he knew absolutely nothing about death. His mother and father and brother and girlfriend told him that in one way or another just about every day. His mother lived and breathed the Trauma Center at San Francisco General. His girlfriend knew absolutely the

worst side of human nature from the cases she handled in the D.A.'s office every day. As for his father,
he saw death in the falling leaves.

Reuben had written six articles and covered two
murders in his time at the **San Francisco Observer.**
And both the women in his life had praised his writing to the skies, and lectured him at length on what
he failed to grasp.

Something his father said came back to him.
"You're innocent, Reuben, yes, but life will teach
you what you need to know soon enough." Phil was
always making rather unusual pronouncements. He
said at dinner last night, "Not a day goes by, when I
don't ask a cosmic question. Does life have meaning?
Or is this all smoke and mirrors? Are we all doomed?"

"You know, Sunshine Boy, I know why nothing
really penetrates with you," Celeste had said later.
"Your mother talks in detail about her surgeries over
shrimp cocktail, and your father will only talk about
what absolutely does not matter at all. I'll take your
easy brand of optimism any day. The fact is, you
make me feel good."

Had that made him feel good? No. Not at all. But
the strange thing about Celeste was that she was far
more affectionate and kindly than her words ever indicated. She was a killer of an attorney, a five-foot-two
firebrand on the job, but with him, she was cuddly
and downright sweet. She fussed over his clothes, and
always answered her phone. She had lawyer friends
on speed dial to answer any questions he encoun-

tered in his reporting. But her tongue? Her tongue was a little sharp.

The fact is, Reuben thought suddenly, secretively, there is something dark and tragic about this house that I want to know. The house made him think of cello music, deep, rich, a little rough, and uncompromising. The house was talking to him, or maybe it would talk to him if he'd stop listening to the voices of home.

He felt his cell phone vibrate in his pocket. Without taking his eyes off the house, he turned it off.

"Oh good gracious, look at you," said Marchent. "You're freezing, dear boy. How utterly thoughtless of me. Come, we must get you inside."

"I'm a San Francisco kid," he muttered. "I've slept all my life on Russian Hill with the window wide open. I should have been prepared."

He followed her up the stone steps, and through the massive arched front door.

The warmth of the room was immediate and delicious, even though it was a vast space, under a high beamed ceiling, its dark oak floors stretching on forever in a kind of airy gloom.

The blazing fireplace was distant but cavernous, facing them directly from across a dark expanse of rather shapeless old couches and chairs.

He'd smelled the oak logs burning earlier, just a whiff here and there as they'd walked on the hillside, and he'd loved that.

She led him to the velvet couch right beside the

hearth. There was a silver coffee service on the large marble coffee table.

"You get warm," she said. And she stood there herself before the flames warming her hands.

There were huge old brass andirons and a fender, and the bricks on the back of the fireplace were black.

She turned and moved about almost silently on the old worn Oriental carpets, turning on the many scattered lamps.

Slowly the room took on a cheerful glow.

The furniture was immense, but comfortable, with worn but serviceable slipcovers and occasional caramel-colored leather chairs. There were a few hulking bronze sculptures, all of predictable mythological figures, very old-fashioned. And a number of dark landscapes in heavy gilt frames hanging here and there.

The warmth was now relentless. In a few minutes he would be taking off his scarf and his coat.

He looked up at the old dark wood paneling above the fireplace, rectangles neatly trimmed in deeply carved egg-and-dart molding, and at the similar paneling that covered the walls. There were bookcases flanking the fireplace, stuffed with old volumes, leather, cloth, even paperbacks, and far to the right over his shoulder he glimpsed an east-facing room that looked like a vintage paneled library, the kind he'd always dreamed of having for himself. There was a fire in there too.

"It takes my breath away," he said. He could see his

father sitting here, shuffling his poems as he made his endless notes. Yes, he would love this place, no doubt of it. It was the place for cosmic reflections and decisions. And how shocked everybody would be if—.

And why wouldn't his mother be glad? They loved each other, his mother and father, but they did not get along. Phil tolerated Grace's doctor friends; and Grace found his few old academic friends an absolute bore. Poetry reading made her furious on general principles. The movies he liked she abhorred. If he spoke his opinion at a dinner party, she changed the subject with the person next to her, or left the room for another bottle of wine, or started to cough.

It wasn't deliberate, really. His mom wasn't mean. His mom was full of enthusiasm for the things she loved, and she adored Reuben and he knew this had given him a confidence many people never enjoyed. It was just that she couldn't stand her husband, and for most of his life Reuben had actually understood.

It was harder to take these days, however, because his mom seemed powerful and timeless, a compulsive worker with a divine vocation; and his father seemed now worn out and obscenely old. Celeste had become his mom's fast friend ("We are both driven women!") and sometime lunch companion, but she ignored the "old man," as she called him. And now and then she even said ominously to Reuben, "Look, do you want to turn out like him?"

Well, how would you like to live here, Dad, Reuben thought. And we'd go walking in the redwoods together, and maybe fix up that old dilapidated guest-house for the poet friends, but of course there's room for all of them in the house, why you could have a regular seminar up here with them anytime you wanted, and Mom could come up when she chose.

That would be never, most likely.

Oh, hell, he couldn't work out the fantasy right now, could he? Marchent was looking sadly into the fire, and he should be asking questions. "Let me get this straight," Celeste would say, "I work seven days a week and you're supposed to be a reporter now and you're going to, what, drive four hours a day to get to work?"

This would be for Celeste the final disappointment, the first being that he didn't know who he was. She'd gone through law school like a rocket and passed the bar at age twenty-two. He'd quit the English Ph.D. program over the foreign-language requirements, and really didn't have a life plan at all. Wasn't it his right to listen to opera, read poetry and adventure novels, go to Europe every couple of months for some reason or another, and drive his Porsche over the speed limit until he found out who he was? He'd asked that once, in just those words, and she'd laughed. They'd both laughed. "Nice work if you can get it, Sunshine Boy," she said. "I'm due in court."

Marchent was tasting the coffee. "Hot enough," she said.

She filled a china cup with coffee for him and gestured to the silver cream pitcher, and the little pile of sugar cubes in the silver dish. All of it so pretty, so nice. And Celeste would think, How dreary, and his mother might not notice at all. Grace had an aversion to all matters domestic, except festive cooking. Celeste said kitchens were for storing Diet Coke. His father would like it—his father had a general fund of knowledge about all manner of things, including silver and china, the history of the fork, holiday customs the world over, the evolution of fashion, cuckoo clocks, whales, wines, and architectural styles. His private nickname for himself was "Miniver Cheevy."

But the point was Reuben liked all this. Reuben loved it. Reuben was Reuben, and Reuben liked the great stone mantelpiece with its scroll supports very much as well.

"So what are you writing in your poetic head just now?" Marchent asked.

"Hmmm. The ceiling beams, they're enormous, and just possibly the longest ceiling beams I've ever seen. The carpets are Persian, all floral designs, except for the little prayer rug there. And there are no evil spirits under this roof."

"'No bad vibrations' is what you mean," she said. "And I agree with you. But I'm sure you realize that I would never be able to stop grieving for Uncle Felix if I stayed on. He was a titan of a man. I'll tell you, it's all come back to me, Felix and his disappearing, I mean, I hadn't brooded over it all for some time. I was eighteen when he walked out that door for the Middle East."

"Why the Middle East?" he asked. "Where was he headed?"

"An archaeological dig, that was often the reason for his trips. That last time it was in Iraq, something about a new city, as old as Mari or Uruk. I could never get any corroboration that sounded right. Anyway, he was unusually excited about where he was going, I remember that. He'd been talking on the phone long-distance to his friends all over the world. I didn't think much of it. He was always going, and always coming back. If it wasn't a dig, then he was off to some foreign library to look at a fragment of manuscript that had just been unearthed in some unpublished collection by one of his many students. He paid them by the dozens. They were always sending information. He lived in his own fully detached and lively world."

"He must have left papers behind," said Reuben, "a man engaged in all that."

"Papers! Reuben, you have no idea. There are rooms upstairs that are filled with nothing but papers, manuscripts, binders, crumbling books. There is so much to be gone through, so many decisions to be made. But if the house sells tomorrow, I'm ready to ship it all to climate-controlled storage and work with it from there."

"Was he searching for something, something in particular?"

"Well, if he was, he never said. One time he did say, 'This world needs witnesses. Too much is lost.'

But I think it was a general complaint. He financed digs, I know that. And often met with archaeology students and history students who didn't work for him. I recall them coming and going here. He would give out his own little private grants."

"What a great thing," Reuben said, "to live like that."

"Well, he had the money, as I well know now. There was never any doubt he was rich, but I didn't know how rich until everything came to me. Come, shall we have a look around?"

How he loved the library.

But it was one of those showplace rooms in which no one ever wrote a letter or read a book. Marchent confessed as much. The old French desk was exquisitely polished and its brass ormolu as bright as gold. It had a clean green blotter, and the floor-to-ceiling shelves were filled with the inevitable classics in leather binding that would have made them awkward to carry in a knapsack or read on a plane.

There was the **Oxford English Dictionary** in twenty volumes, an old **Encyclopaedia Britannica,** massive art tomes, atlases, and thick old volumes whose gilded titles had been worn away.

An awe-inspiring room. He saw his father at the desk watching as the light faded from the leaded windows, or sitting in the velvet-padded window seat with a book. The eastern windows of the house along that wall must have been thirty feet wide.

Too dark now to see the trees. In the morning, he'd come into this room early. And if he bought this house, he'd give this room to Phil. In fact, he could bait his father with a description of all this. He noted the oak parquet with its huge intricate inlaid squares, and the ancient railroad clock on the wall.

Red velvet draperies hung from brass rods, and a great large photograph hung over the mantel, of a group of six men, all in safari khaki, gathered together against a backdrop of banana and tropical trees.

It had to have been taken with sheet film. The detail was superb. Only now in the digital age could you blow up a photo to that size without degrading it hopelessly. But this had never been retouched. Even the banana leaves looked engraved. You could see the finest wrinkles in the men's jackets, and the dust on their boots.

Two of the men had rifles, and several stood quite casually and free with nothing in their hands at all.

"I had that made," Marchent said. "Quite expensive. I didn't want a painting, only an accurate enlargement. It's four by six feet. You see the figure in the middle? That's Uncle Felix. That is the only really current picture I had of him before he disappeared."

Reuben drew closer to look at it.

The names of the men were inscribed in black ink across the mat border just inside the frame. He could barely read them.

Marchent turned on the chandelier for him and

now he could see plainly the figure of Felix, the dark-skinned and dark-haired man who stood near the middle of the group, a very agreeable-looking figure really, with a fine tall physique, and the same lean graceful hands he admired so in Marchent, and even something of the same very gentle smile. A likable man surely, an approachable man, with a near-childlike expression: curious, enthusiastic perhaps. He looked to be anywhere from twenty to about thirty-five.

The other men were undeniably interesting, all with rather abstracted and serious expressions, and one in particular stood out, to the far left. He was tall like the others and he wore his dark hair shoulder length. If it hadn't been for the safari jacket and the khaki pants, he might have looked like an Old West buffalo hunter with that long hair. There was positive radiance to his face—rather like one of those dreamy figures in a Rembrandt painting who seems touched at a particular mystical moment by a key light from God.

"Oh, yes, him," said Marchent rather dramatically. "Isn't he something? Well, that was Felix's closest friend and mentor. Margon Sperver. But Uncle Felix always called him just Margon and sometimes Margon the Godless, though why in the world he called him that I don't know. It always made Margon laugh. Margon was the teacher, said Felix. If Uncle Felix couldn't answer a question, he'd say, 'Well, maybe the teacher knows,' and off he would go to find Margon the Godless by phone wherever he was in the world. There are thousands of photographs of these gentlemen in the rooms upstairs—Sergei, Margon, Frank Vandover—all of them. They were his closest associates."

"And you couldn't reach any of them after he disappeared?"

"Not a single one. But understand. We didn't start trying for about a year. We expected to hear from him any day. His trips could be very short, but then he'd vanish, you know, just drop off the charts. He'd go off into Ethiopia or India beyond anyone's reach. One time he called from an island in the South Pacific after a full year and a half. My father sent a plane to get him. And no, I never found a single one of them, including Margon the Teacher, and that was the saddest part of all."

She sighed. She seemed very tired now. In a small voice, she added: "At first my father didn't try very hard. He came into a lot of money right after Felix disappeared. He was happy for the first time. I don't think he wanted to be reminded about Felix. 'Felix, always Felix,' he would say whenever I asked questions. He and my mother wanted to enjoy the new legacy—something from an aunt, I believe." This was costing her, this painful confession.

He reached out slowly, giving her full warning, and then put his arm around her and kissed her cheek just the polite way that she had kissed him earlier that afternoon.

She turned and melted against him for a moment, kissing him on the lips quickly and then said again that he was the most charming boy.

"It's a heartbreaking story," he said.

"You are such a strange boy, so young yet so old at the same time."

"I hope so," he said.

"And there's that smile. Why do you hide that smile?"

"Do I?" he asked. "I'm sorry."

"Oh, you're right, you certainly are. It's a heart-breaking story." She looked again at the photograph. "That's Sergei," she said, pointing to a tall blond-haired man, a man with pale eyes who seemed to be dreaming or lost in his thoughts. "I suppose I knew him the best. I didn't really know the others that well at all. At first, I thought sure I'd find Margon. But the numbers I found were for hotels in Asia and the Middle East. And they knew him, of course, but they had no idea where he was. I called every hotel in Cairo and Alexandria looking for Margon. As I recall, we tried every place in Damascus too. They'd spent a lot of time in Damascus, Margon and Uncle Felix. Something to do with an ancient monastery, newly unearthed manuscripts. In fact, all those finds are still upstairs. I know where they are."

"Ancient manuscripts? Here? They could be price-less," said Reuben.

"Oh, they probably are, but not to me. To me they're a huge responsibility. What do I do with them to see they're preserved? What would he want done with them? He was so critical of museums and libraries. Where would he want all this to go? Of course his old students would love to see these things, they've never stopped calling and asking, but such affairs have to be carefully managed. The treasures should be archived and under supervision."

"Oh, yes, I know, I've spent my time in the libraries of Berkeley and Stanford," he said. "Did he publish? I mean did he publish his finds?"

"Never to my knowledge," she said.

"You think Margon and Felix were together on this last trip?"

She nodded.

"Whatever happened," she said, "it happened to them together. My worst fear is that it happened to them all."

"All six of them?"

"Yes. Because none of them ever called here looking for Felix. At least not that I ever knew. No more letters from any of them ever came. Before there had often been letters. I had a devil of a time finding the letters, and when I did, well, I couldn't make out the addresses and all turned out to be dead ends. The point is none of them ever contacted anyone here, looking for Uncle Felix, ever. And that's why I'm afraid whatever it was it happened to them all."

"So you couldn't find any of them, and they never wrote again to him?"

"That's it exactly," she said.

"Felix left no itinerary, no written plans?"

"Oh, yes, probably he did, but you see, no one could read his personal writing. He had a language all his own. Well, actually they all used that language, or so it seems from some of the notes and letters I later found. They didn't always use it. But apparently they all could. Wasn't in the English alphabet. I'll show you some of it later. I even hired a computer genius to crack it a few years ago. Couldn't get to first base."

"Extraordinary. You know all this will fascinate my readers. Marchent, this could become a tourist attraction."

"But you saw the old articles about Uncle Felix. It's been written about before."

"But the old articles talk only about Felix, not his friends. They don't really have all these details. I see this as a three-part story already."

"Sounds marvelous," she said. "You do exactly as you please with it. And who knows? Maybe someone out there might know something about what became of them. One never really knows."

Now that was an exciting thought, but he knew not to push it. She'd been living with this tragedy for twenty years.

She led him slowly out of the room.

Reuben glanced back at the agreeable gathering of gentlemen who stared back so placidly from the framed photo. And if I buy this place, he thought, I'll never take that picture down. That is, if she lets me keep it or make a copy of it. I mean shouldn't Felix Nideck remain in some form in this house?

"You wouldn't share that picture with whoever bought the place, would you?"

"Oh, very likely," she said. "I do have smaller copies, after all. You know all this furniture is included." She gestured as they moved across the great room. "Did I say that already? Come, I want to show you the conservatory. It's almost time for dinner. Felice is deaf and nearly blind but she does everything by a clock in her head."

"I can smell it," he said as they crossed the big room. "Delicious."

"There's a girl up from the town helping her. Seems these kids will work for almost nothing just to have a little experience here in this house. I'm starving myself."

The western conservatory was filled with dead plants in colorful old Oriental pots. The white metal framework, holding up the high glass dome, reminded Reuben of bleached bones. There was an old dried fountain in the middle of the soiled black granite floor. This Reuben had to see again in the morning, with the light streaming in from three directions. Right now, it was so damp and cold.

"You can see out that way when the weather's pleasant," Marchent said, pointing to the French doors, "and I remember a party once where people were actually dancing in here, and drifting out there on the terrace. There's a balustrade right at the cliff's edge. Felix's friends were all there. Sergei Gorlagon was singing in Russian, and everyone so loved it. And of course Uncle Felix was having a fabulous time. He adored his friend Sergei. Sergei was a giant of a man. And there was no one quite like Uncle Felix at a large party. Such a vivacious spirit, and how he loved to dance. And my father was skulking about mumbling about the expense." She shrugged. "I'll try to get the place all cleaned up. Should have done it before you arrived."

"I can see it clearly," said Reuben, "filled with potted orange trees and banana palms, and great towering weeping ficus and maybe orchid trees and flowering vines. I'd read the morning papers in here."

She was delighted, obviously. She laughed.

"No, darling, you would read the morning papers in the library which is the morning room. You'd drift in here in the afternoon when the western sun floods the room. Whatever made you think of orchid trees? Ah, orchid trees. And in summer you'd hang about in the early evening here until the sun sinks into the sea."

"I love orchid trees," Reuben confessed. "I've seen them in the Caribbean. I guess all us northern people crave tropic climes. One time we stayed in this small hotel in New Orleans, one of those bed-and-breakfast hotels in the Quarter, and there were orchid trees on either side of the swimming pool, actually dripping purple petals into the water, just a whole sweep of purple petals on the water, and I thought it was the loveliest thing."

"You should have a house like this, you know," she said. A shadow darkened her face, but only for a second. Then she smiled again and squeezed his hand.

They only glanced into the white-paneled music room. The floor there was white-painted wood, and the grand piano, Marchent said, had been long ago ruined by the damp and taken away. "These painted walls in here, all this came right out of some house in France."

"I can believe it," he said admiring the deeply carved borders and faded floral decorations. Now, this was something Celeste would approve of, because Celeste loved music, and often played the piano when she was alone. She didn't attach much importance to her own playing, but now and then Reuben had awakened to hear her playing the small spinet in her apartment. Yes, this she would like.

The great shadowy dining room was a surprise.

"This isn't a dining room," he declared. "It's a banquet room, a mead hall, to say the very least."

"Oh, indeed, it used to be a ballroom in the old days," Marchent said. "The whole country round came to the balls here. There was a ball even when I was a child."

The dark paneling prevailed here as in the great room, as lustrous and beautiful under a high-coffered ceiling of myriad plaster squares scoring a ceiling painted dark blue with bright stars. It was a bold decoration. And it worked.

His heart was beating.

They made their way to the table. It was easily twenty feet long and yet it seemed small in this great space, floating on the dark polished floor.

They sat down opposite each other in red velvet high-backed chairs.

Two massive black wooden hunters' boards stood against the wall behind Marchent, both identically carved with rich Renaissance figures, hunters with their retinue, and piled with heavy silver platters and goblets and stacks of what appeared to be yellow linen, napkins perhaps.

Other imposing pieces loomed in the shadow, what seemed an immense armoire, and a number of old chests.

The fireplace was huge and Gothic, of black marble and replete with solemn-faced helmeted medieval knights. The hearth was high with a medieval battle scene carved in its base. Now surely Reuben would get a well-illuminated photograph of that.

Two baroque candelabra provided the only light, other than the crackling fire.

"You look like a prince at this table," Marchent said with a light laugh. "You look as if you belong."

"You have to be teasing me," he said, "and you look like the grand duchess in this candlelight. I think we are in a Viennese hunting lodge here, not in California at all."

"You've been to Vienna?"

"Many times," he said. He thought of Phil leading him through Maria Theresa's palace there, discoursing on everything from the painted walls to the great ornate enameled stoves. Yes, Phil would love this place. Phil would understand.

They dined on old lavishly painted china, some of it chipped, but still incomparable. And the silver was the heaviest he'd ever used.

Felice, a small shrunken woman with white hair and very dark skin, came and went without a word. "The girl" from the village—Nina—was a robust brown-haired little person who seemed a bit in awe of Marchent, the dining room, and every plate she brought to the table on a silver charger. Amid nervous giggles and sighs, she grinned at Reuben as she hurried out of the room.

"You have a fan," Marchent whispered.

The filet roast was perfect, the vegetables extraordinarily fresh and crisp, and the salad perfectly done with light oil and herbs.

Reuben drank a little more of the red wine than he planned to drink, but it was so smooth, and had that dark smoky taste he associated entirely with the best vintages. He really didn't know wine.

He was eating like a pig. That's what he did when he was happy, and he was happy, remarkably happy.

Marchent talked about the history of the house, the part he'd already researched.

Her great-grandfather—the founding Felix—had been a lumber baron in these parts, and built two sawmills along the coast, along with a small harbor, now gone, for his ships. He'd had the lumber for this house milled and planed on the site, and brought a good deal of the marble and granite up the coast by boat. The stones for the walls of the house came over land and by boat.

"All the Nidecks had European money, apparently," Marchent said, "and they made plenty of money here."

Though Uncle Felix had had the bulk of the family wealth, Marchent's father, Abel, had still owned all the shops in the town when she was growing up. Nearby beachfront lots south of the property had been sold off before she went away to college, but few people had ever really built on that land.

"All that happened while Felix was gone on one of his long trips, my father selling the shops and the beachfront lots, and Felix was so angry when he came back. I recall their arguing about it furiously. But it couldn't be undone." She grew sad. "I wish my father hadn't resented Uncle Felix so much. Maybe if he hadn't, if we'd looked for Uncle Felix sooner. But all that is long past."

The property still comprised forty-seven acres including the protected old-growth redwoods behind the house, and a great many live oaks, and the wooded slopes down to the beach all along the western flank. There was an old tree house out there in the forest, built by Felix, and remarkably high up. "I've never actually been in it," Marchent said. "But my little brothers said it was quite luxurious. Of course they should never have been in it before Felix was officially declared dead."

Marchent really didn't know much about the family other than what everybody knew. They were part of the history of the county. "I think they had money in oil and in diamonds, and in property in Switzerland." She shrugged.

Her trust funds were all conventional investments managed in New York. Same with her younger brothers.

With the settling of Uncle Felix's will had come the revelation of a great deal of money in the Bank of America and the Wells Fargo Bank, more than Marchent had ever expected.

"So you don't need to sell this place," Reuben said.

"I need to sell it to be free," she said. She paused, closed her eyes for a second, and then, making a little fist with her right hand, she tapped her breast. "I need to know that it's over, you see. And then there are my younger brothers." Her face changed, and so did her voice. "They've been bought off not to contest the will." Again came one of her little shrugs, but she looked faintly sad. "They want their 'share.'"

Reuben nodded, but he really didn't understand.

**I'm going to try to buy this place.**

He knew that now, no matter how daunting, no matter how expensive to fix up, to warm up, to maintain. There are times when one simply cannot say no.

But first things first.

She started talking finally about the accident that had killed her parents. They'd been flying back from Las Vegas. Her father was an excellent pilot, and it was a trip they'd made a hundred times.

"They probably never even knew what happened," she said. "It was the most unfortunate thing that they would fly right into that electric tower in the fog."

Marchent had been twenty-eight at the time. Felix had been gone for ten years. She became the guardian of her two younger brothers. "I think I made a mess of it," she said. "They were never the same after the accident. From there on out, it was drugs and booze for them, and the most disreputable friends. I wanted to go back to Paris. I didn't spend enough time with them, then or ever. And they just went from bad to worse."

A year apart, sixteen and seventeen at the time of the accident, they were more like twins, secretive with a personal language of smirks, sneers, and murmurs that few could penetrate or tolerate for very long.

"There were some very fine Impressionist paintings in this room until a few years ago," she said. "My brothers stole them, came up when no one was here but Felice, and sold them off for a pittance. I was furious. But I simply couldn't get them back. I found out later they'd taken some of the silver as well."

"That must have been very discouraging," he said.

She laughed. "It certainly was. The tragedy is these things are gone forever and what did the boys get out of it? A drunken bash in Sausalito raided by the local police."

Felice drifted in, silent, seemingly fragile and unsteady, yet efficiently cleared the plates. Marchent slipped out to pay "the girl," and soon came back.

"Has Felice always been with you?" Reuben asked.

"Oh, yes, along with her son who died last year. He was the man of the place, of course. He managed everything. How he hated my brothers, but then they set fire to the guesthouse twice, and wrecked more than one car. I've hired a couple of men since but it never worked out. There's no man on the place just now. Just old Mr. Galton, down the road, but he contracts for anything and everything we need. You might mention that in your article. Mr. Galton knows this house inside and out. He knows the forest, too. I'm taking Felice with me when I go. There's nothing else to be done."

She paused only long enough for Felice to bring in the dessert of raspberry sherry in crystal glasses.

"Felix brought Felice here from Jamaica," she

said, "along with a load of Jamaican curios and art. He was always coming through the door with some treasure—an Olmec statue, a colonial oil painting from Brazil, a mummified cat. Wait till you see the galleries and storerooms upstairs. There are tablets up there, ancient clay tablets by the boxful—."

"Tablets, you mean actual ancient Mesopotamian tablets? You're talking cuneiform, Babylon, all that?"

She laughed. "I certainly am."

"That has to be priceless," Reuben said. "And that would be worth a story in itself. I have to see those fragments. You will show them to me, won't you? Look, I won't put all this into the story. It would be too distracting. We want the house sold of course, but . . ."

"I'll show you everything," she said. "It's a pleasure. Quite a surprising pleasure actually. It doesn't all seem so impossible now that we're talking about it."

"Look, maybe I could be of assistance in some way, formally, or informally. I did a little time in the field during my summers at Berkeley," he said. "My mother's idea. She said if her boy wasn't going to be a doctor, well, he had to be an educated man. She signed me up for several different trips."

"And you liked that sort of thing."

"I wasn't patient enough for it," he confessed. "But I did enjoy it. I got to spend some time at Çatal Höyük in Turkey—that's one of the oldest sites in the world."

"Oh, yes, I've been there," she observed. "That is simply marvelous," she said. Her face brightened. "And did you see Göbekli Tepe?"

"I did," he said. "The summer before I left Berkeley, I went to Göbekli Tepe. I wrote a piece about it for a journal. Helped me get the job I have now. Seriously, I'd love to see all these treasures. I'd love to play some role in what happens, that is, if that's what you want. How about a separate article, one that wouldn't be published until everything was safely out of here, but you know, a piece on the heritage of Felix Nideck. Is that something you'd like?"

She reflected for a moment, her eyes very calm. "More than I can say," she answered.

It was thrilling to see her interest. Celeste always cut him off when he talked about his archaeological adventures. "I mean, like, where did all that get you, Reuben? What did you take away from those digs?"

"Did you ever want to be a doctor like your mother?" Marchent asked.

Reuben laughed. "I can't remember scientific information," he said. "I can quote you Dickens and Shakespeare and Chaucer and Stendhal, but I can't retain anything about string theory or DNA or black holes in space. Not that I haven't tried. I couldn't possibly have been a doctor. Besides, I fainted once at the sight of blood."

Marchent laughed, but it was a gentle laugh.

"My mother's a trauma center surgeon. She operates five or six times a day."

"And she has been disappointed that you didn't go into medicine, of course."

"A little, more in my older brother, Jim, than me. His becoming a priest was quite a blow. We're Catholic, of course. But that was something my mother had simply never dreamt of, and I have my theory why he did it, you know, the psychological angle, but the truth is, he's a fine priest. He's stationed in San Francisco. He works at St. Francis at Gubbio Church in the Tenderloin, and runs a dining room for the homeless. He works harder than my mother. And they're the hardest-working two people I know." And Celeste would be the third-hardest-working person, wouldn't she?

They talked on about the digs. Reuben had never been one for details, didn't get very far examining potsherds, but he loved what he did learn. He was eager to see the clay tablets.

They talked of other things. Marchent's "failure," as she put it, with her brothers who were never interested in the house or in Felix or in the things that Felix left behind.

"I didn't know what to do after the accident," Marchent said. She rose and wandered towards the fireplace. She poked at the flames, and the fire flared bright again. "The boys had already been through five different boarding schools. Kicked out for drinking. Kicked out for drugs. Kicked out for selling drugs."

She came back to the table. Felice shuffled in with another fifth of the superb wine.

Marchent went on, her voice low and confiding and amazingly trusting.

"I think they've been in every rehab in the country," she said, "and a few overseas as well. They know just what to tell the judge to get sent to rehab, and just what to tell the therapists when they're inside. It's amazing the way they win the doctors' trust. And of course they load up on all the psychiatric meds they can before they're discharged."

She looked up suddenly. "Reuben, you will not write about this ever," she said.

"Unthinkable," he replied. "But Marchent, most journalists can't be trusted. You do know that, don't you?"

"I suppose," she said.

"I had a good friend at Berkeley who died of an overdose. That's how I met my girlfriend, Celeste. He was her brother. Anyway, he had everything, you know, and the drugs just got him, and he died like a dog, in a barroom toilet. Nobody could do a thing."

Sometimes he thought that it was Willie's death that bound them together, him and Celeste, or at least it had for a while. Celeste had gone on from Berkeley to Stanford Law School, and passed the bar as soon as she finished. Willie's death gave the affair a certain gravity, a musical accompaniment in the minor key.

"We don't know why people go that route," Reuben said. "Willie was brilliant, but he was an addict. He was there to stay while his friends were just passing through."

"That's it, exactly. I must have done every drug myself that my brothers ever did. But somehow these things didn't appeal."

"I'm with you," he said.

"Of course they're furious that everything was left to me. But they were little children when Uncle Felix went away. He would have changed his will to take care of them, had he ever come home."

"Didn't they have money from your parents?"

"Oh, definitely. And from grandparents and great-grandparents before them. They went through it with breathtaking speed, giving parties here for hundreds of people, and financing rock bands of druggies like themselves who hadn't a chance of success. They drive drunk, crash the cars and somehow walk away without a scratch. One of these days they'll kill somebody, or kill themselves."

She explained that she would settle quite a lot on them as soon as the property was sold. She didn't have to do it, but she would. The bank would dole it out so that they didn't blow it all as they'd done their inheritance. But they didn't like any of this. As for the house, it had no sentimental value to them whatsoever, and if they thought they could fence Felix's collectibles, they would have stolen them all a long time ago.

"The fact is, they don't know the value of most of the treasures hidden in this house. They break a lock now and then and abscond with some pedestrian item. But mostly, it's extortion—you know, drunken calls in the middle of the night, threatening suicide, and I usually end up sooner or later writing a big check. They bear with the lectures, the tears, and the advice for the money. And then they're gone again, off to the Caribbean, or Hawaii, or down to Los Angeles on another bender. I think their latest scheme is to break into the pornography business. They've found a starlet that they're cultivating. If she's underage they may end up in prison, and perhaps that's inevitable. Our lawyers certainly think so. But we all behave as if there's hope."

Her eyes moved over the room. He could not imagine how it looked to her. He knew how it looked to him, and that he would never forget her as she looked now in the light of the candles, her face slightly flushed from the wine, her lips very red, it seemed, and smoke-colored eyes flashing in the light of the fire.

"What gets me is they were never curious about things, never interested in Felix, never interested in anything, really—not music, not art, not history."

"I can't imagine it," he said.

"But that's what's so refreshing about you, Reuben. You don't have the hard-boiled cynicism of the young." She was still looking around, eyes a little restless as they moved over the dark sideboard, the dark marble mantel, and once again over the round iron chandelier that had not been lighted, its stubby wax candles covered in dust.

"We had such times in this room," she said. "Uncle Felix promised to take me so many places. We had such plans. I had to finish college first, he was adamant. And then we were going to travel the world."

"Are you going to feel a crashing grief when you sell this place?" Reuben ventured. "Okay, I'm a little drunk, not much. But really, will you regret this? How can you not?"

"It's finished here, dear boy," she said. "I wish you could see my house is Buenos Aires. No. This is a pilgrimage, this trip. There's nothing here for me now but loose ends."

He wanted suddenly to say, **Look, I'm buying this place. And Marchent, you can come here, anytime, stay as long as you like.** Pompous nonsense. How his mother would laugh.

"Come," she said. "It's nine o'clock, can you believe it? We'll see what we can upstairs, and leave the rest for the light of day."

They visited a chain of interesting wallpapered bedrooms, and old-fashioned tiled bathrooms with pedestal sinks and claw-foot tubs. There were American antiques galore, and some European pieces, as well. The rooms were spacious, comfortable, inviting no matter how dusty or faded or cold.

And finally, she opened the door to "one of Felix's libraries," more a huge study, really, with blackboards and bulletin boards and walls and walls of books.

"Nothing's been changed in twenty years," she said. She pointed to all the photographs, newspaper clippings, and faded notes tacked up on the boards, and the writing still visible on the blackboards after all this time.

"Why, this is incredible."

"Yes, because, you see, Felice thinks he's coming home, and there were times when I certainly thought so too. I didn't dare touch anything. When I found out the boys had been here and stolen things, I went wild."

"I saw the double locks."

"Yes, well. It came down to that. And the alarm system, though I don't think Felice really sets it when I'm not here."

"These books, these books are in Arabic, aren't they?" he said as he moved along the shelves. "And what's this, I don't even know what this is."

"I don't either," she said. "He wanted me to learn all the languages he knew but I didn't share the knack. He could learn any language. He could almost read people's minds."

"Well, this is Italian, of course, and this is Portuguese."

He paused at the desk. "This is his diary, isn't it?"

"Well, some sort of diary or workbook. I would imagine he took his latest diary with him when he left."

The blue-lined page was covered with curious writing. Only the date was clear and in English: "August 1, 1991."

"Right where he left it," Marchent said. "Now what do you think that language can be? The people who've studied it have several different opinions. It's a Middle Eastern tongue almost certainly, but not derived from Arabic, at least not directly. And there are symbols all through the writing that no one can recognize at all."

"Impenetrable," he murmured.

The inkwell was dried up. A fountain pen lay there, with a name inscribed on it in gold. FELIX NIDECK. And there was a framed picture standing there, of the remarkable gentlemen all together in a more informal gathering, under garlands of flowers, with wineglasses in their hands. Beaming faces—Felix with his arm around the tall blond-haired Sergei with the pale eyes. And Margon the Godless regarding the camera with a placid smile.

"I gave him the pen," she said. "He loved fountain pens. He liked the sound they made when they scratched the paper. I got it at Gump's in San Francisco for him. Go ahead, you may touch it, if you like. As long as we put it back where it was."

He hesitated. He wanted to touch the diary. A chill

had come over him, an overpowering sense of another person or personality, he didn't know quite which. The man appeared so happy in the photograph, eyes crinkled with good humor, dark hair tousled as if by a breeze.

Reuben looked around the room, at the crowded shelves, the old maps taped to the plaster, and back at the desk. He felt a curious love for this man, well, an infatuation, perhaps.

"As I said, if the right buyer presents himself, all of this goes to storage. ASAP. It's all been photographed, you know. Long ago, I had it done. I have files of photographs of every shelf, every desktop, every bulletin board. It's the only kind of inventory I've attempted, so far."

Reuben stared at the blackboard. The chalk writing had surely faded. What was left was scratched into the blackness. But it was in English and he could read it, and he did:

" 'The glow of festal torches,—the blaze of perfumed lamps,—bonfires that had been kindled for him, when he was the darling of the people,—the splendor of the royal court, where he had been the peculiar star,—all seem to have collected their moral or material glory into the gem, and to burn with a radiance caught from the future, as well as gathered from the past.' "

"You read it beautifully," she whispered. "I've never heard it read out loud before."

"I know that passage," he said. "I've read that before. I'm sure I have."

"You do? No one's ever said that before. How do you know it?"

"Wait a moment, let me think. I know who wrote that. Yes, Nathaniel Hawthorne. That's from a story called 'The Antique Ring.'"

"Why, darling, that's quite remarkable. Wait a minute." She began to search the shelves. "Here, here are his favorite writers in English." She pulled an old tattered leather-bound hardcover from the shelf. It had gilt-edged papers. She started turning the pages. "Well, Reuben, you take the prize. Here's the passage, all right, marked in pencil! I would never have ever found this on my own."

He took the book from her. He was flushed with pleasure, and beaming at her. "It's kind of thrilling. First time my master's in English literature ever proved useful."

"Darling, your education is always going to be very useful," she said. "Whoever convinced you otherwise?"

He studied the pages. There were many markings in pencil, and those strange symbols again, dashed off, it seemed, revealing in their opacity what a complex and abstract thing written language is.

She was smiling at him with such obvious affection. But maybe it was a trick of the light from the green-shaded lamp on the desk.

"I should give this house to you, Reuben Golding," she said. "Could you afford to keep it if I did?"

"Absolutely," he said. "But there's no need to give it to me, Marchent. I'll buy it from you." There, he had said it, and now he was blushing again. But he was ecstatic. "I've got to go back to San Francisco—talk to my mother and father. Sit down with my girlfriend. Make them understand. But I can and will buy it, if you're willing. Believe me. Look, I've been thinking about it since the moment I got here. I've been thinking, I'll regret this all my life if I don't, and you see, if I buy it, well, Marchent you'll always find the door open, anytime night or day."

She smiled at him in the most serene way. She was both very present and very far away.

"You have your own means, do you?"

"Yes, always have. Not the means that you have, Marchent, but I have means." He didn't want to go into the details of the real estate magnates who had founded the family fortune, and the trust funds arranged long before he was born. But how his mother and Celeste would scream when he told them. Grace worked every day of her life as if she was penniless. And she'd expected her boys to do the same thing. Even Phil had worked all his life in his own fashion. And there was Jim giving up everything for the priesthood. And here, he would go into his capital for this house. But he didn't care. Celeste would never forgive him. But he absolutely didn't care.

"Rather figured you did," Marchent said. "You're a gentleman reporter, aren't you? Ah, and you feel very guilty about that, too, I see."

"Just a little guilty," he said under his breath.

She reached out with her right hand and touched his left cheek. Her lips moved but she didn't really speak. A tiny frown touched her forehead but her mouth was still soft and smiling.

"Dear boy," she said. "When you write a novel someday about this house, you will call it **Nideck Point,** won't you, and you'll remember me in some way in it, perhaps, you know. You think you might do that?"

He drew close to her. "I'll describe your beautiful smoky-gray eyes," he said, "and your soft golden hair. I'll describe your long graceful neck and how your hands make me think of birds when you gesture. And I'll describe your voice, that crisp, precise way you say your words that make it seem like running silver when you speak."

I will write things, he was thinking. I will write something meaningful and wonderful someday. I can do that. And I'll dedicate it to you because you're the first person who ever made me think I could.

"Who has a right to tell me I have no gift, no talent, no passion. . . ." he murmured. "Why do people say those things to you when you're young? Doesn't seem fair, does it?"

"No, darling, it's not fair," she said. "But the mystery is why you listen."

Then all the old scolding voices went quiet in his head suddenly, and only then did he realize what a loud chorus they'd always been. Did he ever take a breath without hearing that chorus? **Sunshine Boy, Baby Boy, Little Boy, Little Brother, Little Reuben, what do you know about death, what do you know about suffering, what makes you think, why would you ever try, why, you've never focused on any one thing longer than—.** All those words just dried up. He saw his mother. He saw Celeste—saw her small animated face and large brown eyes. But he didn't hear their voices anymore.

He leaned forward and kissed Marchent. She didn't turn away. Her lips were tender, rather like a child's lips, he imagined, though he had never actually kissed a child since he'd been a child himself. He kissed her again. This time, something stirred in her, and when he felt that stirring, the passion was sparked in him.

Suddenly, he felt her hand on his shoulder, squeezing his shoulder, and gently pushing him away.

She turned around and bowed her head like a person catching her breath.

She took his hand and led him towards a closed door.

He was certain this was the entrance to a bedroom and he had made up his mind. It didn't matter what Celeste would think if she ever knew. He had no intention of passing up this opportunity.

She drew him into a darkened room, and turned on a low lamp.

Only slowly did he realize the place was a kind of gallery, as well as a bedroom. There were ancient stone figures standing on pedestals, thick shelves, and on the floor.

The bed itself was Elizabethan, an English relic almost certainly, a coffered chamber of sorts with carved wooden shutters that could be closed against the night's cold.

The old coverlet of green velvet was musty, but he didn't have a care about that in the world.

# 2

HE WOKE UP out of a sound sleep. There was a low light coming from an open bathroom. A thick white terry-cloth robe hung on the hanger on the hook on the door.

His leather bag was nearby on a chair and his pajamas had been laid out for him, along with his fresh shirt for tomorrow, still in its wrapper, and his other personal things. His trousers had been folded. And his discarded socks as well.

He'd left his leather bag in his unlocked car. And this meant she'd gone out there in the dark alone to get it for him, and this made him a little ashamed. But he was a little too happy and relaxed to feel too ashamed.

He was still lying on the velvet cover, but the pillows had been removed from their velvet shams, and the shoes he'd kicked off in his haste were standing neatly together by the chair.

For a long time, he lay there thinking about their lovemaking, and wondered that he had betrayed Celeste so easily. But in truth, it hadn't been easy at all. It had been quick and impulsive but not easy, and the pleasure had been unexpectedly intense. He was not sorry. No, not by any means. He felt that it was something he'd remember forever, and it seemed infinitely more important than most things he'd ever done.

Would he tell Celeste? He wasn't sure. He would certainly not spring it on her, and it would have to be very clear in his mind that she would want to know. That meant talk, talk with Celeste about a lot of things, hypotheticals and realities, and the worst reality of all, that with her, he felt relentlessly defensive and inadequate and this had pretty much worn him out. She'd been too surprised that people liked the articles he'd written for the **Observer.** And that had cut him.

He felt rejuvenated now, and a little elated and guilty, and a little sad. It never occurred to him for a minute that Marchent would invite him into her bed again. In fact, he was certain she wouldn't. And he winced when he thought of her patronizing him, maybe calling him a beautiful boy. Seems she had whispered something like that to him when they were in the thick of it, and it hadn't mattered then. But it mattered now.

Ah, well, he was surprised by this turn of events, and it seemed mixed up with this house and with Felix Nideck and with the mystique of the whole family.

He got up and went into the bathroom. There was his shaving kit unzipped on the edge of the marble washbasin, and on a glass shelf beneath the mirror stood all the toiletries he might need, just as he might find them in a fine hotel. A curtained window faced west, and by day one could likely see the ocean or the cliffs, he wasn't sure.

He showered, brushed his teeth, and then got into his pajamas. Slipping on the robe and his shoes, he quickly turned down the coverlet, and plumped the pillows.

For the first time this evening, he checked his phone and saw he had two messages from his mother, one from his father, two from his brother, Jim, and five messages from Celeste. Well, this wasn't the time to answer them.

He slipped the phone into the pocket of his robe, and then took stock of the room.

Unbelievable treasures, helter-skelter, it seemed, and dusted as best they could be. Tablets. Yes, there were tablets there, tiny fragile baked-clay tablets that might crumble at his touch. He could see the tiny cuneiform writing. And there were figures in jade, and diorite, and alabaster, gods and goddesses he knew, and some he had never known, and inlaid boxes crammed with random bits of paper or fabric, and heaps of coins and what might have been jewelry, and then books. Lots of books, in all the mysterious Asian languages again, and in the languages of Europe too.

All Hawthorne's novels were here, and some very recent novels that surprised him and thrilled him— James Joyce's **Ulysses,** very thumbed and filled with little note tags, and copies of Hemingway and Eudora

Welty and Zane Grey. There were books of old ghost stories, too, elegant British writers, M. R. James, Algernon Blackwood, and Sheridan LeFanu.

He didn't dare to touch these books. Some were bulging with torn bits of paper, and the oldest paperbacks were falling apart. But it gave him the oddest feeling again of knowing and loving Felix, a twinge that was like the fan sickness he'd felt as a kid when he'd fallen in love with Catherine Zeta Jones or Madonna and thought them the most gorgeous and desirable people in the world. It was that kind of simple yearning, to know Felix, to have Felix, to be in Felix's world. But Felix was dead.

A wild fantasy bloomed in his mind. He'd marry Marchent. He'd live here with her. He'd bring the house to life again for her. They'd go through all of Felix's papers together. Maybe Reuben would write a history of the house, and a history of Felix, one of those specialty books, which always include big expensive photographs, books that didn't become best sellers but which were always respectable and valuable. God knows he had such books himself.

Now he was the one telling himself he was dreaming. And in truth, much as he loved Marchent, he didn't want to be married yet to anybody. But the book, maybe he could do the book, and Marchent might cooperate in such a venture, even if she herself went off again to her house in South America. Maybe it would bind them together, deeply, as good friends and fine friends, and that would be something of great value to them both.

He went out of the room and walked about for a while, on the second floor.

He went down the north hallway on the back of the house.

Many doors stood open, and he found himself peering into several little libraries and galleries much like the one he'd just left. More ancient clay tablets. Ah, this took his breath away. More figurines, and even some parchment scrolls. He was fighting himself not to touch.

There were more of the beautifully appointed bedrooms off the east hallway, one with dazzling black-and-gold Oriental wallpaper, and another papered in stripes of red and gold.

Circling back eventually, he was again on the west side of the house. He stood for a moment on the threshold of what was obviously Marchent's bedroom, one door above Felix's bedroom, a haven of white lace curtains and bed trimming, noting her clothes in a heap at the foot of the bed. But Marchent was nowhere around.

He wanted to go up to the attic. There was a staircase at either end of the western hall. But he had no leave to go exploring up there, and so he didn't. And he didn't open closed doors, though he wanted to do that very much too.

He loved the house. He loved the twin candlelike

sconces, the thick wooden crown moldings everywhere, and the dark wooden baseboards and heavy brass-handled doors.

Where was the lady of the house?

He went downstairs.

He heard her voice before he saw her. From the kitchen, he saw her in an adjacent office, amid fax machines or copy machines, computer monitors and mountains of clutter, talking on a landline phone in a low voice.

He didn't want to eavesdrop, and in truth, he couldn't really make out what she was saying. She wore a white negligee now, something very soft, with layers of lace and pearls, it seemed, and her smooth straight hair shimmered like satin in the light.

He felt a stab of desire that was painful, just looking at her hand as it held the receiver of the phone, and seeing the light on her forehead.

She turned, saw him, and smiled, gesturing for him to wait.

He turned and went away.

The old woman Felice was going through the big house and turning off the lights.

The dining room was already dark when he came back through it, and he saw that the fire had been scattered and was no more than embers. The rooms up front appeared to be in total darkness now. And he could see the old woman moving down the hall, reaching for the switches of the sconces one by one.

At last she passed him on her way back to the

kitchen, and this room she plunged into total darkness as well. She went on out then, without a word to Marchent, who was still talking, and Reuben went on back up the stairs.

A small lamp burned on a table in the upstairs hallway. And there was light coming from Marchent's open bedroom door.

He sat down at the top of the stairs, with his back to the wall. He figured he would wait for her and surely she would come up soon.

He knew suddenly he'd do everything in his power to get her to sleep the night with him, and he grew impatient wanting to hold her, kiss her, feel her in his arms. It had been powerfully exciting to sleep with her simply because she was new to him and so very different, yet soft and yielding and utterly self-confident and frankly much more passionate than he'd ever known Celeste to be. She didn't seem like an older woman in any particular way. He knew she was, of course, but her flesh had been firm and sweet, and she'd been a little less muscular than Celeste.

These struck him as crude thoughts; he didn't like these thoughts. He thought of her voice and her eyes and he loved her. He figured Celeste would probably understand. Celeste after all had been unfaithful to him with her old boyfriend twice. She'd been very candid about both of these "disasters," and they'd gotten past it. In fact, Celeste had suffered over them much more than Reuben had.

But he had it in his mind that she owed him one,

and that a woman of Marchent's age wouldn't arouse her jealousy at all. Celeste was uncommonly pretty, effortlessly attractive. She'd let this go.

He went to sleep. It was a thin sleep in which he thought he was awake, but it was sleep. His body felt sublimely relaxed and he knew he was happier than he'd been in a very long time.

# 3

A LOUD CRASH. Glass breaking. He woke up. The lights were out. He couldn't see anything. Then he heard Marchent scream.

He raced down the steps, hand sliding along the broad oak railing, finding his way.

One horrific scream after another drew him straight forward in the blackness, and gradually, by what light he didn't know, he made out the kitchen door.

The beam of a flashlight blinded him, and before he could shield his eyes, someone had caught him by the throat and was pushing him backwards. His head cracked into wall. The guy was strangling him. The flashlight was rolling on the floor. In sheer rage, he rammed his knee into the attacker, while reaching with both hands for the man's face. He caught a hank of hair in his left hand and rammed his fist into the man's eye. The man yelled and gave up the grip on Reuben's throat. But another figure was bearing down on him with another light. Reuben saw the flash of metal, and felt the sharp stab of the blade going into his stomach. He had never felt rage like he was feeling it now, but as the two men beat him and kicked at him, he felt the blood pumping out of his stomach. Again, he saw the flash of the knife raised. He struck out with all the force he could muster, thrusting his shoulder behind the blow, and threw one of his attackers backwards and away.

Again he felt the blade, this time slicing into his left arm.

A sudden torrent of sounds exploded in the shadowy hallway. It had to be the deep roaring growls of a fierce dog. His attackers were screaming, the animal was snapping, roaring, and Reuben himself had slid down in what was surely his own blood.

Once a long time ago, Reuben had seen a dogfight, and what he remembered was not the sight—because it happened too fast and too furiously for anyone to see anything—but the noise.

That's how it was now. He couldn't see the dog. He couldn't see his attackers. He felt the weight of the beast on top of him, pinning him to the floor, and then the bellowing of the two men stopped.

With a savage snarl, the animal grabbed Reuben by his head, the teeth sinking into the side of his face. He felt himself being lifted as his arms flailed. The pain was worse than the wound in his stomach.

Then suddenly the powerful jaws let him go.

He fell back down on top of one of the attackers, and the only sound in the whole world suddenly was the animal's panting breath.

He tried to move but he couldn't feel his legs. Something heavy, the paw of the beast, was resting on his back. "Dear God, help me!" he said. "Dear God, please."

His eyes closed and he went down and down into rolling darkness; but he forced himself back to the surface. "Marchent!" he shouted. Then the darkness rolled over him again.

Utter quiet surrounded him. He knew the two men were dead. He knew that Marchent was dead.

He rolled over on his back, and struggled to reach into the right pocket of his robe. His fingers closed on the cell phone, but he waited, waited in the silence until he was certain that he was truly alone. Then he drew the phone out and up to his face, and punched the button to turn on the small screen.

The darkness rose again, like waves coming up to wash him off the safe white beach. He forced himself to open his eyes. But the phone had slipped from his hand. His hand had been wet and he'd lost it, and as he turned his head, the darkness came again.

With all his strength he fought it. "I'm dying," he whispered. "They're dead, all of them. Marchent's dead. And I'm dying here, and I have to get help."

He reached out, groping for the cell phone, and felt only the wet boards. With his left hand he covered the pain burning in his gut and felt the blood coming through his fingers. A person cannot live with bleeding like this.

Turning on his side he struggled to right himself and climb up on his knees. But when the swoon came this time it took him down at once.

There was a sound somewhere.

A thin winding sound.

It was like a ribbon of light in the darkness, this sound.

Imagining this? Dreaming? Dying.

He had never expected death to be this quiet, this secretive, this easy. "Marchent," he whispered. "I'm sorry, so sorry!"

But there was a second siren, yes, he could hear it, a second shining ribbon in the dark. The two luminous ribbons of sound were weaving in and out, weaving and coming closer and closer. And there was a third siren, yes.

Imagine that.

The sirens were very close now, winding down, someone spooling up that shimmering luminous ribbon and, once again, the sound of breaking glass.

He drifted, feeling the tug of the darkness again. **Ah, well, my friends, you are too late.** It didn't seem so horribly tragic, really. It was all too immediate and exciting, **You are dying, Reuben,** and he didn't struggle, or hope.

Someone was standing over him. Beams of light were crisscrossing above him, sliding down the walls. It was actually beautiful.

"Marchent," he said. "Marchent! They got her." He couldn't say it clearly enough. His mouth was full of fluid.

"Don't talk, son," said the man kneeling beside him. "We're taking care of her. We're doing all we can."

But he knew. He knew by the quiet and the stillness that had surrounded him, and by the sad tone of the man's voice, that for Marchent it was too late. The lovely and elegant woman he had known for less than a day was dead. She'd died right away.

"Stay with me, son," the man said. People were lifting him. Down came the plastic oxygen mask. Someone was ripping open his shirt.

He heard the snap and crackle of the walkie-talkie. He was on the stretcher. They were running.

"Marchent," he said. The glaring light inside the ambulance blinded him. He didn't want to be taken away from her. He panicked but they held him down and then he went out.

# 4

REUBEN WAS IN AND OUT of consciousness for two hours in the Mendocino emergency room; then an air ambulance took him south to San Francisco General where Dr. Grace Golding was waiting with her husband, Phil, at her side.

Reuben was struggling desperately against the restraints that bound him to the gurney. The pain and the drugs were driving him out of his mind.

"They will not tell me what happened!" he roared at his mother, who at once demanded that the police come and give him the answers he was entitled to have.

The only problem with that, said the police, was that he was too drugged to answer their questions and they had more questions than he did at this point. But yes, Marchent Nideck was dead.

It was Celeste who got on the phone with the authorities in Mendocino and came back with the details.

Marchent had been stabbed over sixteen times and any one of ten different wounds might have been fatal. She'd died within minutes, maybe seconds. If she suffered, it was very brief.

Reuben willfully closed his eyes for the first time and went to sleep.

When he woke there was a plainclothes police officer there, and in drug-slurred words, Reuben volunteered that yes, he had had intimate relations "with the deceased," and no, he did not mind if they took a DNA test. He had known the autopsy would reveal all this.

He gave the best account he could of what he remembered. No, he had not made the 911 call; he had dropped his phone, and been unable to recover it. But if the call had come from his phone, well, then, he must have done it.

("Murder, murder." That's what he'd said over and over again? Didn't sound like something he would have said at all.)

Celeste wanted him to stop talking. He needed an attorney. He'd never seen her so anxious, so near to tears.

"No, I don't," Reuben insisted. "I don't need an attorney."

"It's the concussion," Grace said. "You're not going to remember everything. It's a miracle you remember as much as you do."

" 'Murder, murder'?" he whispered. "I said that?"

He so vividly recalled struggling to find the phone and not being able to do it.

Even through the haze of painkillers, Reuben could see how shaken his mother was. She was in her usual green scrubs, her red hair pinned down and flat, her blue eyes red rimmed and tired. He felt a throbbing in her hand as if she were trembling inside where people couldn't see it.

Twenty-four hours later, when he was moved to a private room, Celeste brought the news that the killers had been Marchent's younger brothers. She was powerfully energized by the perfectly outrageous story.

The two had driven a stolen car to the property and, wearing wigs, ski masks, and gloves, had cut off the power to the house, but not before bludgeoning an old housekeeper to death in her bed in the rear servants' quarters. Obviously wanting the attack to look like the work of random junkies, they'd bashed in the dining room window though the back doors of the house were unlocked.

They'd caught Marchent in the kitchen, just outside her office. There was a small gun found near her, with only her fingerprints on the handle. Not a single shot had been fired.

The animal that had killed the brothers was a mystery. No real tracks were found at the scene. The bites had been savage and immediately fatal to the brothers. But what the animal was, the authorities could not at this point say.

As for the locals, some were insisting it was a female mountain lion, long infamous in those parts.

Reuben said nothing. He heard those sounds again, he felt that paw against his back. A violent shock passed through him, a flash of helplessness and acceptance. **I am going to die.**

"These people are driving me insane on this," Grace declared. "One minute it's the saliva of a dog, the next it's the saliva of a wolf, and now they're telling me maybe the bites were made by a human. Something's happened to their lab results. They don't want to admit it. The fact is, they didn't test those wounds properly. Now it was no human being that made these bites on Reuben's head and neck. And it was no mountain lion either. The idea is patently absurd!"

"But why did it stop?" Reuben asked. "Why didn't it kill me the way it killed them?"

"If it was rabid, it was behaving erratically," Grace explained. "And even a bear can be rabid. Mountain lions, no. Maybe something distracted it. We don't know. We only know you're alive."

She went on mumbling about the total lack of hair or fur samples. "Now you know there had to have been fibers at that scene, animal fibers."

Reuben heard that panting breath again. Then the silence. There had been no smell of an animal, but there had been the feel of one, of hair, the long thick coat of a dog or a wolf against him. Maybe a mountain lion. But no scent of a mountain lion. Don't mountain lions have a scent? How would they ever know?

Grace was thankful the paramedics had thoroughly cleaned up Reuben's wounds. That was only proper.

But certainly they could get a decent sampling from the bites on the dead men that would tell them whether the animal had been rabid or not.

"Well, they had a massacre on their hands, Grace," said Celeste. "They weren't thinking about rabies."

"Well, we have to think about rabies, and we're beginning the rabies protocol now." It wasn't nearly as painful as it had been in the old days, she assured Reuben. He'd have to take a series of injections for twenty-eight days.

Rabies was almost uniformly fatal once the symptoms presented. There was no choice but to treat for rabies at once.

Reuben didn't care. He didn't care about the deep pain in his gut, his aching head, or the ice pick of pain that kept stabbing his face. He didn't care about the nausea he felt from the antibiotics. All he cared about was that Marchent was dead.

He closed his eyes and he saw Marchent. He heard Marchent's voice.

He couldn't quite grasp that all life had gone out of Marchent Nideck just that quickly, and that he himself was somehow improbably still alive.

They wouldn't let him watch television news till the next day. People in Mendocino County talked about wolf attacks that happened every few years. And then there were bears up there, no one could deny. But folks in the vicinity of the old house put their money on a mountain lion they'd been tracking for the last year.

The fact was, no one could find the animal, whatever it was. They were combing the redwood forest. People claimed to have heard howling in the night.

Howling. Reuben remembered those gnashing growls and snarls, that savage torrent of sound when the beast had descended on the brothers, as though it could not kill in silence, as if the sounds were part and parcel of its lethal strength.

More medication. More painkillers. More antibiotics. Reuben lost track of the days.

Grace said she wondered if plastic surgery would even be necessary. "I mean this bite has healed remarkably. And I must say, the incision in your stomach is healing too."

"He ate all the right things growing up," said Celeste. "His mother is a brilliant doctor." She winked at Grace. It pleased Reuben so much that they liked each other.

"Yes, indeed, and she can cook!" said Grace. "But this is just marvelous." Gently her fingers moved through Reuben's hair. Gingerly she touched the skin on his neck and then on his chest.

"What is it?" Reuben whispered.

"I don't know," Grace said absently. "Let's say you don't need any vitamins through that IV."

Reuben's dad sat in the corner of the hospital reading **Leaves of Grass** by Walt Whitman. Now and then he said something like, "You're alive, son, that's what matters."

Everything might be healing, but Reuben's headache got worse. He was never fully asleep, only half asleep, and he overheard things he didn't understand.

Grace talking somewhere, perhaps to another doctor. "I see changes, I mean, I know, this has nothing to do with the rabies virus, of course, we have no evidence he's contracted it, but well, you'll think I'm crazy but I could swear that his hair is thicker. You know, the bite marks, well, I know my son's hair, and my son's hair is thicker, and his eyes . . ."

He meant to ask her, **What are you talking about,** but only thought about it dully with a multitude of other tormenting thoughts.

Reuben lay there speculating. If drugs could really numb your consciousness, they'd be a good thing. As it was, they slowed you down, confused you, kept you vulnerable to violent flashes of recall, and then agitated you and made you unsure of what you knew and didn't know. Sounds startled him. Even smells woke him from his shallow uneasy sleep.

Fr. James rushed in a couple of times a day, always late for something back at his church, and with just enough time to tell Reuben he was obviously improving and looking better and better. But Reuben saw something in his brother's face that was entirely new; a kind of fear. Jim had always been protective of his younger brother, but this was deeper. "I gotta say, though," said Jim, "you do look quite ruddy and robust for someone who's been through all this."

Celeste did as much hands-on care as he would

allow. She was amazingly capable. She fed him Diet Coke through a straw, adjusted his covers, wiped his face over and over, and helped him up for his required walk around the ward. She slipped out again and again to call the D.A.'s office, and then she'd be back assuring him he had nothing to worry about. She was efficient, matter of fact, and never got tired.

"The nurses have voted you the most handsome patient on the ward," she told him. "I don't know what they're giving you here, but I could swear your eyes are actually a deeper shade of blue."

"That's impossible," he said. "Eyes don't change color."

"Maybe drugs can change them," she said. She kept looking at him, not in his eyes, but at them. It made him slightly uneasy.

Speculation about the mysterious animal continued. Couldn't Reuben remember anything else, asked his editor Billie Kale, the feminine genius behind the **San Francisco Observer.** She stood beside his bed.

"Honestly, no," Reuben said, pushing hard against the drugs to look and sound alert.

"So it wasn't a mountain lion, you're sure of that?"

"Billie, I saw nothing, I told you."

Billie was a short, rotund woman, with neat white hair and expensive clothes. Her husband, after a long career, had retired from the state senate and bankrolled the paper, giving Billie a second chance at a meaningful life. She was a terrific editor. She looked for an individual voice in each of her reporters. She fostered that voice. And she had liked Reuben from the start.

"I never saw the creature," said Reuben. "I heard it. I heard it and it sounded like a huge dog. I don't know why it didn't kill me. I don't know why it was there."

And that was the real question, wasn't it? Why did this animal wander into the house?

"Well, those crazy junkie brothers tore out half a wall of dining room windows," said Billie. "You should see the photos. What a pair, to murder their own sister like that. And the old woman in back. Good God. Well, look, you get to work on this when you can. You don't look sick to me, by the way. What are they giving you?"

"I don't know."

"Yeah, well, I'll see you when I see you." She went out as abruptly as she'd come in.

When he got a moment alone with Celeste, Reuben volunteered the information about him and Marchent. But she'd already known, of course. It had made the papers, too. That was a blow to Reuben, and Celeste saw it.

"It's not that bad," she said. "Well, just forget that part." She comforted him, as if he was the one who'd been wronged.

Reuben again waved away Celeste's suggestion of legal counsel. Why did he need this? The attackers had beaten and stabbed him. Only the strangest sort of luck had saved his life.

He was almost right.

The fifth day after the killing, he was still in the hospital, his wounds almost healed, and the prophylactic antibiotics still making him wretchedly sick, when he was told that Marchent had willed the house to him.

She'd done this about an hour before she died, speaking with her San Francisco lawyers about it by phone, and faxing several signed documents to them, one of which had been witnessed by Felice, confirming her verbal instructions that the house should go to Reuben Golding, and that she would bear the full cost of gift taxes on the transfer, which would leave Reuben in possession free and clear. She'd arranged for twelve months' prepaid taxes and insurance.

She'd even made arrangements for her brothers to be paid the money they would have received in the event of a sale.

All the papers were found on her desk, along with a list she'd been making "for Reuben" of local vendors, service people, and suppliers.

Her last call had been to her man friend in Buenos Aires. She'd be coming home sooner than expected.

Seven and one-half minutes after that call, the local authorities had received the 911 alert: "Murder, murder."

Reuben was quietly stunned.

Grace sat down wearily after hearing the news. "Well, it's a white elephant, isn't it?" she asked. "How will you ever sell it?"

In a small voice Celeste had said, "I think it's kind of romantic."

This did raise some questions with the authorities. And the Golding family law firm flew into action and response.

But no one really suspected Reuben of anything. Reuben was well off, and had never in his life received so much as a speeding ticket. His mother was internationally known and respected. And Reuben had almost died. The knife wound to his stomach had barely missed vital organs, his throat was badly bruised, and he'd sustained a concussion as well as the vicious animal bite that had almost opened his jugular vein.

Celeste assured him the D.A.'s office knew that no one could inflict that kind of harm on himself. Besides, they had motive for the brothers, and were able to find two confederates who confessed that they had heard about the scheme but thought the boys were just boasting.

Reuben had a solid reason for being on the property, an appointment set up with his editor, Billie, at the **Observer,** and there was no evidence anywhere on the premises that his contact with Marchent had been anything but consensual.

Hour after hour, he lay there in the hospital bed, going over all these different factors. Every time he tried to sleep, he found himself in a hellish tape loop, rushing down that staircase, trying to get to Marchent before her brothers did. Had she known that the men were her brothers? Had she seen through their disguise?

He woke up out of breath, every muscle aching from the strain of making that desperate run. And then all the pain in his face and gut would come back; he'd push the button for more Vicodin and fall again into half nightmare.

Then there were the voices and sounds that kept waking him. Someone crying in another room. A woman arguing furiously with her daughter. "Let me die, let me die, let me die." He woke, staring at the ceiling, hearing that woman.

He could have sworn there was some sort of problem with the vents in this hospital, that he was hearing someone on a lower floor fighting off an attacker. Cars passing. He could hear them too. Raised voices.

"Drug delusions," said his mother. "You've got to be patient with them." She was adjusting the IV for the fluids she insisted he needed. She stared down at him suddenly. "I want to run some more tests."

"What on earth for?"

"You may think me crazy, Baby Boy, but I could swear your eyes are a darker blue."

"Mother, please. Talk about drug delusions." He didn't tell her that Celeste had said the same thing.

Maybe I've at last acquired a distinctive and tragic expression, he thought mockingly, a little gravitas.

She was staring at him as if she hadn't heard him at all. "You know, Reuben, you really are a remarkably healthy boy."

And he was. Everyone said so.

His best friend Mort Keller, from Berkeley, stopped in twice, and Reuben knew how much this meant, since Keller was facing his oral examination for the Ph.D. in English. This was the program Reuben had abandoned. And he still felt the guilt.

"You look better than I've ever seen you," Mort said. He himself had bags under his eyes, and his clothes were wrinkled and even a bit dusty.

Other friends called—guys from school, guys from the paper. He didn't really want to talk. But it was nice that they cared, and he did read the messages. The cousins from Hillsborough called, but he assured them they must not come in. Grace's brother who worked in Rio de Janeiro sent a basket of brownies and cookies big enough to feed the entire ward. Phil's sister, in a nursing home in Pasadena, was too sick to be told what was going on.

Personally, Celeste didn't care at all about his sleeping with Marchent. She was militant with the investigating officers. "What are you saying, he raped her and then she went downstairs and made out a handwritten will leaving him a five-million-dollar piece of property? And then the woman gushed to a lawyer on the phone about all this for an hour? Come on, do I have to do the thinking for all of us here?"

Celeste told the press the same thing. He caught

a glimpse of her on television, firing answers at the reporters, looking adorably ferocious in her little black suit and white ruffled blouse, her fluffy brown hair framing her small animated face.

Someday she'll make legal history, he thought.

As soon as Reuben could keep some food down, Celeste brought him minestrone soup from North Beach. She was wearing the ruby bracelet he'd given her, and a bit of lipstick that was the same color as the ruby. She'd been dressing especially nicely for him all during this ordeal and he knew it.

"Look, I'm sorry," he said.

"You think I don't understand? Romantic coast, romantic house, romantic older woman. Forget about it."

"Maybe you should be the journalist," he murmured.

"Ah, now there's that Sunshine Boy smile. I was beginning to think I'd imagined it." She ran her fingers very gently over his neck. "You know, this is all healed. It's like some kind of miracle."

"You think?" He wanted to kiss her, kiss her smooth cheek.

He dozed off. He could smell food cooking, and then another fragrance, a perfume. That was his mother's perfume. And then there were all these other smells that had to do with the hospital and its chemicals. He opened his eyes. He could smell the chemicals that had been used to bathe these walls. It was as if each fragrance had a personality, a distinct color in his mind. He felt like he was reading a code off the wall.

Distantly, the dying woman pleaded with her daughter, "Shut off the machines, I'm begging you." "Mommy, there are no machines," said the daughter. The daughter cried.

When the nurse came in, he asked about the mother and the daughter. He had the oddest feeling—he didn't dare tell her this—that the woman wanted something from him.

"Not on this ward, Mr. Golding," she assured him. "Maybe it's the drugs."

"Well, just what drugs are they giving me? Last night I thought I heard two guys in a barroom fight."

Hours later, he woke to find himself standing by the window. He'd accidentally ripped the IV out of his arm. His dad was dozing in the chair. Celeste was someplace far away talking rapidly on her phone.

"How did I get here?"

He was restless. He wanted to walk, to walk fast, not just down the hall, dragging that IV pole on wheels with him every step, but out of here and along a street, or into a woods, and along a steep path. He felt such an urge to walk it was painful to be confined here. It was agony suddenly. He saw the woods surrounding Marchent's house, **my house,** and he thought, We'll never walk there together, she'll never get to show me so many things. Those ancient redwoods, those trees that are some of the oldest living things in this world. Oldest living things.

That woods was his now. He had become the guardian of those particular trees. An indefinable energy galvanized him. He began to walk, moving swiftly down the corridor, and past the nurses' station and then down the steps. Of course he was wearing this flimsy hospital gown, tied in the back, thank God, but he certainly couldn't go out for a stroll in the night. But it felt good to be pounding the stairs, making a circuit of another floor and another.

He stopped suddenly. Voices. He could hear them all around him, gentle whispers, too low to interpret, but there, like rippling in water, like breeze moving through trees. Somewhere far off, someone was screaming for help. He stood there, with his hands over his ears. He could still hear it. A boy screaming. **Go to him!** Not in this hospital, but someplace else. Where else?

He was walking through the front lobby on his way out the door when the orderlies stopped him. His feet were bare. "Whoa, I don't know how I got here," he said. He was embarrassed, but they were kind enough as they took him back upstairs.

"Don't call my mother," he said ominously. Celeste and Phil were waiting for him.

"You went AWOL, son?"

"Dad, I'm so restless. I don't know what I was thinking."

The next morning, he lay half asleep listening. His mother was talking about the tests they'd run. "It makes no sense, a sudden surge of human growth hormone in a twenty-three-year-old man? And all this calcium in his blood, these enzymes. No, I know it's not rabies, of course it's not rabies, but I wonder if the lab didn't simply make a mistake. I want them to run everything all over again."

He opened his eyes. The room was empty. Silence. He got up, showered, shaved, looked at the wound on his abdomen. You could hardly see the scar.

More tests. There was no evidence now that he'd ever had a concussion.

"Mom, I want to go home!"

"Not quite yet, Baby Boy." There was a very elaborate test that could find any infection in any part of the body. Took forty-five minutes. He'd have to lie perfectly still.

"May I call you Baby Boy, too?" whispered the nurse.

An hour later Grace came in with the laboratory technicians.

"Can you believe they have lost every single specimen they took?" She was "fit to be tied," as she liked to say. "Now this time they'd better get it right. And we are not giving anyone another DNA sample. If they screwed that up, it's their problem. Once was enough."

"Screwed it up?"

"That's what they're telling me. We're having a laboratorial crisis in Northern California!" She folded her arms and watched through cold narrow eyes as the techs drew his blood into vial after vial.

Toward the end of the week, Grace was almost manic over his speedy recovery. He was spending most of the day walking around, or in the chair reading the newspaper accounts of the massacre, the Nideck family, the mystery of the rabid animal. He demanded his laptop. His phone was still with the police, of course, so he asked for another.

The first person he called was his editor Billie Kale. "I don't like being the subject of all these stories," he said. "I want to write my own."

"That's what we're dying to have, Reuben. You e-mail it to me. We're on."

His mother walked in. Yes, he could be discharged if he insisted. "My heavens, just look at you," she said. "You do need a haircut, Baby Boy."

One of the other doctors, a good friend of Grace's, had dropped by, and they stood chatting in the hall. "And can you believe they have completely screwed up the lab tests again?"

Long hair. Reuben got out of bed to look at it in the bathroom mirror. Hmm. His hair was bushier, longer, bigger, without doubt.

For the first time, Reuben thought of that mysterious Margon the Godless and his shoulder-length hair. He saw the distinguished gentleman of the photograph over Marchent's library fireplace. Maybe Reuben would wear his long like the impressive Margon the Godless. Well, for a while.

He laughed.

As soon as he walked into the door of the house on

Russian Hill, he made for his desk. He was firing up his desktop as the private-duty nurse took vitals.

It was early afternoon, eight days since the massacre, and one of those clear sunny days in San Francisco when the bay is vibrantly blue and the city is still white in spite of its many glass buildings. He went out on the balcony and let the cold wind sweep over him. He breathed it in as if he loved it, which frankly he never had.

He was so glad to be back in his own room, with his own fireplace, his own desk.

He wrote for five hours.

By the time he hit the key to send the text by e-mail to Billie, he was happy enough with the blow-by-blow account. But he knew that the drugs were still clouding his recall and his sense of the rhythm of what he'd written. "Cut where you feel you should," he had written. Billie would know what to do. Ironic that he, one of their most promising reporters, as they always put it, was the subject of headlines in other papers.

In the morning, he woke up with one thought in mind. He called his lawyer, Simon Oliver. "It's about the Nideck estate," he said. "It's about all the personal property up there and, most especially, the personal effects and papers of Felix Nideck. I want to make an offer on all of it."

Simon started to advise patience, taking things one step at a time. Reuben had never gone into his capital before. Why, Grandfather Spangler (Grace's father) had only been dead now five years, and what would he have thought of this rash expenditure? Reuben interrupted. He wanted everything that had belonged to Felix Nideck, unless Marchent had made arrangements otherwise, and then he hung up the phone.

Not like me to talk like that, is it, he thought. But he hadn't been rude, really, just eager to advance the plot.

That afternoon, after his article had gone to press at the **Observer,** he was dozing, half awake, looking out the window at the fog rolling in over San Francisco Bay, when Oliver called to say that the Nideck estate lawyers were very receptive. Marchent Nideck had discussed her frustration at not knowing what to do with all that Felix Nideck had left behind. Did Mr. Golding want to make an offer on the entire contents of the house and all its related buildings?

"Absolutely," said Reuben. "Everything, furniture, books, papers, whatever."

He closed his eyes. He cried for a long time. The nurse looked in once, but obviously not wanting to intrude, left him alone. "Marchent," he whispered. "Beautiful Marchent."

He told the nurse he had an intolerable craving for some beef broth. Could you get in the car and find some, you know, just some really good fresh beef broth?

"Well, I'll make it," she said. "Just let me go to the store and get what I need."

"Superb!" he said.

He was dressed before her car left the curb.

Slipping out the front door before Phil was the wiser, he was off walking, pounding down Russian Hill towards the bay, loving the feel of the wind, loving the spring in his legs.

In fact, his legs felt stronger than they ever had, it seemed to him. He might have expected a little stiffness after so many days and nights in bed. But he was really sprinting along.

It was dark when he found himself in North Beach. He was moving along past the restaurants and bars, eyeing people, feeling strangely separate from them, that is, able to look at them as if they couldn't see him. Of course they did see him, but he didn't feel as if he was being seen, and that was something entirely new in his brain.

All his life, he'd been conscious of how people saw him. He'd been far too visible for his own comfort. And now it didn't matter. It was as if he was invisible. He felt so free.

He went into a dimly lighted bar, took one of the stools near the end, and ordered a Diet Coke. Didn't matter to him what the bartender thought, for the first time in his life.

He drank it down and the caffeine sizzled in his brain.

He fell to watching the passersby through the glass doors.

A man came in, large boned, with a thick knotted

forehead, and sat down a couple of stools away. He wore a dark worn leather jacket and he had two thick silver rings on his right hand.

There was something decidedly ugly about this guy, about the way he hunched forward over the bar, and the way he told the bartender he wanted a beer. The guy seemed to reek of some malevolent power.

Suddenly he whipped around. "You like what you see?" he demanded of Reuben.

Reuben regarded him calmly. He felt not the slightest urgency to respond. He continued to look at him.

Suddenly, in a fury, the man got up and moved out of the bar.

Reuben calmly watched. He knew intellectually that the man had become angry, and that the situation was one which men in general sought to avoid: making a big guy angry in a bar. But none of this much mattered. He was considering all the little details of what he'd seen. The man was guilty of something, very guilty. The man was uncomfortable just being alive.

Reuben left the bar.

All the lights had come on. Daylight was absolutely gone. The traffic had thickened, and there were more people on the streets. An atmosphere of gaiety surrounded him. There were cheerful faces everywhere that he turned.

But then he heard voices, voices from far off.

For one second, he couldn't move. A woman

somewhere was fighting with a man. The woman was angry but frightened. And the man threatened the woman and the woman began to scream.

Reuben was paralyzed. His muscles were tense, hard. He stood there caught by the sounds he was hearing, but utterly unable to place them. Slowly he realized that someone had approached him. It was the surly uncomfortable man from the bar.

"You still looking for trouble?" the man snarled. "Faggot!" He placed his open hand on Reuben's chest and tried to shove him backwards, but Reuben didn't budge. His right fist shot up and struck the man right under his nostrils, sending him off the sidewalk and into the gutter.

People around them were gasping, whispering, pointing.

The man was astonished. Reuben watched him, watched his shock, watched the way he reached for his bloody nose, watched the way that he backed up, almost into the traffic, and then sauntered off.

Reuben looked down at his hand. No blood, thank God.

But he had an uncontrollable desire to wash his hand nevertheless. He stepped out in the street and hailed a cab and went home.

Now all this must mean something. He had been overpowered by two thug druggies who'd nearly killed him. And now he was able very easily to defend himself against a big lumbering guy who two weeks ago might have scared him out of his wits. Not that he was a coward, no. He just knew what all men know: you don't tangle with some belligerent weather-beaten guy who outweighs you by seventy-five pounds and has arms that are half a foot longer than your arms. You get out of the way of violent men like that. Fast.

Well, not now.

And it must mean something, but he had trouble caring what it meant. He was still wrapped up in the details.

Grace was in hysterics when he got home. Where had he been?

"Out, Ma, what do you think?" he asked. He went to the computer. "Look, I've got to get to work."

"What is this," she stammered, gesturing wildly, "delayed adolescent rebellion? I mean is that what's happening now, you're going through some sort of adolescent recharge of your whole system?"

His father spoke up from his book.

"Son, are you sure you want to offer two hundred thousand dollars for the personal possessions of this Nideck family? Did you really tell Simon Oliver to do that?"

"It's a steal, Dad," he said. "I'm trying to do what Marchent would want."

He started writing. **Oh, forgot to wash my hand.**

He went into the bathroom and began to scrub. Something didn't feel right about his hand. He stretched out his fingers. Well now, this can't be. He examined his other hand as well. Bigger. His hands were bigger. No doubt about it. He didn't wear a ring. If he had, he'd have known before now.

He went to his dresser, and pulled out a pair of his leather driving gloves. He couldn't get them on.

He stood there taking stock. His feet were aching. They'd been aching all day. It hadn't mattered much. He'd been enjoying himself and it had been a minor annoyance, but now he realized what it meant. His feet were bigger, not a whole lot bigger, just slightly bigger. He took off his shoes and that felt good.

He walked into his mother's room. She was standing against the window, with her arms folded, merely looking at him. That's much the way I've been looking at people, he thought. She's staring, studying, taking stock. Only she isn't looking at everybody that way, just at me.

"Human growth hormone," he said. "They found that in my blood."

She nodded slowly.

"You're still technically an adolescent. You're still growing. You probably will be until you're maybe thirty. So your body puts out human growth hormone still when you sleep."

"So I could have a growth spurt still."

"A small one, perhaps." She was concealing something. She was not herself at all.

"What's wrong, Mom?"

"I don't know, baby, I'm just worried about you," she said. "I want you to be all right."

"I'm fine, Mamma. Never better."

He went to his room, fell across his bed, and slept.

After dinner the next night, his brother sought him out and asked if they could talk alone together.

They went up to the roof deck, but it was just too cold. After a few minutes, they settled in the living room before the fireplace. The room was small, like all the rooms in the Russian Hill house, but beautifully appointed and cozy. Reuben was in his father's leather chair, and Jim was sitting on the couch. Jim wore his "clerics," as he called them, meaning his black shirtfront and white Roman collar with the usual black coat and pants. He was never one for going around in regular clothes.

His ran his fingers back through his brown hair and then he looked at his brother. Reuben felt that same odd detachment he'd been feeling for days. He studied his brother's blue eyes, his pale skin, his thin lips. His brother simply wasn't as flashy as Reuben was, Reuben thought, but he was a good-looking man.

"I'm worried about you," Jim said.

"Of course, why wouldn't you be?" said Reuben.

"See, that's just it. That's the way you've been talking. Kind of soft and direct and strange."

"It's not strange," said Reuben. Why add anything to that? Didn't Jim know what this had been like? Or didn't Jim know enough to know he couldn't know what this had been like? Marchent dead, that house his now, Reuben nearly dying. All that.

"I want you to know we're all with you," Jim said.

"That's an understatement," said Reuben.

Jim smiled grimly and shot him a sharp flashing glance.

"Tell me something," Reuben said. "You meet a lot of people down there in the Tenderloin, I mean very unusual people, and you hear confessions. You've been hearing them for years."

"Right."

"Do you believe in evil, a disembodied principle of evil?"

Jim was speechless.

Then he ran his tongue over his lips and replied. "These killers," he said. "They were addicts. It's all much more mundane. . . ."

"No, Jim, I'm not talking about them. Yeah, I know their story. I mean . . . do you ever think you can feel evil? Feel it coming out of someone? Feel a person about to do something evil?"

Jim appeared to be reflecting.

"It's situational and psychological," he said. "People do destructive things."

"Maybe that's it," said Reuben.

"What?"

He didn't want to recount the story of the man in the bar. After all, it really wasn't a story. Hardly anything had happened. He sat there thinking, thinking about what he had felt about that man. Maybe he had a heightened sense of the man's destructive power or tendencies. "Much more mundane . . . ," he murmured.

"You know," said Jim, "I've always teased you about living a charmed life, about being the sunshine boy, the happy one."

"Yes," said Reuben drawing out the word sarcastically. "Well, I always was."

"Well, nothing like this has ever happened to you before and . . . I'm worried."

Reuben didn't answer. He was thinking again. He was thinking about the man in the bar. And then he thought about his brother. His brother was gentle. His brother had a remarkable calm. It occurred to him suddenly that his brother had a kind of simplicity that others never achieve.

When Jim spoke up again, his voice startled Reuben.

"I would give anything in this world to make you better," said Jim, "to have the expression on your face come back to what it was before, to have you again look like my brother, Reuben."

What a remarkable statement. Reuben didn't answer. What was the point of saying anything? He had to think about that. He was drifting. For a moment, he was with Marchent, walking up the slope to Nideck Point.

Jim cleared his throat.

"I understand," Jim offered. "She screamed and you tried to reach her, but you couldn't reach her in time. That's going to make a difference, even though you know you did your very best to get to her. That's bound to make any man feel a lot of things."

Reuben thought, Yes, that's true. But he felt no necessity to say anything about it. He thought of how easy it had been to punch that man in North Beach right in the face. And easy enough to do that and nothing else, to let the guy stagger and decide to move on.

"Reuben?"

"Yeah, Jim, I'm listening," he said. "But I wish you wouldn't worry. Look, we'll talk when it's time for us to talk."

Jim's phone was ringing in his pocket. He jerked it out angrily, studied the small screen, rose to his feet, kissed Reuben on the top of his head, and left.

Thank God, Reuben thought.

He sat there looking into the fire. It was a gas-log fire but a good one. He thought of that roaring untidy oak blaze in Marchent's living room fireplace. He smelled the burning oak again, and her perfume.

You are alone when something like this happens. Doesn't matter how many people love you and want to help you. You are alone.

When Marchent died, she was alone.

He had a sudden overwhelming sense of it. Marchent had probably rested her face against the kitchen floor and bled out alone.

He got up and went down the hall. The door to his father's darkened office was open. City lights glowed in the tall white frame windows. Phil was in his robe and pajamas and was sitting back in his big leather desk chair, listening to music under the obvious black headphones. He had his feet up. He was singing in a low voice with the music, that eerie, disembodied singing that comes from people who are hearing a music we can't hear with them.

Reuben went up to bed.

Sometime around 2:00 a.m., he awoke with a start. I own the place now, he thought. So I'll be connected all my life to what's happened. All my life. Connected. He'd been dreaming of the attack again, but not in the usual repetitive and fragmentary way. He'd been dreaming of the animal's paw on his back, and of the sound of the creature breathing. In his dream it had not been dog, wolf, or bear. It had been some force in the darkness that savaged the young killers, and then left him alive for reasons he could not understand. **Murder, murder.**

In the morning, the Nideck lawyers and the Golding lawyers came to a settlement on all the personal possessions. The original handwritten codicil signed by Marchent and witnessed by Felice had been filed, and within six weeks, Reuben would take possession of Nideck Point, a name, by the way, that Marchent had referenced in her papers—and all that Felix Nideck had left behind when he vanished.

"Now of course," Simon Oliver said, "it's too much to be hoped for that no one will contest this codicil or the will in general. However, I've known these lawyers at Baker, Hammermill a very long time, especially Arthur Hammermill, and they say they've been all through this question of heirs and inheritance already, and that there are no heirs to the Nideck estate. When Felix Nideck's affairs were settled, they tracked every conceivable family connection, and there are simply no living heirs. This man friend of Ms. Nideck in Buenos Aires, well, he signed all the appropriate papers a long time ago, guaranteeing he would make no claim on Ms. Nideck's wealth. She left the man quite a lot, by the way. This was a generous woman. She's left quite a bit to worthy causes, as we say. I'll tell you the sad thing here. A lot of this woman's money is going to go unclaimed. But as far as the Mendocino property—and the personal possessions on the premises—well, my boy, I think you're home free."

He'd talked on and on about the family, how they'd sprung up "out of nowhere" in the nineteenth century, and how the Nideck lawyers had searched exhaustively for family connections during those years when Felix Nideck had been missing. They'd never found anyone in Europe or America. Now the Goldings, and the Spanglers (Grace's people), well, they were old San Francisco families, going way back.

Reuben was going to sleep. All he cared about was that land, that house, and what was in that house.

"All of it's yours," Simon said.

Before noon, Reuben decided to cook lunch like in the old days just so everybody would think he was all right. He and Jim had grown up preparing meals with Phil, and he found it soothing, the rinsing, chopping, frying. Grace joined in whenever she had the time.

They sat down to lamb chops and salad as soon as Grace got in.

"Listen, Baby Boy," she said. "I think you should put the house up there on the market as soon as you can."

Reuben burst out laughing. "Sell the place! Mom, that's insane. This woman left it to me because I loved it. I loved it at first sight. I'm ready to move up there."

She was horrified. "Well, that's a bit premature," she said. She glared at Celeste.

Celeste put down her fork. "You're seriously thinking of living up there? I mean, like, how can you even think of going into that house after what happened? I never thought—."

There was something so sad and vulnerable in her expression that it cut Reuben to the quick. But what was the use of saying anything?

Phil was staring at Reuben.

"What on earth is the matter with you, Phil?" Grace asked.

"Well, I don't know, really," said Phil. "But look at our boy. He's gained weight, hasn't he? And you're right about his skin."

"What about my skin?" Reuben asked.

"Don't tell him all that," said Grace.

"Well, your mother said there was a bloom to it,

you know, almost like a woman gets when she's pregnant. Now I know you're not a woman and you're not pregnant, but she's right. There's a bloom to your skin."

Reuben started laughing again.

They were all looking at him.

"Dad, I want to ask you something," said Reuben. "About evil. Do you believe evil is a palpable force? I mean do you think there is such a thing as evil apart from what men do, a force maybe that can get into you and turn you to evil?"

Phil answered without missing a beat. "No, no, no, son," he said, scooping a forkful of salad into his mouth, "the explanation of evil is a hell of a lot more disappointing than that. It's blunders, people making blunders, whether it's raiding a village and killing all the inhabitants, or killing a child in a fit of rage. Mistakes. Everything is simply a matter of mistakes."

No one else said a word.

"I mean look at Genesis, son," said Phil. "The story of Adam and Eve, it's a mistake. They make a mistake."

Reuben was pondering. He didn't want to answer, but he thought he should.

"That's what I'm afraid of," he said. "Dad, do you have a pair of shoes I can borrow? You're a size twelve, right?"

"Oh, sure, son. I've got a closetful of shoes I never wear."

Reuben drifted off into his thoughts.

He was thankful for the silence.

He was thinking about the house, thinking about all those little clay tablets covered with cuneiform, and about that room where he'd slept with Marchent. Six weeks. It seemed like forever.

He got up and walked slowly out of the dining room and up the steps.

A little later he was sitting by his window looking out at the distant towers of the Golden Gate, when Celeste came in to say she was headed back to the office.

He nodded.

She put her arm around his shoulders. Slowly he turned and looked up at her. How very pretty she was, he thought. Not regal or elegant like Marchent, no. But so fresh and pretty. Her hair was such a very glossy brown and her eyes were so deeply brown, and she had such an intense expression. He'd never thought of her as fragile before, but she seemed fragile now—fresh, innocent, and definitely fragile.

Why had he ever been so afraid of her, afraid of pleasing her, afraid of measuring up to what she expected, afraid of her energy and her smarts?

Suddenly she drew back. It was as if she'd been startled. She moved several steps away. She stared at him.

"What on earth is the matter?" he asked. He actually didn't want to say much of anything, but it was clear something had made her very uncomfortable and it seemed the decent thing to ask.

"I don't know," she said. She forced a smile. Then

gave up on it. "I could have sworn, it was like, well, you seemed like a different person—a different person looking out of Reuben's eyes at me."

"Hmmmm. It's just me," he responded. Now he was the one smiling at her.

But her face was puckered, fearful. "Good-bye, sweetie," she said quickly. "I'll see you at dinner." He figured he'd cook a roast for dinner. He looked forward to having the kitchen to himself.

The nurse was in the door. She'd come to give him an injection. This was her last day.

# 5

It was Friday.

The call came while he was going over the first sheaf of papers from the title company regarding the Mendocino property.

Kidnapping: an entire busload of students from the Goldenwood Academy in Marin County.

He threw on one of Phil's old corduroy jackets, the one with the leather patches on the elbows, and rushed down the stairs and into the Porsche and headed over the Golden Gate.

He had the news blaring from the radio all the way. All that was known was that the entire student body of forty-two students, aged five years old through eleven, and three teachers had vanished without a trace. A sack containing the teacher's cell phones and a couple of phones that had belonged to the students had been found at a call box on Highway One, with a printed note:

"Wait For Our Call."

By three o'clock, Reuben was in front of the huge old brown shingle Craftsman style building that housed the private school, along with a mob of local cameramen and reporters, as more and more people arrived from the local news.

Celeste confirmed by phone. No one knew where the students had been taken or how, and no ransom demand had been received.

Reuben managed to get in a few words with a volunteer at the school who described conditions there as idyllic, and the teachers as "earth mothers" and the gentlest "flower children" in the world. The kids had been en route for a field trip in nearby Muir Woods, which included some of the most beautiful redwoods in the world.

Goldenwood Academy was private, unconventional, and expensive. But the school bus, specially made for Goldenwood, had been old and without a GPS tracker or its own phone.

Billie Kale had two researchers on it at the city room.

Reuben's thumbs were going as he typed on his iPhone, describing the picturesque three-story building, surrounded by venerable oaks, and masses of wildflowers, including poppies, and marguerites and azaleas blooming on the shady grounds.

Parents were still arriving, and the authorities were shielding them from the press as they rushed them inside. Women were crying. Reporters were pressing too close, trampling the flowers, even shoving. The police were getting testy. Reuben chose a spot well to the rear.

These were mostly doctors, lawyers, and politicians, these parents. Goldenwood Academy was experimental but prestigious. No doubt the ransom demand would be outrageous. And why bother to keep asking if the FBI had been called in?

Sammy Flynn, the young photographer from the **Observer,** found him finally, and asked what Reuben thought he should do. "Get the whole scene," said Reuben a little impatiently. "Get the sheriff up there on the porch; get the feel of the school itself."

But how is this going to help, Reuben wondered. He'd covered five criminal cases before this, and in each he'd thought the press played some laudatory role. He wasn't so sure here. But then maybe somewhere somebody had seen something, and in watching this spectacle flashing on every home television in the area, somebody would see this, remember, make a connection and then make a call.

He stood back, on the roots of a low gray live oak, and rested against the rough bark. The woods here smelled of pine needles and green things, and reminded him very much of that walk with Marchent over the Mendocino property, and a little fear came to him suddenly. Was he unhappy to be here, instead of there? Was that unlikely and remarkable inheritance going to lure him away from his job?

Why hadn't that crossed his mind before?

He closed his eyes for a moment. Nothing much was happening. The sheriff was now repeating himself endlessly, as the same questions kept flying at him from different voices in the crowd.

Other voices intruded. For a second, he thought they were coming from the people around him, but then he realized they were coming from the distant rooms in the house. Parents sobbing. Teachers babbling platitudes. People reassuring one another when they had no real basis for reassurance.

He felt uneasy. No way in the world was he going to report these voices. He shut them out. But then it came to him. **Why the hell am I hearing this? If I can't report it, well, what's the point?** The fact was, there was nothing much to report.

He typed in what was obvious. Parents were breaking down under the strain. No ransom call. He felt confident enough to verify that. All those voices told him there had been none, even the low drone of the crisis manager, assuring them that such a call would likely come.

People around him talked about the famous Chowchilla school bus kidnapping of the seventies. No one had been hurt in that one. The teachers and the kids had been taken off their bus and moved by van to an underground quarry, from which they'd later managed to escape.

What can I do, really do, to help this situation? Reuben was thinking. He was exhausted suddenly and agitated. Maybe he wasn't ready to go back to work. Maybe he didn't want ever again to go back to work.

By six o'clock, when nothing had changed in the

situation, he headed back across the Golden Gate and home.

He was still suffering waves of unusual exhaustion, no matter how robust he looked, and Grace said this was a simple aftereffect of the anesthesia used in the abdominal surgery he'd endured. And then those antibiotics. He was still on them and they were still making him sick.

As soon as he hit the house, he hammered out a visceral "on the scene" piece for the morning's paper and e-mailed it in. Billie called a minute and a half later to say she loved it, especially the stuff about the crisis counselors, and the flowers getting totally trampled by the press.

He went downstairs for supper with Grace, who was not her usual self for a number of reasons, among them that two patients had died on the table that afternoon. Of course, no one had expected either one to survive. But even a trauma center surgeon takes two losses painfully, and he sat just a little longer at the table with her than he might have done otherwise. The family talked about "The School Bus Kidnapping," with the television on mute in the corner of the room so Reuben could watch for developments.

Then Reuben was back at work, writing up a review of the old Chowchilla kidnap case, including updates on the kidnappers who were still to this day behind bars. They'd been young men his age at the time of the kidnapping. He wondered what had really become of them during their long years of incarceration. But that wasn't the focus of his piece. He was optimistic. All of the kids and teachers had survived.

This was the busiest he'd been in one day since the massacre in Mendocino. He took a long shower, and went to bed.

An extraordinary restlessness came over him. He got up, paced, went back to bed. He was lonely, hideously lonely. He hadn't really been with Celeste since before the massacre. He didn't want to be with Celeste now. He kept thinking that if he was with Celeste, he'd hurt her, bruise her somehow, run roughshod over her feelings. Wasn't he doing that these days without their putting it to the bedroom test?

He turned over, clutched his pillow and imagined he was alone at Nideck Point, in Felix's old bed, and that Marchent was with him. Just a useful incoherent fantasy to get to sleep. When sleep did come he went down deep into the dreamless darkness.

When next he opened his eyes, the clock said midnight. The television was the only light in the room. Beyond the open windows, the city burned bright in spectral towers on the crowded hills. The bay was the absence of light: pools of blackness.

Could he really see all the way to the hills of Marin? It seemed so. It seemed he saw their outline way beyond the Golden Gate. But how was that possible?

He looked around. He could see all the details of the room with remarkable clarity, the old plaster crown moldings, even the fine cracks in the ceiling. He could see the grain in the wood of his dresser. He had the oddest feeling of being at home in the artificial twilight.

There were voices in the night. They sizzled just below the level of meaning. He knew he could pick out any one and amplify it, but why could he do that?

He got up and went out on the deck, and put his hands on the wooden railing. The salty wind iced him all over, quickening him and refreshing him. How invulnerable he felt to the cold, how energized by it.

There was a limitless reservoir of heat inside of him, and now it broke out on the surface of his skin as if every hair follicle on his body was expanding. He'd never felt such exquisite throbbing pleasure, such raw, divine pleasure.

"Yes!" he whispered. He understood! But what, what did he understand? The realization escaped him suddenly, yet it didn't matter. What mattered was the wave after wave of ecstasy passing through him.

Every particle of his body was defined in these waves, the skin covering his face, his head, his hands, the muscles of his arms and legs. With every particle of himself he was breathing, breathing as he'd never breathed in his life, his whole being expanding, hardening, growing stronger and stronger by the second.

His fingernails and toenails tingled. He felt the skin of his face, and realized that it was covered in soft silky hair, indeed soft thick hair was growing out of every pore, covering his nose, his cheeks, his upper lip! His fingers, or were they claws, touched his teeth and they were fangs! He could feel them descending, feel his mouth lengthening!

"Oh, but you knew, didn't you? Didn't you know this was inside of you, bursting to come out? You knew!"

His voice was guttural, roughened. He began to laugh with delight, low and confidential and utterly yielding to the laughter.

His hands were thickly covered with hair! And the claws, look at the claws.

He tore off his shirt and shorts, shredding them effortlessly and letting them drop to the boards of the deck.

The hair was pouring out of his scalp, it was rolling down to his shoulders. His chest was now completely covered and the muscles in his thighs and calves sang with ever-increasing strength.

Surely this had to peak, this orgasmic frenzy, but it didn't peak. It went on and on. He felt his throat open with a cry, a howl, but he didn't give in to it. Staring up at the night sky, he saw the layers and layers of white clouds beyond the mist; he saw the stars beyond the reach of human eyes, drifting into eternity.

"Oh, God, good God!" he whispered.

On all sides the buildings were alive with pulsing

lights, tiny busy windows, voices throbbing inside, as the city breathed and sang around him.

**You should ask, shouldn't you, why this is happening? You should stop, shouldn't you? You should question.** "Nooo!" he whispered. It was like reaching for Marchent in the dark; it was peeling back her soft brown wool dress and finding her naked breasts beneath him.

**But what is happening to me! What is this that I am?**

An imperative as strong as hunger told him he knew, he knew and he welcomed it. He'd known it was coming; he'd known it in his dreams and in his waking ruminations. This strength had to find its way out of him, or it would have torn him limb from limb.

Every muscle in his body wanted to leap, to run, to spring loose of this confining spot.

He turned around and, flexing his powerful thighs, sprang up to the ledge beneath his parents' window, easily springing from that to the roof of the house.

He laughed it was so easy, so natural. His bare feet hugged the asphalt. And bounding across the roof he went, leaping forward as an animal might leap and then walking a few steps and leaping again.

Before he'd even meant to do it, he had cleared the entire width of the street and landed on the roof of the house opposite. There hadn't been a chance of his falling.

He stopped thinking. He gave in to it and raced across the rooftops. Never had he known such power, such freedom.

The voices were louder now, the chorus rising and falling, and rolling as he turned around and round, and he was searching those voices for one dominant note, what was it? What did he want to hear, to know? Who was calling him?

From one house to another he sped, going lower and lower as he made his way down towards the traffic and noise of North Beach, flying so fast now that he scarce touched down on the smaller slopes, his clawed hands flying out to grasp whatever he needed to hoist his easy weight and send him flying over the next street or alleyway.

Alleyway! He stopped. He heard the sound. A woman screaming, a woman terrified, a woman who had become her scream in fear of her life.

He was down on the ground before he even willed it, landing soft and soundless on the greasy pavement, the walls rising up on either side, the light from the sidewalk showing in horrifying relief the figure of a man tearing off the woman's clothes, his right hand clutching her by the throat, strangling her as she kicked at him helplessly.

Her eyes rolled in her head. She was dying.

A great effortless roar came out of Reuben. Growling, snarling, he bore down on the man, ripping him loose from the woman, Reuben's teeth sinking into the man's throat, the hot blood spurting in Reuben's face, as the man screeched in pain. A hideous scent rose from the man, if indeed it was a scent. It was as if the man's intent was a scent, and it maddened Reuben. Reuben tore at the man's flesh, growls coming out of his mouth as his teeth tore at the man's shoulder. It felt so good to sink his teeth deep into the muscle and feel it split. That scent overpowered him, drove him on. Scent of evil.

He let the man go.

The man fell to the pavement, the arterial blood pumping out of him. Reuben chomped at his right arm, tore it almost loose from the shoulder, and then flung the helpless broken body by this arm against the far wall so that the man's skull cracked on the bricks.

The woman stood stark still, her arms crossed over her breasts, staring at him. Feeble, choking sounds came out of her. How utterly miserable and pitiable she was. How unspeakable that anyone would do such evil to her. She was shaking so violently that she could scarce stand, one naked shoulder visible above the torn red silk of her dress.

She began to sob.

"You're safe now," Reuben said. Was this his voice? This low and rough and confidential voice? "The man who tried to hurt you is dead." He reached out towards her. He saw his paw like a hand reaching for her. Tenderly he stroked her arm. What did it feel like to her?

He looked down at the dead man who lay on his

side, his eyes gleaming like glass in the shadows. So incongruous, those eyes, those bits of hard-polished beauty embedded in such reeking flesh. The scent of the man and the scent of what the man was filled the space around him.

The woman backed away from Reuben. She turned and ran, her loud shrill screams filling the alleyway. She went down on one knee, rose again, and continued, running right towards the traffic of the busy street.

Reuben easily sprang up out of the alley, gripping the bricks as surely as a cat might grip the bark of a tree as he went straight up to the rooftop. In less than a second, he had left the entire block behind, bounding towards home.

There was only one thought in his mind. Survive. Get away. Get back to your room. Get away from her screams and from the dead man.

Without a conscious thought, he found his house, and came down from the roof to the open deck outside his bedroom.

He stood there in the open door staring at the little tableau of bed, television, desk, fireplace. He licked the blood on his fangs, on his lower teeth. It had a salty taste, a taste that was ugly yet tantalizing.

How quaint and small the bedroom seemed, how painfully artificial, as if it was fabricated from something as fragile as eggshells.

He moved inside, into the dense unwelcome warm

air, and closed the windows behind him. It seemed absurd to slide the tiny brass lock shut; what a curious little thing it was. Why, anyone could break one of the small white framed panes in the glass door and easily open it. One could easily break all of the panes, and fling the window, frame and all, out into the darkness.

In this close place, he heard his own easy breathing.

The light from the television was flashing white and blue over the ceiling.

In the full-length mirror on the bathroom door, he saw himself, a great hairy figure with a long mane covering his shoulders. **Man wolf.**

"So this was the manner of beast that saved me in Marchent's house, was it?" He laughed again that low, irresistible rolling laughter. Of course. "And you bit me, you devil. And I didn't die from the bite and now it's happened to me." He wanted to laugh out loud. He wanted to roar with laughter.

But the dark little house was too close around him for that, too close for throwing open the doors and howling at the drifting stars, though he so wanted to do it.

He drew closer to the mirror.

A daylight scene on the television screen laid bare every detail. His eyes were the same, large and deeply blue, but his eyes. He could see himself in them, yet all the rest of his face was thick with dark brown hair, revealing a small black-tipped nose that only faintly resembled that of a wolf, and a long lipless mouth with glaring white teeth and fangs. **The better to eat you with, my dear.**

His frame was bigger, taller, taller by perhaps four inches than it had been, and his hands or paws were enormous, sprouting thin deadly white claws. His feet were huge as well, and his calves and thighs so powerfully muscled, he could see this beneath the hair. He touched his private parts, then drew back from the slight hardness he discovered there.

But it was hidden, all that, by a soft underfur, as well as the coarser hair that covered most of his body. Indeed this soft underfur was everywhere, he realized. It was just thicker in some places than others— around his private parts, and on his inner thighs, and on his lower belly. If he parted the fur, or the coarser outer hair, gently with his claw, he felt a rippling, dazzling sensation.

It made him want to go out again, to travel over the rooftops, to seek out the voices of those in need. He was salivating.

"And you are thinking, feeling, watching this," he said. Once again, the low timbre of his voice startled him. "Stop it!"

He looked at his palms, which had thickened into hairless pads for the paws his hands had become. There was a thin webbing between what had been his fingers. But he had thumbs, still, did he not?

Slowly, he made his way to the bedside table. The room felt much too warm. He was thirsty. He picked up the small iPhone, and it was difficult to grasp it with these huge paws, but he managed.

He went into the bathroom, turned on the full electric light, and stared at himself in the mirrored wall opposite the shower.

Now, in this intense illumination, the shock was almost too much for him. He wanted to turn, cower, shut off the light. But he forced himself to study the image in the mirror.

Yes, a black-tipped nose, and a nose that could smell a multitude of things such as an animal could smell, and powerful jaws, though they did not protrude, and such fangs, ah!

He wanted to cover his face with his hands. But he didn't have hands. Instead, he held up the iPhone and clicked a picture of himself. And again and again.

He rested back against the marble tile beside the shower.

He pushed his tongue through his fangs. He tasted the dead man's blood again.

The desire rose in him again. There were more like the reeking rapist, and the sobbing woman. The voices were still all around him. If he wanted, he could reach into that slow rolling ocean of sound and hook another voice, and bring himself to it.

But he didn't. He was paralyzed, finished.

The impulse to cry came to him, but there was no real physical pressure to it. It was just an idea: cry, pray to God, beg to understand; confess your fear.

No. He had no intention of doing it.

He turned on the tap and let the basin fill with water. Then he drank it in fierce laps until he was satisfied. It seemed he'd never tasted water before, never known how purely delicious it was, how sweet and cleansing it was, how invigorating.

He was struggling to hold a glass and fill it with water when the change began.

He felt it as he had the first time, in the millions of hair follicles covering his body. And there was a sharp contraction in his stomach, not painful, just a spasm that was almost pleasure.

He made himself look up. And he made himself remain standing, though it became harder and harder to do so. The hair was retracting, disappearing, though some of it fell to the tile floor. The black tip of his nose was paling, dissolving. His nose was shrinking, becoming shorter. The fangs were shrinking. His mouth tingled. His hands and feet tingled. Every part of him was electrified with sensation.

Finally, the acute physical pleasure overwhelmed him. He couldn't watch, couldn't be attentive. He was near to fainting.

He staggered into the bedroom and fell across the bed. Deep orgasmic spasms ran through the muscles of his thighs and calves, through his back, his arms. The bed felt wondrously soft, and the voices outside had become a low vibrant hum.

The darkness came, as it had during those despairing moments in Marchent's house, when he'd thought he was dying. But he didn't fight it now as he had then.

He was asleep before the transformation was finished.

It was broad daylight when the ringing of his phone awakened him. Where was it coming from?

It stopped.

He turned and got up. He was cold and naked, and the raw light of the overcast sky hurt his eyes. A sharp pain in his head scared him, but then it left as suddenly as it had come.

He looked around for the iPhone. He found it on the bathroom floor and at once clicked back to the pictures.

He was certain, certain, he would find nothing there but a photograph of good old Reuben Golding. Just that, and nothing more, and incontrovertible proof that Reuben Golding was going flat-out crazy.

But there it was: the man wolf, staring back at him.

His heart stopped.

The head was immense, the brown mane falling well beyond the shoulders, the long black-tipped nose more than evident, and the fangs cutting below the black-rimmed edge of the mouth of the thing. **Blue eyes, your blue eyes.**

He covered his mouth with his hand. He was shaking all over. He felt of his own, natural lips, well formed, faintly pink, as he studied himself in the mirror. And then he looked at that mouth again, rimmed in black. This could not be; and this was. This was a lupine man—a monster. He clicked through one picture after another.

Dear God . . .

The creature's ears were long, pointed, cleaving to its head, half hidden by the luxuriant hair. Its forehead protruded, but did not really conceal the large eyes. Only they retained their human proportion. The beast looked like nothing he'd ever seen before—certainly not the teddy bear monster of old werewolf movies. It looked like a tall satyr.

"Man wolf," he whispered.

**And is this what almost killed me in Marchent's house? Is this what lifted me in its mouth and almost tore open my throat as it had done to Marchent's brothers?**

He synced the images one by one to his computer.

Then, sitting down before the thirty-inch monitor, he brought them up one by one. He gasped. In one picture, he'd been holding up his paw—and it was him, wasn't it? No point to calling it "it." And now he studied the paw, the big hairy webbed fingers and the claws.

He went back into the bathroom and looked at the floor. Last night he'd seen hairs dropping off him as they would off a shedding dog. They weren't there now. There was something there, something wispy—tiny tendrils, almost too thin to see that seemed to disintegrate when he tried to catch them up in his fingers.

So it dries up, it dissolves, it flies away. All the evidence is inside me or gone, burnt up.

**So that's why they'd never found any fur or hair in Mendocino County!**

He remembered that spasm in his gut, and the waves of pleasure washing over him, pervading every limb the way music reverberates through the wood of a violin or the wood of a building.

On the bed, he found the same fine, vanishing hairs, dissolving at his touch, or simply scattering far and wide.

He began to laugh. "I can't help it," he whispered. "I can't help it." But this was an exhausted, desperate laughter. Sinking down on the side of the bed, his head in his hands, he gave in to it, laughing under his breath until he was too exhausted to laugh anymore.

An hour later, he was still lying there, with his head on the pillow. He was remembering things—the scent of the alleyway, garbage, urine; the scent of the woman, a tender perfume suffused with an acid smell, almost citruslike—the smell of fear? He didn't know. The whole world had been alive with scents and sounds, but he'd been focused only on the reek of the man, the pumping smell of his fury.

The phone rang. He ignored it. It rang again. It didn't matter.

"You killed somebody," he said. "Are you going to think about that? Stop thinking about scents, and sensations, and leaping over rooftops, and jumping some twelve feet in the air. Stop it. You killed somebody."

He couldn't be sorry. No, not at all. The man was going to kill the woman. He had already done irreparable damage to her, terrifying her, strangling her, forcing his fury upon her. The man had harmed others. The man lived and breathed to hurt and harm. He knew this, knew this from what he saw, and oddly enough from that powerful reek. The man was a killer.

Dogs know the scent of fear, don't they? Well, he knew the scent of helplessness, and the scent of rage.

No, he wasn't sorry. The woman was alive. He saw her running down that alley, falling, rising again, running not only towards the busy street, the lights, the traffic, but towards her life, her life yet to be lived, a life of things to learn, and things to know and things to do.

He saw Marchent, in his mind's eye, rushing out of the office with the gun in her hand. He saw the dark figures close in on her. She fell hard on the kitchen floor. She died. And there was no more life.

Life died around her. The great redwood forest outside her house died, and all the rooms of her house died. The shadows of the kitchen shrank; the boards beneath her shrank. Until there was nothing, and the nothing closed her in and shut her up. And that was the end of it for Marchent.

If there was a great blossoming on the other side, if her soul had expanded in the light of an infinite and embracing love, well, how are we to know it, until we go there too? He tried for a moment to imagine God, a God as immense as the universe with all its millions of stars and planets, its unchartable distances, its inevitable sounds and its silence. Such a God could know all things, **all things,** the minds and attitudes and fears and regrets of every single living thing, from the scampering rat to every person. This God could gather a soul, whole and complete and magnificent, from a dying woman on a kitchen floor. He could catch it up in His powerful hands, and carry it heavenward beyond this world to be forever united with Him.

But how could Reuben really know that? How could he know what lay on the other side of the silence in the hallway when he'd been struggling there to breathe and live, and those two dead bodies had been tangled with his body?

He saw the forest die again, and the rooms shrink and vanish; every visible thing collapsed—and all life winked out for Marchent.

He saw the rapist's victim again, running, running towards her life. He saw the entire city take shape around her with myriad scents and sounds and exploding lights; he saw it expand in all directions from her running figure. He saw it tumbling and boiling towards the dark waters of the bay, the distant invisible ocean, the faraway mountains, the rolling clouds. The woman was screaming and reaching for life.

No, he didn't regret it. Not one bit. Ah, the hubris, the greed of that man as he'd clutched at her throat, as he'd sought to take her life. Ah, the gluttonous arrogance of those two crazed brothers as they sank the knife over and over again into that magnificent living being that had been their sister.

"No, not at all," he whispered.

Somewhere in the back of his mind he was aware that he had never thought of such things before. But observing himself just now was not the point. He was observing them, the others. And he had no regrets at all, only a marvelous calm.

Finally, he got up. He went to wash his face and comb his hair.

Only absently did he glance at his own reflection. But it shocked him. He was Reuben, of course, not the man wolf, but he wasn't the Reuben he used to be. His hair was fuller, and longer. And he was slightly bigger all over. Whatever he'd become, a factory of alchemical changes, he was different now externally. He housed a crucible that required a more durable body, didn't he?

Grace had talked about hormones, his body being flooded with hormones. Well, hormones make you grow, don't they? They lengthen your vocal cords, add inches to your legs, increase the growth of your hair. This involved hormones, all right, but secret hormones, hormones infinitely more complex than the hospital tests had been able to measure. Something had happened to his entire body that was very much like what happens to the erectile tissue of his organ when a man is sexually aroused. It increases marvelously in size, no matter what the man wants to happen. It goes from something flaccid and secret to becoming a kind of weapon.

That's what had happened to him; he'd increased all over, and all the processes that govern any hormonal change in a man had been greatly accelerated.

Well, Reuben never really understood science. And maybe now he was trying to understand magic. But he sensed the science behind the apparent magic. And this capacity to change, how had he acquired it? Through the saliva of the beast that had bitten him, the creature who might have given him the fatal virus, rabies. The beast had given him this. And was the beast a man wolf such as Reuben had become?

Had the beast heard Marchent's screams just as Reuben had heard the screams of the rape victim in the alley? Had the beast smelled the evil of Marchent's brothers?

Of course, it had to be. And he understood for the first time why the beast had released him. The beast had known suddenly that Reuben was no part of the evil that had ended Marchent's life. The beast knew the scent of innocence as well as evil.

But had the beast meant to pass on its obvious power?

Something in the beast's saliva had traveled into Reuben's bloodstream, just as a virus might travel, sought a pathway to his brain, perhaps, to the mysterious pineal gland, perhaps, or the pituitary gland, that little pea-sized thing we all have in our brain that controls what? Hormones?

Hell.

He didn't really know. These were guesses. If ever in his life he wanted to talk to Grace about "science," it was now, but not a chance. Not a chance!

Grace was not to know about this! Grace must never know. And no one like her must ever know.

Grace had done too many damned tests already.

No one was to know about this.

He had a vivid memory of being strapped to that gurney in Mendocino County as he shouted at those doctors, "Tell me what happened!" No. No one must know because not a single person in this world could be trusted not to incarcerate the thing he'd become, and he had to know infinitely more about what had happened and whether it would happen again and when and how. This was his journey! His darkness.

And up there, somewhere in that redwood forest, was another creature like himself, surely, a beast man who was responsible for what was happening to him. But what if it wasn't a beast man? What if it was more nearly a beast, and Reuben himself was some hybrid creature?

This was maddening.

He pictured that creature now moving through the darkness of Marchent's hallway, ravaging those evil brothers with its fangs and claws. And then lifting Reuben in its jaws, ready to do away with him in the same fashion. Then something had stopped it. Reuben wasn't guilty. No, and the beast had let him go.

**But had the beast known what would happen to Reuben?**

Again, his own reflection in the mirror startled him, brought him back to the moment.

His skin had this unmistakable luster. Yeah, that was it, it was a luster, as if he'd been rubbed with a tiny bit of oil all over, and the hands that had anointed him with it had polished his cheekbones and jawline and his forehead.

No wonder they'd all been staring at him.

And they didn't even begin to guess what was happening. How could they? It hit him that all he was doing was guessing himself, that he didn't know a particle of it, truly. There was so much to find out, so much—.

There was a loud knocking at the door. Someone tried the knob. He heard Phil calling him.

He put on his robe, and went to answer.

"Reuben, son, it's two o'clock in the afternoon. The **Observer**'s been calling you for hours."

"Yeah, Dad, I'm sorry," he said. "I'll go in. Just got to take a shower."

The **Observer.** That was the last place he wanted to go, damn it. He locked himself in the bathroom, and turned on the hot water.

There was so much else he wanted to do, so much thinking, pondering, and delving.

But he knew it was extremely important to go to

work, to get out of this room and out of himself and at least show up for Billie Kale, and for his mother and his father.

But never had he wanted so much to be alone, to be studying, thinking, searching for answers to the mystery that was engulfing him.

# 6

REUBEN DROVE THE PORSCHE too fast on the way to work. The car was always a chained lion in the city. With all his heart, he wanted to be on the road to the Mendocino forest behind Marchent's house, but he knew it was way too soon for that. There was much more he had to know before he went searching for the monster who had done this to him.

Meanwhile the radio news was filling him in on the Goldenwood school bus kidnapping. No ransom call had been received, and there were still no leads as to who had taken the busload of children or where.

He made a quick call to Celeste. "Sunshine Boy," she said, "where the hell have you been? The town's forgotten about the children. It's Werewolf Fever. If one more person asks me, 'What does your boyfriend have to say about this?' I'm going to cut out of here and barricade myself in my apartment." She went on and on about the "crackpot" woman from North Beach who thought she'd been saved by a combination of Lon Chaney Jr. and the Abominable Snowman.

Billie was texting him, "Get in here."

He could hear the mingled voices of the city room before he got out of the elevator. He made straight for Billie's office.

He recognized the woman sitting in front of Billie's desk. But for a moment he couldn't place her. At the same time there was a scent in the room that was distinctly familiar and connected to something out of the ordinary, but what? It was a good scent. The scent of the woman, of course. And he could detect Billie's scent, too. Quite distinctive. In fact, he was picking up all kinds of scents. He could smell coffee and popcorn the way he'd never smelled them before. He was even picking up the scents from the nearby bathrooms, and they weren't particularly unpleasant!

So it's going to be like this, he figured. I'm going to pick up scents like a wolf, and sounds, too, no doubt.

The woman was petite, brunette, and crying. She was dressed in a light wool suit, with her neck covered by a tightly wound silk scarf. One eye was swollen shut.

"Thank God you're here," she said the minute she saw Reuben. He smiled as he always did.

She immediately grabbed for his left hand, and almost pulled him down in the chair next to her. Her eyes welled with tears.

**Good God, it's the woman from the alleyway.**

Billie's words came as if from a blast furnace.

"Well, you took your sweet time getting in here, and Ms. Susan Larson here doesn't want to talk to anyone else but you. Small wonder, isn't it, with the entire city making fun of her."

She threw the front page of the **San Francisco Chronicle** at him. "That's the extra that hit the streets while you were getting your beauty sleep, Reuben. 'Woman Saved by Wolf Man.' CNN went with 'Mysterious Beast Attacks Rapist in San Francisco Alleyway.' This went viral right after noon. We're getting calls from Japan!"

"Can you start at the beginning?" Reuben said. But he understood only too well.

" 'The beginning'?" Billie demanded. "What's with you, Reuben? We've got a busload of kids missing, and a blue-eyed beast creature stalking the back alleys of North Beach, and you ask me to start from the beginning?"

"I'm not insane," said the woman. "I saw what I saw. Just like you saw it up there in Mendocino County. I read your description of what happened to you!"

"But I didn't see anything up there," said Reuben. He hated this. Was he going to try to make her think she was crazy?

"It was the way you described it!" the woman said. Her voice was thin and hysterical. "The panting, the snarls, the sound of the thing. But it wasn't an animal. I saw it. It was a beast man, all right. I know what I saw." She moved to the edge of the chair, and stared into his eyes. "I'm not talking to anybody but you," she said. "I'm sick of being laughed at and made fun of. 'Woman Rescued by Yeti!' How dare they make this into a joke."

"Take her into the conference room and get the whole story," said Billie. "I want your view on this from start to finish. I want the details the rest of the press has been all too happy to miss."

"I've been offered money for this interview," broke in Ms. Larson. "I turned it down to come to you."

"Just hold it here, Billie," said Reuben. He held Ms. Larson's hand as warmly as he could. "I'm not the person to do this story and you know perfectly well why. It's been two weeks since that disaster in Mendocino, and you're expecting me to cover another animal attack—."

"You're damn right I am," said Billie. "Who else? Look, everybody's been calling you, Reuben. The networks, the cable news—the **New York Times,** for heaven's sakes! They want your comment. Is this the beast from Mendocino? And if you don't think the people from Mendocino have been calling, well, you have another think coming. Now you're telling me you won't cover this for **us.**"

" 'Us' should have a little loyalty here, Billie," Reuben shot back. "I'm not ready to—."

"Mr. Golding, please, I'm asking you to listen to me," said the woman. "Don't you understand what this is like? I was nearly killed last night. This thing saved me, and now I'm an international joke for describing what I saw."

Reuben went speechless. The blood was pounding in his face. **Where the hell are Lois Lane and Jimmy Olsen?** He was saved by Billie's phone. She listened attentively for fifteen seconds, grunted, and clicked it off. He heard the words too.

"Well, the coroner's office has confirmed it was an animal, all right, canine or lupine, but an animal. That much is out of the way."

"What about hair or fur?" Reuben asked.

"It wasn't an animal," the woman protested. She was almost screaming. "I'm telling you, it had a face, a human face, and it spoke to me. It spoke words! It tried to help me. It touched me. It was gentling me! Stop saying it was an animal."

Billie got up and beckoned for them to follow.

The conference room was windowless, sterile, with an oval mahogany table and several scattered Chippendale chairs. The two television monitors near the ceiling were flashing CNN and Fox silently with flowing captions.

Suddenly a lurid painting of a werewolf, comic-book style, filled up one screen.

Reuben flinched.

In a flash he saw that hallway in Marchent's house, this time illuminated by his imagination, and the beast man there, descending on those two men who'd been trying to kill him.

He covered his eyes, and Billie grabbed at his wrist, "Wake up, Reuben," she said. She turned to the young woman. "Sit down here and tell Reuben everything you remember." She was hollering at her assistant, Althea, to bring some coffee.

The woman put her face in her hands and cried.

Reuben felt a rising panic. He moved in closer to the woman and put his arm around her. One of the monitors was running a clip from the Lon Chaney Jr. **Wolf Man.** And there suddenly was the first panoramic shot of Nideck Point that he'd ever seen on the television screen—his house with its peaked gables and diamond-pane windows.

"No, no," said the woman, "not like that. Can you make them turn that thing off? He didn't look like Lon Chaney and he didn't look like Michael J. Fox!"

"Althea," Billie shouted. "Turn that damn TV off."

Reuben had the urge to just walk out now. But that was out of the question.

"What about the kidnapping?" Reuben murmured.

"What about it? You're off it. You're on the wolf man full-time. Althea, get Reuben's tape recorder."

"Don't need it, Billie," said Reuben, "got my iPhone." He set the iPhone to record.

She slammed the door as she went out.

For the next half hour, he listened to the woman, his thumbs busy as he wrote his notes, his eyes returning again and again to the woman's face.

But again and again, he faded out on her words. He couldn't stop trying to picture "the beast" that had almost killed him.

Again and again, he nodded, he squeezed her hand, and at one point he took her in his arms. But he was not there.

Finally her husband showed up and insisted she leave, though the woman herself wanted very much to go on talking, and Reuben ended up walking them to the elevator doors.

Back at his desk, he stared at all the little paper phone messages taped to his computer monitor. Althea told him Celeste was on line 2.

"What did you do with your cell phone?" Celeste demanded. "What's going on?"

"I don't know," he mumbled. "Tell me something. Is the moon full?"

"No. Not at all. I think we're in the quarter moon. Hold on." He heard the keys of her computer clacking. "Yeah, quarter moon, so you can forget about that. But why are you asking? They just got a ransom demand from the kidnappers, for heaven's sakes. And you're talking about the wolf man thing?"

"They put me on the wolf man story. There's nothing I can do. How much is the ransom demand?"

"That's the most insulting and demeaning thing I ever heard," Celeste stormed. "Reuben, stand up for yourself. Why, because of what happened to you up north? What is Billie thinking? The kidnappers have just demanded five million dollars or they will start killing the kids one by one. You should be on the way to Marin. The ransom's to be transferred to an account in the Bahamas, but you can be sure it will pass through that account like lightning and vanish into the cyber-banking twilight zone. It might never even reach that bank. They're saying these kidnappers are tech geniuses."

Billie was suddenly standing over his desk.

"What did you get?"

He hung up the phone. "A lot," he said "Her perspective. Now I need some time to catch up on the coverage out there."

"You haven't got time. I want your exclusive on the front page. You realize the **Chronicle**'s going to offer you a job, don't you? And you know what? Channel Six is making noises about wanting you. They have been since you were attacked in Mendocino."

"That's ridiculous."

"No, it isn't. It's your looks. That's all broadcast news cares about, your looks. But I didn't offer you this job for your looks. I'm telling you, Reuben, the worst thing that could possibly happen to you is to go into broadcast news at your age. Give me the Reuben take on all this in your own voice, your distinctive voice. And don't disappear on me again the way you did this morning."

She was gone.

He sat there staring in front of him.

All right, the moon's not full. It meant that what had happened to him had nothing to do with the moon, and that it could happen again anytime. It might happen again tonight. So much for the old legends, and why was he trapped here when he should be investigating every shred of fact or fancy that had to do with "beast men"?

A memory came back to him, of gliding over the rooftops, his legs throbbing with their new strength. He'd looked up and seen the quarter moon behind the clouds that surely veiled it from human eyes.

And will this happen again as soon as it's dark?

How beautiful it had looked, that quarter moon hanging amid so many vibrant stars. He felt himself again flying with arms out as he cleared the street before him, landing effortlessly on the sloped roof. He felt a powerful exhilaration. And then the horrifying thought came: **Will this happen every night?**

Althea put down a fresh cup of coffee for him. She smiled and waved as she moved away.

He stared at all the people around him, coming and going from their white cubicles, some glancing his way, a few nodding, others passing in inevitable silence, locked in their thoughts. He stared at the row of television monitors that ran the length of the far wall. Images of the empty school bus, the Goldenwood Academy. A woman crying. Lon Chaney Jr. again looking like a giant teddy bear rushing through the misty English forest, his lupine ears standing up.

He turned away in his swivel chair, picked up the phone, and punched in the number of the coroner's office and agreed to hold.

I don't want to do any of this, he was thinking. I can't do any of it. It's all slipping away from me in the blaze of what's happened. I can't. Sure, I'm sorry for Miss Larson and what she suffered, and that nobody believes her, but hell, I saved her life! I don't belong here doing this. I'm the last person who should be doing it. None of this matters, that's the problem. At least not to me.

A kind of cold settled over Reuben. One of his colleagues, a very friendly woman named Peggy Flynn, appeared with a plate of cookies for him. He flashed the inevitable warm smile. But he felt nothing, not even that he knew her, or had ever been connected with her, or that they even shared the same world.

That was it; they didn't share the same world. Nobody shared the world in which he lived right now. Nobody could.

Except maybe that thing that had attacked him in Mendocino. He closed his eyes. He felt those fangs biting into his scalp, into his face, that deep horrific pain in the side of his face when those teeth sank in.

And if he hadn't killed that man in the North Beach alley, would that man have gone on to become a beast thing, too, just like Reuben! He shuddered. Thank God, he'd killed the guy. Oh, now, wait a minute. What kind of a prayer was that!

He went blank.

The coffee in his cup looked like gasoline. The cookies looked like plaster.

And it wasn't reversible, was it? It was no matter of choice; in fact he had not the slightest control at all.

The voice of the coroner's assistant snapped him back to life. "Oh, it was an animal all right. We can tell by the lysozyme in the saliva. Well, humans don't have this amount of lysozyme in their saliva. Humans have a lot of amylase, which starts to break down the carbohydrates that we eat. But an animal doesn't have amylase, and it does have a powerful amount of lysozyme, which kills the bacteria it ingests, which is why

a dog can eat from a garbage dump or a rotted carcass and we can't. But I'll tell you something strange
about this beast, whatever it is. It had more lysozyme
than any dog would ever have. And there were other
enzymes in the saliva that we can't properly analyze
here. Tests on this are going to take months."

No, no hair, no fur, nothing like that. They'd collected some fibers, or thought they had, but then they
came up with nothing.

His heart was pounding when he put down the
phone. So he'd become something other than human,
without a doubt. It all got back to the hormones,
didn't it? But that was as far as he could understand.

What he did understand was that he had to be
locked in his room before it got dark.

And it was fall now, almost winter, and this was
one of those damp gray days with no real sky at all,
just a wet roof over San Francisco.

By five o'clock, he was finished with his story.

He'd checked in covertly with Celeste, who verified the **Chronicle** account of the woman's bruises
and torn clothes. He'd checked in with San Francisco
General but no one would say anything and Grace
was in surgery.

He'd also checked out all the main versions of the
mystery animal attack online. The story was galloping
around the globe, all right, and almost all accounts
mentioned the "mysterious" attack on him in Mendocino. Only now as he tracked the news of Mar-

chent's murder did he realize this had traveled the globe as well. "Mystery Beast Strikes Again?" "Bigfoot Intervenes to Save Lives."

He'd also checked out the YouTubes of reporters in North Beach describing the "back-alley beast."

Then he hit the computer keyboard with the woman's words.

> "It had a face, I tell you. It spoke to me. It moved like a man. A man wolf. [She'd used that very term, his term, "man wolf."] I heard its voice. Dear God, I wish I hadn't run from it. It saved my life, and I ran from it as if it was a monster."

He made the story personal, yes, but only in tone. Following her own vivid descriptions, a review of the forensic evidence and the inevitable questions, he wrote in conclusion:

> Was it some sort of "Man Wolf" that saved the victim from her assailant? Was it a beast of intelligence that so recently spared the life of this reporter in the darkened hallway of a Mendocino house?
>
> We have no answers now to these questions. But there can be no doubt as to the intentions of the North Beach rapist—already connected to a string of unsolved rapes—or the drug-crazed

killers who took the life of Marchent Nideck on the Mendocino coast.

If science cannot yet explain the forensic evidence found at both sites, or the emotional testimony of the survivors, there is no reason to believe that it won't in time be able to explain all. For now, we must, as so often happens, live with unanswered questions. If a Man Wolf—**the Man Wolf**—is stalking the alleyways of San Francisco, to whom exactly is this beast a threat?

Last, he added the title:

San Francisco's **Man Wolf:** Moral Certainty in the Middle of a Mystery

Before he filed the story, he Googled the words "man wolf." Just as he suspected, the name had been used—for a minor character in the Spider-Man comics, and for another minor character in the manga-anime series **Dragon Ball.** But he also noted a book called **The Man-Wolf and Other Tales** by Émile Erckmann and Louis-Alexandre Chatrian, first translated into English in 1876. Good enough. It was in the public domain as far as he was concerned.

He hit the SEND button to file the story with Billie, and walked out.

# 7

THE RAIN STARTED before Reuben ever got home, and by the time he locked himself in his room, it was coming down hard in that dreary windless way it so often did in Northern California, slowly, relentlessly drenching everything, and quenching the light of the dying sun, the moon, and the stars completely. He was sorry to see it. This rain meant that "the rainy season" had begun and there might not be another clear day until next April.

Reuben hated the rain, and immediately lighted his fireplace, turning down the lamps so the flickering of the fire could provide some tangible comfort.

But it tantalized him to think about how it might not matter one whit to him once he was transformed, if indeed the transformation was coming.

What is hating rain to me now, he thought. He thought of Nideck Point and wondered how the redwood forest would be in the rain. Somewhere on his desk was a map of the property sent to him by Simon Oliver. On that map for the first time he'd seen the actual layout of the land. The point of land where the house stood was just south of a huge bluff and jutting cliffs that obviously protected the redwood forest to the east and behind the east side of the house.

The beach itself was small, with access uncertain, but whoever had built the house had certainly chosen a blessed location, as it overlooked both sea and forest.

Well, there was time to think about all that. Now he had to barricade himself in and go to work.

He'd bought a hot sandwich and soda on the way home, and he devoured these impatiently, Googling "werewolves," "werewolf legends," "werewolf movies," and a host of other such subjects with his right hand.

Unfortunately he was fully capable of hearing the entire discussion going on downstairs at the dining table.

Celeste was still personally outraged that the **Observer** had taken Reuben off the Goldenwood kidnap for this crazy wolf man story, and Grace was positively disgusted, or so she said, that her son could never stand up for himself. This monstrous attack in Mendocino was the last thing her baby needed. Phil was mumbling that Reuben might become a writer after all and writers had a way of "redeeming everything that ever happens to them."

Reuben perked up at that thought, and even jotted it down on the pad next to his keyboard. Good old Dad.

But the Committee on Reuben and Reuben's Life now included new members.

Rosy, the darling and deeply beloved housekeeper who'd returned this morning from her yearly trip to Mexico, was weighing in that she could never forgive herself for being "gone" when Reuben most needed her. She said flat out it was the "loup garoo" who had gotten him.

Reuben's best friend, Mort Keller, was also there, apparently having been drafted for the meeting before anybody realized that Reuben was going to lock himself in his room and refuse to talk to anyone. This made Reuben furious. Mort Keller was finishing his Ph.D. at Berkeley and didn't have time for nonsense like this. He'd come to the hospital twice, and that had been heroic, as far as Reuben was concerned, considering Mort was getting maybe four hours of sleep a night, and having a hell of a time with preparing for his oral examination.

Now Mort had to listen—and so did Reuben—to the "whole story" of how Reuben had changed since the tragic night in Mendocino, and Grace's theory that he'd caught something from that rabid animal that bit him.

Caught something! Understatement. And what was up there in the Mendocino forest? Did he talk? Did it walk? Or was it—? He stopped.

Of course it talked. "Murder, murder." He'd always known he didn't make that 911 call. It was the beast thing that had picked up his phone.

A great relief coursed through him. Okay, so it wasn't so degenerate and transformed that it had become a mindless monster. No, it was inhabited by some civilized force just like the back-alley beast of

San Francisco. And if that was the case, perhaps it knew—it knew—what was happening to the man it had nearly killed in Marchent's hallway.

Was that good? Or was that bad?

The voices from downstairs were driving him crazy.

He got up, found a CD of Mozart, a piano concerto that he loved, shoved it into the Bose player by his bed, and turned it up to full volume.

Now that worked. He couldn't hear them. He couldn't hear anybody—not even that low rolling hum of the voices of the city around him. He hit the REPEAT DISK button on the machine, and relaxed.

With the fire flickering away, and the rain tapping at the windows, and the lovely rippling Mozart filling the room, he felt almost normal.

Well, for a moment.

He was soon skimming one scholarly source after another. Little of what he found proved a surprise. He'd always known lycanthropy was perceived by many historically as a mental illness in which you imagined you were a wolf and behaved like one; or some kind of demonic shape-shifting in which you did indeed become a wolf until someone shot you with a silver bullet and your lupine body changed back to human form as you died, maybe with a placid expression on your face, and an old gypsy woman pronounced that you would now have rest.

As for the movies, well, he'd seen a good many of them—an embarrassing number, in fact. It was easy to find seminal scenes on YouTube, and as he tracked back through **Ginger Snaps** and then Jack Nicholson's **Wolf,** something pretty ghastly came to him.

This was fiction, of course, but it presented the phase he was in as transformative and not final. Only in the early stages were some werewolves anthropoid. By the end of **Wolf,** Jack Nicholson had been a full-blown four-footed animal of the forest. By the end of **Ginger Snaps,** the unfortunate girl wolf had become a great hideous and repulsive porcine demon.

But then it spoke, he thought, flashing on Mendocino. It used a phone, for the love of hell. It punched in 911 and brought help for the victim. How old was it? How long had it been around? And what the hell was it doing in the redwood forest up there?

Celeste had said something, what was it? That there had always been wolves up there in Mendocino County? Well, the local population certainly didn't agree. He'd seen enough of them reporting on television that wolves were extinct in their part of the world forest.

Okay. Forget about the movies answering any questions. What do the movies know? Though there was one little thing worth salvaging: in several movies, the power to become a werewolf was referred to as a "gift." He liked that. A gift. That was more in keeping with what was happening to him certainly.

But in most of the movies, the gift didn't have much of a purpose. In fact, it was unclear exactly why cinema werewolves went after their victims. All they did was rip random people to pieces. They didn't even drink the blood or eat the meat. They didn't behave like wolves at all. They behaved as if . . . they had rabies. True, in **The Howling,** they had fun making out, but other than that, what was the good of being a movie werewolf? You howled at the moon; you couldn't remember what you did, and then somebody shot you.

And forget silver bullets too. If there was science behind that, well, he wasn't Reuben the Man Wolf.

Reuben the Man Wolf. That was the term he liked most of all himself. And it had been ratified by Susan Larson. Pray Billie left his headline intact.

**Is that so wrong, to want to think of myself as Man Wolf?** Again, he tried to muster some compassion for the rapist he'd killed. But he could not.

At about eight o'clock, he took a break. He shut off the Mozart and worked at shutting out the voices on his own.

Wasn't as hard as he'd thought. Celeste was no longer in the house. In fact, she'd gone off to a café with Mort Keller, who'd always been sort of in love with her, and Phil and Grace were talking about that very development right now, and they weren't really saying a whole lot. Grace had gotten a call from a specialist in Paris who was very interested in the wolf killings, but she hadn't had much time to talk with the man. Easy to shut them out.

Reuben brought up the pictures he'd taken of himself last night, which he had buried in an encrypted file that was password protected. Staring at them was horrifying and tantalizing.

He wanted it to happen again.

He had to face that. He was looking forward to it as he had never looked forward to anything in his entire life, not even his first night in bed with a woman, or Christmas morning when he was eight years old. He was waiting for it to happen.

Meantime he reminded himself that it hadn't happened until midnight the night before. And he went back to surfing classics on lycanthropy and mythology. Actually the lore of wolves in all cultures was fascinating him as much as werewolf stories proper, and old medieval traditions pertaining to a village Brotherhood of the Green Wolf charmed him with their descriptions of country people dancing wildly around bonfires into which the "wolf" was now and then symbolically tossed.

He was about to call it a night when he remembered that collection, **The Man-Wolf and Other Tales,** by those two nineteenth-century French writers. Why not try it? It was easy to find. On Amazon.com, he punched in an order for one of several reprints, and then decided to try to find the title story online.

No problem. On horrormasters.com, he found a free download. He probably wouldn't read all of it, just have a look in the vain hope that some nugget of truth might be mixed in with the fiction.

About Christmas time in the year 18—, as I was lying fast asleep at the Cygne at Fribourg, my old friend Gideon Sperver broke abruptly into my room crying—

"Fritz, I have good news for you; I am going to take you to Nideck. . . .

Nideck!
The next sentence read, "You know Nideck, the finest baronial castle in the country, a grand monument of the glory of our forefathers."

He could not quite believe his eyes. There was Marchent's last name in a story called "The Man-Wolf."

He broke off and Googled "Nideck." Yes, it was an actual place, a real Château de Nideck, a famous ruin, on the road from Oberhaslach to Wangenbourg. But that really wasn't the point. The point was the last name had been used over a hundred years ago in a short story about a werewolf. And the story had come into English in 1876, right before the Nideck family moved to Mendocino County and built their immense house overlooking the ocean. This family that came out of nowhere, apparently, if Simon Oliver was right, was named Nideck.

He was stunned. This had to be a coincidence, and certainly it was a coincidence that no one had noticed and which no one might ever notice.

But there was something else in those first few lines. He brought up the story again. Sperver. He'd seen that name before too, somewhere, and it had something to do with Marchent and Nideck Point. But what? He couldn't remember. Sperver. He could almost see the name written in ink, but where? Then it hit him. It was the last name of Felix Nideck's very dear friend and mentor, Margon, the man Felix had called Margon the Godless. Hadn't his name been written on the mat inside the framing of the big photograph over the fireplace? Oh, why hadn't he written down those names? But he was certain of it. He remembered Marchent saying the name Margon Sperver.

No, this simply could not be a coincidence. One name, yes, but two names? No. Impossible. But what in the world could this possibly mean?

He experienced a deep frisson.

Nideck.

What had Simon Oliver, his lawyer, told him? He'd talked on and on about this in phone call after phone call, as if reassuring himself of this rather than Reuben.

"The family's hardly what you would call ancient. It comes out of nowhere in the 1880s. There was an exhaustive search for relatives after Felix disappeared, for anyone who might have information on the man. They found nothing. Of course the nineteenth century is filled with new men, self-made men. A timber baron who comes out of nowhere and builds a huge house. Par for the course. The point is, you aren't likely to be challenged on all this by any long-lost heirs. They don't exist anywhere."

He sat staring at the computer screen.

Could that family name have been contrived for a reason? No. That's absurd. What would have been the reason? What, these people read an obscure werewolf story and they took the name Nideck from it? And then over a century later—. No, this was nonsense. Sperver or no Sperver. It just couldn't be. Marchent never knew of any such family secret.

He saw Marchent's radiant face, her smile, heard her laughter. So wholesome, so possessed of an inner . . . an inner what? An inner happiness?

But what if that dark house contained the proverbial dark secret?

He spent the next quarter hour skimming the short story "The Man-Wolf."

It was predictably entertaining, and typically nineteenth century. Hugh Lupus was the werewolf, of Nideck Castle, under a family curse, and the story involved tantalizing but for Reuben's purposes meaningless elements like a dwarf who answered the gates of the castle and a powerful witch called the Black Plague. Sperver was the huntsman of the Black Forest.

What could all this have to do with the reality of what Reuben had endured? Surely he didn't believe the obvious cliché that a werewolf curse hung over Nideck Point.

How could he know?

He couldn't dismiss it, that was certain.

He thought of that big photograph over Marchent's library fireplace, of those men deep in the tropical forest—Felix Nideck and his mentor, Margon Sperver. Marchent had mentioned others' names, but he couldn't clearly remember them—except that they didn't appear in the story.

Ah, he had to make an exhaustive search of all werewolf literature. And at once he set about ordering books specifically on werewolf fiction, legends, and poetry, including anthologies and studies, to be delivered overnight.

But he felt he was grasping at straws. He was imagining things.

Felix was long dead. Margon was probably dead. Marchent had searched and searched. What absurd nonsense. And the beast thing came into that house from the forest, certainly, through the shattered dining room windows. It heard the screams just as you hear screams; he smelled the evil as you smell evil.

Romantic nonsense.

A sadness came over him suddenly that Felix was dead and gone. But still: names from a man wolf story. And what if there is, what, some degenerate beast cousin roaming the forest . . . keeping guard over the house?

He felt tired.

Suddenly a warm feeling came over him. He heard the low roar of the gas fire; he heard the rain singing in the gutters. He felt warm all over, and light. The voices of the city throbbed and rumbled, and gave him the oddest feeling that he was connected to the whole world. Hmmm. It was just the opposite of the alienation he'd felt earlier when talking to real identifiable people at the **Observer.**

"You belong to them now, maybe," he whispered. The voices were too homogenized. Words, cries, pleas, hovered just below the surface.

God, what is it like to be You and hear all those people all the time everywhere, begging, imploring, calling out for anything and anyone?

He looked at his watch.

It was just past ten o'clock. What if he took off now in the Porsche for Nideck Point? Why, the drive would be nothing. Just several hours in pouring rain. Very likely he could get in the house. He'd break a little windowpane if he had to. Why would there be a problem? The house would be legally his within a few weeks. He'd already signed all the documents the title company required of him. He'd already taken over the utility bills, hadn't he? Well, hell, why not go there?

And the beast man out there, in the forest. Would he know that Reuben was there? Would he pick up the scent of the one he'd bitten and left alive?

He was burning to go up there.

Something startled him. It wasn't a sound exactly, no, but something . . . a vibration—as if a car with a pounding sound system was passing in the street.

He saw a dark woods, but it wasn't the woods of

Mendocino. No, another woods, a misty tangled woods that he knew. Alarm.

He got up and opened the doors to the deck.

The air was gusty and bitter cold. The rain struck his face and his hands. It was divinely bracing.

The city shimmered beneath its veil of rain, thicket upon thicket of lighted towers crowding in on him so beautifully. He heard a voice whispering as if in his ear: "Burn him, burn them." This was an ugly, acid voice.

His heart was thudding, and his body tensed. All over his skin came the ecstatic rippling sensation. A fount inside him let loose with a gushing power that straightened his back.

It was happening, all right, the wolf-hair was covering his body, the mane descending to his shoulders, and the waves of ecstatic pleasure were coursing over him, obliterating all caution. The wolf-hair grew from his face as though invisible fingers coaxed it, and the keening pleasure made him gasp.

His hands were already claws; as before, he tore off his clothes, and kicked off his shoes. He ran his claws over his thick hairy arms and chest.

All the sounds of the night were sharpened, the chorus rising around him, mingled with bells, fleeting streaks of music, and desperate prayers. He felt the urge to escape the confines of the room, to spring off into the darkness, utterly indifferent to where he might land.

Wait; photograph it. Get to the mirror and witness it, he thought. But there was no time for that. He heard the voices again: "We'll burn you alive, old man!"

He leapt up to the rooftop. The rain scarcely touched him. It was no more than a mist.

Towards the voice he bounded, clearing one alley and street after another, scaling the taller apartment houses and flying free over the lower buildings, springing over the broader avenues effortlessly, and heading towards the ocean, buoyed by the wind.

The voice grew louder, mingled with yet another voice, and then came the cries of the victim. "I won't tell you. I won't tell you. I'll die but I won't tell you."

He knew where he was now, traveling at his greatest conceivable speed over the buildings of the Haight. Ahead he saw the great dark rectangle of Golden Gate Park. Those woods, yes, that dense fairy forest with its secret hollows. Of course!

He plunged into it now, moving along the wet grassy ground and then up into the fragrant trees.

Suddenly he saw the ragged old man running away from his pursuers, through a tunnel in the bracken, surrounded by a sylvan camouflage in which other witnesses cowered under shining tarps and broken boards as the rain came pouring down.

One of the attackers caught the man by the shoulder and dragged him out into a grassy clearing. The rain soaked their clothes. The other attacker had stopped, and was setting afire a torch of curled newspapers, but the rain was putting out the fire.

"The kerosene!" shouted the man who held the victim. The victim was punching, and kicking. "I'll never tell you," he wailed.

"Then you'll burn with your secret, old man."

The scent of the kerosene mingled with the scent of evil, the stench of evil, as the torchbearer splashed the fluid on his torch and it burst into flame.

With a deep rolling roar, Reuben caught the torchbearer, his claws digging into the man's throat and all but splitting his head from his shoulders. The man's neck snapped.

Then he turned on the other assailant who had dropped the shuddering victim and was loping across the clearing in the downpour towards the shelter of the far trees.

Effortlessly Reuben overtook him. His jaws opened instinctively. He wanted so with all his being to dig out the man's heart. His jaws were hungry for it, aching for it. But no, not the teeth, not the teeth that could give the Wolf Gift, no, he could not risk that. His snarls coming like curses, he tore at the helpless man. "You would have burned him alive, would you?"—clawing the flesh off his face, and the skin from his chest. His claw raked through the carotid artery and the blood spurted. The man sank down on his knees and fell over, as the blood soaked his old denim coat.

Reuben turned back. The kerosene had spilled in the grass and was burning, spitting and smoking in the rain, giving the ghastly scene a hellish light.

The old man who had been the victim knelt huddled, his arms tightly wrapped around his body, staring at Reuben with large unquestioning eyes. Reuben could see the old man flinching in the rain, flinching as the cold rain beat down on him, but Reuben couldn't feel the rain.

He approached the man and reached out to help him to his feet. How powerful and calm he felt, the blaze flickering near him, the warmth barely touching him.

The dark undergrowth surrounding them was swarming with movement and whispers, with desperate accolades and ejaculations of fear.

"Where do you want to go?" Reuben asked.

The man pointed to the darkness beyond the low-hanging oaks. Reuben lifted him and carried him under the low boughs. The earth was dry and fragrant here. The matted vines formed veils. A shack of broken boards and tarpaper hung amid the swallowing ivy and giant shuddering ferns. Reuben put the man down on his nest of rags and woolen blankets. He shrank back amid the bundles that surrounded him, pulling the covers up to his neck.

The scent of dusty cloth and whiskey filled the little enclosure. The scent of raw earth surrounded them, of wet and glistening green things, of tiny animals burrowing in the dark. Reuben pulled away as if the little man-made space were a form of trap.

He moved off, quickly, taking to the sturdy treetops, arms reaching for one limb after another, as the forest grew thicker, moving back towards the dim yellow lights of Stanyan Street with its steady traffic hissing on the asphalt along the eastern border of the world of Golden Gate Park.

He seemed to fly across the breadth of the street, into the soaring eucalyptus trees of the Panhandle, the narrow arm of the park that went east.

He traveled as high as he could in the giant weed-like eucalyptus, breathing the strange bittersweet scent of their long thin pale leaves. He followed the ribbon of park, almost singing aloud as he moved from giant tree to giant tree with fluid movements, and then he made for the roofs of the Victorians that climbed the Masonic Street hill.

Who could see him in the darkness? No one. The rain was his friend. He went up over the slippery roof tiles with no hesitation and found himself traveling to the blackness of yet another small woodland— Buena Vista Park.

Out of the low simmering melee that was the voices, he picked out another despairing plea. "To die, I want to die. Kill me. I want to die."

Only it wasn't spoken aloud; it was the drum-beat behind the moans and cries he heard that were beneath or beyond language.

He landed on the roof above the victim, high atop a grand four-story mansion that bordered the steep hill leading up to the little park. Down the front of the house, he made his way, clutching the pipes and ledges, until he saw through the window the ugly spectacle of an old woman, skin and bones and bleeding sores, tied to a brass bed. Her pink scalp shone beneath her thin hanks of gray hair in the light of one small lamp.

Before her on the tray was a plate with a steaming pile of human feces, and the hunched figure of a young woman across from her held out a spoon of the loathsome mess, pressing it to the old woman's lips. The old woman shuddered and was near to fainting. Stench of filth, stench of evil, stench of cruelty. The young woman sang her bitter taunts.

"You never fed me anything but slop in all your life, you think you will not pay for it now?"

Reuben shattered the mullions and the panes as he broke into the room.

The young woman screamed and backed away from the bed. Her face was full of rage.

He bore down on her as she scrambled to pull a gun from a drawer.

The shot rang out, deafening him for one split second, and he felt the pain in his shoulder, sharp, ugly, disabling, but at once, he moved beyond it, a deep growl rising out of him as he snatched her up, the gun falling, and slammed her into the plaster wall. Her head broke the plaster; he felt the life go out of her, the curses dying in her throat.

In a snarling frenzy, he hurled her through the broken window. He heard the body strike the paving of the street.

For a long second he stood there, waiting for the

pain to return, but the pain didn't return. There was nothing there but pulsing warmth.

He moved towards the wraithlike figure that was tied with tape and bandages to the brass headboard. Carefully he ripped loose her fetters.

She had her thin face turned to one side. "Hail Mary, full of grace," she prayed in a dry, whistling whisper, "the Lord is with thee. Blessed art thou among women, and blessed is the fruit of thy womb, Jesus."

He bent down, removing the last of the bonds from her waist.

"Holy Mary, Mother of God," he said under his breath as he looked into her eyes. "Pray for us sinners—us sinners!—now and at the hour of our death."

The old woman moaned. She was too weak to move.

He left her, padding softly down the carpeted hallway of the house, and into another spacious room where he found a phone. It was so difficult to punch in the numbers. He was laughing to himself, thinking of the beast of Mendocino, tapping them out on the screen of an iPhone. When he heard the voice of the operator a wild exultant urge went through him, to say **Murder, murder,** but he did not. That would have been sheer madness. And he hated himself suddenly for thinking it so very funny. Besides, it wasn't true. "Ambulance. Break-in. Old woman top floor. Held prisoner."

The operator was questioning him, and rattling off the address for verification.

"Hurry," he said. He left the phone off the hook.

He listened.

The house was empty except for the old woman—and one other silent person who slept.

It took him only a few moments to move down to the second floor and find that helpless invalid, an old man, bound as the woman had been bound, bruised and frail, and deep asleep.

Reuben explored, finding the light switch, and flooded the scene with light.

What more could he do to bring help to this creature and the other, to make certain no colossal blunder was made?

In the hallway, he saw the dim outline of himself in a high gold-framed mirror. He smashed it, the giant shards clattering to the floor.

He picked up the old-fashioned glass-shaded lamp from the hall table and heaved it over the railing so that it was smashed on the floor of the lower front hall.

The sirens were coming, winding together, just like those unraveling sounds he heard in Mendocino. Ribbons in the night.

He could go now.

He made his escape.

For a long time, he remained in the high dark cypress woods of Buena Vista Park. The hilltop trees were slender, but he had easily found one strong enough to support him, and he watched through a mesh of branches the ambulances and the police cars collected below on the hillside outside the mansion. He saw the old woman and the old man taken away. He saw the corpse of the vengeful tormentor collected from the pavement. He saw the sleepy disheveled spectators finally wander away.

A great exhaustion came over him. The pain in his shoulder was gone. In fact, he'd forgotten about it entirely. These paws of his could not feel like hands, he realized. They could not read the texture of the sticky fluid matted in his hair.

He was becoming ever more tired, positively weak.

Yet it was a simple matter to make the secretive and rapid journey home.

Back in his room, he again confronted himself in the mirror.

"Anything new to tell me?" he asked. "What a deep voice you have."

The transformation had begun.

He gripped the soft fur between his legs even as it was shrinking, vanishing, and then he felt his fingers emerging again to touch the wound in his shoulder.

There was no wound.

No wound at all.

He was so tired now he could scarcely remain standing, but he had to make sure of this. He moved towards the mirror. No wound. But was there a bullet locked inside him, a bullet that could infect him and kill him? How could he know?

He almost laughed out loud thinking of what Grace would say if he said, **Mom, I think I got shot last night. Can you run an X-ray to see if there's a bullet lodged in my shoulder? Don't worry, I don't feel a thing.**

But no, that wasn't going to happen.

He fell into his bed, loving the soft clean smell of the pillow, and as the pewter light of morning filled the room, he went fast asleep.

## 8

REUBEN AWOKE at ten, showered, shaved, and went immediately to Simon Oliver's office to pick up the keys to Nideck Point. No, Marchent's lawyers didn't care if he visited the place; indeed the handyman needed to see him, and the sooner he could take over having some repairs made the better. And would he make his own inventory, please? They were worried about "all that stuff up there."

He was on the road before noon, speeding across the Golden Gate towards Mendocino, the rain a steady drizzle, the car filled with clothes, an extra computer, a couple of old Bose DVD players, and other things he would leave in his new refuge.

He needed this time alone desperately. He needed to be alone tonight with these powers—to study, to observe, to seek to control. Maybe he could stop the transformation at will or modulate it. Maybe he could bring it on.

Whatever the case, he had to get away from everything, including the voices that had drawn him into the slaughtering of four people. He had no choice but to head north.

And . . . and, there was always the remote possibility that something lived up there in those northern woods that knew all about what he was and might just share with him the secrets of what he'd become. He didn't really hope for that, but it was possible. He wanted to be visible to that thing. He wanted that thing to see him roaming the rooms of Nideck Point.

Grace had been at the hospital when he'd slipped out, and Phil had been nowhere around. He'd talked to Celeste briefly, listening numbly as she recounted the horrors of last night to him in boiling detail.

"And this THING just threw the woman out of the window, Reuben! And she landed smack-dab on the pavement! I mean the city is going crazy! It ripped apart two bums in Golden Gate Park, gutting one of them like a fish. And everybody loved your story, Reuben. The Man Wolf—that's what they're calling him. You could get a cut from the mugs and the T-shirts, you know. Maybe you should trademark 'Man Wolf.' But who's going to believe what that crazy woman in North Beach said? I mean, what is the thing going to do next: scrawl a poetic message on a wall in the victim's blood?"

"That's a thought, Celeste," Reuben had murmured.

When traffic stalled on the Waldo Grade, he called Billie.

"You scored again, Boy Wonder," said Billie. "I don't know how you do it. It's been picked up by the wire services and websites around the world. People are linking to it on Facebook and Twitter. You gave this monster, the Man Wolf, some metaphysical depth!"

Had he? How had that happened—with his attention to Susan Larson's descriptions, and her account of the creature's voice? He couldn't even remember what he'd written now. But they were calling him the Man Wolf and that was a small score.

Billie was raving about what had just happened. She wanted him to talk to the Golden Gate Park witnesses and the neighbors on Buena Vista Hill.

Well, he had to go up north, he had no choice, he told her. He had to see the scene of the crime where he was almost killed.

"Well, of course, you're looking for evidence of the Man Wolf up there, right? Get some pix of that hallway! You realize we never had any pix inside that house? Have you got your Nikon with you?"

"What's happening with the kidnap?" he demanded.

"These kidnappers aren't giving any assurance that the kids will be returned alive. It's a standoff, with the FBI saying don't transfer the money till the kidnappers come up with a plan. They aren't telling us everything, but my contacts in the sheriff's office say they're dealing with real professionals here. And it doesn't look good. If this damned San Francisco Man Wolf is so hot to bring superhero justice and vengeance to the world, why the hell doesn't he go find those missing children?"

Reuben swallowed. "That's a good question," he said.

**And just maybe the Man Wolf hasn't gotten his act together yet, and is gaining confidence night by night, ever think of that, Billie?** But he didn't say it.

A wave of sickness came over him. He thought of the bodies of those dead men in Golden Gate Park. He thought of the corpse of that woman on the pavement. Maybe Billie should visit the morgue, and take a look at the human wreckage "the superhero" was leaving behind. This was no series of capers.

His sickness was short-lived, however. He was keenly aware that he had no pity for any of those creatures. And just as keenly aware that he'd had no right to kill any of them. So what?

The traffic was moving. And the rain had picked up. He had to go. The noise of the traffic was muting the voices around himself somewhat, but he could still hear them, like a bubbling brew.

He started surfing the radio for news and talk, turning it up loud to seal every other sound out.

It was either the Goldenwood kidnapping or the Man Wolf, with all the predictable jokes and ridicule of the beast and his dubious witnesses. The name "Man Wolf" was a favorite, all right. But there was still plenty of talk of a Yeti, Bigfoot, or even a Gorilla Man. One caramel-voiced commentator on National Public Radio compared the rampages and their ambiguous physical evidence to "The Murders in the Rue Morgue" and speculated that this could be a beast manipulated by a human handler; or a powerful man dressed in furred costume.

In fact, the more Reuben listened, the more it came clear that the idea of a costumed perpetrator was gaining favor. People weren't accepting evidence or testimony to the contrary. And certainly nobody thought or guessed that this creature had any special power to search out injustice; it was assumed he'd stumbled on the situations in which he'd intervened. And nobody suggested that he could or ought to catch the Goldenwood kidnappers. Billie had been way ahead on that one. And so was Reuben himself.

Why not try to find those children? Why not cancel this trip north and start driving the back roads of Marin County scanning for those children and those three adults?

Reuben couldn't get that out of his mind. Didn't it stand to reason that the kidnappers could not have transported those forty-five victims very far at all?

Some talk show hosts were thoroughly disgusted that anybody was focusing on anything other than the Goldenwood kidnapping. And one parent had broken with the FBI and the sheriff's office to publicly condemn both for not paying the ransom on demand.

The power Reuben had enjoyed last night, and make no mistake, he had enjoyed it, was nothing when he thought of the missing children, and those

parents sobbing behind closed doors at the Goldenwood Academy. What if? But how exactly? Should
he simply drive the back roads in the vicinity of the
kidnapping, listening with his new acute hearing for
the victims' cries?

The trouble was, his hearing wasn't very acute early
in the day. It sharpened as night came on, and that
would be hours from now.

The rain came down heavier as he pushed north.
For long stretches, people drove with their headlamps
on. When the traffic slowed to a crawl in Sonoma
County, Reuben realized he'd never make it to Nideck
Point and back before dark. Hell, it was twilight now
at 2:00 p.m.

He pulled off in Santa Rosa, tapped his iPhone
for the address of the nearest Big Man XL clothing store, and quickly bought two of the largest and
longest raincoats they had, including a tolerable-
looking brown trench coat that he actually liked, several pairs of superbig sweatpants, and three hooded
sweatshirts, and then found a ski store for ski masks
and the largest ski mittens they carried. He threw in
five brown cashmere scarves that would be good for
hiding his face right up to a pair of giant sunglasses,
if the ski masks didn't work or were too frightening, and the giant sunglasses he found in the drug-
store.

Walmart had giant rain boots.

All this was powerfully exciting.

He went back to the news as soon as he was on the road again. The rain was almost torrential. The traffic moved sluggishly and sometimes not at all. He would definitely be spending the night in Mendocino County.

Around four o'clock, he reached the forest road leading directly to Marchent's house—well, our house, that is. The news sang on.

On the Man Wolf front, the coroner's office had now confirmed that the dead woman of Buena Vista Hill had been only distantly related to the old couple she'd been torturing. And the woman's own mother had died in mysterious circumstances two years before. As for the dead men in Golden Gate Park, both were now linked by fingerprint evidence to two baseball bat murders of homeless men in the Los Angeles area. The victim in Golden Gate Park had been identified as a missing Fresno man, and his family had been overjoyed to be reunited with him. The would-be rapist of North Beach was a convicted killer, just released from prison after serving less than ten years for a rape-murder.

"So whoever this mad avenger is," the police spokesman said, "he has an uncanny knack for intervening in the right situations and in the nick of time, and that's all very commendable, but his methods have now made him the target of the largest manhunt in San Francisco history."

"Make no mistake," he went on to say when the frenzy of questions had been allowed to crest, "we are dealing here with a dangerous and obviously psychotic individual."

"Is he a man wearing some kind of animal costume?"

"We'll address this question when we've had more time to process the evidence."

So tell them about the abundant lysozyme in the saliva, Reuben thought, but of course you won't. That would only exacerbate the hysteria. And he'd left no saliva evidence last night, just whatever might have come from the claws with which he'd slashed his victims.

One thing was clear. People weren't fearing for their lives with the Man Wolf. But nobody, or so the radio call-ins seemed to indicate, believed the Man Wolf had actually spoken words to the North Beach victim and witness.

Reuben was about to shut the radio off when the news came in that the body of one little eight-year-old Goldenwood Academy student had been found two hours ago in the surf at Muir Beach. Cause of death: blunt force trauma.

There was a press conference in progress at the sheriff's headquarters in San Rafael. It sounded like a lynching.

"Until we have a concrete plan for the return of the children and the teachers," said the sheriff, "we cannot accede to the kidnappers' demands."

Enough. Reuben couldn't take any more. He turned off the radio. A little girl dead on Muir Beach. So these "tech geniuses" had done that, had they?

Simply murdered one of their numerous victims to show they meant business? Of course. When you have forty-five potential victims, why not?

He was in a fury.

It was five o'clock, and dark, and the rain showed no sign of slacking. And the voices of the world were very far away. In fact, he heard no voices. That meant, obviously, that he could no more hear over an infinite distance than an animal. But what were the actual limits of his powers? He had no idea.

Little girl found dead in the surf.

That was all the more reason, wasn't it, to conclude that the other victims were not very far away at all.

Abruptly, he came to the top of the final rise, and in the beam of his headlamps he saw the enormous house looming ahead of him, a giant phantom of itself in the rain, far more grand than memory had allowed him to envision it. There were lights in its windows.

He was awed by the sight of it, awed by the moment.

But he was also miserable. He couldn't stop thinking about the children—about that little girl on that cold beach.

As he pulled up to the front door, the outside lamps went on, illuminating not only the steps and the door itself, but flashing upwards on the façade at least as far as the top of the second-floor windows. What a glorious place it was.

Oh, how very far he was from the innocent young

guy who'd first crossed that threshold with Marchent Nideck.

The door opened and the handyman appeared in a yellow rain slicker and came down to help Reuben with his bundles and suitcase.

The big room already had a roaring fire. And Reuben could smell the rich aroma of coffee.

"I've got some supper for you on the stove," said the handyman, a tall lean gray-eyed person, very weathered and wrinkled, with sparse iron-colored hair and a colorless but agreeable smile. He had one of those pleasant, accentless California voices that gave no hint of his home base or origins. "My wife brought that up here for you. She didn't cook herself, of course. She got it at the local Redwood House down in the town. And some groceries, too. She took the liberty—."

"I'm so pleased," said Reuben at once. "I thought of everything but food, thank you. And I was absolutely crazy to think I could get here by four o'clock. I am so sorry."

"No bother," the man said. "My name's Leroy Galton and everybody calls me Galton. My wife is Bess. My wife's lived here all her life, used to cook and clean up here now and then when there were parties." He took the suitcase from Reuben, and hefting the bundles in one hand he headed back the hallway towards the stairs.

Reuben felt the breath go out of him. They were

nearing the spot where he'd struggled with Marchent's attackers, the spot where he'd nearly died.

He hadn't remembered the dark oak wainscoting. No bloodstains were visible. But some seven feet of carpet stretching from the stairs to the kitchen door was obviously brand-new. It did not match the wide Oriental runner on the stairs.

"You'd never know it even happened!" declared Galton triumphantly. "We scrubbed those floorboards. There must have been two inches of old wax on them anyway. You would just never know."

Reuben stopped. No memory attached itself to the spot. All he remembered was darkness, and he slipped into the darkness, compulsively reliving the attack, as though he was making the Stations of the Cross in St. Francis at Gubbio Church on Good Friday. Teeth like needles driving into his neck and skull.

**Did you know what would happen to me when you let me live?**

Galton let loose with a long, truly awe-inspiring string of clichés and platitudes to the effect that life goes on, life belongs to the living, these things happen, nobody's safe, you know, you never knew why things happened, one day you would know why things happened, and even the best boys can go bad these days with the dope the way it is, and we just have to get over these things and move on.

"I'll tell you this much," he said suddenly in a low, confidential voice. "I know what did it. I know what got you. And it's a miracle it let you live."

The hair stood up on the back of Reuben's neck. His heart was thudding in his ears. "You know what did it?" he asked.

"Mountain lion," said Galton, narrowing his eyes and lifting his chin. "And I know which mountain lion too. She's been in these parts too long."

Reuben shook his head. He felt a surge of relief. Back to the old mystery. "It couldn't have been," he said.

"Oh, son, we all know it was that mountain lion. She's out there somewhere now with her litter. Three times I've gotten a clear shot at her and missed. She took my dog from me, young man. Now you never knew my dog. But my dog was no ordinary dog."

Reuben felt a surge of relief at all this, because it was utterly off the mark.

"My dog was the most beautiful German shepherd I ever saw. Panzer was his name, and I reared that dog from a six-week-old pup myself and trained him never to take a morsel of food except from my hand, gave him all the commands in German, and he was the finest dog I ever had."

"And the mountain lion got him," Reuben murmured.

The old man lifted his chin again and nodded solemnly. "Dragged him off, right out of my yard down there and into the woods, and there was hardly anything left of him when I found him. She did that. She and her litter, and that litter's almost grown. I went after her, went after the brood. I'll get her, permit or no permit! They can't stop me. Just a matter of time.

But you be careful if you go walking in these woods. She's got her young cats with her. I know she has, she's teaching them to hunt, and you have to be careful at sundown and at dawn."

"I'll be careful," Reuben said. "But it really wasn't a mountain lion."

"And how do you know that, son?" the man asked.

Why was he arguing? Why was he even saying a word? Let the old man believe what he wanted to believe. Isn't that what everybody was doing?

"Because I would have smelled it if it had been a mountain lion," he confessed, "and the scent would have been on the dead men and on me."

The man pondered that for a moment, reluctantly, but seemingly honestly. He shook his head. "Well, she got my dog," he confessed, "and I'm going to kill her just the same."

Reuben nodded.

The old man started up the broad oak stairway.

"Did you hear about that poor little girl in Marin County?" Galton asked over his shoulder.

Reuben murmured that indeed he had.

He could scarce breathe. But he wanted to see everything, yes, every single thing.

The place looked so clean, polished floorboards gleaming on either side of the old Oriental carpet. The little candlelike sconces were all lighted as they had been that first night.

"You can put me in that last bedroom back there,"

he said. This was the last one at the end of the western hall, Felix's old room.

"You don't want the master bedroom on the front of the house? Gets a lot more sun, that front room. Beautiful front room."

"Not sure yet. This is fine for now."

The man led the way, snapping on the light quickly enough as though he was entirely familiar with the house.

The bed was freshly made up with a cheap flowered polyester bedspread. But Reuben found fresh sheets and pillowcases underneath and some very old but clean towels in the bathroom.

"My wife did the best she could," said Galton. "The bank wanted the place decent, they said, soon as the police released the crime scene."

"Gotcha," said Reuben.

The man was cheerful and kind, but Reuben wanted this part of it all to be over.

They walked through a number of the rooms, chatted, talked about simple repairs, a doorknob here, a window painted shut there, some Sheetrock crumbling in a bathroom.

The master bedroom was indeed impressive, with its original brilliant flowered William Morris wallpaper, and the best bedroom on the front of the house.

It occupied the southwest corner, had windows on two sides and a very spacious marble bathroom with a windowed shower. The fire had been lighted there especially for Reuben, in the big deep stone hearth beneath the scrollwork mantel.

"In the old days, there was an iron stairs in that left corner," said Galton, "that went up to the attic room above. But Felix couldn't have that. He had to be private up there and he made his nephew and his nephew's wife take out that stairs." Galton enjoyed the role of tour guide. "All this is the original furniture, you know." He pointed to the huge walnut bed. "That's Renaissance Revival, broken-arch style. You see those urn finials? That headboard's nine feet, solid walnut. Those are burl panels." He gestured to the marble-top dresser. "Broken-arch style," he said pointing to the high mirror. "And that's the original washstand too. Berkey and Gay made this furniture in Grand Rapids. Same with that table. Don't know where the big leather chair came from. Marchent's father loved that chair. Had his breakfast up here every morning, with the papers. Somebody had to go get the papers. Nobody would deliver them out here. These are real American antiques. This house was built for furniture like this. It was Felix who brought in all the European furniture in the library and great room downstairs. That Felix was a Renaissance man."

"That I can see," said Reuben.

"We fixed up this room special for you with the best sheets. Everything you need is in the bathroom. Those flowers on the table came from my garden," he said.

Reuben was grateful, and he said so. "I'll make

my way here eventually," he said. "It's surely the best room in the house."

"It's the best view of the sea, from here," Galton said. "Of course Marchent never used it. It was always her parents' room to her. Her bedroom's just down the hall."

Shades of Mrs. Danvers, thought Reuben quietly. He felt one of those delicious chills to which he was becoming all the more susceptible. **This is my house now, my house.**

He wanted so badly for Phil to see this place, but he couldn't bring Phil up here just now. That was simply out of the question.

The southeast bedroom of the house was just as quaint as the master, and so were the two central front bedrooms that faced south. These three had the heavy impressive Grand Rapids furnishings and the dazzling floral William Morris paper, but the paper was coming down in places and moldy in others, badly in need of repair. None of these bedrooms had been renovated yet, confessed Galton. Didn't have enough electric outlets, and the fireplaces needed work. And charming as the old bathrooms were, with old pedestal sinks and claw-foot tubs, they would have been uncomfortable to use. "Felix would have gotten to all this," said Galton, shaking his head.

Even the long wide front hallway had a neglected aspect to it with threadbare carpet.

They moved on to several other eastern bedrooms that had the American antiques as well—sometimes massive bedsteads and scatterings of old Renaissance Revival chairs.

"Now all this here is renovated," Galton said proudly, "and all this is wired for cable, every bedroom in the place. You've got central heat in these rooms and working fireplaces. Felix saw to that. But Marchent never installed televisions. And the old televisions are long gone. Marchent wasn't much of a one for television, and, well, after the boys were banned from the place, there just was no point. She brought friends here all the time, of course. Why, she brought a whole club of people here one time from South America. But they didn't care about television. She said it was just fine."

"You think you could mount a good flat screen for me in that master bedroom, with full cable service?" asked Reuben. "I'm a news junkie. Get the top of the line. Wouldn't mind a good flat screen in the library downstairs either. And maybe something small in the kitchen. As I said I cook for myself."

"No problem, I'll get right on it," said Galton with obvious glee.

They went back down the oak stairs, and through the vestibule of death.

"Now, you do know I have two other fellas working with me," said Galton, "and so they'd be in and out of here too, but one's my cousin and one's my stepson. It's the same as having me. We can do just about anything you want done."

They went back downstairs, and Galton showed

Reuben proudly how the broken dining room windows had been "restored" so you could hardly tell they were not the originals. And that was no easy thing to do what with diamond-pane leaded glass like this.

Those miserable brothers had raided the little silver pantries on both sides of the broad door to the great room, dragging out silver platters and teapots and leaving them strewn all over the alcove, just to make it look like a robbery, as if anyone was stupid enough to fall for that.

"Well, all of that has been put right," he said. He opened the doors on either side for Reuben to see. "You have plenty enough pantries in this house," he said, "what with those two pantries, and the butler's pantry right there before you go into the kitchen. Hope you're looking forward to a big family and lots of kids. There's a closet down at that other end off the hallway and that's full of china and silver, too."

Bracing himself Reuben followed the man into the kitchen. Very slowly, he turned to survey the floor, and discovered that the white marble had been covered by a series of oval braided throw rugs. Somewhere under all that was Marchent's blood, probably visible in the grouting if not in the marble. He had no idea where she had fallen. He knew with all his heart he did not want to be in the room, and the idea of ladling up stew from the steaming pot on the stove was revolting to him. Revolting.

Eating right after a "death" had always revolted him. He remembered when Celeste's brother had died in Berkeley. Reuben had not been able to eat or drink anything for days, without vomiting.

He was doing a very good job of concealing his distress. Galton was watching him, waiting.

"Look, you go ahead," said Reuben. "I give you carte blanche on the repairs." He opened his wallet and drew out a wad of bills. "This ought to start things off. And stock the freezer and the pantry, you know, with all the usual stuff. I know how to defrost and cook a leg of lamb. Get me a sack or two of potatoes, carrots, and onions. I can fend for myself. You just tend to everything. The main thing with me is privacy. I ask that nobody, I mean nobody, be admitted to the place except your workmen and only then when you're with them yourself."

The man was pleased. He put the wad of bills in his pocket. He nodded to everything. He explained "those reporters" had been all around, snooping on the outside, but none had dared to come in, and then when the kidnapping happened, the reporters had vanished. "That's the way it is today, with the Internet and all," said Galton. "Everything's a flash in the pan, though now of course they're talking about this Man Wolf in San Francisco, and people have been calling up here, you know. The police drove by here twice earlier."

Besides, the alarm had been connected since the police left the place. He had personally set the alarm as soon as the investigators were out. The family lawyer had seen to all that. Once that alarm was set, the entire ground floor was covered by motion detectors, glass breaker alarms, and contacts on all doors and windows.

"When that alarm goes off, it rings my house, and the local police station simultaneously. I call. They call. But no matter what they barrel on up here."

He gave Reuben the alarm code, showed him how to punch it in, and told him there was a keypad on the second floor that he could use to take off the motion detectors before he came downstairs in the morning. "Now, if you want it on while you're still moving around, then you punch in the code and press HOME, and your windows and doors are covered without the motion detectors.

"Oh, and you have to have my e-mail. I check my e-mail all day. You e-mail me about anything you find wrong up here. I'm on it." He held up his iPhone proudly. "Oh you just call me. This phone's right by my bed all night."

Not to worry about the furnaces either. The old gas furnaces were relatively new, considering the age of the place, and there was absolutely no asbestos in the place. They were keeping the house at about sixty-nine degrees, which was how Marchent had liked it. Of course a lot of the vents were closed off. But wasn't it warm enough in here now?

And by the way, there's a cellar under this house, a small cellar, with a stairs under the main stairs. Forgot about that. Nothing down there, however, because all the furnaces were moved out back into the service wing years ago.

"Yes, fine," said Reuben.

The Internet service was connected too, just as Miss Marchent had had it before. The service covered the whole house. There was a router in her office and in the second-floor electrical room at the end of the hall up there.

Reuben was happy about all that.

Reuben walked Galton to the back door.

For the first time under the high floodlights in the trees he saw a broad parking area and the back two-story servants' wing to the far left where, apparently, Felice had been murdered. It was obviously a later addition to the house.

He could see almost nothing of the forest beyond the lights, just here and there a bit of green and the streak of light on the bark of a tree.

**Are you out there? Are you watching? Do you remember the man you spared when you killed the others?**

Galton had a brand-new Ford truck and discoursed on its virtues for several minutes. Few things made a man feel better than a brand-new truck. Reuben might want to keep a truck on the property, would come in handy. But then Galton's truck was at Reuben's disposal. Then he was off with the promise that he could be here in ten minutes if Reuben rang his cell or house phone.

"One last question," Reuben said. "I have the surveyor's maps and all, but is there any kind of fencing around this property?"

"No," said the man. "The redwoods run on for miles, with some of the oldest trees on the coast out there. But you don't get many hikers. This is too off the beaten path. They're all headed for the state parks. The Hamiltons live north and the Drexel family used to live east but I don't think there's anybody out there anymore. That place has been for sale for years. I did see a light out there a couple of weeks ago. Probably just a real estate agent. They've got trees on that property as old as your trees."

"I can't wait to walk the woods," Reuben murmured but what he was registering was that he was really alone here. Alone.

Come to think of it, what could be better when the change came—than to walk these woods as the Man Wolf, seeing and hearing—and perhaps tasting things—as never before?

And what about the mountain lion and her brood? Were they really close? Something in him stirred at the thought of it—a beast as powerful as a mountain lion. Could he outrun such an animal? Could he kill it?

He stood for a moment in the kitchen door listening as the sound of Galton's truck died away, and then he turned around and faced the empty house and everything that had happened there.

# 9

HE HADN'T BEEN the least bit afraid of anything when he'd come here the first time. And now he was far more removed from fear than he'd been then. He felt quietly powerful, resilient, and self-confident in a way he'd never felt before the transformation.

Nevertheless he did not entirely like being this alone, this utterly alone, and he really never had much liked it.

He'd grown up in the crowds of San Francisco, squeezed into the high narrow house on Russian Hill with its small elegant rooms, and the constant vitality of Grace and Phil and Grace's friends coming and going. He'd spent his life in groups and gatherings, just steps from the foot traffic of North Beach and Fisherman's Wharf, minutes from his favorite restaurants on busy Union Street, or Union Square—loving cruise-ship family vacations and wandering with bands of intrepid students through Middle Eastern ruins.

Now he had the solitude and quiet he'd been craving, dreaming of, the solitude and quiet that had seduced him so powerfully that first afternoon here with Marchent, and it settled over him and he felt more alone than ever in his life, and more alienated from everything, even the memory of Marchent, than he'd ever been.

If there was something out there in the night, something that knew more about him perhaps than anyone did, he couldn't feel it. He couldn't hear it. He heard small sounds, sounds without menace. That was all.

And he couldn't really hope for that creature to come either.

He felt too alone.

Well, time to get to work—to learn the place, and learn whatever else he could.

The kitchen was cavernous and spotlessly clean. Even the braided throw rugs were new, and dreadfully unsuited for the white marble floor. Copper-bottomed pans hung from iron hooks above the central island with its butcher-block surface and small fancy sinks. Black granite countertops gleamed along the walls. Behind the glass doors of the white enameled cabinets he saw row upon row of china in different patterns, and the more utilitarian pitchers and bowls of a large kitchen. A long narrow butler's pantry ran between kitchen and dining room, and there was more china and a lot of linen in the glass-doored cabinets there.

Slowly, he glanced in the direction of Marchent's office. Then he made his way into the small darkened room, and stared at the blank desk. This place had been carved out of the western end of the kitchen, and the marble floor ran on underneath. All the clutter he'd glimpsed that fatal night had apparently been gathered into white storage boxes, each labeled in black felt-tip writing with numbers and abbreviations that must have meant something to the police who'd come to investigate Marchent's murder. The floor had been swept and mopped, obviously. Yet a faint perfume lingered in the room—**Marchent.**

He felt a surge of love for her and unspeakable pain. He held tight waiting for it to pass.

Everything was dusted and still. The computer was there, though what was left on its hard drive, he could not guess. The printer and fax machine stood ready for action. There was a copy machine with a glass window, for copying from books. And there was a photograph on the wall, a single portrait, under framed glass, which Reuben had not seen before, of Felix Nideck.

It was one of those formal front-facing portraits that appear to be staring right at you. Sheet film again, he reasoned, because you could see the tiniest details so clearly.

The man's hair was dark and wavy. His smile was immediate, his dark eyes warm and expressive. He wore what appeared to be a tailored jacket of faded denim, and a white shirt open at the neck. He seemed about to speak.

In black ink in the left-hand corner was written: "Beloved Marchent. Don't forget me. Love, Uncle Felix, '85."

Reuben turned his back and closed the door.

He hadn't expected all this to hurt so very much.

"Nideck Point," he whispered. "I accept all you have to give me." But he didn't so much as glance towards the hallway outside the kitchen door where he'd almost been killed.

**Let's take it one thing at a time.**

He stood quiet. He could not hear a sound in the night. Then far away he heard the sea banging on the coast, banging, the waves sounding like big guns as they thundered on the beach. But he'd had to reach for that sound, reach beyond these placid well-lighted rooms.

He took some stew on a plate, found a fork in a drawer of silver, and went into the eastern breakfast room, sitting down at the table in front of the windows.

Even this room had its wood fire—though it wasn't lighted—in a black iron Franklin stove in the corner, and there was a big oak hutch of painted plates along the back wall.

A finely carved Black Forest cuckoo clock hung just to the right of the hutch. Phil would love that, Reuben thought. Phil had once collected cuckoo clocks, and their constant chiming and tweeting and cooing had driven everybody at home a little nuts.

Black Forest. He thought of that story, "The Man-Wolf," and of the character of Sperver. And the Nideck connection. Black Forest. He had to go look at that picture in the library, but there were so many pictures upstairs to check as well.

One thing at a time.

The windows here covered most of the eastern wall.

He'd never liked sitting before naked windows at night, especially when one could see nothing in the dark world beyond, but he did it consciously and deliberately now. To anyone out there in the forest he must be strikingly visible here, as if he were on a lighted stage.

**So if you are out there, degenerate cousin of the great Nidecks, well, for the love of heaven, make yourself known.**

There was no doubt in his mind that he would change later, of course, as he had the night before and the night before, even if he did not know why or when. But he was going to try to bring it on sooner. And he wondered if that creature, that creature who just might be out there watching, would wait for that transformation before he or it appeared.

He ate the beef, the carrots, the potatoes, whatever he could spear with the fork. It was pretty good, actually. So much for being disgusted by food. He lifted the plate and drank the broth. Nice of Galton's wife to arrange this.

Suddenly he set the fork down and he rested his forehead in his hands, elbows on the table. "Marchent, forgive me," he whispered. "Forgive me for forgetting for one moment you died here."

He was still sitting there quietly when Celeste called him.

"You're not afraid up there?"

"Afraid of what?" he asked. "The people who attacked me are dead. They've been dead since it happened."

"I don't know. I don't like to think of you up there. You know what's happened. They found this little girl."

"I heard on the way up here."

"There're reporters camped outside the sheriff's office."

"I'm sure of it. I'm not going there just now."

"Reuben, you're missing the biggest story of your career."

"My career's six months old, Celeste, I have a long way to go."

"Reuben, you have never had your priorities straight," she said gently, emboldened obviously by the miles between them. "You know, nobody who knows you expected you to write such interesting articles for the **Observer** and you should be writing right now. I mean when you took that job, I thought, Yeah, sure, and How long will this last? and now you're the one who's given the Man Wolf his name. Everybody's referencing your description—."

"The witness's description, Celeste—." But why was he bothering to argue, or to talk at all?

"Look, I'm here with Mort. Mort wants to say hello."

Now that was cozy, wasn't it?

"How're you doing, old buddy?"

"Fine, just fine," said Reuben.

Mort went on for a little while about Reuben's article on the Man Wolf. "Good stuff," he said. "Are you writing something on the house up there?"

"I don't want to draw any more attention to this house," he said. "I don't want to remind anybody about it anymore."

"That figures. Besides, this is one of those stories that will be over before it ever grows legs."

You think so?

Mort mentioned he might take Celeste to a movie in Berkeley, and he wished Reuben was there to come with them.

Hmmmm.

Reuben said fine, he'd catch up with them both in a few days. End of phone call.

So that was it. She was with Mort and she was having too good a time and she felt guilty and so she rang me. And what is she doing going to a movie with Mort when the whole city's looking for the kidnappers or the Man Wolf?

Since when did Celeste want to be in a Berkeley art house with those kinds of things going on? Well, maybe she was falling for Mort. He couldn't blame her. The fact was, he did not care.

After he'd put the plate and fork in one of the three dishwashers he discovered under the counter, he started his real tour of things.

He went all through the ground floor, peering into the closets and pantries that were everywhere, finding all as it had been, except that old abandoned conservatory had been thoroughly cleaned, and all the dead plants taken away, and the black granite floor tidily swept. Even the old Grecian fountain had been scoured apparently, and someone had fixed a neat note, "Needs pump," to the side of it with Scotch tape.

Beneath the main stairs, he found the steps to the cellar, and it was small, a cement room about twenty feet square, lined with darkly stained wooden storage cabinets, floor to ceiling, filled with stained and torn linen that had seen its day. One dusty obsolete furnace still stood against the wall. He could see where other furnaces had once been. The ductwork was gone, the ceiling patched. A broken dining room chair stood in one corner, and an old electric hair dryer, and an empty steamer trunk.

Now came a key moment, one he'd anticipated as he deliberately put it off: the library and the distinguished gentlemen of the jungle in their gilt frame. He headed back upstairs.

He entered the library as if it were a sanctum.

Turning on the overhead chandelier, he read the names written in ink on the framing mat.

Margon Sperver, Baron Thibault, Reynolds Wagner, Felix Nideck, Sergei Gorlagon, and Frank Vandover.

Quickly he typed them into an iPhone e-mail and sent it to himself.

What remarkable and cheerful faces these men had. Sergei was a giant as Marchent had mentioned, with very blond hair and bushy blond eyebrows and a long rectangular face. Quite Nordic looking, indeed. The others were all slightly smaller, but varied in physiognomy quite a bit. Only Felix and Margon were dark skinned, as if they had some Asian or Latin blood.

Were they sharing some kind of personal joke in this photo? Or was this just a marvelous moment during a great adventure shared by close friends?

Sperver; Nideck. Maybe it was just coincidence and nothing else. The other names didn't mean anything much to Reuben at all.

Well, they'd be here forever now; and he could spend hours with them later this evening or tomorrow or tomorrow after that.

He went upstairs.

Now came more very special moments. He opened the doors that had been locked that first night. All were unlocked now.

"Storerooms," Galton had said dismissively.

He saw the crowded shelves he'd anticipated with such relish, the countless statues in jade or diorite or alabaster, the scattered books, fragments. . . .

He went from room to room, hoping to capture the scope of it.

And then he pounded up the bare steps at the front of the house to the third floor, and groping for a light switch, quickly found himself in a vast room beneath the sloping roofs of the southwest gable, gazing at wooden tables scattered with books, papers, more statues, and curios, boxes of cards covered in scribbled writing, blank books, what seemed to be ledgers, even bundles of letters.

This was the room above the master bedroom, the one that Felix had sealed off. Indeed he saw the square of replaced flooring where the iron stairs had once been.

There were big old sagging comfortable chairs in the center of this room beneath an old black iron chandelier.

On the arm of one chair, he found a small dusty paperback book.

He picked it up.

## Pierre Teilhard de Chardin
### How I Believe

Now this was most curious. Had Felix been a reader of Teilhard de Chardin, one of Catholicism's most elegant and mysterious theologians? Reuben didn't really have a mind for abstract philosophy or theology, any more than he did for science. But he loved the poetic dimension of Teilhard and always had. So did his brother, Jim. Reuben found a kind of promise in Teilhard, who'd been not only an ardent believer in God but a believer in the world, as he had often put it.

Reuben opened the book now. The paper was aged and brittle. Copyright 1969.

**I believe that the universe is an evolution.**
**I believe that evolution proceeds toward**
   **spirit.**
**I believe that spirit is fully realized in a form**
   **of personality.**
**I believe that the supremely personal is the**
   **Universal Christ.**

Well, bully for Teilhard, he thought bitterly. He felt a deep sadness suddenly, a bit of anger and then something akin to despair. Despair wasn't in his nature really. But he knew it in moments like this. He was about to put the book back when he saw there was something scribbled in ink on this page:

**Beloved Felix,**
**For You!**
**We have survived this;**
**we can survive anything.**
**In Celebration,**
**Margon**
**Rome '04**

Well, this was his now.

He shoved the small relic into his coat pocket.

Far to the back of the room, he saw the discarded iron stairs, all of a circular piece lying on its side in the dust. There were boxes there, boxes he wouldn't try to search just now.

For the next hour, he roamed, finding two other

isolated gable attic rooms like this first one, and another that was empty. All were reached by closeted staircases from the front hall below.

Then he went back down to Felix's old room that he would occupy tonight, and he felt a little panic that he'd been here so far away from the television news that had sustained him since he'd been old enough to turn it on at the age of four. But then he had his computer, of course. And maybe it was all just as well.

It was the night that the power went out in Berkeley that he'd finished Joyce's **Finnegans Wake** by the light of a candle. Sometimes you need to be forced to study what's right in front of you.

He surveyed Felix's shelves. These items in his bedroom must have been the most important to him. Where would he begin? What would he examine first?

Something was missing.

At first he thought, No, I've just made a mistake. I've misremembered. But as he quickly scanned every shelf in the room, he realized he was right.

The tablets, the tiny Mesopotamian tablets, the priceless tablets covered in cuneiform, were gone. Every single one of them, every single fragment of them, was missing.

He went down the hall and examined two other storerooms. Same result. No tablets.

He went back up to the attics.

Same thing. Treasures galore but no tablets.

And now in the dust he could see where things had been that were no longer there.

Everywhere he searched he found evidence that small items—the tablets—had been carefully collected and removed, leaving shiny blank places in the dust.

He went back to the room he knew best and double-checked. The tablets were indeed gone, and the dustless places were clearly visible and he could see here and there fingerprints.

He panicked.

Someone had come into this house and stolen the most valuable parts of Felix's collection. Someone had taken the most significant finds he'd brought back with him from years of traveling in the Middle East. Someone had raided the treasure that Marchent had wanted so to protect and to bequeath. Someone had . . .

But that was ridiculous.

Who could have done that? Who could have done that and left so very much here utterly undisturbed— statues that were surely worth a fortune, even old scrolls that must have been priceless to scholars and curators? Who would have left the little boxes of ancient coins and, look there, a medieval codex in plain sight, and he'd seen others upstairs, books that libraries would have paid a fortune for.

He couldn't figure this out! What sort of person would have known what the tablets were, when in fact some of them had looked like pieces of dirt, or plaster or even dried cookie or biscuit?

And imagine the care of this august thief, ferreting out these precious fragments from amid so much valuable clutter and slipping away leaving all else undisturbed.

Who would have had the knowledge, the patience, the skill, to do this?

Didn't make sense, but the tablets were gone. There was not a fragment left in the house with the precious cuneiform writing.

And just maybe a lot of other things were gone and Reuben simply wasn't aware of it.

He began to rummage through items on the bedroom shelves. Here were books from the seventeenth century, pages soft and disintegrating, but still turnable, readable. Yes, and this statuette was genuine, he could see and feel that as he set it back down.

Oh, there was so much here that was worth a fortune.

Why, on one shelf he found an exquisite necklace of soft, pliable gold worked into engraved leaves that was surely ancient.

He was very careful to put it back exactly as he had found it.

Reuben went down to the library and rang Simon Oliver on his home phone.

"I need some information," Reuben said. "I need to know if the police photographed every single thing in this house when they investigated, I mean did they photograph all the rooms they didn't disturb. Can you get me those photographs?"

Simon protested that that wouldn't be easy, but the

Nideck law firm had photographed everything right after Marchent's death.

"Marchent took photographs of all of it, she told me," said Reuben. "Can you get those photographs?"

"I honestly don't know. I'll see what I can do. You'll get the law firm's inventory, of that I'm quite sure."

"The sooner the better," said Reuben. "Tomorrow, e-mail me whatever photographs of the place you can."

He rang off and called Galton.

The man assured him: no one but him and his family had been in the house. He and his wife had been in and out for days, and yes, his cousin and his stepson, along with Nina, the little girl from the town who had often helped Felice, okay, yeah, she'd been in there too. Nina liked to hike the woods back there. Nina wouldn't touch a thing.

"Remember the alarm," said Galton. "I set that alarm as soon as the investigators left." That alarm never failed. If Miss Nideck had had that alarm set the night she was attacked, why it would have gone off the minute those windows had been smashed.

"Nobody's been in that house, Reuben," he insisted. Galton said he lived just off the road ten minutes below the point. He would have seen or heard any traffic headed up that way. Yes, there had been reporters and photographers, but that had only been in those first few days and, even then, he'd been up there most of the time keeping an eye on them, and they couldn't have gotten past the alarm.

"You have to realize, Reuben," said Galton, "that place is hard to get to. Not many people want to drive up this road, you know. Except for the nature lovers, you know, the hikers, well, nobody goes around there at all."

Right. Reuben thanked him for everything.

"If you're getting uneasy up there, son, I'll be glad to come back up and sleep in the back."

"No, that's fine, Galton, thanks." Reuben rang off.

He sat at the desk for a long time, looking across the room at the big photograph of Felix and Company over the fireplace.

The draperies had not been drawn, and he was surrounded with dark mirrorlike glass. The fireplace was laid with oak logs and kindling but he didn't want to light the fire.

He was a little cold, but not too cold, and he sat there pondering.

There was a distinct possibility here. One of these men, one of Felix's old friends, that is, had read of Marchent's murder in this house, read it somewhere far away, maybe on the other side of the globe, where such news would never have penetrated in pre-Internet days—and that person had taken time to research the whole story. And having researched the whole story, that person had come here, entered surreptitiously, and collected those priceless tablets and tablet fragments.

The story of Marchent's murder had gone viral all right, no question of that. He'd checked that last night.

Now if this was so, it could mean a lot of things.

It could mean that Felix's precious tablets were in good hands, collected and saved by a concerned fellow archaeologist who might soon return them to Reuben when he learned of Reuben's honorable intentions, or who might take better care of the tablets than Reuben could.

It gave him a little peace to think of this.

And furthermore: this person, this person might very well have some information about what had happened to Felix. At least it would be a connection, wouldn't it, to somebody that knew Felix.

Of course that was about the most optimistic and reassuring spin that could be put on this little mystery, and if Reuben had still been in the habit of hearing Celeste's critical voice in his head, which he wasn't, he would have heard her say, **You're dreaming!**

But that's just it, Reuben thought, I'm not hearing her voice every minute, am I? And she's not texting me or calling me. She's at the movies with Mort Keller. And I'm not hearing my mother's voice either, and what the hell do either of them know about it? And Phil wasn't listening when I told him about the tablets, he was reading **Leaves of Grass,** and I didn't tell Mort, did I? I'd been too groggy with painkillers and antibiotics to tell Mort anything when he came to the hospital.

Reuben went upstairs, unpacked his laptop computer and brought it down to the library.

There was an old typewriter stand to the left of the desk, and he set up the computer there, verified the wireless connection, and went online.

Yes, before the Man Wolf of San Francisco had ever attacked, Marchent's story had made headlines as far away as Japan and Russia. That was clear enough. And he knew enough of French, Spanish, Italian, et al., to see that the mysterious beast who'd slain the killers had been given substantial play everywhere. The house was described, even the forest behind the house, and the mystery of the beast of course had been part and parcel of the appeal.

Yes, a friend of Felix could have seen the entire configuration: the house, the coast, and the mysterious name: Nideck.

He left off tracking the story. He checked on the Goldenwood kidnapping. Nothing had changed except parents were breaking faith with the sheriff's office and the FBI and blaming them for the little girl's death. Susan Kirkland. That was her name. Little Susan Kirkland. Eight years old. Her smiling face was now available in full color—a sweet-eyed little being with blond hair and pink plastic barrettes.

He checked his watch.

It was already eight o'clock.

His heart started to pound, but that's all that happened. Closing his eyes, he heard the inevitable sounds of the forest, and the incessant song of the rain. Animals out there, yes, things rustling in the dark. Birds in the night. He had a strange, disoriented feeling that he was falling into the sounds. He shook himself awake.

Apprehensive, uncertain, he got up and closed all the velvet draperies. A bit of dust was stirred, but it soon settled. He turned on a few more lamps—beside the leather couch and the Morris chair. And then he started the fire. Why the hell not have the fire?

He went into the great room, and built up that fire too, with a couple more short logs. He banked it well. And made sure the screen in front of it—which had not been there that first night—was secure.

Then he went into the kitchen. The coffeepot had long ago gone off. It didn't take a genius to figure out how to make another pot.

And within a few minutes, he was drinking a tolerable brew from one of Marchent's pretty china cups, and pacing the floor, soothed by the crackling noises from the fireplace, and the steady song of the rainwater flowing in the gutters, and down drainpipes, and over roof tiles, and down windows.

Funny how he heard it now so distinctly for the first time.

**Trouble is, you're not paying enough attention to all these little details. You are not being scientific.**

He set the coffee down on the library desk and started pounding away on the matter in a password-protected document that nobody could have made head or tail of anyway.

A little while later he stood at the back door, look-ing out into the darkness. He had killed the big lights, and he could see the trees now very distinctly and beautifully, and the high slate roof of the servants' wing, covered in tangled ivy and flowering vine.

He closed his eyes and tried to bring on the trans-formation. He pictured it, evoking those dizzying sensations, letting his mind go blank except for the metamorphosis.

But he couldn't bring it on.

Again, there came that sense of aloneness—that he was in a truly deserted place.

"What are you hoping for? What are you dreaming?"

That somehow it's all related, the creature that changed you, the name Nideck, even the theft of the tablets because maybe, somehow, the ancient tablets contained some secret that has to do with this, with all this?

Nonsense. What had Phil said about evil? "It's blunders, people making blunders, whether it's raid-ing a village and killing all the inhabitants, or killing a child in a fit of rage. Mistakes. Everything is simply a matter of mistakes."

Maybe somehow this was a matter of blunders, too. And he'd been lucky, damned lucky, that the people he'd so thoughtlessly slaughtered had been "guilty" in the eyes of the world.

What if a brute beast was responsible for the bite that had changed him—not some wise man wolf, but simply an animal—like this famous mountain lion?

What then? But he didn't believe that at all. How many human beings since the dawn of time have been attacked by beasts? They don't turn into monsters.

At nine o'clock, he woke up in the big leather chair behind the desk. His shoulders and neck were stiff and his head aching.

He had an e-mail from Grace. She'd spoken again to "that specialist in Paris." Would Reuben please call?

Specialist in Paris? What specialist in Paris? He didn't call. Quickly, he typed out an e-mail. "Mom, I don't need to see a specialist in anything. I am well. Love, R."

**I am after all sitting here in my new house waiting patiently to turn into a werewolf. Love, your son.**

He felt restless, hungry, but not hungry for food. It was something much worse. He looked around him at the big dark room with its crowded bookcases. The fire had gone out. He felt anxious, as though he had to move, had to get out, had to be somewhere.

He could hear the soft murmuring sounds of the forest, the lisping of the rain falling through the dense branches. He could not hear a large animal. If there was a mountain lion out there, perhaps she was fast asleep with her cubs. Whatever the case she was a wild thing, and he was a human being waiting, waiting in a house with glass walls.

He e-mailed Galton a list of things to buy for the house, though probably most of the stuff was there. He wanted a lot of new plants for the conservatory—

orange trees, ferns, and bougainvillea—could Galton handle that? What else? There had to be something else. The restlessness was driving him crazy.

He went online and ordered a laser printer for this library, and a desktop Mac to be delivered as soon as possible, and a number of Bose CD players, and a whole slew of Blu-ray. Bose CD players were the only obsolete technology he loved.

He unpacked the Bose players he'd brought— both of which were also radios—and put one in the kitchen and the other in the library on the desk.

He was not hearing any voices. The night was empty around him.

And the change was not happening to him.

For a while he drifted about the house, pondering, talking aloud to himself, thinking. He had to keep moving. He put signs where the televisions should be installed. He'd sit down, get up, pace, climb the stairs, roam the attics, come down.

He went outside into the rain, roaming the back part of the house. Under the overhang he looked into the various lower bedrooms of the servants' quarters, each of which had a door and a window on the stone walkway. All seemed in order, with simple somewhat rustic furnishings.

At the end of the wing he found the shed, stacked with a huge amount of firewood. A worktable ran along one side, with axes and saws hung on hooks on the wall. There were other tools, anything a man might need for repairs large and small.

Reuben had never held an ax in his hands. He took down the largest of the axes—it had a three-foot wooden handle—and felt the edge of the blade. The blade itself must have weighed about five pounds and was a good five inches long. And sharp. Very sharp. All his life he'd seen men in movies and television programs splitting logs with an ax like this. He wondered how he might like doing that out here himself. The handle itself didn't weigh much at all; and surely the weight of the blade gave the ax its force. If it hadn't been raining, he would have looked for the place where the wood had been split.

But something else occurred to him—that this was the only weapon he had.

He carried the ax back into the house with him and set it down beside the fireplace in the big room. It looked simple enough there—the paint had long ago peeled from the wooden handle—between the pile of firewood and the fire, almost out of sight.

He felt he could get to that quickly enough if he ever had a need. Of course—before some two weeks ago, it had never occurred to him that he could defend himself with any weapon, but he had not the slightest qualm now.

The restlessness was almost unsupportable.

Was he resisting the change? Or was it just too damned early? It had never come on him this early. He had to wait.

But he couldn't wait.

His hands and feet were tingling. The rain was

acutely loud now, and he thought he could hear the surf again, but he wasn't sure.

He couldn't bear it here any longer. He made a decision. He had no choice.

He took off his clothes, hung them up neatly in the closet, and put on the big loose clothing he'd bought in Santa Rosa.

He was swallowed by the giant hooded sweatshirt and oversized pants, but it didn't matter. The brown trench coat was simply too big to wear, but he'd take it with him.

He took off his shoes and slipped into the huge rain boots. He put the scarf around his neck, tucked it in, and put the sunglasses in the coat pocket along with his phone and his wallet and his keys, and picking up the ski mittens, and his computer, he went out.

He almost forgot to set the alarm, but he remembered it and punched in the code.

All the lights were still on.

As he drove away, he could see in his rearview mirror the lights burning all over the first and second floors. He liked it. The house looked alive and safe and good to him.

Oh, this was glorious to own this house, to be here in this dark forest once again, to be close to this immense mystery. It felt good to work his feet as he drove. He stretched his fingers, then closed them tight on the leather-covered steering wheel.

The rain was washing over the windshield of the

Porsche, but he could see through it quite easily. His headlamps flashed over the uneven bumpy road ahead, and he found himself singing as he rode along, pushing the speedometer as high as he dared to go.

Think. Think like a kidnapper who has to hide forty-two children. Think like a ruthless tech genius that can bludgeon a little girl to death and throw her on a lonely spit of beach in the rain, and get back to where he's warm and comfortable, where he's got his computer handy for routing his bank demands and his calls.

Why, those kids are probably right under everybody's nose.

# 10

REUBEN KNEW THE BACK ROADS of Marin County the way he knew the streets of San Francisco. He'd grown up visiting friends in Sausalito and Mill Valley, and taking the inevitable hikes on Mount Tamalpais and through the breathtaking paths of Muir Woods.

He didn't need to visit the sheriff's office before beginning his little dragnet, but he did it anyway, because he was hearing the voices now clearly, all around him, and he knew he'd be able to hear their voices inside without their ever knowing it, of course, and they just might know something they were not telling the world.

He parked near the San Rafael Civic Center and took up his stand in the trees, far from the gaggle of reporters camped before the doors.

His shut his eyes, and sought with all his will to home in on the voices within the office, surfing for the likely words these people would be repeating, and within seconds he was picking up the threads. Yes, the kidnappers had called again, and they weren't going to tell that to the public, no matter who was demanding it. "We tell what serves a purpose!" a man insisted. "And there is no purpose." "And they're threatening to kill another child."

Babble and protest; point and counterpoint. The bank in the Bahamas would give them absolutely no cooperation, but in truth their hackers weren't finding out anything there that was helpful on their own.

But the body of the little girl, rain or no rain, surf or no surf, had yielded soil samples from shoes and clothing that connected her to Marin. Of course that wasn't conclusive; but the absence of any other soil samples was a good sign.

And it was all Reuben needed to confirm what he already suspected.

Cop cars were crawling the forest and mountain roads.

There were random checkpoints and house-to-house searches.

So law enforcement was his only enemy now as he began his search.

He was getting back in the car when something caught him off guard. It was the scent—the scent of evil that had been so unmistakable in the nights before.

He turned his head, uncertain, not willing to be drawn off on any errand other than the kidnap, and then the voices came clear to him from the melee of the reporters—two youthful, mocking voices, offering innocent questions, relishing answers that gave them information they already possessed. Sinister, particular, undeniable. "For our school paper, we just thought we'd come out here. . . ." "And did they really just beat her to death, poor little girl!"

He felt the tingling all over the surface of his skin, as sweet and pervasive as the revulsion.

"Well, we're off now, we have to get back to San Francisco. . . ." But that wasn't where they were going!

He went to the edge of the little thicket in which he'd been hiding. He saw the two young men—Princeton haircuts, blue blazers—waving good-bye cheerily to their reporter comrades.

They were hurrying across the parking lot towards a waiting Land Rover with its lights on. Driver inside anxious, scared out of his wits, **Will you come on!**

It was all a matter of sharp ugly musical sounds to him, the snickering, boasting. The syllables were almost unimportant. How they were wallowing in the excitement, the intrigue, as they piled into the car. The driver was a sniveling coward without a particle of empathy for the victims. He could smell that too.

He sped around the periphery of the parking lot, easily picking up their trail as they headed towards the coast.

He had no need to see their taillights; he could hear every word of their ugly banter. **No one knows shit!**

The driver was near hysterical. He didn't like this, he wished to God he'd never got into it. He was stammering that he wasn't going back there, no matter what they said. That was just nuts, driving up there, and mingling with the reporters. The other two ignored him, congratulating each other on a triumph.

The scent was in the wind and the scent was strong.

On through the night Reuben followed them. The conversation had turned to technicalities. Should they dump the body now tonight on the Muir Woods Road or wait a few hours, maybe closer to dawn?

The body; Reuben caught the scent of it; they had it in the car with them. Another child. His vision sharpened; he saw them up ahead in the blackness, saw the silhouette of one laughing young man against the back window; caught the frantic curses of the driver who struggled to see through the rain.

"I'm telling you Muir Woods Road is too damn close," said the driver. "You're pushing it, just pushing it."

"Hell, the closer the better. Don't you see the perfection of it? We should dump it across the street from the house." Laughter.

Reuben brought the car up closer, caught the scent so thick he could scarce breathe. And the smell of decomposition. It made him gag.

His skin was crawling with sensation. He felt the spasms in his chest, the riot of pleasurable feeling in his scalp. The hair was coming slowly all over his body. It felt like loving hands were everywhere stroking him, coaxing the power.

The Land Rover picked up speed.

"Look, we'll give them till five a.m. If they haven't responded by then by e-mail, we dump the body. It will make it seem like we just killed him."

So it was a little boy.

"And if there's nothing by noon, I say we dump the teacher with the long hair."

Good God, were they all already dead?

No, that wasn't possible. They just weren't making any distinction between the living and the dead because they were planning to kill all of them.

On he drove as his rage mounted.

He was sitting higher in the seat, and his hands were covered in hair. Hold on, hold on tight. His fingers were retaining their shape. But the mane had come down around his shoulders, and his vision was growing ever sharper, clearer. He felt he could hear every single sound for miles.

The car seemed to be driving itself.

The Land Rover made a sharp turn up ahead. They were cruising now into the deeply wooded town of Mill Valley, following a winding road.

Reuben dropped back.

Then another chorus of sounds flooded his ears.

It was the children, the children crying, and sobbing, and the women's voices crooning to them, singing, comforting them. They were in an airless place. Some of them were coughing, others moaning. He had a sense of utter darkness. He was almost there!

The Land Rover again picked up speed and turned down a neglected dirt road. The trees swallowed the red taillights.

Reuben knew exactly where the children were. He could feel it.

He pulled the Porsche over into a thicket of oaks

on a bluff quite high above the deep valley into which the Land Rover had gone.

He got out of the car, and stripped off the awkward uncomfortable clothes and boots. The change had now taken full possession of him, with the inevitable wash of ecstasy.

He had to force himself to hide the clothing inside the car, but he knew that was essential, just as it was to lock the car, and hide the key in the roots of the nearby tree.

The Land Rover was way down there, just turning into the grassy clearing before a large impressive house with sprawling decks off each of its three well-lighted stories. Beside the house, and to the rear of the property, shrouded by trees, stood an old vine-covered barn.

The children and the teachers were in the barn.

The mingled voices of the kidnappers rose like smoke to his nostrils.

Down the slope he bounded, covering the yards and yards between him and his victims, leaping from one tree after another, passing one small sleeping hillside house after another, until he landed in the clearing just as the young men were entering the house.

The place glowed like a wedding cake beyond them against the night.

A roar came out of Reuben before he willed it, ripping from his chest and his throat. That anything but a beast could roar like that was impossible.

All three of the young men turned in the vestibule of the house, and saw him plainly rush towards them. They were nineteen, maybe twenty years old. Their screams were lost in the sounds of his own growls. One man fell down but the other two—the crafty ones, the exultant ones—turned to run.

He caught the first man easily and ripped his neck open, watching the blood spurt. With all his soul, he wanted to devour the man, to close his jaws on his flesh, but there was no time. He lifted the broken body, squeezing it greedily in his paws, and then relinquished it, heaving it far away from him, out towards the distant road.

Oh, too little, too quick!

With a flying leap, he caught the other two struggling to get out of the back door which was apparently locked. One of them was clawing hysterically at the glass.

The other had a gun. Reuben caught it, clearly breaking the man's wrist as he wrenched it from the man and cast it aside.

He was going to close his jaws on this one; he couldn't stop himself, he had to do it. He was so hungry for it! And why not, because he would never never allow this man to live.

He couldn't stop his ravening growls as his teeth sank into the man's skull and throat. He clamped down as hard as he could, and felt the bones crack. He heard them crack. A whine came out of the dying man.

It thrilled Reuben to run his tongue over the blood pouring down the man's face. **Killer, filthy killer.**

He bit deep into the man's shoulder, and tore loose both cloth and flesh. The taste of the flesh was rich and overpowering, mixed with the stench of evil, the stench of viciousness, the stench of utter corruption. He wanted to unwrap the man and gorge himself on his naked flesh. This was always what he'd wanted to do; and why didn't he give in to it?

But where was the other culprit? He could not let that last of the trio escape.

No chance of that. The third man was helpless. He had slipped down into the corner and was shaking violently. He held out his two hands. Water was gushing out of his mouth or was it vomit? He had urinated on himself, and the urine was puddling around him on the tiled floor.

The hideous spectacle of him maddened Reuben. **Murdered the children, murdered them. The room is rank with the stench of it. And rank with the stench of cowardice too.** He lunged for the man and caught his chest in both paws, crushing it, hearing the bones snap, and staring at the man's white and shuttering face until the eyes went dim. **Oh, you died too soon, you craven animal.**

He slammed the jangled body against the floor. Still unsatisfied, his growls as loud as before, he picked up the corpse and threw it against the side window of the room and the glass shattered as the body vanished in the falling rain.

A sudden terrible disappointment gripped him. They were all dead. He moaned aloud. A rough sob came out of his chest. It had been way too fast, and he threw back his head and roared again as he had before. His jaws ached. He clenched and opened and roared again. It was the worst craving he'd ever felt. He could have torn at the frames of the doors with his teeth; he wanted to lock his teeth again on anything that he could find.

The saliva was dripping from his mouth. He wiped at it angrily. His paws were streaked with gouts of blood. **But the children, have you forgotten the children? Have you forgotten why you are here?**

He staggered through the house back towards the front door. He slammed at the mirrors and the framed pictures that covered the walls. He wanted to smash the furniture. But he had to get to the children.

An alarm keypad caught his eye, like the one in Mendocino. He hit the blue medical alert button and the red button for fire.

At once a whooping shrieking wail erupted in the stillness.

He covered his ears as he cried out. The pain was unbearable; his head throbbed. There was no time to find the source of this deafening sound and stop it.

He had to hurry. The sound was driving him mad.

He reached the doors of the barn in a split second, and ripped off the locks, fracturing and splintering the doors as they fell in.

There in the bright light from the house, he saw

the bus, draped in chains and tied around and around with duct tape—a torture chamber.

The children were squealing in a frenzy, their cries thin, and shrill, the whooping clarion of the alarm almost swallowing the sound. He could smell their terror, their desperate excitement. They thought they were about to die. In a matter of seconds they would know they had been saved. They would know that they were free.

His claws tore the tape as if it were tissue paper. With one paw he smashed the glass of the door and then ripped the door off the bus.

A revolting smell assailed his nostrils—feces, vomit, urine, sweat. Oh, the cruelty of it. He wanted to howl.

He backed up. The blaring alarm was disorienting him, crippling him. But the job was nearly done.

He made his way out of the barn, back into the rain, the ground mushy beneath his feet, wanting desperately to recover the dead child from the Land Rover, and put its body where it would surely be found, but he could not endure the noise anymore. They would have to find it, and surely they would. Yet it felt wrong to leave it. Wrong, not to somehow prepare for them the entire scene.

Out of the corner of his eye he saw the figures, large and small, scrambling from the bus.

They were moving towards him. And surely they saw him, saw what he was, saw in the lights from the windows behind him the blood drenching his paws, his fur.

They were going to be more afraid! He had to get away.

He made for the wet shining trees at the back of the property, and headed for the great silent forest that lay directly west—Muir Woods.

# 11

MUIR WOODS STRETCHED for some five hundred and fifty acres, including some of the oldest redwoods yet standing in California, trees that soared over two hundred feet, and had been alive for over a thousand years. At least two creeks ran through the deep canyon of the park. And Reuben had traveled its hiking trails many a time.

He plunged into the enveloping stillness now, hungry for the solitude that had driven him to Mendocino, and glorying in his strength as he climbed the immense trees, leaping from the branches of one to another as if he had wings. Everywhere the scent of other animals tantalized him.

Deeper into the park he went, only dropping down to the soft leafy floor when all the human voices of the night had died, and only the rain sang to him, and the muted sounds of a thousand little creatures, nestled in the ferns and the leaves, whose names he couldn't know. Above, the birds rustled in the branches.

He was laughing out loud, singing nonsense syllables, roaming, staggering, and then scaling a tree again, as high as he could go, the rain falling like needles on his eyes, until the trunk was too thin for his weight and he had to seek another perch and then another and descend once more to dance in circles with his arms out.

He threw back his head and roared again, and then let the roar round itself into a deep howl. Nothing answered him in the night except the crackling flight of other living things, living things that fled from him.

Suddenly descending to all fours he ran as a wolf would run, swiftly through the dense foliage. He caught the scent of an animal—**bobcat**—fleeing before him, flushed from its lair, and after that scent he went with unstoppable hunger until he reached out, and caught the furry snarling creature in his claws, and drove his fangs into its throat.

This time nothing held him back from the feast.

He stripped succulent muscle from bone, and crunched both in his jaws as he devoured the beast with its brittle yellowish fur, slurping up its blood, its soft innards, the rich sack of its belly, all in all some forty pounds of it, leaving only its paws and its head, with yellow eyes staring at him bitterly.

He lay down on a bed of leaves panting and crying softly, licking at his teeth for a last taste of the warm flesh and blood. Bobcat. Scrumptious. And cats never beg for mercy. Cats snarl until the end. Even more succulent.

A great disgust came over him, a horror. He'd run on all fours as an animal runs. He'd feasted like an animal.

He walked after that, dreamily through the dense

forest, crossing the broad stream on a thick moss-
covered log, his clawed feet easily clinging to it, and
he ventured even further into the canyon, beyond
the places he'd known, and further up the flank of
Mount Tamalpais.

At last he fell down and lay against the bark of a
tree, peering through the dark, and seeing for the first
time many more creatures than he'd ever dreamed
were harbored in the brush. Scent of fox, squirrel,
chipmunk—how did he know what each was?

An hour passed; he'd been snuffling, crawling on
all fours, wandering.

The hunger was on him again. He knelt beside a
creek, his eyes easily tracking the swift progress of the
winter salmon, and when his paw came down, he had
a large fish, helpless, squirming and flapping, which
he tore open at once with his teeth.

He savored the raw flesh, and how distinctly different it was from the meat of the juicy sinewy bobcat.

This wasn't hunger he was satisfying, was it? This
was something else—a great flexing and exercising of
what he was.

He climbed again, high, fumbling for birds' nests
in the shivering branches, and devoured the eggs shell
and all as the screeching mother bird circled him,
pecking at him vainly.

Back down beside the creek, he bathed his face
and his paws in the icy water. He walked out in it
and bathed all over, splashing the water over his head

and shoulders. All the blood must be washed away. The water felt refreshing. He knelt and drank as if he'd never satisfied thirst in his whole life before, lapping, guzzling, gulping the water.

The rain sparkled on the rippling, tossing surface of the stream. And beneath it, the indifferent fish swam speedily past him.

He climbed up again and traveled in the trees, high above the valley floor. Never mind, little birds. I don't want to torment you.

**Thou shalt not seethe a kid in its mother's milk,**—indeed.

As had happened before he could see the stars through the thick mist. What a glorious thing it was, the open heavens rising above the thick layer of fog and damp that shrouded this earth. It seemed the tumbling rain carried with it a silvery light in its busy descent. It sparkled and sang on the leaves around him. Then down from the upper branches it became rain again to the lower branches, and from then on down to the world below, rain and rain and rain, until it fell soft on the tiny quaking ferns and on the deep mulch of dead leaf, so rich, so fragrant.

He couldn't really feel the rain on his body, except for his eyelids. But he could smell it, smell it as it changed with every surface it cleansed and nourished.

Slowly, he dropped down once more and walked, his back very straight, the strong desire to feast having left him, and he felt a wondrous safety in the dark forest, musing with a smile that he had encountered nothing that was not afraid of him.

The annihilation of the three evil men revolted him. He felt light-headed and liable to weep. Could he weep? Did savage animals actually weep? A low laughter came out of him. It seemed the trees were listening to him, but that was most certainly the most preposterous of illusions that these thousand-year-old guardians knew or cared that anything else whatever was actually alive. How monstrous were the redwoods, how out of scale with all the rest of the natural earth, how divinely primitive and magnificent.

The night had never seemed sweeter to him in all his existence; it was conceivable that he could live this way forever, self-sufficient, strong, monstrous, and utterly unafraid. If that was what the Wolf Gift had in store for him, perhaps he could bear it.

Yet it terrified him that he might surrender his conscious soul to the heart of the beast pumping within. For now, poetry was still with him—and the deepest moral considerations.

A song came to him, an old song. Where he'd heard it he couldn't recall. He sang it in his head, putting its half-forgotten words in proper order, only humming under his breath.

He came out into a grassy clearing, the light from the low gray heavens increasing, and after the closeness of the woods, it seemed beautiful to see the shimmering grass in the thin rain.

He began to dance in large slow circles singing the song. His voice sounded deep and clear to him, not the voice of the old Reuben, the poor innocent and fearful Reuben, but the voice of the Reuben he was now.

**'Tis the gift to be simple,**
**'tis the gift to be free**
**'Tis the gift to come down**
**where we ought to be,**
**And when we find ourselves**
**in the place just right,**
**'Twill be in the valley of love and delight.**

Again, he sang it, dancing a little faster and in greater circles, his eyes closed. A light shone against his eyelids, a dim, distant light, but he took no note of it. He was dancing and singing—.

He stopped.

He'd caught a strong scent—an unexpected scent. Something sweet and mingled with an artificial perfume.

Someone was very near to him. And as he opened his eyes, he saw the light shining on the grass, and the rain sparkling gold in it.

He caught not the slightest hint of danger. This human scent was clean, innocent—fearless.

He turned and looked to his right. Be gentle as you are careful, he reminded himself. You will frighten, perhaps terrify, this blundering witness.

Yards away, on the rear porch of a small darkened house, there stood a woman looking at him. She held a lantern in her hand.

In the total darkness that had been the night, the light of the lantern expanded widely, thinly; and surely in this light she could see him.

She stood very still, apparently gazing at him across the expanse of wild soft grass, a woman with long hair parted in the middle, and large shadowy eyes. Her hair appeared to be gray but this might have been a mistake. For as well as he could see, he couldn't quite make out the details of what he saw. She wore a long-sleeved white nightgown and she was utterly alone. No one in the dark house behind her.

**Don't be frightened!**

It remained his first and only thought. How small and fragile she looked standing on the porch, a tender animal, holding the lantern up as she stared at him.

**Oh, please, don't be afraid.**

He began to sing again, the same stanza, only more slowly, in the same clear deep voice as before.

He moved slowly towards her, and watched in secret astonishment as she moved along the porch and to the head of the back steps.

She wasn't afraid. That was plain. She wasn't afraid at all.

He moved closer and closer, and again he sang the words. He was now full in the strong light of the lantern. And yet she stood still as before.

She looked utterly curious, fascinated.

He came closer until he stood at the foot of the small steps.

Her hair was gray, actually, prematurely gray surely as her face was as smooth as a china mask. Her eyes were a large glacial blue. She was fascinated, all right, and unshakable, as if she'd lost herself utterly in gazing at him.

And what did she see? Did she see his eyes gazing at her with the same curiosity, the same fascination?

Deep in the pit of his loins the desire rose, surprising him in its intensity. He was growing hard for her. Did she see that? Could she see it? That he was naked, unable to conceal his desire, excited him further, strengthened him, emboldened him.

He'd never felt desire precisely like this desire.

He started up the steps, soon towering over her as she stepped backwards on the porch. But she hadn't stepped back in fear. No, it seemed she was welcoming him.

What was this remarkable fearlessness, what was this seeming serenity as she looked up into his eyes? She was thirty perhaps, perhaps a little younger, small boned, with a thick well-shaped sensuous mouth and strong though small shoulders.

He reached out tentatively, allowing her plenty of time if she meant to run away. He took the lantern from her in both his paws, oblivious to the obvious heat of the thing, and set it down on a wooden bench near the wall. A door stood partially open. Beyond he caught a bit of very pale light.

He wanted her, wanted to rip the white flannel nightgown off of her.

Very cautiously he reached out for her, and took her in his arms. His heart was pounding. The desire for her was as strange and undeniable as the desire to kill, or the desire to feast. Beasts are creatures of imperatives.

Her flesh was white in the light of the lantern, sweet, tender—and her lips opened and she gave a little gasp. Carefully, ever so carefully, he touched her lips with the edge of his paw.

He picked her up, easily lifting her legs over his left arm. She weighed nothing, absolutely nothing. She put her arms around his neck, letting her fingers slide into the thick hair.

And with these simple gestures, she drove him right over the edge. A low secretive growl came out of him.

He had to have her if she would allow it. And she was surely allowing it.

He carried her towards the door, and gently pushing it back, carried her into the warmer, sweeter air of the house.

All the domestic scents swirled around him—of polished wood, scented soap, candles, a touch of incense, the smell of a fire. And her perfume, her lovely natural perfume and a tasty citrus essence she'd added to it. Oh, flesh, oh blessed flesh. There came that low caressing growl from him again. Is that how it seemed to her? Caressing?

There were embers in the small black stove. A digital clock gave its numbers with a tiny bit of light.

A small bedroom materialized around him. He made out an antique bed against the wall, with a high back of golden oak, and white covers that looked as soft as foam.

She was clinging to him. She reached up and touched his face. He could barely feel her touch through the hair, but then it began to zing right to the roots. She touched his mouth, the thin ribbon of black flesh that he knew was there. She touched his teeth and his fangs. Did she realize he was smiling down at her? She closed the thick hair of his mane in her hand tightly.

He kissed the top of her head, and he kissed her forehead, hmmmmm, satin, kissed her upturned eyes and made them close.

The flesh of her eyelids was like silk. A silk and satin little being, hairless, fragrant, petal soft.

How naked and vulnerable she seemed; it maddened him. Oh, please, my dear, do not change your mind!

They sank down together on the bed, though he did not put his full weight on her. He would have hurt her if he had done that, but he nestled close to her, cradling her with his arms, stroking her hair back from her forehead. Blond and gray, with lots and lots of softer gray.

He bent to kiss her lips and her lips opened. He breathed into her mouth.

"Gently," she whispered, her fingers pushing the hair back from his eyes, smoothing it back.

"Oh, beautiful, beautiful," he said. "I won't hurt you. I would rather die than hurt you. Tender stem. Little stem. I give you my word."

# 12

THE LITTLE CLOCK on her bedside table said 4:00 a.m. in bright digital numerals. Just this clock gave the room all the light his eyes needed.

He lay beside her, staring at the dark beaded wood paneling of the ceiling covered in a thick and lustrous varnish.

This had been a porch once, this bedroom, and it ran along the entire back of her house. Above the surrounding wainscoting were small-paned windows on three sides. And he could well imagine how lovely this would be when the sun came, and the dark forest which he could see would close in visibly for human eyes with its reddish trunks and feathery green leaves.

He could smell the woods here, smell it as deeply as he had when he was out in it. This was a little house of the woods made by someone who had loved the woods and wanted to be in it without disturbing it.

She lay against him, sleeping.

A woman of thirty, yes, and her hair was an ashen blond, but mostly grayish white now, and long and loose and natural. He'd ripped open her nightgown all right, destroyed it, freeing her from it bit by bit, with her irresistible compliance, and the remnants of it lay beneath her like feathers in a nest.

It had taken all his control not to batter her in the lovemaking, man and beast had worked together, gloried in it together, and her heated desire had been like melting wax. With complete abandon, she'd received him, moaning as spontaneously as he had moaned, thrusting against him hard, and then stiffening in ecstasy beneath him.

There was something about her fearlessness that was beyond trusting.

She'd slept beside him in childlike comfort.

But he hadn't dared to sleep. He'd lain there thinking, reflecting, calling man and beast to account, and yet feeling a kind of muted bliss, bliss in her arms as the beast that she'd welcomed.

If he hadn't feared to wake her, he would have gotten up and looked around—maybe sat in the large wooden rocking chair she had, maybe looked more closely at the framed photographs on her bedside table. From where he lay he could see a picture of her in hiking gear, with a backpack and a staff, smiling for the camera. There was another picture of her with two small blond-haired boys.

How different she looked in that picture—with coiffed hair and pearls around her neck.

There were books on the table, old and new, all having to do with the forest, the wildlife, or the plants native to Muir Woods and to the mountain.

Not surprising.

Who else would live in such an unguarded place except a woman for whom the forest was the world, he figured. And what a gentle child of that world she seemed. But oh so foolishly trusting. Way too trusting.

He felt powerfully drawn to her, bound to her by the secret of this, that she'd welcomed him into her bed as he was. And then there was the heat of it. He looked down at her, wondering who or what she was, what she was dreaming.

But he had to leave now.

He was just beginning to feel tired.

If he didn't move fast through the forest, the change might come way too far from the car he'd left hidden on the bluff high above the kidnap scene.

He kissed her now with this lipless mouth, feeling his own fangs pressing against her.

Her eyes snapped open, large, alert, glistening.

"You'll welcome me again?" he asked, a low husky voice, soft as he could make it.

"Yes," she whispered.

It was almost too much. He wanted to take her again. But there simply wasn't time. He wanted to know her, and he wanted—yes, wanted her to know him. Oh, the greed of it, he thought. But he was overcome again by the realization that she hadn't run from him in fear, that she'd nestled with him here in the fragrant warmth of this bed for hours.

He lifted her hand and kissed it and kissed her again.

"Good-bye then for a little while, beautiful one."

"Laura," she said. "My name is Laura."

"I wish I had a name," he answered. "I'd gladly give it to you."

He was up and out of the house without another word.

He moved fast through the treetops, back through Muir Woods, and southeast, seldom if ever touching down until he had emerged from the park itself and was roaming the wooded thickets of Mill Valley.

He found the Porsche without ever consciously thinking about it, right where he'd left it, safe under the shelter of a grove of scrub oaks.

The rain had slacked off finally to a drizzle.

The voices rustled and whistled in the shadows.

Far below he could hear the radios of the police who still swarmed over the "kidnap scene."

He sat down beside the car, hunched over, and tried to induce the transformation.

Within seconds it began, the wolf-hair melting away, as paralytic waves of pleasure gripped him.

The sky was growing light.

He was weak to fainting.

He dressed in the loose baggy clothes, all he'd brought with him. But where was he to go? He couldn't make it to Nideck Point. That was out of the question. Even the short journey home seemed out of the question. He couldn't be at home, not now.

He forced himself to get on the road. He could hardly keep his eyes open. Chances were the reporters had booked the Mill Valley Inn, and every other motel or hotel for miles. He headed south for the

Golden Gate, struggling again and again to stay awake as the sunrise broke through the fog with a steely heartless light.

The rain had begun again as he entered the city.

As soon as he saw a big commercial motel on Lombard Street, he pulled off, and got a room. What had caught him were the individual balconies of the top floor, right under the roof. He got a suite up there on the back, "away from the traffic."

Closing the blinds, and stripping off his uncomfortable rough clothes, he climbed onto the king-size bed as if it were a lifesaving raft, and fell fast asleep against the cool white pillows.

# 13

FATHER JIM LOCKED UP St. Francis at Gubbio Church in San Francisco's Tenderloin as soon as it was dark. By day, the homeless slept in the pews, and took their meals at the dining room down the street. But at nightfall, for safety's sake, the church was locked.

Reuben knew all this.

He also knew that by 10:00 p.m.—which it was now—his brother would be sound asleep in his own small spartan apartment, in a flophouse building just across the street from the entrance to the church courtyard.

The old rectory had been Jim's place of residence for the first couple of years. But now it housed parish offices and storage. Grace and Phil had sprung for the apartment, with the archbishop's approval. They'd even bought the building, which Jim was slowly transforming into a decent hotel of sorts for the more stable and dependable residents of the old downtown neighborhood.

Reuben, in his brown trench coat and hoodie, clawed feet bare, and paws bare, had traveled over the roofs to reach the church, and dropped down into the dark courtyard. The transformation had come over him three hours ago. He'd been fighting the voices since then, the voices calling to him from all around him. But he could fight no more.

He rang his brother now on his cell, a little more adept at handling it now that he had a bit of practice.

"I need to go to Confession, in the church," he said in the deep guttural voice that was now all too familiar to his own ears, but not at all recognizable to Jim. "I need the confessional. I must do it there."

"Ah, right now, huh?" His brother was struggling to wake up.

"Can't wait, Father. I need you. I need God. You will forgive me for this when you hear me."

Well, maybe.

Reuben adjusted the scarf up around his mouth and pushed the sunglasses in place as he waited.

Jim, ever the devoted and tireless priest, entered the gate and, surprised to see that the penitent was already inside, and maybe a little awed by the size of the guy, nevertheless nodded, and unlocked the heavy wood door of the nave.

What a risk, Reuben thought. I could easily hit him over the head and rob the church of its gold candlesticks. He wondered how often Jim had done this kind of thing, or why Jim's life was such a round of sacrifice and exhausting work, how it was Jim could ladle up soup and corned beef hash every day for people who so often let him down, or go through the same ritual every morning at the altar, as if it really was a miracle when he consecrated the bread and wine and gave out "the Body of Christ" in tiny white wafers.

St. Francis was one of the most ornate and colorful churches in all the city, built long before the Tenderloin had become the city's premier and most legendary slum. It was large with old heavily carved scrollwork pews, and walls covered with richly painted and gilded murals. The huge paintings embraced its altar under a trio of Roman arches, then moved behind its side altars—to St. Joseph and the Blessed Virgin Mary—and down the sides to the very back, where, on the far right side, stood the old wooden confessionals, each a little tripartite wooden house with booths for penitents to kneel on either side of a central place where the priest sat as he pulled back the wooden panel that covered the screen through which he could hear the confession.

It was not strictly necessary to be in such a booth when one confessed. You could confess on a park bench or in a room, or anywhere for that matter. Reuben knew all that. But this had to be utterly official, utterly secret, and he wanted it this way, and so he had requested it.

He followed Jim towards the first confessional, the only one of late that Jim ever really used, and he watched patiently as Jim took out his small satin stole and put it around his neck, this to assure the man behind him that he was now ready officially to offer the Sacrament of Penance.

Now silently, Reuben removed the glasses and pushed down the scarf, exposing his face.

Only casually did Jim glance back as he gestured for "the man" to open the door of the little booth. But the glance was enough.

He saw the bestial face hovering just over him and he gasped as he fell back against the confessional.

Immediately Jim's right hand flew up to his forehead and he made the Sign of the Cross. He closed his eyes, opened them again, and confronted what he saw.

"Confession," said Reuben and he opened the door of the booth. He was the one gesturing now with his paw for Jim to take his place inside.

It took a minute for Jim to recover.

It was so very strange to see Jim in this moment, when Jim did not know this monster he was looking at was his brother, Reuben. When do we ever see a brother or sister staring at us as if we are perfect strangers?

He knew things about his brother now that he could never know in their day-to-day contact—that his brother was even braver and more dedicated than he'd ever imagined. And that his brother could handle fear calmly.

Reuben went into the penitent's booth and pulled the velvet curtain behind him. It was tight in here, made for small men and women. But he knelt on the padded kneeler, and faced the screen as Jim pulled back the panel. He saw Jim's hand raised in blessing.

"Bless me, Father, for I have sinned," Reuben said. "And all I tell you now is under the absolute Seal of the Confessional."

"Yes," said Jim. "Are your intentions sincere?"

"Completely. I'm your brother, Reuben."

Jim didn't utter a word.

"I'm the one who killed the rapist in North Beach and the men in Golden Gate Park. I slew the woman on Buena Vista Hill who was torturing the old couple. I killed the kidnappers in Marin when I liberated the children. I was too late there to save them all. Two were already dead. Another little girl, a diabetic, died this morning."

Silence.

"I am indeed your brother," Reuben said. "This began for me with the attack in Mendocino County. I don't know what manner of beast attacked me up there, or whether or not it meant to give me this power. But I know what manner of beast I am."

Again, utter silence. Jim appeared to be staring forward. It seemed his elbow was resting on the arm of his chair. And that his hand was near to his mouth.

Reuben went on:

"The change is coming earlier and earlier in the evening. It came on tonight about seven. I don't know whether or not I can learn to block it or bring it on at will. I don't know why it leaves me around dawn. But I do know it leaves me near dead with exhaustion.

"How do I find the victims? I hear them. I hear them and I smell them—their innocence and fear.

And I smell the evil of those attacking them. I smell it like a dog or a wolf smells his prey.

"You know the rest, you've read it in the papers, heard it on the news. I have nothing more to tell you."

Silence.

Reuben waited.

It was stiflingly hot for him in this little box. But he waited.

Finally Jim spoke. His voice was thick and low, almost unrecognizable.

"If you are my little brother, then you must know something, something only he would know, something that you can tell me to assure me that's who you are."

"For Chrissake, Jimmy, it's me," Reuben said. "Mom doesn't know anything about this; neither does Phil. Neither does Celeste. No one knows, Jim, except for one woman and that woman doesn't know who I really am. She's only known me as the Man Wolf. If she's called the police or the FBI, or the NIH, or the CIA, there's been no word made public on it. I'm telling you, Jim, because I need you, I need you to hear these things. I'm alone in this, Jim. I'm completely alone. And yes, I'm your brother. Aren't I **still** your brother, Jim? Please answer me."

Dimly, Reuben saw Jim put his hands up over his nose and Jim made a short sound, like a cough.

"Okay." He sighed, sitting back. "Reuben. Just give me a minute. You know the old story. You can't shock a priest in Confession. Well, I think that applies to

people who haven't been changed into some sort
of . . ."

"Animal," said Reuben. "I'm a werewolf, Jim. But
I'd rather call myself a man wolf. I do actually retain
my full consciousness in this state, as ought to be
plain enough to you. But it's not that simple. There
are hormones flooding me in this state and they work
on my emotions. I am Reuben, yes, but I'm Reuben under a new series of influences. And no one
really knows to what extent hormones and emotions
influence free will and conscience and inhibition and
moral habit."

"Yes, that's so true, and nobody would word
that quite like you just did except my little brother,
Reuben."

"Phil Golding didn't bring up any sons who
couldn't obsess over cosmic questions."

Jim laughed. "And where is Phil now when I need
him?"

"Don't go there," said Reuben. "What we say here
is sealed."

"Amen, that's without question."

Reuben waited.

Then he said:

"It's easy to kill, easy to kill people reeking of guilt.
No, that's not it. They don't reek of guilt. They reek
of intent to do evil."

"And other people, innocent people?"

"Other people smell just like people. They smell
innocent; they smell healthy; they smell good. That

must be why the beast in Mendocino let me go. He caught me in the midst of his attack on two killers. And he let me go, perhaps knowing what he'd done to me, what he'd passed on to me."

"But you don't know who or what he is."

"No. Not yet. But I'm going to find out, that is, if there is any way that I can. And there's more to it all than meets the eye, I mean, more connecting what happened to that house and the family. But it's too soon to try to make sense of it yet."

"Tonight. Have you killed tonight?"

"No, I have not. But it's early, Jim."

"The whole city's looking for you. They've got more traffic-light cameras put up. They have people watching the rooftops. Reuben, they have satellite capabilities now to watch the rooftops. They know that's how you travel. Reuben, they're going to catch you. They're going to shoot you down! They're going to kill you."

"It won't be that easy, Jim. Let me worry about that."

"Listen, I want you to turn yourself over to the authorities. I will go home with you. We will call Simon Oliver and get the litigator in the firm, what's-his-name, Gary Paget, and—."

"Stop it, Jim. Not going to happen."

"Little Boy, you can't handle this on your own. You're tearing human beings limb from limb—."

"Jimmy, stop."

"You expect me to give you absolution for—."

"I didn't come for absolution. You know that. I came for this to be secret! You can't share this with anyone, Jim. You've made that promise to God, not just to me."

"That's true, but you must do as I tell you. You must go to Mom and explain all this. Look, let Mom run tests, let her figure out what the physical components of this thing are, how or why it's happening. Mom's been contacted by some specialist from Paris, some Russian doctor, really bizarre name, Jaska, I think, but this doctor claims to have seen other cases, cases in which strange things have happened. Reuben, this is not the first time—."

"Not on your life."

"We don't live in the Dark Ages, Reuben. We're not roaming around nineteenth-century London! Mom is the perfect person to shed real light on—."

"Are you serious? You think Mom is going to set up a Frankenstein-style lab with this Jaska guy and research this little project on her own? Will they get a humpbacked helper named Igor to run the MRIs and mix the chemicals? You think she's going to strap me to an iron chair when the sun sets so I can froth and roar in a little prison cell? You're dreaming. One word to Mom and I'm finished, Jim. She'll have to call in the finest scientific minds of her generation, the Paris specialist be damned. That's the way she's made. That's what the world would expect of her, that she'll get on the phone to the NIH. And in the meantime, she'd seek with all her power to confine me so I couldn't 'harm' anyone else and that would be the end, Jim. The end. Or the beginning of Reuben's life as an experimental animal under lock and key and government supervision. How long do you think it would be before I disappeared completely into some government facility? She couldn't stop that from happening.

"Let me tell you what happened to me when I entered that Buena Vista house two nights ago. The woman shot me. Jim, the wound had vanished by morning. There's nothing wrong with my shoulder where the bullet passed through. Nothing.

"Jim, they'd be drawing my blood day in and day out for the rest of my life, trying to isolate what gave me that kind of recuperative power. They'd biopsy every organ I've got. They'd biopsy my brain, if nobody stopped them. They'd be studying me with every instrument known to man to figure out how and why I change into this thing, and what hormones or chemicals govern my increase in size, the descent of the fangs and the claws, the rapid production of wolf-hair, the increase in muscular strength and aggression. They'll seek to trigger the change and control it. They'll catch on soon enough that what's happening to me has implications not only for longevity but for national defense—that if they can breed a corps of elite wolf soldiers they'll have a powerful tool for guerrilla warfare in places around the globe where conventional weapons are useless."

"All right. Stop. You've thought this through."

"Oh, yes, absolutely," Reuben said. "I've been lying in a motel room all day, listening to the news, and thinking about nothing else. I've been thinking about the hostages in the jungles of Colombia, and how easy it might be for me to get to them. I've been thinking about—everything. But not as clearly as I'm thinking it through now." He hesitated. His voice broke. "You don't know what it means to talk about it with you, Jim. But let's really talk about it; I mean let's really face what's happening to me."

"There's got to be somebody, somebody you can trust," said Jim. "Someone who can study this without jeopardizing you."

"Jimmy, there just isn't. That's why the werewolf movies end the way they do, with a silver bullet."

"Is that realistic? Can a silver bullet kill you?"

Reuben laughed under his breath.

"I have no idea," he said. "Probably not. I do know a knife or an ordinary bullet doesn't work. I know that much. You know, there could be something very simple that could kill me. Some toxin. Who knows?"

"All right. I understand. I understand why you can't trust Mom. I get it. Frankly, I think Mom could be persuaded to keep this secret because she loves you, Little Boy, and she's your mom. But I could be wrong, very wrong. It would . . . it would drive Mom right over the edge, that much is certain, no matter what she decided to do."

"That's another thing, isn't it?" Reuben said. "Protecting those I love from this secret because of what it will do to their minds and their lives."

**That's why I want to get out of here and find Laura in that Marin forest again. That's why I want so much to be in her arms because for whatever reason, she just wasn't afraid, wasn't repelled. In fact, she held me, she let me hold her. . . .**

Some thoughts for the confessional.

"There's this woman," he said. "I don't really even know who she is. I did some Internet searching. I think I know who she is, but the point is, I came on her unexpectedly and I lay with her."

" 'Lay with her,' you sound like the Bible. You mean you had sex with her?"

"Yeah, only I like to think of it as 'lay' because it was, as they say, you know, the old cliché, beautiful."

"Oh, this is great. Look, you can't handle this on your own. You can't handle the power, and from what you're telling me you can't handle the loneliness."

"And who is going to handle it with me?"

"I'm trying," Jim said.

"I know."

"You have to get someplace safe for the night, now. They're out everywhere searching for you. They think you're a madman dressed like a wolf, that's what they think."

"They don't know anything."

"Oh, yeah, they do. They expedited the DNA evidence from the saliva left on your victims. What if they find out it's human DNA and that it's mutated? What if they find unusual sequences in the DNA?"

"I don't understand those things," said Reuben.

"They're having problems with the tests, problems they don't want the public to know about. But that could mean they're making more sophisticated tests. Celeste says they think the evidence is being manipulated in some way."

"What do you mean?"

"The Man Wolf's playing tricks with them, planting bizarre evidence at the scenes of the crimes."

"That's ridiculous. They should have been there!"

"And they are connecting these attacks with Mendocino. Mom's connecting it to Mendocino. Mom's pushing for more tests on those dead junkies. They're going over everything."

"So you mean they'll figure out that it's different DNA up there, and that they have two man wolves roaming the world."

"I don't know. Nobody knows. Look, don't underestimate the web they can weave to snare you with their tests. If your DNA is in the system, Reuben, and they make a match—!"

"It's not in the system. Mom said something went wrong with their sample. Besides, I'm not . . . I wasn't a criminal. I'm not in the criminal system."

"Oh, and they play by the rules? They have a sample from Marchent Nideck's autopsy, don't they?" Jim was becoming more and more agitated.

"Yes, they probably do have that," said Reuben.

"And Mom said they've been calling, asking if they can get more of your DNA. Mom's been telling them no. Apparently, this Paris doctor advised Mom not to agree to any more tests."

"Please, Jim, try to keep calm. I can't follow you on this. You should have been a doctor like Mom."

Silence.

"Jim, I've got to go."

"Reuben, hang on! Go where?"

"There are things I have to find out, and first and foremost it's how to control the change, how to stop it, how to shut it down cold."

"So this has got nothing to do with the moon."

"It's not magical, Jim. No, it's got no connection to the moon. That's fantasy. It's like a virus. It's working from within. At least, that's how it seems. There has been a change in the way I view the world, a change in the moral temperature of things. I don't know what to make of all that yet. But it's not magic, no."

"If it's not supernatural, if it's simply a virus, then why are you killing only bad people?"

"I told you. It's a matter of scent and hearing." A chill came over Reuben. What did this mean?

"Since when does evil have a scent?" Jim asked.

"I don't know that either," said Reuben. "But we don't know why dogs smell fear, do we?"

"Dogs pick up on tiny physical signals. They can smell sweat, maybe even hormones like adrenaline.

You're going to tell me evil has some sort of hormonal dimension?"

"It could have," Reuben said. "Aggression, hostility, rage—maybe they all have scents, scents that human beings can't ordinarily measure. We don't know, do we?"

Jim didn't answer.

"What, you want it to be supernatural?" Reuben asked. "You want it to be diabolical?"

"When have I ever talked to you about anything being diabolical?" said Jim. "Besides—you're rescuing innocent victims. Since when does the devil care about innocent victims?"

Reuben sighed. He couldn't put all his thoughts into words. He couldn't begin to explain how his thinking had changed, even when he wasn't under the power of the transformation. He wasn't sure he wanted to tell Jim everything.

"I know this much," he said. "As long as I change like this unpredictably and with no control, I'm completely vulnerable. And I'm the only one who can work this out, and you're damn right, they have my DNA from Marchent, if from no other source. It's right under their noses, and so am I, and I have to get going."

"Where are you going?"

"Up to Nideck Point. Now listen to me, Father Jim. Come up there anytime that you can. And you can talk to me about this, in private, if you feel the need. I give you permission. But never to anyone else, or in front of anyone else."

"Thank you." Jim was obviously relieved. "Reuben, I want permission to read on this, to do research."

Reuben understood. A priest couldn't really act on a confession any more than he could talk about it or bring it up to the man who had confessed. Reuben said yes.

"I went by the house earlier today, got some books I'd ordered," Reuben explained. "Just legend, fiction, poetry, that kind of thing. But there have been incidents in America, you know, sightings—."

"Mom's been talking about those things," said Jim. "So has this Dr. Jaska. Something about the Beast of Bray Road."

"That's nothing," said Reuben. "Just a sighting in Wisconsin of a strange creature, a Bigfoot, maybe, something like that. Not much to go on. But I am searching myself for anything and everything that can shed light on this, and there is a bizarre coincidence having to do with the name Nideck, and I'm trying to figure it out. I just don't have anything yet. And yes, yes, you can do research, of course."

"Thank you," said Jim. "Now I want you to stay in touch with me, Reuben."

"Yes, Jim, I will."

Reuben reached for the curtain.

"Wait," Jim said. "Wait. Please, say whatever Act

of Contrition you can. Say it from your heart." Jim's voice was breaking. "And let me give you Absolution."

It hurt Reuben's heart, the sound of Jim's voice.

Reuben bowed his head and whispered: "God forgive me. God forgive me for my murderous heart, my heart that glories in this, my heart that doesn't want to give it up, that will not give it up, that wants somehow to possess it yet to be good." He sighed. He quoted St. Augustine: "'God make me chaste; just not today.'"

Jim was deep into the recitation of the Absolution and perhaps some other prayer, Reuben didn't know.

"May God protect you."

"And why would He do that?" Reuben asked.

Jim's voice came back with childlike sincerity:

"Because He made you. Whatever you are, He made you. And He knows why and for what purpose."

# 14

REUBEN WENT over the roofs back to the motel,
and locked himself in. All night long he tried to bring
about an end to the transformation. He couldn't use
his computer, not with these enormous claws. He
couldn't read the new books he'd ordered. They irri-
tated him. What had legendary werewolves to do
with him?

He didn't dare attempt to drive. He'd had a good
taste of how difficult that was when he'd followed
the kidnappers. He couldn't risk being seen or appre-
hended in his own car, even if he could endure the
difficulties.

He didn't dare go out either.

No matter how he wished for it, he couldn't work
the change. At least not right away.

All around him in the night he could hear the
voices. He'd been hearing them all the time he was
with Jim.

He didn't dare to focus on any one thread of sound
now. If one voice snared him, he'd be going out to
answer it.

It made him miserable to think that he could have
been saving someone from suffering, even death. He

crouched down in the corner, and tried to sleep, but that too was impossible.

At last around 3:00 a.m., much earlier than ever before, he did change.

It came on as always with a riot of orgasmic sensation, weakening him into a delirium as he went from beast to man. He watched it in the mirror. He snapped pictures on his iPhone. At last he stood staring at the old Reuben Golding he thought he knew so well, and neither had a word for the other that mattered. His hands looked delicate to him, and he wondered that he didn't feel a vulnerability as a human, but he didn't feel that vulnerability. He felt uncommonly strong, uncommonly able to resist whatever might threaten him in this form or the other form.

He was not very tired. He took a shower, and decided he'd sleep for a while before hitting the road.

It had now been two days since he'd spoken with anyone at home, and Jim could not, according to the old sacrosanct rules, so much as tell anyone he had even seen Reuben.

He had phone and e-mail messages from virtually everybody, including Galton, who'd installed the televisions for him the way that he'd asked. Galton had another piece of news for him. Orchid trees. Two very large orchid trees had arrived at the house, express shipped from Florida, apparently ordered by Marchent Nideck the night she died. Did Reuben want those trees?

Reuben felt a lump in his throat. For the first time

he knew what that cliché meant. Yes, he wanted the orchid trees. That was terrific. Would Galton order any other plants that he could?

He sent a number of e-mails, confident nobody would be up yet to answer. He told Grace he was okay, and doing errands and handling loose ends at Nideck Point. He told Phil pretty much the same thing. He told Billie he was writing a long piece on the modus operandi of the Man Wolf. He told Celeste he needed to be alone right now, and he hoped she'd understand.

He had to let Celeste go. He desperately needed her friendship right now, but the rest had taken on a nightmarish hue, and it wasn't her fault. No, not at all her fault. He was racking his brain for a way to disconnect romantically, a way that was gentlemanly and kind.

He added: "I hope you and Mort had a good time. I know how fond you are of Mort."

Was that a nudge towards Mort, or did it sound like a passive-aggressive snipe at her for being with Mort? He was in no condition to decide. He wrote: "You and Mort were always good together. As for me, I'm changed. We both know it. It's time for me to stop denying it. I'm just not the person I used to be."

It was about four-thirty, still dark outside, and he was not sleepy and he was restless. It wasn't painful, this restlessness, as it had been in Mendocino, but it wasn't all that pleasant.

Suddenly, he heard a gunshot. But where had it come from? He got up from the little motel desk and went towards the windows. Nothing out there but Lombard Street and a few late-night cars crawling the asphalt under the bright streetlamps.

His muscles were on alert. He was hearing something, something distinct and sharp. A man whimpering, crying, telling himself that he had to go through with it. And a woman, a woman pleading with the man. **Don't hurt the children. Please, please, don't hurt the children.** Then came another shot from the gun.

The spasms came from deep within, nearly crippling Reuben. He bent over, feeling his pores breathing, the hair breaking out all over his chest and arms. The change was happening, and happening more rapidly than ever. An ecstatic feeling gripped him, then a paralytic wave of pleasure and strength.

Within seconds, he'd left the room and was moving over the roofs.

The man was bawling, whining, pitying himself and those he "had" to kill, and the wife who was already dead. Reuben moved towards the man's voice.

The stench hit his nostrils, almost rancid, scent of cowardice and hate.

Reuben cleared the street with a long leap, and moved as fast as he could towards the white stucco house at the end of the block, coming down behind it on a second-floor iron balcony.

He broke the glass and stepped into the room. The only light was from outside. It was a neat, lovingly furnished room.

The woman lay dead on the four-poster bed, blood flowing from her head. The man stood over her, shirtless and barefoot, in pajama bottoms, holding the gun, blubbering and slobbering. The smell of liquor was overpowering and so was the scent of seething, convicting anger. They deserved it, they were making him do it, they'd driven him out of his mind, and they would never leave him alone.

"Have to do it, have to finish it!" the man protested to some unseen questioner. His bleary eyes looked at Reuben, but it wasn't clear that he saw anything in front of him. He was wobbling, whimpering. He cocked the gun again.

Reuben stepped up to him quietly, took the gun from his hand, and squeezed the man's thick slippery neck until his windpipe broke. He squeezed tighter, snapping the man's spinal cord.

The man dropped in an awkward heap to the floor.

Reuben set the gun down on the dressing table.

On the gilt-framed mirror above it was scrawled in lipstick an incoherent suicide note. He could scarcely make out the words.

He moved quickly down the small narrow hallway of the house, tracking the scent of children, the sweetest loveliest scent—his feet silent on the hardwood floor. Behind a door, he heard a child whispering.

Slowly he opened the door. The little girl was crouched in the bed, knees drawn up under her nightgown, and a toddler crouched beside her, a little boy, maybe three at most, with fair hair.

The little girl's eyes grew large as she looked at Reuben.

"The Man Wolf," she said, with the most radiant expression.

Reuben nodded. "After I'm gone, I want you to stay in this room," he said softly. "I want you to wait until the police come, do you hear me? Don't go down the hall. Wait here."

"Daddy's going to kill us," said the little girl in a small but very firm voice. "I heard him tell Mommy. He's going to kill me and Tracy."

"Not now, he's not," said Reuben. He reached out and touched each child on the head.

"You're a gentle wolf," said the little girl.

Reuben nodded. He said, "Do as I say."

He went back the way he came, punched in 911 on the bedroom phone, and said to the operator, "Two people are dead. There are little children here."

He was back at the motel just before the sun rose. Someone might have seen him come down from the roof onto the third-floor balcony. Not likely, no, but possible. The situation was untenable. He had to change now.

And indeed the change happened immediately, almost as if some merciful wolf god had heard him and forced it. Or maybe he'd forced it himself.

Fighting exhaustion, he packed up and was gone within minutes.

He made it as far as the Redwood Highway just north of Sausalito. Spying a small old one-story adobe style motel, he pulled off and managed to score the room at the very back which opened on a broken asphalt alley at the foot of a hill.

In the early afternoon, he woke.

He was in near despair. Where should he go? What should he do? He knew the answer—that Mendocino provided safety, solitude, and rooms in which to hide, and that it was only up there that he might find the "other one" who might be able to help him. He wanted to be with the distinguished gentlemen on the library wall.

**Damn you, I wish I knew who the hell you were.**

But he couldn't stop thinking about Laura. He didn't want to go up there, because Laura was here.

Over and over in his mind, he played the details of their few hours together. Of course, Laura may have already called the authorities about what happened. But there had been something utterly strange and steely about Laura that caused him to hope that that had not happened.

He got some coffee and sandwiches from a nearby café, brought them back to the room, and started work on the computer.

It didn't take a brain surgeon to figure out that Laura was in some way professionally connected to

the forest, to the outdoors, to the wilderness surrounding her house. Yesterday, he'd found one tour
guide website featuring tours for women—by an L. J.
Dennys. He scanned that website now again looking
for clues. But the only pictures of L. J. Dennys made
it quite impossible to tell who she was beneath her
hat and behind her sunglasses. Her hair was scarcely
visible.

He found random references to L. J. Dennys, naturalist and environmentalist, all over the place. But
no really good pictures.

He keyed in Laura J. Dennys, and let fly. There were
several false leads, and then something entirely unexpected: a four-year-old news story from the **Boston
Globe** concerning a Laura Dennys Hoffman, widow
of a Caulfield Hoffman who'd died, with his two
children, in a boating accident off Martha's Vineyard.

Well, probably another false lead but he punched
it, and up came the picture he'd been looking for.
This was the wearer of the pearls, the mother of the
two boys in the photo on Laura's night table—staring
out from a society picture of Laura with her late husband, a formidably handsome man with secretive
eyes and very white teeth.

She was poised, quietly beautiful—the woman
he'd held in his arms.

Within seconds, he was scanning any number of
hits on the drowning at sea of Caulfield Hoffman
and his sons. Laura had been in New York when the

"accident" had happened, and the accident, it turned out, was no accident. After a lengthy investigation, the coroner had ruled it a murder-suicide.

Hoffman had been facing serious criminal charges in connection with insider trading and mismanagement of funds. He'd been arguing with his wife about a possible separation and custody of the boys.

That wasn't all there was to Laura's story. The Hoffmans had lost their first child, a baby girl, to a hospital infection when she was less than one year old.

It didn't take much ingenuity now to close in on the life story of Laura J. Dennys.

She was the daughter of the California naturalist Jacob Dennys, who had written five books about the redwood forests of the northern coast. He'd died two years ago. His wife, Collette, a Sausalito painter, had died of a brain tumor twenty years before. That meant Laura had lost her mother very young. Jacob Dennys's oldest daughter, Sandra, had been murdered in a liquor store holdup in Los Angeles when she was twenty-two, one of several innocent bystanders "in the wrong place at the wrong time."

It was a breathtaking litany of tragedies. It surpassed anything Reuben might have imagined. And part and parcel of it was that Jacob Dennys had suffered from Alzheimer's in his last years.

Reuben sat back and drank a little of the coffee. The sandwich looked to him like paper and sawdust.

He was stunned by all this. And felt vaguely guilty

reading it, even ashamed. Yes, he was spying on Laura, and, yes, to uncover a mystery in her, and maybe he'd hoped that she was something so exceptional that she could accept him for what he was.

But this was too much.

He thought of those two little kids in the house in San Francisco, nestled together in that bed. He felt a secret exultation that he'd saved them, and a deep resentment that he hadn't been there in time to save the mother. He wondered where those little kids were now.

No wonder Laura had come home to disappear into the California forest. The L. J. Dennys website was three years old. She'd probably taken care of her elderly father. And then he'd left her, inevitably, like all the rest.

A terrible sadness for Laura settled over Reuben. **I'm ashamed, ashamed that I want you and that it sustains me to think, just to think, that because of all you've lost, you might love me.**

He could not conceive of being that alone, no matter what he was going through even now. In fact, the new isolation he was experiencing was driving him crazy.

But even in this, he was surrounded by love—intimately connected to Grace and Phil and, of course, his beloved brother, Jim. He had Celeste still, who would do anything for him, and Mort, his true friend. He had the warm hub of the Russian Hill house and the great gang of friends drawn perpetually into the family circle by all its vibrant members. And Rosy, beloved Rosy. Even Phil's tiresome professor friends were a staple of Reuben's life, like so many gracious old uncles and aunts.

He thought of Laura and that small house on the edge of the wood. He tried to assess what it would mean to marry, and then lose your entire family. Unspeakable pain.

Now a life like that, he figured, could make one tentative and fearful perhaps. Or it could make you remarkably strong, and what people called philosophical—and fiercely independent. Maybe it could make you careless of your own life, indifferent to danger, and determined to live exactly as you pleased.

Reuben knew a dozen other ways to find out information about Laura—credit score, car registration, personal net worth—but that simply wasn't fair. In fact, it was obscene. However, there was one more tiny item that he did want, and that was her address, and he found that quickly enough. The house in which she lived had been the subject of a couple of articles. It had belonged to her grandfather, Harper Dennys, and was quite literally grandfathered; no one could have built such a house so deep into the protected forest area today.

He wandered outside and walked around the small motel. The rain was a drizzle. It would be easy after dark to slip out of his room and go up the wooded slope and over the summit and into the thickly forested hills of Mill Valley. From there it would be simple to get to Muir Woods.

Very likely no one was looking for him here now. After all, he had only hours ago killed a man in San Francisco.

That is, nobody was looking for him here unless Laura J. Dennys had told the authorities what happened.

Could she have done that? **And would they have believed a word of it?**

He didn't know. He couldn't imagine her telling anyone.

If there was a television in that small house, if there were newspapers delivered to the door, or brought home from the grocery store in town, then she had to know what had been happening.

Maybe she understood that the Wild Man of the Wood would rather die than bring harm to her—unless harm was his love for her, and his near-mad desire to see her again.

Just before dark, Reuben hit a store for some cheap clothes that actually fit him, clean underwear and socks and such, and stowed all this in a bag that would stay permanently in the Porsche. He was sick of roaming around in the oversized hoodie and trench coat. But he didn't bother to change now.

As the sun set, he drove into Mill Valley in a thin noiseless rain, and up Panoramic Highway till he found Laura's house—a small gray-shingled cottage way back from the road, scarcely visible for the trees that surrounded it.

He drove past it and found a small gulley in which to hide the Porsche, and there inside the car, he fell into a fitful uneasy sleep. The change woke him much sooner than he expected.

# 15

THE HOUSE WAS EMPTY when he entered it, the door unlocked and open to the back porch.

He'd come down through the trees. There was no one anywhere near; no stakeout, certainly; no police voices in the vicinity—in fact, there were no voices at all.

The back bedroom was the sweet picture that he remembered. All the same sweet scents were there.

The high-backed oak bed was draped with a soft beautifully crafted patchwork quilt. A small brass lamp burned on the night table, giving a warm light through its parchment shade. And nestled among the pillows in the oak rocking chair was a faded handmade rag doll with a carefully stitched face of almond-shaped button eyes, rose-red lips, and long yellow yarn hair. A small bookshelf held row after row of books by Harper Dennys and Jacob Dennys. And even a book by L. J. Dennys on the wildflowers of Mount Tamalpais and the surrounding area.

The bedroom opened onto the kitchen, divinely rustic with its big black stove and blue-and-white china cups on hooks beneath the open white shelves.

Potato vines grew from glasses on the windowsill above the sink. Bright white and gold daisies filled a blue vase in the center of the small white table. And a bright impressionistic landscape of a walled rose garden hung on the wall. The signature was "Collette D."

Beyond was a spacious bathroom with its own small iron fireplace, a huge shower, and a claw-foot tub. Opposite, a narrow stairs went up to a second floor.

Then came the large dining room with its vintage round oak table and heavy press-back chairs, a hutch filled with more antique blue-and-white china, and a living room of comfortable old chairs, draped with artful quilts and blankets, gathered as if for a tête-à-tête before the fieldstone hearth. A small fire was burning deep in the fireplace, well protected by a screen. A corner floor lamp, old-fashioned brass, gave a soft, agreeable light.

There were large bright garden paintings by Collette D. throughout the house, rather tame and predictable, perhaps, but brilliantly colorful and comforting and sweet. And lots of photographs everywhere—many including the cheerful weathered face of Jacob Dennys, white-haired even as a young man.

There was a flat-screen television in the living room, and even a small one in the kitchen, on the counter. There were recent newspapers by the living room hearth. "Man Wolf Frees Kidnapped Children" screamed the front page of the **San Francisco Chronicle.** The Mill Valley paper had opted for: "Children Found Safe in Mill Valley; Two Dead." Both papers had very similar drawings of the Man Wolf—an anthropoid figure with lupine ears and a ghastly fanged snout.

It was a house full of windows, and everywhere they sparkled with the soft, whispering rain. Walls were carefully painted in deep earth tones, and the woodwork was natural, and gleaming with wax.

He was in the living room by the fire when she came in the back door. He slipped into the hallway. He could see her in the kitchen, setting down a brown paper sack of groceries and what looked like a folded newspaper.

Her hair was tied back by a black ribbon at the nape of her neck. She slipped off her heavy corduroy jacket and threw it aside. She wore a soft gray high-neck sweater and a long dark skirt. There was a weariness, a dissatisfaction, in her gesture. Her sweet scent slowly filled the house. He knew now he'd know this scent anywhere—its unmistakable blend of personal warmth and that subtle citrus perfume.

He was rapt looking at her, at her tapering hands and her smooth forehead, at the soft white hair that framed her face, at her ice-blue eyes sweeping absently over the room.

He drew closer to the kitchen door.

She was anxious, uncertain. She moved dejectedly to the white table and was about to sit down when she saw him standing in the hall.

"Beautiful Laura," he whispered. **What do you see? The Man Wolf, the monster, the beast that rips his victims limb from limb?**

In shock, she clapped her hands to her face, staring at him through her long fingers. And her eyes filled with tears. Suddenly she began to cry aloud in deep heartrending sobs.

She opened her arms as she ran to him. He stepped forward to embrace her, and he pressed her warmly to his chest.

"Beautiful Laura," he whispered again, and picked her up as he had before, and carried her into the rear bedroom and set her on the bed.

He tore the ribbon from her hair. It came down in waves around her—white, streaked with yellow in the light of the nearby lamp.

He could scarcely keep from stripping off her clothes. It seemed an eternity that she struggled with buttons and clips as she peeled them away. Finally she was naked and pink against him, her nipples like petals, and the dark hair between her legs the color of smoke. He covered her mouth with kisses, and heard that deep growl come out of his chest, that animalian growl that a man could never make. He couldn't stop himself from kissing her all over, on her throat and her breasts and her belly and on the insides of her silky thighs.

He cradled her head in his hands as she ran her fingers over his face, digging deep into the undercoat of soft wolf-fur beneath the long coarser hair.

She was still crying, but in his ears it was like the rain on the windows—like a song.

# 16

WHILE SHE SLEPT, he built up the living room fire. He wasn't cold, no, not at all, but he wanted the spectacle of it, the flicker against the ceiling and the walls. He wanted the bright blaze itself.

He was standing with one foot on the low hearth when she came into the room.

She'd put on a white flannel nightgown, like the one he'd torn up so greedily the first night. It had thick antique lace at the wrists and around the collar. Little pearl buttons glinted in the dark.

Her hair was brushed and lustrous.

She sat down in the old chair to the left of the fire, and pointed tentatively to the bigger chair, the battered and worn chair to the right, which was large enough for him.

He sat down and gestured for her to come.

She quickly moved to his lap, and he held her shoulders in his right arm and she rested her head on his chest.

"They're searching for you," she said. "You know that."

"Of course." He still was not used to the depth of this voice or its huskiness. Maybe he was lucky that he had a voice at all.

"You're not afraid here, alone, in this house?" he asked. "I see that you aren't. I'm asking why."

"What is there to fear?" she answered. She was speaking confidentially, naturally, her hand playing with the long hair on his shoulder. Gradually her fingers found the nipple amid the hair of his chest. She pinched it.

"Wicked girl!" he whispered. He winced. He gave that low hungry growl again and heard her muted laughter.

"Truly," he said. "I'm afraid for you; I'm afraid for you alone in this house."

"I grew up in this house," she said simply, without drama. "Nothing has ever hurt me in this house." She paused, then said: "You've come to me here in this house."

He didn't answer. He was stroking her hair.

"You're the one I fear for," she said. "I've been sick with fear for you since you left. Even now, I'm afraid that they've followed you here, or someone's seen you. . . ."

"They haven't followed me," he said. "I would hear them if they were out there. I would pick up their scent."

They were quiet for a while. He was watching the fire.

"I know who you are," he said. "I read your story."

She didn't answer.

"Everyone today has a story; the world's an archive. I read about the things that have happened to you."

"Then you have the advantage, as they say," she replied. "Because I do not have the slightest idea who you really are. Or why you came here."

"I don't know myself at the moment," he said.

"Then you weren't always what you are now?" she asked.

"No." He laughed under his breath. "Most certainly not." His tongue pressed against his fangs, ran against the silky black liplike tissue around his mouth. He shifted comfortably in the chair, and her weight was like nothing to him.

"You can't stay here, I mean in the city, I mean here. They'll find you. The world's too small now, too controlled. If they catch the slightest hint that you're in the forest, they'll swarm over it. It only looks like a wilderness. It's not."

"I know that," he said. "I know that very well."

"But you take risks, terrible risks."

"I hear voices," he said. "I hear voices and I go to them. It's as if I can't help but go to them. Someone will suffer and die if I don't."

Slowly, he described it to her, pretty much the way he'd described it to Jim—the scents, the mystery of the scents. He talked about the various attacks, how the victims had been crying out in the darkness, how it had been so clear to him who was evil and who was good. He told her about the man who shot his wife.

"Yes, he would have killed the children," she said. "I heard the story on the way home tonight in the car."

"I didn't get there in time to save the woman," he said. "I am not infallible. I am something that can make terrible mistakes."

"But you're careful, so very careful," she insisted. "You were careful with that boy up north."

"The boy up north?"

"The reporter," she said, "the handsome one, in the house in Mendocino—up north."

He hesitated. Current of pain. Pain in the heart.

He didn't answer.

"They surprised that woman, didn't they?" she whispered.

"Yes."

"If they hadn't, you would have—." She stopped.

"Yes," he said. "They surprised her. And they surprised me."

He went quiet.

After a long time, she asked softly, tentatively, "What brought you down this far?"

He didn't understand.

"Was it the voices, that there are so many more here?"

He didn't answer. But he thought he understood. She was thinking he'd come down from the forests to the cities of the Bay Area. It made a kind of sense.

He was burning to pour it all out for her, burning. But he couldn't. Not yet. And he couldn't forsake holding her like this, the power of it, the protective and loving power. He couldn't tell her that he wasn't always like this, that he was in fact "that boy up north." If he confessed that to her and she turned from him in scorn or indifference it would cut him to his soul.

**That boy up north.** He tried to picture himself as just Reuben, Celeste's Sunshine Boy, Grace's baby, Jim's little brother, Phil's son. Why would that vapid "boy" interest her? It seemed absurd to think that he would. After all, Marchent Nideck hadn't really been interested in him. She'd thought him sweet and gentle and a poet, and a rich boy with the means to take Nideck Point off her hands. But that was not interest, really; and that was hardly love.

What he felt for Laura was love.

His closed his eyes and listened to the slow rhythm of her breathing. She'd fallen asleep.

The forest whispered beyond the windows. Scent of bobcat. It maddened him. He wanted to stalk it, kill it, feast on it. He could taste it. His mouth was watering. Sound of the creeks running deep in the redwoods; sound of the owls in the high branches, of things unnamable slithering in the brush.

He wondered what Laura would think if she saw him as he was in the forest, crushing that thrashing hissing bobcat and gorging on his hot flesh. That was the thing about these feasts: the flesh was so fresh. The blood was still pumping in it, the heart still quivering. What would she think if she really saw what it was like?

She had no idea, really, what it meant to see a man's arm ripped out by the root, to see a head torn off a neck. She had no idea. We human beings live perpetually insulated from the horrors that happen all around us. No matter what she'd suffered, she had not witnessed the viscous ugliness of that kind of death. No, it had to be unreal to her, even Laura who had endured so much.

Only those who work day in and day out with the killers of the world know what they really are. It hadn't taken him long as a reporter to realize that— why the cops he'd interviewed were so very different from other people, why Celeste was becoming so different as she worked on more and more cases for the district attorney, or why Grace was different because she saw the bodies rolled into the emergency room with the knives in their bellies and the bullet wounds in their heads.

But even those people, cops, lawyers, doctors, learned what they learned from the aftermath. They weren't there when the killer tore at his victim; they didn't smell the scent of evil; they didn't hear the cries to heaven for something, someone, to intervene.

A frightening sadness had come over him. He wanted her so much. But what right did he have to tell her these things? What right had he to seduce her with "stories" that made it all sound so meaningful when it was perhaps not meaningful—when it was violent and primitive and dark?

Just let me have these moments with her, he mused. Let me just hold her here by this fire, in this small house of simple things, and let this be all right for now.

He drifted off, feeling her heart next to his heart.

An hour must have passed, perhaps more time than that.

He opened his eyes. The forest was at peace, from one border to another.

But something was wrong out there. Something was very wrong. A voice pushed at the layers and layers of muffled sound that surrounded him. A voice rose thin and reedy and desperate.

It was a man screaming for help. Far beyond the forest. He knew the direction. He knew the scent would come.

He carried her to the back of the house and laid her gently in the bed. She woke with a start, rising up on her elbows.

"You're going."

"I have to go, it's calling me," he said.

"They'll catch you. They're everywhere!" she pleaded. She started to cry. "Listen to me!" she pleaded. "You've got to go back up north, to the forests, away from here."

He bent quickly to kiss her.

"You'll see me again very soon."

She rushed after him but he was halfway across the clearing in a second and he leapt high up into the redwoods and began his swift journey towards the coast road.

Hours later, he stood in a small grove of trees looking out at the great cold Pacific under a lowering silver sky. The moon hung behind those rain clouds. The moon shone through to the tilting, shifting surface of the sea. Oh, if the moon only had a secret, if the moon only held a truth. But the moon was just the moon.

He'd tracked the car in which the man had been imprisoned, descended from the trees onto the roof of it, and when it slowed for a dangerous curve on Highway 1, he had torn the doors open, and dragged the ugly, hardened thieves out into the dark. They'd shot the man's companion—but kept him alive, bound, gagged, suffocating in the trunk of the car. They'd meant to force him to an automatic teller window, for the few hundred dollars they could get from him, then kill him as they had the other man.

He'd feasted on both of the thieves before he freed the prisoner and left him on the cliff above the sea with the promise that help would soon come. After that, he had roamed the cliffs in the salt wind, letting the gusting rain wash away the blood from his paws, from his mouth, from his chest.

Now it was approaching dawn and he was exhausted and lonely as if he'd never held Laura in his arms.

**We all need love, don't we, even the worst killers, the worst animals! We all need love.**

He traveled back fast to where he'd left his Porsche off the Panoramic Highway, and waited there in the glade until the change came on. Again, it surprised him, seemed more amenable to his will. He flexed and forced it to greater and greater speed.

He drove the car into Mill Valley and put up at the charming and beautiful little hotel called the Mill Valley Inn. Best place to hide right on Throckmorton Street in the very center of town. Because now they really would be looking for the Man Wolf in Marin County and he had to see Laura before he went north, perhaps for a long time.

# 17

AROUND NOON, he had just parked downhill from Laura's house when she suddenly came out, got into an olive-green four-door Jeep, and drove down into the center of town, from which he'd only just come.

She went into a cheerful little café, and he saw her take her place at a table inside the front window alone.

He parked, and went inside.

She appeared wrapped in solitude as she sat there, snug in her corduroy coat, her face fresh and lovely as it had been last night. Her hair was tied back again with a black ribbon, and the symmetry of her face was flawless. It was the first time he'd seen her in the light of day.

He sat down opposite her without a word. He was dressed now more like his old self in a halfway-decent khaki jacket and a clean shirt and a tie—clothes he'd bought yesterday—and he'd scrubbed himself in the shower for an hour before checking out of the hotel. His hair was too thick and too long, but it was thoroughly combed.

"Who are you!" she demanded. She set the menu down and glanced angrily towards the back of the restaurant for the waiter.

Reuben didn't answer. There was no waiter visible in the back of the restaurant just now. Only a couple of other tables were occupied.

"Look, I'm dining here alone," she said politely but firmly. "Now, please go."

Then her face changed. It went from anger and annoyance to thinly concealed alarm. At once her eyes hardened and so did her voice:

"You're the reporter," she said accusingly. "The one from the **Observer.**"

"Yes."

"What are you doing here?" She had become furious. "What do you want with me?" Her features were transformed into an obdurate mask. Inside, she was roiling with panic.

He leaned forward and he spoke in a warm intimate voice.

"I'm that boy from up north," he said.

"Yes, I know that," she said, not getting the connection. "I know just who you are. Now kindly explain: what do you want with me?"

He reflected for a moment. And again, she looked desperately for a waiter but none was in the main room. She started to get up. "Very well, I'll have my lunch someplace else," she said. She was trembling.

"Laura, wait."

He reached out for her left hand.

Reluctantly, suspiciously, she sank back down in the chair.

"How do you know my name?"

"I was with you last night," he said softly, "most of the night. I was with you until early morning when I had to go."

He'd never in his life seen anyone so perfectly astonished. She was frozen, staring at him across the table. He could see the blood pounding in her pale cheeks. Her lower lip quivered but she didn't speak a word.

"Reuben Golding is my name," he went on in a low trusting voice. "It started up there for me, in that house, up north. That's how it began."

She took a deep ragged breath. The sweat broke out on her forehead and on her upper lip. He could hear her heart pounding. Her face softened and her lips were trembling. The tears rose in her eyes.

"Good heavens," she whispered. She looked at the hand with which he was clasping hers. She looked at his face. She was taking his full measure and he felt it keenly, and the tears almost sprang to his eyes, too. "But who—? How—?"

"I don't know," he admitted. "But I do know that I have to leave here now. I'm going back up there. The place is mine—the house in Mendocino where it happened. It belongs to me. And I want to go there. I can't stay here any longer, not after last night. Will you come with me?"

There it was, and he fully expected her to shrink from him, to pull her hand out of his and draw it down away from his reach. Her Man of the Wild was not a Man of the Wild after all.

"Look, I know you have your work, your tours, your customers. . . ."

"It's the rainy season," she said in a weak small voice. "There are no tours right now. I don't have any work." Her eyes were glassy, huge. She took another heaving breath. Her fingers wrapped around his.

"Oh . . . ," he said stupidly. He didn't know what else to say. Then, "Will you come?"

It was unbearable to sit there quietly under her scrutiny, to wait until she spoke again.

"Yes," she said suddenly. She nodded. "I'll come with you." She looked certain but dazed.

"You realize what you're doing if you come with me."

"I'm coming," she said.

Now he really did have to fight the tears, and it took him a moment. He held tight to her hand but looked out the window, at rainy Throckmorton Street and the crowds hurrying to and fro under their umbrellas, in front of the many little shops.

"Reuben," she said. She pressed his hand now tightly. She'd recovered herself and she was very serious. "We should leave now."

As he steered the Porsche towards the Panoramic Highway, she began to laugh.

She laughed harder and harder. It was a great release, this laughter. And she obviously couldn't hold it in.

He was baffled, uncomfortable. "What is it?" he asked.

"Well, you have to see the humor of this surely," she said. "Look at you. Look at who you are."

His heart sank.

She stopped laughing abruptly. "I'm sorry," she said in a small crestfallen voice. "It wasn't right to laugh, was it? I shouldn't have laughed. It's not a time for laughing at all. It's just, well, let me put it this way: you've got to be one of the handsomest men I've ever seen."

"Oh," he whispered. He couldn't look at her. Well, at least she hadn't called him a kid or a boy. "Is that good?" he asked. "Or is that bad?"

"You serious?"

He shrugged.

"Well, it's just surprising," she confessed. "I'm sorry, Reuben. I shouldn't have laughed."

"It's all right. It's not important, is it?"

They had reached her gravel driveway. He turned to her. She looked so genuinely concerned. He couldn't help but smile to reassure her, and at once her face brightened.

"You know," she said with the utmost sincerity. "In the story of the prince and the frog, there's always a frog. This story . . . it has no frog."

"Hmmm. It's a different story, Laura," he responded. "It's **Dr. Jekyll and Mr. Hyde.**"

"No, it's not," she said reprovingly. "I don't think it's that story at all. It's not 'Beauty and the Beast' either. Maybe it's a new story."

"Yes, a new story," he agreed eagerly. "And I think the next line of the story is 'Get the hell out of Dodge now.' "

She leaned forward and kissed him—him; not the big hairy wolf-beast, but him.

He took her face in both hands and kissed her slowly, lovingly. It was altogether different, the old rhythm, the old way of things, and oh, so indefinably sweet.

# 18

IT TOOK HER LESS than fifteen minutes to pack and call a neighbor who would pick up her car downtown and check on her house while she was gone.

The drive to Nideck Point took almost four hours, just as it had before, largely due to the rain.

On the way, they talked nonstop.

Reuben told her everything that had happened. He explained it all from the start, and in minute detail.

He told her who he'd been before it ever began—all about his family, about Celeste, about Jim, and a multitude of other things, the stories tumbling out effortlessly and sometimes without coherence, her questions always sensitive, and only slightly probing, her fascination obvious even with the things of which he'd always been a little embarrassed or downright ashamed.

"It was a fluke that I got hired by the **Observer.** Billie knows my mother and it started out as a favor. Then she actually liked what I wrote."

He explained how he was Sunshine Boy to Celeste, and Baby Boy to his mother, and Little Boy to Jim, and lately his editor, Billie, had been calling him Boy Wonder, and only his father called him Reuben. She broke into laughter again over that and had a bit of a time stopping herself.

But it was easy to talk to her, and agreeable to listen to her, too.

Laura had seen Dr. Grace Golding on the morning talk shows. She'd met Grace once at a black-tie benefit. The Goldings supported wildlife causes. "I've read all your articles in the **Observer,**" she said. "Everybody likes what you write. I started reading you because somebody told me about your pieces."

He nodded. That might have meant something if all of this had not happened.

They talked about Laura's years at Radcliffe, her late husband, and briefly the kids. She wasn't going to linger on those things; Reuben picked up on that quickly. She spoke of her sister, Sandra, as if Sandra were still living. Sandra had been her best friend.

Her dad was the mentor of her life. She and Sandra had grown up in Muir Woods, gone off to eastern schools in their teens, to Europe during the summers, but the rich, near-fantastical paradise of Northern California had been their sustaining life.

Yes, she'd imagined Reuben a wild man come down out of the northern forests, some secret species at one with nature and caught off guard by the routine horrors of urban life.

The little house in the forest had belonged to her grandfather, and he'd still been alive when she was a little girl. There were four bedrooms on the second floor, all empty now. "My boys got to play in the woods for one summer," she said in a small voice.

Their stories poured out of them easily and completely.

He talked about his Berkeley days and the digs overseas, about his love of books, and she talked about her time in New York, and how her husband had swept her off her feet. As for her father, she'd been utterly devoted to him. And he'd never uttered a word of criticism of her for marrying Caulfield Hoffman against his candid but gentle advice.

She'd lived a life of parties, concerts, operas, receptions, and benefits in New York with Caulfield that now seemed like a dream. Their town house on Central Park East, the nannies, the frantic pace and richness of life, all of that was like something that had never happened. Hoffman had been ruined when he killed himself and the children. Everything they'd owned together had been lost. Every single thing.

She woke in the night sometimes unable to believe that her children had ever really existed, let alone died in those cruel ways.

They went back to the mysterious life in which Reuben now found himself, and to the night Reuben had been attacked in the hallway of the Mendocino house. They speculated on what might have happened.

He confided to her his wild theories about the name Nideck, but the connection seemed quite feeble. He circled back to the fact that the creature who'd passed on the "gift" to him, as he called it, might well have been a vagrant monster passing through this part of the world on a journey to parts unknown.

He went over every detail of the transformation. He recounted his confession with his brother, Jim.

She wasn't Catholic. She didn't really trust the Seal of the Confessional, but she accepted that he and Jim believed in it, and she certainly respected his love for Jim.

She had a slightly better grasp of science than he did, but said several times that she was no scientist. She asked questions about the DNA testing that had been done which he couldn't answer. He figured he'd left DNA evidence at the scene of every little massacre over which he'd presided. He couldn't begin to understand what the tests would reveal.

They both agreed that the DNA testing was the most dangerous tool that others possessed against him. And neither of them knew what he should do.

Certainly going to the Mendocino house was the best thing right now. If the creature was up there, if the creature had secrets to divulge, well, then they should give the creature a chance.

Yet Laura was fearful.

"I wouldn't assume," she said, "that this thing is capable of love and conscience as you are. That might not be true at all."

"Well, why not?" Reuben asked. What could that mean—that he himself perhaps was progressing beyond conscience and emotion? That was his worst fear.

They stopped for supper in a little inn on the coast right before dark. It was a glorious spot, even with the relentless rain and the featureless gray skies. They had a table by a window over the sea, and a view of desolate yet majestic rocks.

The tables were draped in lavender linen, with lavender napkins, and the food was subtly spiced, special. He ate ravenously, consuming everything offered down to the last crumb of bread.

The place was rustic with a low sloping ceiling, the expected roaring fireplace, and old weathered plank floors.

It comforted him, made him a little too happy. Then there came the inevitable gloom.

The sea beyond the glass was darkening. The waves below looked black with silvery-white foam.

"You realize what I've done to you," he whispered.

Her face had a soft radiance in the light of the candles. Her eyebrows were just dark enough to give her a definite serious expression and her blue eyes were always beautiful even when they looked a bit cold. He'd seldom seen blue eyes so light yet so intense. Her face was wonderfully expressive, full of obvious fascination and what certainly seemed to be love.

"I knew the things you'd done when I first saw you," she said.

"You're an accessory now, after the fact."

"Hmmm, to a very strange series of violent incidents, indeed."

"This is not a fantasy."

"Who knows that better than me?"

He sat there in silence wondering, inevitably, if he left her now would she be free? He had a vague sense that it would be a disaster for her if he left her. But maybe he was simply confused. It would be a disaster for him if he were to lose her.

"Some mysteries are simply irresistible," she said. "They have components that alter a life."

He nodded.

He realized he felt utterly possessive of her, proprietary, in a way he'd never felt with anyone, not even Celeste. It was stoking his passion to think of it. There were rooms upstairs in this inn. He wondered what it would be like, the two of them just as they were.

But how long did he have tonight? He was longing for the transformation; he was yearning to be more fully and completely himself.

Now that was one horrible revelation. She was saying something but he didn't hear her. Who and what am I now, he thought, if the other is my true self?

". . . ought to get going now."

"Yes," he said.

He stood to help her with her chair, to hold her coat.

She seemed touched by these gestures. "Who taught you your Old-World manners?" she asked.

# 19

It was nine o'clock.

They were sitting on the leather couch in the library, with the fire going, watching the large television to the left of the fireplace. Laura had changed into one of her white nightgowns. And he'd put on one of his old sweaters and a pair of old jeans.

The man in the red tie on the television screen was in deadly earnest.

"This is the worst kind of psychopath," he said. "There can be no doubt of it. He thinks he's on our side. The public adulation is no doubt feeding his obsessions and his pathology. But let's be very clear on this: he rips his victims apart without mercy; he devours human flesh."

The man's name and credentials flashed beneath his picture: CRIMINAL PSYCHOLOGIST. The camera cut to the interviewer, a familiar face on CNN news, though at the moment Reuben could not recall his name:

"But what if this is some sort of mutation—?"

"Out of the question," said the expert. "This is a human being like you or me, using a series of sophisticated methods to surround his killings with the aura of an animal attack. The DNA is unequivocal. He's human. Oh, yes, he has access to the bodily fluids of animals—this is most certainly true. He's contaminated the evidence. And certainly he's using prosthetic teeth, or fangs. That part is certain. Some sort of sophisticated mask covers his entire head. But he's a human being, and probably the most dangerous human being that criminal pathology has seen in recent times."

"But what accounts for the man's strength?" asked the commentator. "I mean this man clearly overpowers two and three people at a time. How is a man in an animal mask supposed to—."

"Well, the element of surprise, for one thing," said the expert, "but his strength has probably been wildly exaggerated."

"But the evidence, I mean three bodies left mangled and one decapitated—."

"Again, we are rushing to conclusions here." The expert was getting testy. "He may well use some sort of gas to disorient or disable his victims."

"Yes, but he threw a woman out of a window so that she landed over seventy-five feet from the house—."

"It does us no good to hyperbolize what this man is capable of. Witnesses can't be counted on—."

"And you're confident that they are telling us everything they know about the creature's DNA."

"No, not at all," said the expert. "Undoubtedly they're withholding information, trying to make sense of the data they have. And they've got their hands full trying to quell the hysteria. But the rhapsodic nonsense in the press about this individual is completely irresponsible and likely to goad him into even more vicious attacks."

"But how does he find his victims?" asked the commentator. "That's what is so baffling here. How did he find a woman on the third floor of a San Francisco house or a homeless man being attacked in Golden Gate Park?"

"Oh, he's been lucky, that's all." The expert was becoming visibly disgusted. "And we don't know how long he trolled for these people or stalked them before closing in."

"But the kidnappers, he found the kidnappers in Marin County when no one else could—."

"For all we know he may have been connected with the kidnapping," said the commentator. "There was nobody left alive there to explain anything let alone who all was involved. Or maybe it was sheer luck."

Reuben hit the remote for another channel.

"I'm sorry, I can't listen to that," he said.

At once, a woman's face filled the screen. She was a picture of grief and distress. "I don't care what my son did," she said. "He was entitled to due process of law like any other American; he didn't deserve to be torn limb from limb by a monster who holds himself to be judge, jury, and executioner. And now people are singing the praises of his killer." She started to sob. "Has the world gone mad?"

Cut away to the news anchor, a long-haired dark-skinned woman with a rich mellow voice.

"Who is this mysterious being now known around the globe as the San Francisco Man Wolf—who comforts little children, carries a homeless man back to his hiding place, and frees an entire busload of kidnap victims after setting off an alarm to summon help? Right now authorities have more questions than they have answers. [Shots of City Hall, officials gathered before microphones.] But one thing is certain. People do not fear the San Francisco Man Wolf. They are celebrating him, bombarding the Internet with sketches of him, poems to him, even songs."

The camera closed on a pair of youngsters in cheap garish orange gorilla costumes holding a hand-painted sign: MAN WOLF WE LOVE YOU! Cut to a teenage girl with a guitar singing: "It was the Man Wolf, it was the Man Wolf, it was the Man Wolf with the big blue eyes!"

Woman on the street before a reporter's handheld mike: "It's troubling that they are keeping these witnesses from talking directly to the press! Why are we hearing all about what these people saw but not hearing from them ourselves?"

"Well, how do you expect people to feel?" said a tall man, questioned on a busy street corner against a backdrop of the Powell Street cable car clanging noisily downhill. "Is there any one of us who doesn't want to strike back at all the evil in this world? Look, these kidnappers murdered two kids. A third died from a ketoacidosis coma. And who's afraid of the guy, may I ask? I'm not. Are you?"

Reuben hit the OFF button.

"I've had enough," he said apologetically.

Laura nodded.

"So have I," she said. She walked soundlessly to the fireplace and gave the logs a nudge with the brass poker, then returned to the couch, snuggling up against the white pillow she'd brought down from upstairs, and covering up with a white blanket. She had Reuben's new collection of books on werewolf literature. She'd been reading them on and off since they arrived.

The room was comfortably lighted by the brass lamp on the desk. All the draperies were closed. Reuben had closed them throughout the house—quite a chore, but they had both wanted it.

Reuben wanted for all the world to snuggle up with her now, either here or upstairs in the regal bed of the master bedroom.

But they were both on tenterhooks. All Reuben could think about was "the transformation." Would it come? Would it not come? And if it did not come, how bad would the restlessness get? He was already feeling it.

"If only I knew," he said with a sigh. "Will this be something that happens to me every night for the rest of my life? If only I knew some way to predict or control it."

Laura was quietly entirely sympathetic. She asked for one thing: to stay close to him.

Their first couple of hours at the house had been blissful. Reuben had loved revealing the place room by room to Laura, and she had fallen in love with the master bedroom, as he'd hoped.

Galton had installed a great many new plants in the conservatory, and even sought to arrange them in some decent fashion.

The orchid trees were magnificent, well over eight feet tall and filled with pinkish-purple blossoms, though some had been a little damaged in transit. They were in wooden pots. It took Reuben's breath away to think that Marchent had ordered these right before her life came to an end. These trees flanked the fountain, and a white marble-top table with two white iron chairs now stood right in front of it.

The fountain had been reinvigorated and the water was rumbling beautifully from the small basin atop its fluted column into the broad flat basin below.

Reuben's computer equipment and printer had arrived, along with the Blu-ray films. And all of the many television sets were fully equipped and working.

Reuben had spent some time answering e-mails, principally to head off trouble. Celeste had reported that the DNA findings for the Man Wolf case were "frustrating everybody," but she hadn't elaborated on what that meant.

And Grace had insisted that he needed to come home for more tests. But that if anyone asked him for another DNA sample, he was to refuse. And he should know they could not take it from him against his will without a warrant. She was looking into the matter of a private facility in Sausalito, recommended by the Russian doctor from Paris, that might be the perfect place for some confidential research.

She'd also cautioned him sternly against talking to reporters. With every new revelation concerning the Man Wolf, the reporters grew bolder in their search for a comment from Reuben, even showing up at the door of the Russian Hill house now, or calling the family's private landline.

Billie wanted some deep reflection on the Man Wolf craze.

Maybe now was the time to offer it. He'd watched as much of the national news as he could endure, and had surveyed enough online to have a feel for the range of public responses.

It was good here, being alone with Laura. The silence, the crackle of the fire, the whispers of the forest beyond the curtains. Why not work? Who said that he couldn't work? Who said that he could not go on working?

Finally he began.

After passing over the cases to date in some choice detail, Reuben went on to write:

> Our way—the Western Way—has always been a "work in progress." Questions of life and death, good and evil, justice and tragedy— these are never definitively settled, but must be

addressed again and again as personal and public worlds shift and change. We hold our morals to be absolutes, but the context of our actions and decisions is forever changing. We are not relativists because we seek to re-evaluate again and again our most crucial moral positions.

So why do we romanticize the Man Wolf who seemingly punishes wrongdoing without hesitation in ways that we ourselves cannot countenance?

Why does a noisy public cheer him on in his nocturnal frenzy when in fact his cruelty and violence should repel all of us? Can a monster who embodies the most primal and detestable urge we know as humans—the urge to kill with utter abandon—be hailed as a superhero? Certainly not. And surely if we sleep soundly in our beds during these extraordinary times, it is because we are certain that those upon whom we depend for our daily safety are in fact on the trail of this most challenging of aberrations.

The social fabric no matter how resilient cannot subsume the Man Wolf. And no sustained embrace of the creature by the popular media can alter that fact.

It is perhaps worth remembering that we are all, as a species, prey to dreams and nightmares. Our art is built upon the irrepressible stream of images rising from a secret fulcrum that can never be trusted. And though these images can delight and amaze, they can also paralyze and terrify. There are times when we are shamed by the most fleeting savage fancy.

Surely the Man Wolf seems the stuff of nightmare. But a dream he most certainly is not. And therein lies our responsibility, not only to him, but to all that he seeks to undermine in his unconscionable rampages.

Reuben e-mailed this at once to Billie, and printed out a copy for Laura. She read it in silence, then slipped her arm around him and kissed him. They were side by side then. He was staring into the fire, his elbows on his knees, his fingers running through his hair, as if he could somehow get to the thoughts in his head that way.

"Tell me the truth, if you will," he had said. "Are you disappointed that I am not the Man of the Wild you imagined? I think you saw me as something pure, unburdened by moral constraint. Or maybe, maybe having to live up to an entirely different code because I was something not human."

"Disappointed . . ." She pondered. "No, I'm in no way disappointed. I'm deeply in love." Her voice was quiet, steady. "Let me put it to you like this. Maybe you'll understand. You're a mystery the way a sacrament is a mystery."

He turned and looked at her.

He wanted desperately to kiss her, to make love to her, right here in the library, or anywhere for that matter, anywhere that she would permit. But it was firmly lodged in his mind that she didn't want him the way he was now. How could she? She wanted the other. They were waiting for the other, for him to become her lover, not simply "one of the handsomest men" she'd ever seen.

Time can tick when there is no clock.

He started kissing her. The heat was immediate and she slipped her arms around him. He found her naked breasts beneath the white flannel and laid claim with his left hand. He was ready, oh, too ready after waiting so long.

They moved down to the carpet together, and he heard her pulse quicken just as the scent of desire rose from her, something secretive and smoky and delicate. Her face was flushed under him, oh, so warm.

They removed their clothes, hurriedly, silently, and came together again, in a tangle of kisses that were almost tormenting for him.

Suddenly he felt the violent spasm in his belly and in his chest; the ecstasy moved over the surface of his entire body; the prickling pleasure paralyzed him. He fell to one side, and sat up, doubled over.

He heard her gasp.

His eyes were closed. Had it always happened that way before? Yes, at the very moment when he felt the hairs erupting from every pore, when the pleasure was one volcanic wave after another, he couldn't actually see.

When he did open his eyes, he was standing, the

mane thick and heavy over his shoulders, his hands transformed into claws. The fur was thickening into a ruff around his neck and between his legs. His muscles were singing with the power, his arms expanding, his legs pulled upwards as if by unseen hands.

He looked down at her from his new height.

She was on her knees staring up at him in obvious shock.

Shakily, she rose. She murmured some half-strangled prayer under her breath, and reached out cautiously and then quickly to touch him, to slide her fingers as she had done before into the thick outer coat that was growing denser and longer all over him.

"Like velvet!" she whispered, running her hands over his face. "So silken smooth."

He could scarcely hold back from lifting her off her feet so that he could put his lips on hers. He had all of her, naked and small and beating with passion, in his arms.

"Laura," he said in the new voice, the real voice. A divine relief coursed through him. She opened her mouth to his. That deep throbbing sound was coming from him, as if his body were a drum.

The forest crept to the windows. The rain was hissing and splashing in the gutters and in the downspouts, and rushing over the flags. The ocean wind drove at the rain and pushed against the walls.

He could hear a low vibration of the wind in the rafters, and in the softly groaning branches of the trees.

All the scents of the night had broken through the solid shell of the house, rising like steam from a thousand tiny whispering chinks and crannies. But central to all scents was the scent of her, and it went right into his brain.

# 20

HE STOOD in the front door, the rain pelting him, and the wind whistling under the eaves.

Out there, south of here, in the redwoods that ran to the east and upwards, he heard the snorting, snuffling animal he wanted. **Mountain lion slumbering. Oh, you are a worthy prey.**

Laura hovered close to him, the loose collar of her nightgown held tight at her throat against the cold.

"You can't go," she said. "You can't risk it. You can't bring them up here."

"No. It's not the voices," he said. He knew he was staring glaze-eyed at the forest. He could hear the low almost guttural sound of his words. "No one will mourn this victim. She and I are creatures of the wild."

He wanted that animal, that huge hulking animal that had killed Galton's dog, that powerful beast that was secreted deep in the brush so very close by with three of her grown cubs, big cats themselves, breathing deep in sleep, but ready to break from their mother into the savage world. The scents mingled in his nostrils.

He had to go. He could not refuse this. The hunger and restlessness would be unendurable.

He turned and bent to kiss Laura again, fearing to hurt her as he held her face gently, very gently, with his paws.

"Wait for me by the fire. Stay warm, and I promise you, I won't be long."

He began to run as soon as he left the orbit of light surrounding the house. Swiftly, he entered the living whispering forest, running on all fours at such speed he scarce saw anything around him, the scent of the cats pulling him like a vibrant cord.

The coast winds died in the deep redwoods, and the rain was a mist against his eyes.

As he drew near the sleeping cat, he moved upwards into the lower branches of the trees, easily traveling as fast as he had on all fours, gaining on the lair of the cat, as the cat, catching his scent perhaps, woke and rattled the undergrowth around it, alerting the cubs whose low growls and hisses he could hear.

He knew instinctively what the cat would do. It was crouching low, fully expecting him to pass near to it, when it would spring with the full power of its hind legs and seek to overtake him from behind. It would sink its teeth into his spine if it could, disabling him immediately, and then tear out his throat. He saw this, saw it as if the scent carried the modus operandi.

Ah, poor brave and senseless animal that it would become the prey of a man beast who could outwit it and outfight it; his hunger, his rage for it, only grew.

As he neared the lair now the cubs, great sixty- to

seventy-pound cats themselves, bolted from the wet foliage; the mother cat crouched, ready to spring. It was powerful, this tawny creature, perhaps a hundred and fifty pounds, and it sensed it was in danger. Did it know by his scent what he was?

If you do, you know more than I may ever know, he thought.

He let out a huge roar to give it fair warning, and then leapt from one tree to another before it, enticing it to pounce.

It took the bait, and as fast as it sprang for him, he whipped around and descended on it, his arm going around it as he sank his fangs into the tough layer of muscle covering its neck.

Never had he felt a creature this powerful, this big, this filled with the brute drive to survive. In a frenzy of snarling sounds, they went down together, his face pressed to its thick, odiferous fur, scrambling and struggling in the thorny vines and crashing wet leaves. Again and again, Reuben sank his fangs, wounding, maddening the animal, and then shredding the thick resistant layer of living meat with all the strength he had in his jaws.

The cat would not give up. Its long powerful body convulsed, its hind legs kicking. It gave a deep whining and furious cry. Only as he came round on top of it, forcing its head back with his left claw, was he able to kill it, piercing the softer underside of its neck, fangs closing deep on its spine.

The flesh and the blood were his now. But the

cubs had come. They had surrounded him and they moved in. Firmly holding the carcass of the mother in his teeth, he sprang up the thick bark of an old redwood, easily climbing higher than the cats could climb. It felt good to his aching jaws to carry the kill ever upwards, the cat's heavy body bouncing against his chest.

He settled high above against a thick lattice of branches and rough splintery leaves. Creatures of the heights fled from him. The upper reaches rustled and sang with the swift retreat of winged things.

He feasted on the salty meat of the cat slowly, devouring great pieces of dripping flesh.

For a long moment, after he was satisfied, he watched the angry, menacing cubs below, their yellow eyes flashing and glinting in the dark. He heard their low growls.

He shifted the thick body of the mother against his left arm so that he could feast on her belly, and rip into the soft juicy tissue inside.

He was in a kind of delirium again, because he was able to eat until his hunger was gone. Simply gone. He lay back against the crunching branches and half shut his eyes. The rain was a soft sweet veil of silver around him. As he glanced upwards the heavens opened as if for a laser beam, and he saw the moon, the full moon, the meaningless and irrelevant full moon in all its blessed glory, floating in a wreath of clouds, against the distant stars.

A deep love of all he saw settled over him—love

for the splendor of the moon and the sparkling fragments of light that drifted beyond it—for the enfolding forest that sheltered him so completely, for the rain that carried the dazzling light of the skies to this shimmering bower in which he lay.

A flame burned in him, a faith that a comprehending Power existed, animating all this that it had created, and sustaining it with a love beyond anything that he, Reuben, could imagine. He prayed for this to be so. He wondered if, somehow, the whole forest was not praying for this, and it seemed to him then that all the biological world was alive with prayer, with reaching, with hope. What if the drive to survive was a form of faith, a form of prayer?

He felt no pity for the cats circling restively below in the darkness. He had thought of pity, yes, but he did not feel it; he seemed deeply part of a world where such an emotion made little or no sense. After all, what would the cats have thought of pity? The cats would have torn him apart if they could. The mother would have feasted on him at any opportunity. The mother had brought the long happy life of Galton's cherished dog to a violent close. How easy a prey to her Reuben must have seemed.

The horror was that he was worse than anything known in the realm of the cat, wasn't he? Even the bear could not have outfought him, he figured. But then he would have to see about that, wouldn't he, and the thrill of the possibility made him laugh.

How wrong people were about the werewolf,

imagining him to devolve into a mindless frenzy. The werewolf was not a wolf, no, nor a man, but an obscene combination of the two, exponentially more powerful than either one.

But right now, it did not matter. The language of thought was . . . just the language of thought. Who could trust language? Words like "monster," "horror," "obscene." The words he'd written so recently to Billie, what were these words but weightless tissuelike membranes too weak to support the essence of any fragrant or pulsing thing.

**Big cat, dead cat, cat who killed the warm and loving thing that was Galton's dog. Dead. I loved every second of it!**

He was half dreaming. He lapped at the great gash in the cat's stomach, and sucked up the blood as if it were syrup. "Good-bye, sister cat," he whispered, nuzzling its grinning mouth, running his tongue along its dead teeth. "Good-bye, sister cat; you fought well."

And then he let go of her, his trophy, and she went down, down, down through the net of branches and fell to the soft hungry earth amongst her brood.

His mind wandered. If only he could bring Laura with him up into this shining realm, enfolding her safely in his arms. He dreamed that she was with him, safe against him, dozing as he dozed—as the wet breeze stirred the wilderness around them, and a universe of tiny creatures lisped and fluttered, lulling him to half sleep.

What of the distant voices that he could not hear? Was anyone calling to him from the cities to the north or the south? Was anyone running from danger, screaming for his help? A sense of his ever-growing power filled him with a dark pride; how many nights could he ignore the voices? How many nights could he flee "the most dangerous game"?

But he was hearing something now!

Something had pierced the leafy portals of this sanctuary.

Somebody **was** in danger, terrible danger—and he knew this voice! "Reuben!" came the ragged scream. "Reuben!" It was Laura calling for him. "—I am warning you," she was sobbing, "don't you come a step closer!" Laughter—low vicious laughter, and the voice of another: "Oh, come now, little woman, are you going to kill me with that ax?"

# 21

HE SPED through the forest on all fours, darting in and out of the trees, hitting speeds he'd never achieved before.

"—My dear, you're making this all too easy for me. You don't know how it distresses me to shed innocent blood."

"—Get away from me. Get away from me!"

It wasn't the scent of evil that guided him because there was no discernible scent. What was a voice so menacing without a scent?

In two leaps he crossed the broad stone terrace and pitched his weight against the door, tearing the locks out of the wood.

He landed on the floorboards, and slammed the door behind him without looking back.

Laura, trembling, terrified, stood to the left of the huge stone fireplace, clutching the long wooden handle of the ax as she held it up with both hands.

"He's come here to kill you, Reuben!" she said, her voice thick.

Across from her, to the right, stood a small slender and composed figure, a dark-skinned man. His features had a slightly Asian cast. He appeared to be perhaps fifty years old and he had short insignificant black hair and small black eyes. He wore a simple gray jacket and pants, and a white shirt open at his neck.

Reuben moved in front of him, coming between him and Laura.

The small man very gracefully gave way.

He was taking the measure of Reuben. He appeared as detached as a man taking the measure of a stranger on a street corner.

"He says he has to kill you," Laura was saying, her words ragged and choked. "He says he has no choice. He says he has to kill me too."

"Go upstairs," said Reuben. He moved closer to the man. "Lock yourself in the bedroom."

"No, I don't think we have time for that at all," said the man. "I see the descriptions of you were not at all exaggerated. You are a remarkable example of the breed."

"And what breed is that?" asked Reuben. He stood a couple of feet from the man now, peering down at him, confounded by the utter absence of scent. Oh, there was a human scent that came from him, yes, but no scent of hostility or evil intent.

"I regret what's happened to you," said the man. His voice was even and eloquent. "I should never have wounded you. This was an unforgivable mistake on my part. But it's done and I have no choice now but to undo it."

"And you are the one behind it all," said Reuben.

"Most definitely, though it was never my intention."

He seemed entirely reasonable, and certainly far too slight of build to be of any danger to Reuben, but Reuben knew this was not the final form, no, not by any means, that the man would take. Would it be better to kill him now before the change started? When he was weak and defenseless? Or to drag out of him whatever precious information he might give up? Think of the secrets he might possess.

"I've been guarding the place for so long," said the man, taking another step backwards as Reuben advanced. "It just went on for so very long. And I was never a very good guard, really, and sometimes not here at all. Yet it is unforgivable and if I'm to be shown the slightest mercy I must correct what I've done. I'm afraid my poor young 'Man Wolf,' as you call yourself, you should never have been born."

Only now did a sinister smile come over his face, and with it the transformation coming on so rapidly that Reuben could scarce measure the changes before his eyes. The man's clothes were ripped apart as his chest expanded and his arms and legs began to lengthen and swell. He ripped off his gold wristwatch and dropped it at his side. Fine shiny black hair sprouted all over him, thickening like foam. His shoes were torn into tatters by his clawed feet. He reached up and stripped the remnants of his shirt and jacket away, and brushed off the ragged fragments of his pants. The inevitable deep growl came out of his chest.

Reuben's eyes narrowed: smaller, shorter arms, but

who can calculate the power or the skill? And what huge paws he had and huge feet. His lower limbs were thicker than Reuben's or so it seemed.

Laura drew closer to Reuben. Out of the corner of his eye he saw her against the fireplace with the ax still held high against her right shoulder.

Reuben held steady; he drew in his breath and reached for the quiet strength he knew he possessed. You're fighting not just for your life but for Laura's life, he thought.

The man was now a foot taller than he had been, his black mane like a mantle, but nowhere near as tall as Reuben in Reuben's lupine form. His face had lost all recognizable sympathetic expression, eyes small and porcine and the mouth a muzzle with long curving fangs.

A pink tongue flashed behind his white teeth as he flexed his powerful thighs. All of his hair was black, even the undercoat of fur; and his ears had a hideous peaked lupine appearance that sickened Reuben because he feared that his own ears looked the same.

Hold steady, that was Reuben's only thought. Hold steady. He was in a rage, but not a shuddering, trembling rage that causes one's legs to turn to water or one's hands to flail. No, not at all.

Something is causing this being to hesitate; something is not as this being would have it. Take another step forward.

He did and the dark wolfen creature stepped back.

"And so, what now? You think you're going to dispose of me?" asked Reuben. "You think you can destroy me because of your mistake?"

"I have no choice," said the creature, his voice a deep resonant baritone. "I told you. It should never have happened. I would have killed you with the others, the guilty ones, if I had known. But surely you know how utterly distasteful it is to shed innocent blood. When I saw my error, I released you. There's always the chance, you see, that the Chrism won't be passed, that the victim will simply recover; or that the victim will shortly die. That's what so often happens. The victim simply dies."

"The Chrism? That's what you call it?" asked Reuben.

"Yes, the Chrism—that's what we've called it for ages. The gift, the power—there are a hundred ancient words for it—what does it matter?"

" 'We'?" asked Reuben. "You said 'we.' How many are there of creatures like us?"

"Oh, I know you're burning with curiosity for what I might tell you," said the creature with subtle contempt. His voice went on with a maddening restraint. "I remember that curiosity more clearly than I remember anything else. But why should I tell you anything—when I can't let you live? Am I indulging myself now, or you? It's easier for me to be kind as I kill you, believe me. It's not my intent to make either of you suffer. Not at all."

It was grotesque, the cultured, polished voice coming from such a bestial face. And so this is how I look to them, Reuben thought—just this hideous and monstrous.

"You'll let the woman go now," said Reuben. "She can take my car. She can get clear of this place—."

"No, I will not let the woman go, now or ever," said the beast. He went on with perfect equanimity. "You sealed the woman's fate, not I, when you gave her the secret of who and what you are."

"I don't know the secret of who and what I am," Reuben said. He was buying time. He was calculating. How do I best attack him? Where is he most vulnerable? Is he vulnerable at all! He took a step closer to the beast, and to his surprise the beast reflexively stepped back.

"None of it matters now, does it?" asked the beast. "That's the horror."

"It matters to me," said Reuben.

What a macabre spectacle this must make for Laura, two such monsters sparring with words. Reuben took another step and the beast again gave ground.

"You're young, hungry for life," said the beast, words coming just a little more rapidly, "hungry for power too."

"We're all of us hungry for life," said Reuben. He kept his voice low. "That is what life demands of us. If we aren't hungry for life, we don't deserve to live."

"Oh, but you're especially hungry, aren't you?" said the beast spitefully. "Believe me, it gives me no pleasure to execute one so strong." His small dark eyes flashed malevolently in the light of the fire.

"And if you don't execute me, what happens then?"

"I'm held accountable for you, for your prodigious achievements," he said contemptuously, "which have all the world clamoring to take you captive, cage you, narcotize you, laboratize you, and put you under the glass."

Again, Reuben advanced, but the creature stood firm, raising one paw as if to fend Reuben off, a weak defensive gesture. How many other small cues was Reuben receiving?

"I did what seemed natural for me to do," said Reuben. "I heard the voices; the voices called me; I caught the scent of evil and I tracked it. It was as natural as breathing to do what I did."

"Oh, believe me," said the other thoughtfully. "I am deeply impressed. You cannot imagine how many stumble, sicken, die in the first few weeks. It's so unpredictable. All aspects of it are unpredictable. No one can conceivably know what will happen when the Chrism hits the pluripotent progenitor cells."

"Explain this to me," said Reuben under his breath. "What is the Chrism?" He pressed closer, and the creature again stepped back, as if he couldn't stop himself. His thighs were still flexed, and his arms were slightly curved at his sides.

"No," said the beast coldly. "If only you'd been a little more reticent, a little more wise."

"Oh, so I'm to blame for this, am I?" Reuben asked

calmly. Again, he edged closer and the beast took two steps back. He was close to the paneled wall. "And where were you when the Chrism began to work? Where were you to guide me or advise me, to warn me what I might expect?"

"Long gone," said the beast with the first touch of real impatience. "Your truly fabulous exploits caught up with me halfway around the world. And now you will die for them. Were they worth it? Do tell me. Has this been the pinnacle of your existence so far?"

Reuben said nothing. It was now, he thought, now that he should strike.

But the beast spoke again. "Don't think it doesn't rip at my heart," he said, baring his fangs as if in an ugly smile. "Had I chosen you for the Chrism, you would have been magnificent, the finest of Morphenkinder, but I did not choose you. You're no Morphenkind." It was the German word for "child," the way he said it, pronounced as if it were spelled **kint.** "You're odious, loathsome, an offense, that's what you are!" His voice was angry, but steady. "I would never have chosen you, never even noticed you. Now all the world notices you. Well, this will end now."

Now he's the one playing for time, Reuben thought. Why? Does he know he can't win this?

"Who put you to guard this house?" said Reuben.

"One who won't tolerate what's happened," he said. "Not here of all places, not here." He sighed. "And you, you contemptible boy, having your way with Marchent, **his** precious Marchent, and Marchent dead." His eyes quivered and again he bared his teeth and his fangs without a sound.

"Who is he? How is he connected to Marchent?"

"You were the cause of her death," said the creature in a small voice. A low rolling growl escaped him. "I turned my back because of you, not to spy on you and Marchent—you and your antics—and in that interval death came to Marchent! It was all you! Well, you will not remain while I draw breath."

This infuriated Reuben, but he pressed on.

"Felix Nideck? Is that who told you to guard the house?"

The beast tensed, drew up his shoulders, and crooked his arms. Again, that rolling growl came out of him.

"You think these questions advance your case?" the creature snarled. A gnashing contemptuous sound came out of him, fully as eloquent as his words. "I'm done with you!" he roared.

Reuben rushed at him, claws out. He slammed the beast's head into the dark paneling, and lunged for the beast's throat.

In snarling outrage, the monster kicked at Reuben and drove frantically against Reuben's face with his powerful paws. He held off Reuben with an iron strength.

Reuben yanked him forward by the hair of his mane and then hurled him against the stone mantel and the beast let out a strangled roar. He raked at Reuben's arms with his fierce claws, and then brought up his knee and kicked Reuben again, this time in the lower gut, with tremendous force.

The wind went out of Reuben. He staggered backwards. Everything went dark. He felt the creature clutching his neck, the claws digging deeply into the fur trying to find the toughened flesh, the hot breath on his face.

In a roaring frenzy Reuben broke loose of him, slamming the creature's inner arms with two monstrous blows from the backs of his paws and shattering the creature's grip.

Again, Reuben hurled him backwards and his head again struck the wall. Instantly, he recovered and sprang at Reuben, those powerful thighs catapulting him forward, his paws driving Reuben back and down, scrambling, to the floor.

Reuben rose up under him, and with his right arm dealt him one fine blow that stunned him. But he came down over Reuben again, his fangs snapping above Reuben and then sinking into Reuben's throat.

Reuben felt the pain, felt it infinitely more intensely than he had that night. In a positive fury, his paws thrust the creature up and away. He felt the blood gushing, the heat of it. He was on his feet, and this time he slashed wildly at the creature, kicking the creature as the creature had kicked him, raking the creature's face with his claws, gashing open the creature's right eye. The creature bellowed, and thrashed at Reuben, and Reuben lunged again and clamped his teeth down on the side of the creature's face. He drove his fangs deeper and deeper, his teeth grinding the creature's jawbone, the creature screaming in pain.

I can't overpower him, Reuben thought wildly, but he's not able to overpower me. Again came the creature's knee, his foot, and those iron arms held him back. They were dancing together away from the wall. Hang on, hang on!

With a fierce growl Reuben ripped with his teeth, ripped as he had at the flesh of the mountain lion, and he knew in that instant that he hadn't dared to use that full savagery until this minute. And now he must use it or die.

Again and again his left claw tore at the creature, at the creature's gushing eye socket, while he held fast to his head with his aching jaws.

The creature was bawling, cursing, cursing in a language Reuben could not understand.

Suddenly the creature went limp. The iron arms dropped. A loud gurgling cry came out of him.

Reuben saw the beast's one good eye staring forward, as the beast slumped but did not fall.

Reuben released him, released his torn and bleeding face.

The thing stood helpless staring upwards with that one good eye while the other eye socket pumped blood. And Laura stood directly behind the beast, glaring at him.

As the monster doubled over, Reuben saw the ax embedded in the back of the creature's skull.

"I knew it!" the beast roared. "I knew it! I knew it!" He wailed in rage. Frantically he sought to reach behind himself for the ax handle but he couldn't command his arms, couldn't make them stop shuddering, couldn't bring his paws down on the ax handle. Blood and foam poured from his gaping mouth. He turned round and round, staggering to stop himself from falling, maddened, howling, gnashing his teeth.

Reuben pulled out the ax blade by its long handle, and as the creature reeled, he struck at the creature's neck with his full strength. The blade crashed through the mane and the fur and sank into the flesh, severing the neck halfway. The monster went silent, jaws loose, slobbering, giving only a low hissing sound.

Reuben yanked the ax free and swung it with all his might again. Mercifully the blade went through, and the creature's head fell forwards and crashed to the floor.

Before he could stop himself, Reuben had grabbed it by its thick hair and flung it into the fire. The body, as if deflated, collapsed heavily on the Oriental rug.

Laura let out a series of gasping cries. He saw her in front of the flames, bent double, moaning, rocking, pointing at the fire, and then she fell backwards against the nearby chair and tumbled to the floor.

Hysterically she screamed, "Reuben, get it out of the fire, out of the fire! Please, for the love of God!"

The flames were licking at the thing, licking at its bleeding staring eye. Reuben couldn't stop himself. He snatched it free of the blazing logs and dropped it on the floor. The smoke rose from it like dust. A few errant sparks flared in its writhing hair.

Then it was a swollen and bleeding thing, a ruined thing, tangled with blood, and blind. And dead.

Come poetry, come fantasy, come wild imagination, come dreams. The gleaming black hair began to fall away from the head and the body which lay only a few feet away. With no force to retract it, it fell away as the head appeared to shrink, and the body to shrink, and in a nest of hair, hair dissolving slowly around them and under them, body and head were the man again, naked, and slashed and seeping blood and dead.

# 22

REUBEN SANK DOWN on his knees and sat back on his heels. All his muscles ached. His shoulders ached. The heat in his face was almost unbearable.

**So I'm not a Morphenkind. So I'm odious, loathsome, an offense. Well, this offense to the species has just killed this Morphenkind with a little help, of course, from his beloved and her ax.**

Laura began to cry desperately, almost as if she was laughing, her sobs and cries erupting uncontrollably. She knelt down beside him and he took her in his arms. He saw the blood being smeared all over her white gown, all over her hair.

But he held her close, stroking her, trying to calm her. Her cries were heartbroken. Finally, she sobbed without making a sound.

Reuben gently kissed the top of her head, and her forehead. He brought up a knuckle of his paw and touched her lips. Smeared with blood. Too much blood. Unspeakable.

"Laura," he whispered. She held fast to him as if she was drowning, as if some invisible wave might sweep her away.

The man's remains were hairless now, as if there

had never been any hair at all. Only a coarse and barely visible dust covered him and the surrounding carpet.

For a long moment, they remained still, Laura crying ever more softly, exhausting herself in her tears, and then finally growing quiet.

"I have to bury him now," said Reuben. "There are shovels back there in that shed."

"Bury him! Reuben, you can't." Laura looked up at him as if awakened from a nightmare. She wiped at her nose with the back of her hand. "Reuben, you can't simply bury him. Surely you realize how valuable, how utterly priceless, this body is—to you!"

She climbed to her feet and looked down at the man from a little ways off as if she was afraid to go closer. The head now lay on its side, the left eye half closed and yellowish. The flesh of the face and body was faintly yellowish too.

"In this body are all the cellular secrets of this power," Laura said. "If ever you are to find out, if ever you are to know. Why, you can't discard this thing. That's unthinkable."

"And who's going to do the studying of this body, Laura?" asked Reuben. He was so exhausted that he feared the change would come, too soon. He needed his strength to dig a hole deep enough for this being's grave. "Who's going to biopsy the organs, remove the brain, do the autopsy? I can't do those things. You can't do those things. Who can?"

"But there has to be some way to preserve it, to save it so that someone eventually can."

"What? Stow it in a freezer? Risk having somebody find it here, connect it to us? You are seriously suggesting we conceal this body on the premises of this house where we live?"

"I don't know," she said frantically. "But Reuben, you can't simply take this thing, this mysterious thing, and consign it to the dirt, you can't just bury it. My God, this is an unimaginable organism, of which the world knows nothing. It points the way to understanding—." She broke off. She stood quiet for a moment, her hair tumbling down on either side of her face like a veil. "Could it be put somewhere . . . where someone else would find it? I mean miles from here."

"Why, to what purpose?" Reuben asked.

"What if it were found, and analyzed and blamed for all the crimes that have occurred?" She looked at Reuben. "Just think about it for a minute. Don't say no. This thing tried to kill us. Say, we left it somewhere off the highway, in plain sight, so to speak, and what if they found some strange mixture of human DNA and wolf fluids . . . the Chrism, as he called it—."

"Laura, the mitochondrial component of the DNA would prove that this wasn't the being who slaughtered the others," Reuben said. "Even I know that much science."

He stared at the head again. It seemed even more

shriveled than before, and to be darkening slightly like a piece of fruit ripening into decay. The body too was shrinking and darkening, the trunk particularly, though the feet were shriveling to nubs. Just nubs.

"And do you realize what this creature told us?" said Reuben, patiently. "He sentenced me to death for the trouble I caused, the 'prodigious achievements,' as he called them, the fact that I'd attracted notice. These things want secrecy; they depend on it. And how do you think the other Morphenkinder would respond if I dumped this body unceremoniously into the public domain?"

She nodded.

"There are others, Laura! This thing managed to tell us a great deal."

"You're right, on all counts," she said. She too was watching the subtle changes in the body and the head. "I could swear it's . . . disappearing," she said.

"Well, shriveling, drying up."

"Disappearing," she said again.

She came back to him and sat down beside him. "Look at it," she said. "The bones inside are disintegrating. It's flattening out. I want to touch it, but I can't."

Reuben didn't answer.

The body and the head were deflating, flattening; she was right. The flesh now looked powdery and porous.

"Look!" she said. "Look at the carpet. Look where the blood—."

"I see it," he whispered. The blood was a tissue-thin glaze on the surface of the rug. And the glaze was silently cracking into a million tiny bits and pieces. The blood was turning into infinitesimal flakes. And the flakes were dissolving. "Look, look at your gown."

The blood was crusting, flaking off there as well. She crumpled the flannel, brushed at it. She reached up to grasp the flaky residue that still clung to her hair. It was all crumbling.

"I see now," Reuben said. "I understand. I understand everything." He was in awe.

"Understand what?" she asked.

"Why they keep saying the Man Wolf is human. Don't you see? They're lying. They don't have proof of this or anything else. This is what happens to us, to all particles of us, to all fluids. Look. They don't have any samples from the Man Wolf. They took samples of what they found at the crime scenes, and probably even before they'd completed their work, the samples were no good, dissolving, dissolving like this."

He crawled forward and leaned down over the head. The face had fallen in. The head was a small puddle on the rug. He sniffed at it. Decomposition, human scent, animal scent—a mixture, subtle, very subtle, so subtle. Was he himself scentless like this to others, or only to others of this species?

He sat back again on his heels. He looked at his own paws, at the soft pads that had replaced his palms, and the shining white claws which he could so easy retract or extend.

"All of it," he said, "the transformed tissue, it dissolves. That is, it dehydrates and breaks into particles too fine to be seen, and finally too fine to be measured, even in whatever laboratory chemicals or preservatives that they have. Oh, it explains everything—the ridiculous contradictions from the Mendocino officials, and from the San Francisco laboratories. I see now what's happened."

"I don't follow."

He explained to her about the failure of the tests on him at San Francisco General. They'd gotten some results, then gone back only to find that all the original material was useless, or contaminated or lost.

"In the beginning, with my tissues, perhaps the process of dissolution was slower. I was still evolving. What did the man say about the cells . . . . you remember . . ."

"I do. He referred to pluripotent progenitor cells, cells we all have in our bodies. We're a tiny mass of pluripotent progenitor cells when we are embryos. Then those cells get signals, chemical signals to express themselves in different ways—to become skin tissue cells, or eye cells, or bone cells—."

"Right, of course," he said. "Stem cells are pluripotent progenitor cells."

"They are," she said.

"So we all still have such cells inside us."

"Yes."

"And the wolf fluid, the Chrism, it caused those cells to express themselves to make me into a Morphenkind, into this."

"Chrism," she said, "it has to be in the saliva, a metaphysical word for a toxin or a serum in the bodily fluids of the Morphenkind that triggers a whole string of glandular and hormonal responses for a new kind of growth."

He nodded.

"And you're saying that even right after you were bitten, while you were still evolving, the tests they took still went bad."

"More slowly, but yes, the specimens definitely went bad. They lasted long enough to get results about hormones, and extraordinary amounts of calcium in my system, but my mother said that eventually all the lab results failed."

He sat quiet for a long while, thinking about it.

"My mother knows more than she's letting on," he said. "She must have realized after the second battery of tests that something in my blood itself was causing the specimens to destruct. She couldn't tell me this. She might have been trying to protect me from it. God knows what she feared was happening. Oh, Mamma. But she knew. And when the authorities came back to her, asking for another DNA sample from me, she said no."

He felt a heavy sadness that he couldn't talk to Grace, couldn't present her with all of this, and have her loving counsel, but what right had he to dream of such a thing?

All her life Grace had saved lives. She couldn't live without saving lives. And he would not ask her sympathy and complicity now for what he was. It was bad enough that he had brought Laura into this. Bad enough that he'd given Jim troubled sleep for the rest of his days.

"You do realize what this means," said Laura. "All that talk on the television about human DNA and manipulating the evidence."

"Oh, yes, I certainly do realize it. It's just talk." He nodded. "That's what I was saying. It's talk. Laura, they have no evidence of any kind against me at all."

They looked at one another.

Reuben reached up, felt the fur at his neck where the monster had bitten him in his most effective and dangerous strike. No blood there. The blood was gone.

They both stared at the head and the body. They were now heaps of what looked like ash. A wind could have swept them into invisibility. But even the ash was growing lighter, fainter.

There were only gray streaks, like streaks of dust on Laura's white gown.

For a quarter of an hour they continued to watch. Nothing now remained of the monster but a few dark streaks on the woven fabric of the carpet, streaks dissolving into the rosy flowers and the twining green leaves.

Even the blade of the ax was clean as if it had never struck a blow.

Reuben gathered up the creature's shredded clothes. There was nothing personal, no identification, nothing in the jacket pockets or the pants pockets.

The shoes were soft expensive heelless moccasins—and small. The jacket and pants had Florentine labels. None of this was cheap. But none of it identified the man or gave a hint of where he had come from. He'd obviously come here prepared to lose these clothes, which might mean that he had a lodging and a vehicle close by. But there was one thing—the gold wristwatch. Where was it? It had become almost invisible against the flowered pattern of the rug.

He picked it up, examining its large face of Roman numerals; then he looked at the back. The name MARROK was inscribed there in Latin block letters.

"Marrok," he whispered.

"Don't keep it."

"Why not?" he said. "All the evidence is gone. That includes the evidence that might have been on this watch . . . prints, fluids, DNA."

He put it on the mantel. He didn't want to argue, but he couldn't destroy it. It was really all he had that gave him any clue as to the identity of the beast.

They put the rags on the fire, and watched them burn.

He was now painfully tired.

But he had to try to fix the front door and its broken locks before he reverted back to Reuben Golding who could barely turn a screwdriver or drive in a nail.

And he and Laura attended to that now.

It took much longer than either of them expected, but Laura knew all about how to stuff little splinters into the gouged-out screw holes, which filled them up and allowed the screws to catch and secure the lock mechanisms, and so it got done. Galton could take care of the rest.

He needed sleep.

He needed for the transformation to come, but he had the sense that he himself was holding it off. And he was a little afraid of its coming, of being weakened and unable to defend himself if another one of these creatures appeared.

He couldn't think anymore, couldn't analyze, couldn't absorb. Chrism, Morphenkinder. Did these poetic terms help?

The horror was this: the others. How would the others respond when they knew this Morphenkind had been destroyed?

There could be a tribe of them, couldn't there? There could be an entire race.

And Felix Nideck had to have been one of them, and maybe he was alive now, a Morphenkind still. **His Marchent.** Felix was the primary other. He had come here and taken the tablets, hadn't he? Or was it that thing that had done it?

He pondered. He had caught no scent from the

man wolf who had come to kill them! No scent at all, no scent of animal or man, no scent of evil.

All through the battle with the creature there had been no scent of evil to intoxicate him, and drive him forward.

And perhaps that meant that the dead Morphenkind had not detected any scent of evil from Reuben as well, no scent of malice, no scent of the will to destroy.

Was this why they had struggled so clumsily, so hopelessly with one another?

**And if I can't detect a scent from them, I will not know if they come here and are close by.**

He wouldn't tell this to Laura.

He got up slowly and made a round of the house.

Neither he nor Laura could figure how the creature had gotten in. They'd locked all the doors. He'd checked the locks all over the first floor when he'd arrived.

Yet Laura explained that the beast had come upon her as she was sleeping in the library and awakened her with a steady stream of low explanations as to why her life had to be forfeit much as he disliked to shed innocent blood. He'd said that he loathed killing women, he'd wanted her to know that, that he wasn't "insensible" to her beauty. He'd compared her to a flower that had to be crushed underfoot.

The cruelty of it made Reuben wince.

Perhaps he had come in through an upper window. Such was conceivable.

Reuben went through all the rooms, even the smaller northern bedrooms that faced the forest behind the house. He could find no window that was not securely latched.

For the first time, he searched all the linen closets, and extra coat closets and bathrooms off the inside walls of the four hallways, and found no openings or secret staircases to the roof.

He went through the gable attic rooms on all four sides of the house and could find only locked windows there as well. None contained a rear stairway. In fact he could not quite figure how anyone could get to the roof of this house.

Tomorrow, he vowed, he'd walk the property and search for some vehicle that the creature had driven to the house, or some hiding place in the forest where he might have left a backpack or duffel bag hidden in the trees.

It was growing light.

The change had still not come.

Laura was in the master bedroom when he found her. She'd bathed and dressed in a fresh nightgown and brushed her long hair. She was pale with exhaustion but looked as fresh and tender to him as she always had.

For fifteen minutes or more he argued with her furiously, that she should leave here, take his car, go south back to her home in the Marin woods. If Felix Nideck was coming, if he was the primary other, who knew what strength and cunning he possessed? It was all in vain. Laura wasn't leaving him. She never raised her voice; she never became agitated. But she never budged.

"My only chance with Felix is to appeal to him, to talk to him, to somehow——." He gave off, too tired to go on.

"You don't know that it is Felix."

"Oh, it has to be one of the Nidecks," he said. "It has to be. This creature knew Marchent, had protective feelings for Marchent, was told to guard this house. How could it not be a Nideck?"

But there were so many unanswered questions.

He went into the master shower and let the water stream over him for a long time. It washed the blood of the mountain lion in pale reddish rivulets down the copper drain. But he barely felt this water. His hairy body craved the icy water of a forest stream.

The morning was brightening. The view from the window wall of the shower was marvelously clear. He could see the sea to the far left, pale and colorless and glittering under the white sky.

Just opposite and to his right, the cliffs rose, blotting out the view of the ocean and its winds, as they extended further north.

Something could be up there on the cliffs, Felix Nideck, up there watching, waiting to avenge the dead Marrok.

But no. If Felix was near at hand, why would Marrok have come? Marrok had clearly indicated that he feared the eventual meeting with the one who'd appointed him as guardian, that he meant to annihilate his "mistake" before that meeting came to pass.

And if Felix Nideck was living, why did he allow his death to be made official, and his property passed on?

Too many possibilities.

Think about the good news. You've left nothing at the site of any kill. Absolutely nothing. Your fears on that score are over; there is no threat now from "the world" to you or Laura. Well, almost. There was the matter of Marchent's autopsy, wasn't there?—and their intimate contact before his DNA had begun to change. But what did that matter if they had nothing, absolutely nothing, from the kills? He wasn't thinking clearly anymore at all.

Reuben folded his arms around himself and willed the change to come. He willed it with all his strength, feeling the heat teem in his temples, and feeling his heart beat faster in his ears. **Change now, leave me, dissolve into me and outside me.**

It **was** happening, as if his body had obeyed him, as if the power had acknowledged him. He was almost weeping at this small progress. The pleasure crawled over him, subduing him, making him groggy, the hair dropping off of him, the convulsions stretching him and making him shudder divinely even as he reverted to his regular form.

Laura was waiting for him when he came out. She'd been reading a book. It was the little book by Teilhard de Chardin that had belonged to Felix—given him by Margon. Reuben had found it in his jacket pocket when he'd moved his clothes in here from Felix's old room.

"Did you see the inscription?" he asked. She had not. He opened to the third page and held it out for her to read.

**Beloved Felix,**
**For You!**
**We have survived this;**
**we can survive anything.**
**In Celebration,**
**Margon**
**Rome '04**

"What do you think it means, 'We have survived this; we can survive anything'?"

"I can't imagine."

"What the book means to me at any rate is that Felix is a theological thinker, a person interested in the destiny of souls."

"Perhaps, perhaps not." She hesitated, then. "You do realize . . ."

"What?" he asked.

"I hesitate to say it, but it's true, really. Catholics, sometimes, seem to be all a little insane."

He laughed. "I suppose that is true," he said.

"Well, Felix Nideck might not be Catholic," she said soberly, "and he might not be a theological thinker. The destiny of souls might not mean a thing to him at all."

He nodded. He smiled. But he didn't believe it. He knew Felix. He knew something of Felix. Enough to love him, and that was quite a lot.

She put her arms around him and gently urged him towards the bed.

They fell into each other's arms.

Then they climbed under the covers of the big bed and went to sleep.

# 23

JIM ARRIVED in the late afternoon.

Reuben had been out walking in the woods with Laura. They'd found no vehicle or backpack or anything to connect with Marrok. And they still did not know how he'd gained access to the house.

Jim had managed to get the evening off at St. Francis, which was quite a rare thing, and he had prevented Grace and Phil and Celeste from coming on the promise that he would go and see why Reuben wasn't answering his cell, or e-mail, and if everything was all right. He had time for an early dinner, yes, but then he'd have to be on the road for home.

Reuben had to confess he was glad to see him. Jim was in his full clerics, and Reuben couldn't prevent himself from hugging Jim as if he hadn't seen him in a year. It felt that long. It felt wretched. The whole separation from his family felt wretched.

After a fairly perfunctory tour of the house, they took a pot of coffee with them to the eastern breakfast room that opened off the long kitchen and sat down to talk.

Laura understood this was "Confession" as Reuben had explained, and she'd gone upstairs to answer e-mails on her laptop. She'd chosen the first western bedroom behind the master as her office, and they would have this cleared out for her as soon as possible. In the meantime, she'd set up her books and papers in there, and was more than comfortable, with a partial view of the sea, and a splendid view of the wooded cliffs.

Reuben watched as Jim took out the small purple stole and put it around his neck to hear Confession.

"Is it sacrilege for me to allow you to do that?" Reuben asked.

Jim said nothing for a moment and then in the softest voice suggested, "Come to God with your best intentions."

"Bless me, Father, for I have sinned," said Reuben. "I'm trying to find my way to contrition." He looked out the eastern window as he spoke, into the dense but airy grove of gray live oaks that ran on out to the redwood forest. These trees were thick and gnarled, and the ground beneath them soft and speckled with yellow and green and brown leaves, and the ivy grew rampant over many a massive trunk and up into the winding, reaching branches.

The rain had stopped before dawn. The blue sky shone through the mass of enclosing foliage that was the treetops. And warm sunlight came from the west, slanting down on the pathways through the trees. Reuben was lost in thought for a moment looking at it.

Then he turned and, resting his elbows on the table, and his face in his hands, he started talking, telling Jim absolutely everything that had happened. He told him of the strange coincidence of the names Nideck and Sperver. He explained everything in minute and obviously horrifying detail.

"I can't tell you that I want to give up this power," he confided. "I can't tell you what it's like to be moving through the forest as this thing, this beast, this creature that can run for miles on all fours and then go up, up there into the canopy and climb for hundreds of feet, this thing that can so easily satisfy its needs. . . ."

Jim's eyes were moist, and his face sort of broken with sadness, with worry. But he only nodded, waiting patiently, every time Reuben paused, for him to go on.

"Every other form of experience is paling in the face of it," Reuben said. "Oh, I miss you and Mom and Phil so much, so much! But everything is paling."

He described feasting on the mountain lion, and what it had been like up there in that haven of branches when the lethal cubs had been circling beneath, how he had wanted to take Laura up there in that sanctuary. How could he convey this to Jim, the seduction of this new existence? How could he break through the tragic expression on Jim's face with some flash of how dazzling and even sublime this was?

"Is this impossible for you to grasp?"

"I don't know that I need to grasp it," said Jim. "Let's go back now to this Marrok and what you've learned."

"But you can't forgive me if you don't grasp it," said Reuben.

"I'm not the one who has to forgive, am I?" asked Jim.

Reuben looked off again, beyond the gravel driveway, at the oak forest, so close, so dense, so filled with shadow and light.

"So what you know now is this," said Jim. "There are 'others' and these others may include Felix Nideck, though you can't be sure. This man, Margon Sperver, he too may be a Morphenkind, with the names being deliberate clues, that's what you suspect. These creatures have a terminology—Chrism, Morphenkinder—and that indicates tradition, that they've been around for a long time. The creature hinted they'd been around for a long time. You know that the Chrism that made you into this can sicken and can kill, yet you survived. You know that your cells have been altered so that once severed from the life force in you they disintegrate. And once that life force is extinguished, the corpse disintegrates. And that's why the authorities have no indication of who you are."

"Yes, that's it, so far."

"Well, not quite. This Marrok gave you the impression that you'd been brash, destructive, courting publicity that threatens the species, right?"

"Yes."

"And so you think the 'other' or 'others' may come to harm you, even kill you, and kill Laura as well.

You've killed one of them, and they may want to kill you for that as well as everything else."

"I know what you're going to say," said Reuben. "I know what you're going to tell me. But there is no one who can help us with this. No one. And don't tell me to call this or that authority! Or to confide in this or that doctor. Because any such move would spell the complete end of my freedom and Laura's freedom, and the complete end of our lives!"

"But what is your alternative, Reuben? Live here and fight this power? Fight the lure of the voices? Fight the urge to go into the woods and kill? And when will you be tempted to bring Laura into this, and what if the Chrism or the serum or whatever it is kills her exactly as this Marrok indicated it could?"

"I've thought of that, of course," he said, "I've thought of that." And he had.

He'd always thought it a stupid cliché of horror films that "the monster" wants a mate, or spends eternity chasing a lost love. Now he understood that completely. He understood the isolation and the alienation and the fear. "I will bring no harm to Laura," he said. "Laura isn't asking for the gift."

"The gift, you call this a gift? Look, I'm a man of imagination. I always have been. I can imagine the freedom, the power——."

"No, you can't. You won't. You refuse."

"Okay, then I know I can't imagine the freedom and the power and they must be seductive beyond my most feverish dreams."

"Now you're getting it. Feverish dreams. Have you ever wanted to bring agony to someone who hurt you, ever wanted them to feel pain for what they did? I brought that agony to those kidnappers, to others."

"You killed them, Reuben. You killed them in their sins! You terminated their destiny on this earth. You snatched from them any chance for repentance, for redemption. You took that from them. You took it all, Reuben. You snuffed out forever the years of reparation they might have lived! You took life itself from them and you took it from their descendants, and yes, even from their victims, you took what their amends might have been."

He stopped. Reuben had closed his eyes, and was holding his forehead in his hands. He was angry. Took from their victims? They had been slaughtering their victims! There would have been no "amends" for their victims. There would have been death if Reuben had not intervened. Even all the children of the kidnap had been in mortal peril. But that was not the point, was it? He was guilty of killing. He could not deny it and he could not feel remorse.

"Look, I want to help you!" Jim pleaded. "I don't want to condemn you, or drive you away from me."

"You won't do that, Jimmy." **It is I who am moving inexorably away from you.**

"You can't keep going with this alone. And this woman, Laura, she's beautiful and she's devoted to you. And she's no child or fool, I can see that. But she doesn't know any more about this than you do."

"She knows what I know. And she knows that I love her. If she hadn't struck Marrok with the ax when she did, I might not have been able to defeat him. . . ."

Jim clearly didn't know how to answer.

"So what are you saying?" Reuben asked. "What then do you want me to do?"

"I don't know. Let me think. Let me try to figure who could be trusted, who could study this, analyze, figure some way perhaps to reverse it—."

"Reverse it? Jim, Marrok evaporated! Ashes to ashes. He disappeared. You think something this powerful can be reversed?"

"You don't know how long this creature had had the power."

"That's another thing, Jim. A knife or a gun can't hurt me. If that creature had had a few more seconds, he could have removed that ax from the back of his skull, and his skull, even his skull, and his brain might have healed. I decapitated him. Nothing can survive that. Remember, I healed from a bullet wound, Jim."

"Yes, I know that, Reuben, I remember. I didn't believe you when you told me this before, about being shot. I have to say, I didn't believe you." He shook his head. "But they found the bullet in the wall of that Buena Vista house. Celeste told me. They found the bullet and the trajectory indicated the bullet had been deflected somehow. The bullet had passed through something before it lodged in the plaster of the wall. And there was no tissue on that bullet, not even the tiniest particle of any tissue."

"And what does that mean, Jim? What does that mean about . . . my body and about time?"

"Don't go thinking you're immortal, Little Boy," he said under his breath. He reached out and pinched the loose flesh right above Reuben's left wrist. "Please don't go thinking that."

"But what if we have great longevity, Jim? I mean, I don't know, but that Marrok creature. I got the distinct impression that the thing had been around for a long time."

"Why do you say that?"

"Something he said about remembering, remembering his early curiosity when he couldn't remember anything else. I don't know. I confess, I'm guessing, going by my gut."

"It could be the opposite," Jim said. "You just don't know. You're right about the forensics. There's no other explanation as to why they have nothing, and Celeste says they have nothing. . . . And Mom says they can't explain it but the materials they gather simply self-destruct."

"I knew it. And Mom knows that's what happened to the specimens they took from me."

"She hasn't said so. But Mom knows something. And Mom is afraid. Also Mom's obsessed. This Russian doctor, he's supposed to arrive here tomorrow, and take her to see this little hospital in Sausalito—."

"That is a dead end!"

"I understand, but I don't like it. I mean, I want you to tell Mom, but I don't like it, this Paris doctor, what he's got in mind. Dad doesn't like it either. He's already had it out with Mom that she better not be suggesting committing you against your will."

"What?"

"Look, I'm telling you what I've been hearing. Mom and Dad can't find any mention of this hospital on the Internet or any doctor that's ever heard of such a place."

"Well, what the hell is Mom thinking?"

"I do not see how much more harm you could do to Mom by telling her the whole truth. But I'd get her alone to do that, away from this Paris doctor, whoever he is. Reuben, you can't let yourself fall into private hands. That's worse than any scenario you've imagined."

"Private hands!"

Jim nodded. "I don't like it. I don't know that Mom actually likes it. But Mom's desperate."

"Jim, I can't tell her. Private hospital, government hospital, it doesn't matter. Fearing your son has become a monster is one thing; hearing him confess it in detail would be too much. Besides, it's not going to happen. That is not the path for me. If I had it to do over again, I wouldn't have told you."

"Don't say that, Little Boy."

"Listen to me. I fear what you fear—that this thing will consume me, that I will lose my inhibitions one by one, that I will lose all perspective finally and obey its physical imperatives without question—."

"Dear God."

"—but Jim, I will not go into this without a fight. I am not bad, Jim. I am good. I know it. I feel it. My soul is me. And I am not a creature without conscience, without empathy, without the capacity for good."

Reuben opened his right hand on his chest.

"In here, I know this," he said. "And I'll tell you something else."

"Please."

"I am not progressing with this, Jim. I've reached a kind of plateau. I battle it, I seek to come to terms with it, I learn new things from it every time it happens, but I am not devolving, Jim."

"Reuben, you said yourself everything else was paling in comparison to what you think and feel when this change comes! Now you're saying that's not so?"

"My soul is not decaying," said Reuben. "I swear it. Look at me and tell me that I'm not your brother."

"You're my brother, Reuben," he said. "But those men you killed, they were your brothers, too. Damn, what can I say to make it any clearer? The woman you killed was your sister! We are not beasts of the wild, for the love of heaven, we are human beings. We are all kin! Look, you don't have to believe in God to believe that. You don't have to believe doctrine or dogma to know what I'm saying is true."

"Okay, Jimmy, take it easy, take it easy." Reuben reached for the carafe of coffee and refilled Jim's cup.

Jim sat back, trying to get control, but the tears were in his eyes. Reuben had never seen Jim cry. Jim was almost ten years older than him. Jim had been a tall, clever, and self-possessed adolescent by the time Reuben crawled out of toddlerhood. He'd never known Jim as a child.

Jim was looking out into the woods. The afternoon sun was traveling west and the house cast a big shadow now over the nearest grove of trees, but it broke through gloriously in the distance where the woods ran uphill towards the southern end of the redwood forest.

"And you don't even know what brings on the change, or how to control it," Jim murmured almost absently, his eyes distant, and his voice dispirited. "Will you change into this thing every night of your life from now on?"

"That's impossible," Reuben said. "This species, Morphenkinder, it couldn't survive if it changed every night, if it lived like this. I have to believe that's not how it works. And I'm learning how to control it. I'll learn how to bring it on and how to make it stop. That thing, that guardian, Marrok, he changed at will, just like that, when he was ready. I'll learn."

Jim sighed. He shook his head.

A quiet fell between them. Jim kept looking at the forest. The winter afternoon was dying fast. Reuben wondered what Jim could hear, what scents he could detect. The forest was living, breathing, gasping, whispering. The forest was redolent with the smell of life and death. Was that a form of prayer? Was that a striving towards the spiritual? Was that spiritual in itself? He wanted so to talk about these thoughts with Jim, but he couldn't. He couldn't expect that of Jim now. He stared off beyond the oak forest at the ghostly haze of the redwoods that lay far beyond. The world went to dusk in shades of blue. He felt himself drifting, drifting away from this table, this conversation, this confession.

Suddenly, softly, Jim's voice brought him back.

"This is an exceptional place, this," Jim said. "Ah, but what a price you've paid for it."

"Don't I know?" Reuben pressed his lips together in a bitter smile.

He put his hands together in an attitude of prayer and began the Act of Contrition: " 'O my God I am heartily sorry' . . . heartily sorry, I am; with all my heart, I swear it, I am heartily sorry; please show me the way. God, please show me what I am, what manner of thing I am. Please give me the strength, against all temptation, to do no harm to anyone, somehow to do no harm, but to be a force for love in Your Name."

He meant these prayers, but he did not deeply feel them. He had a sense of the world around him, insofar as he could grasp it, and of the tiny speck that was the planet Earth, spinning in the galaxy of the Milky Way, and of how tiny was that galaxy in the vast far-flung universe beyond human grasp. He had the sinking feeling that he was speaking not to God but to Jim, and for Jim. But hadn't he spoken to God in another way last night? Wasn't he speaking to God in his own way when he looked out there at the living, striving forest and he felt in all his parts that that striving of all living things was a form of prayer?

The silence was filled by sadness. They were united in sadness. Reuben said, "Do you think Teilhard de Chardin could have been right? That we fear that God does not exist because we can't **spatially** grasp the immensity of the universe; we fear that personality is lost in it when maybe it is a superpersonality that holds it all together, a superconscious God who planted evolving consciousness in each of us—." He broke off. He'd never really been good at abstract theology or philosophy. He hungered for theories he could understand and repeat when he needed to repeat them, in which every single thing everywhere in the seemingly hopeless reaches of space had a meaning and a destiny—even Reuben himself.

"Reuben," Jim answered, "when you take the life of a single sentient being, innocent or guilty, you go against that great redeeming power, whatever it is, however it might be described—you annihilate its mystery and its force."

"Yes," said Reuben. He kept his eyes on the oaks that were fading into shadow as he watched. "I know that's what you believe, Jim. But it doesn't feel that way when I'm the Morphenkind. It feels like something else."

# 24

REUBEN HAD PUT the lamb shanks on for supper before he'd ever gone out in the woods. The meat and vegetables were simmering in the Crock-Pot all afternoon.

After Laura made a particularly luscious salad, of lettuce, tomato, and avocado tossed in the most delicate olive oil with herbs, they sat down to dinner in the breakfast room and Reuben, as usual, devoured everything in sight while Jim touched a little of this and a little of that.

Laura had put on what Reuben thought was an old-fashioned dress. It was made of yellow-and-white-checkered cotton and had sleeves with carefully sewn cuffs and white floral buttons. Her hair was loose and shining. And she smiled spontaneously at Jim when she drew him into conversation about the church and his work.

Conversation between them became easy; they talked about Muir Woods and Laura's research on the "understory" there, that is, the floor of the forest and how to prevent it from being destroyed by the constant foot traffic of the thousands of people who, understandably enough, wanted to see the unbelievable beauty of the redwoods for themselves.

Laura spoke not at all of her past, and Reuben certainly didn't feel he had the right to move the conversation into the dark waters, and Jim spoke with enthusiasm about the St. Francis dining room and the number of Thanksgiving meals they hoped to serve this year.

In the past, Reuben had always helped serve on Thanksgiving at St. Francis, and so had Phil and Celeste and even Grace when she could.

A heavy gloom fell over Reuben. He would not be there this year, he sensed it. And he would not be home for Thanksgiving either, when the family gathered at 7:00 p.m. for the traditional meal.

Thanksgiving had always been a sparkling, convivial event in the house on Russian Hill. Frequently Celeste's mother joined the family, and Grace thought nothing of asking any intern or resident working with her, especially if he or she was far from home. Phil wrote a new poem each year for the occasion, and one of his old students, an eccentric genius who lived in a Haight-Ashbury flophouse, frequently wandered in and stayed until someone inevitably challenged him on his intense conspiratorial views of society being destroyed by a clandestine organization of the rich and powerful, after which he would storm out.

Well, Reuben was not going to be there this year.

He walked Jim to the car.

The wind had come up off the ocean. It was dark at six o'clock, and Jim was anxious and cold. He agreed to tell the family Reuben needed this time alone, but he begged Reuben to stay in contact.

At about that moment, Galton drove up in his shining pickup truck and announced jubilantly, as his feet hit the flagstones, that the mountain cat that killed his dog had been "got."

Jim, in his inevitably polite manner, showed great interest in what Galton was saying. So Galton pulled his collar up against the wind and told the whole story of the dog again, how the dog had once read minds, sensed danger, saved lives, worked miracles, and turned off a light switch regularly with its paws.

"But how did you find out the big cat is dead?" Reuben asked.

"Oh, they found her out there this afternoon. She'd been tagged by the university four years ago, tagged on her left ear. It was her, all right, and whatever got her gave her what for! There's a bear out there in those woods, now you be careful, you and that pretty girl."

Reuben nodded. He was turning to ice, but Galton seemed impervious to the cold in his goose-down jacket. He railed against the mountain cat. "They should have given me a depredation permit to shoot that sucker," he said. "But oh, no, they were going to wait till she killed a human being and, believe me, she would have, too."

"What about her cubs?" Reuben asked with a little bit of concealed glee. He was gloating inwardly that he had slain the cat and half devoured it, and it gave him a sinister pleasure that Jim knew this, because he had told Jim, and Jim could say nothing, and Galton would never know. He felt ashamed of these feelings, but mostly he remembered the cat, the feast, the bower in the trees, and he was gleeful and that was all.

"Oh, those cubs will scatter now and find new territory. Maybe one of them will hang around here, who knows? There are likely five thousand of those big cats in California. One come into town and took a walk in north Berkeley, right past the shops and restaurants, not so very long ago."

"I remember that," said Jim. "Caused a little panic. But I've got to run. It was nice meeting you, Mr. Galton, and I hope to see you again."

"So you have your very own priest in the family," said Galton as Jim drove his old Suburban towards the forest, the taillights soon disappearing in the dark. "And you drive the Porsche, huh, son, and he drives the old family car."

"Well, it's not as if we don't try to get him a decent set of wheels," said Reuben. "My mom bought him a Mercedes, and he lasted with that about two days. He just took so many wisecracks from the homeless in his parish, and then he brought it right back."

He took Galton's arm. "Come inside," he said.

At the kitchen table, he poured Galton a cup of coffee, and asked what Galton had known of Felix Nideck.

"What kind of a man was he?"

"Oh, the finest. An Old World aristocrat, if you ask me. Not that I know a hell of a lot about aristocrats. I guess in truth I don't. But he was larger than life, if you know what I mean. Everybody out here loved him. There never was a more generous man. When he left these parts everybody was the loser. Course we didn't know we'd never see him again. We always thought we would."

"How old was he when he disappeared?"

"Well, they said later on that he was sixty years old. That's what the papers said when they started really looking for him. But I never dreamed he was that age. He didn't look a day over forty. I was forty myself when he disappeared. If he was a day older, well, you couldn't prove it by me. But come to find out, he'd been born in 1932. That was news to me. Of course he wasn't born here, you understand. He was born overseas, and came out here later on. I knew him for a good fifteen years, I'd say. That's about right. I never could quite figure out how he could have been sixty years old. But that's what they said."

Reuben only nodded.

"Well, I've got to get going," Galton said finally. "This coffee's warmed me up. I only came to check on things, make sure you're all right, and by the way, did that fella ever find you, that old guy, that friend of Felix's?"

"What fella?" asked Reuben.

"Marrok," said Galton. "I saw him a couple of nights ago down at the Inn. He was having a drink down there. And he asked if I knew when you were coming back."

"Tell me about him."

"Well, he's been around for years. He was Felix's friend, as I said. He always stayed up here at the house when he came, at least until Marchent would throw him out. She did that from time to time. Marchent couldn't stand him, really. But she always let him back in. He'll be coming around, probably just out of respect for Felix and the family, that's all. He's not nosy. He probably just wants to know the house is all right, in good hands. I told him it was in very good hands."

"Marchent and he didn't get along?"

"Well, they did when she was a little girl, I guess, but after Felix disappeared, I don't know. She wasn't too keen on him and one time she told me she'd get rid of him if she could. My wife, Bessie, said that he was in love with Marchent, you know, coming on to her and all, and Marchent didn't like it. Marchent wasn't going to stand for any of that from him."

Reuben didn't respond.

"And the brothers hated him," Galton said. "He was always getting the brothers in trouble. They'd be up to something, stealing a car, getting some liquor, you know, that they weren't old enough to be buying, and he'd turn them in.

"Their father couldn't much stand the man either. Abel Nideck was nothing like Felix Nideck, no, nothing at all. He didn't run Marrok off, he just didn't have the time of day for him. Then of course they weren't here a lot of the time and neither was Marchent. Marchent argued for him for Felix's sake, I figured. Sometimes he slept in the back bedroom upstairs, and sometimes he slept out in the woods. He would camp out there in back. Liked to do that. Liked to be alone."

"Where did he come from? Do you know?"

Galton shook his head. "There were always people coming to see Felix, friends of his from . . . heck, all over the world. This fella's Asiatic, Indian perhaps, I don't know. He's kind of dark skinned with black hair, very well spoken, like all of Felix's friends. But he certainly was too old for Marchent, though he was like Felix, you know, he doesn't show his age. I know how old he is because I remember. He was here when Marchent was a little girl." He looked to each side as though someone was going to sneak up on him and then he said in a confidential voice, "I'll tell you what Marchent said to Bessie, she said, 'Felix told him to look out for me, to protect me. Well, who's going to protect me from **him**!'" He drew back laughing, and swallowed another mouthful of coffee. "But he's really all right. Why, when Abel and Celia were killed, he came up here and stayed with Marchent so she wouldn't be alone. That's about the only time she ever really needed him, I suppose. Didn't last that long. You sure as hell don't have to let him hang around this place, you know. This place is yours now, son, and people have got to get used to that. It's not Felix's house. Felix is long gone."

"Well, I'll be on the lookout for him," Reuben said.

"Like I was saying, he isn't really a bad fella. Everybody knows him around here. He's just one of those strange international drifters that was always around. But this is your house now."

He walked Galton to the door.

"You come down to the Inn tonight if you want to have a drink with us," he said. "We'll be celebrating that the cat that got my dog has been got!"

"The Inn? Where's the Inn?"

"Son, you can't miss it. Come on down to Nideck. Nideck's got one main street. It's right there."

"Oh, the bed-and-breakfast, yes, I saw it the first day I came up here," Reuben said. "It was for sale."

"Still is, and will be for a long time to come!" Galton laughed. "Nideck's twelve miles inland. Why would anybody ever come to a bed-and-breakfast in Nideck? You join us tonight. We'd love to see you both there."

Reuben shut the door behind him and went into the library.

He opened the folder with the papers that Simon Oliver had sent him pertaining to the house. There was a handwritten list of contractors and service people that Marchent had made for him during that last hour before she'd been killed. Just maybe . . .

He had the copy somewhere.

He found it.

He went down the list quickly. There it was, Thomas Marrok. "Friend of the family who appears from time to time. May ask to sleep in the woods out back. Old friend of Felix. Up to you. No special favors recommended. Your call."

He went upstairs and found Laura in her office.

He told her everything Galton had told him.

They got into the Porsche and drove down to Nideck.

There was a cozy dinner crowd in the main room of the Inn when they entered. It was rustic, with rough wood walls and an old man in the corner playing a guitar and singing some mournful Celtic song. The place had red-and-white-checkered tablecloths and candles.

The innkeeper was in his little office, with his feet up on the desk, reading a paperback novel and watching a rerun of **Gunsmoke** on his little TV.

Reuben asked him if he knew a man named Marrok, and if the man had had a room here in the last week.

"Oh yeah, he's been around," said the man. "But he didn't stay here, no."

"You don't know where he comes from, do you?" asked Reuben.

"Well, he travels all over, to hear him tell it. I think he said last night that he'd been in Mumbai. I know one time he said he'd just come back from Cairo. I don't know that he has a permanent home. He always got his mail at the old house, as far as I know. Wait a minute, I think he got a letter here today, as a matter of fact. Postman said he had no authority to be delivering his mail up there any longer. Left it here in case he comes back."

"Maybe I could give him the letter," said Reuben. "I'm from the Nideck house."

"Yes, I know that you are," said the man.

Reuben introduced himself and apologized for not having done so before.

"That's all right," said the man. "Everybody knows who you are. We're glad there's a new family in the old house. Glad to see you."

The man went out into the Inn's dining room and came back with the letter. "My wife opened it before she saw what it was. Then she saw it was for Tom Marrok. So I'm sorry about that. You can tell him we're to blame for that."

"Thank you," said Reuben. He had never stolen a piece of federally protected mail before, and he felt his cheeks color.

"If he comes in, I'll tell him you're up at the house and you've got the letter."

"That would be fine," said Reuben.

Galton waved from the bar and lifted his beer stein as Reuben and Laura went out the door.

They drove back to the house.

"You can't believe anything Marrok told you," said

Laura, "not about 'the other' or his intentions. It was lies."

Reuben stared straight ahead. He had but one thought in his head and that was that Marrok had been in the house yesterday before they even arrived.

As soon as they were safe inside the great room again, he opened the letter. He was certain this had been the property of the dead creature, so what was the point of scrupling about it now?

The letter was in that strange spidery script that he'd seen only once before—in Felix's diary upstairs.

There were three pages to the letter, and not a single word was discernible to him, of course. But there was what might be a signature.

"Come with me," he said and led Laura up the stairs to Felix's small studio. He snapped on the overhead light.

"It's gone," he said. "Felix's diary. It was right there on that desk."

He began to search the desk. But he knew it was useless. Whoever had taken the tablets from all over the house had taken the diaries of Felix Nideck too.

He looked at Laura. "He's alive," he said. "I know he is. He's alive, and he wrote to this man, Marrok, telling him to come back here, to—."

"You don't know what he told him," Laura said reasonably. "You don't really know that this letter is from Felix. You only know these people share a language, a script."

"No. I know. He's alive. He's always been alive.

Something stopped him from coming back here and claiming his identity and his property. Maybe he wanted to disappear. Maybe he couldn't pretend to be his age any longer, because he simply wasn't aging. And he had to disappear. Though I can't believe he would have done such a painful thing to Marchent or her parents—as to simply disappear."

He was still for a moment, surveying the familiar clutter of the little room. The blackboards, the bulletin boards—all appeared unchanged. There was the same faded chalk writing, the same yellowed newspaper clippings with their map tacks. The same photographs everywhere of the smiling Felix and the smiling Sergei and the other mysterious men.

"I have to reach him some way, I have to talk with him, beg him to understand what happened to me, that I didn't know what this was, that I—."

"What is it?"

He let out a long exasperated sigh. "It's the restlessness," he said. "It's the restlessness that comes when I can't change, when I don't hear the voices calling me. I've got to get out of here. I've got to walk. But we can't remain here; we can't remain like sitting ducks, just waiting for him to strike."

He paced the floor, surveying the shelves again. There had probably been other diaries, tucked in the shelves here, but the shelves had never been full, and he couldn't know. Was it Marrok who had entered the house and taken these things? Or was it Felix himself?

The door stood open to the adjacent bedroom—
the northwest-corner bedroom where he and Marchent had made love. That sense of the man came
over him again, the keeper of these rooms, the man
who'd chosen that great ornate black four-poster bed,
all carved with tiny intricate figures, who had placed
the black diorite figure of a cat near the lamp, who
had left, what, a book of poems by Keats there on
that little inlaid table by the chair.

He picked up the book. A faded burgundy ribbon
marked a page. "Ode on Melancholy." And on the
page there was written a black check mark in ink by
the first stanza, and a long line beside it, and scrib-
bles in that fleecy writing—the Felix writing—that
looked like a drawing of the sea.

"Here, here is what he marked a long time ago."
He gave it to Laura.

She took it to the lamp and gently read it aloud:

**No, no! go not to Lethe, neither twist**
  **Wolf's-bane, tight-rooted, for its poisonous**
    **wine;**
**Nor suffer thy pale forehead to be kiss'd**
  **By nightshade, ruby grape of Proserpine;**
**Make not your rosary of yew-berries,**
  **Nor let the beetle, nor the death-moth be**
    **Your mournful Psyche, nor the downy owl**
**A partner in your sorrow's mysteries;**
  **For shade to shade will come too drowsily,**
    **And drown the wakeful anguish of the soul.**

The agony of this, wanting so much to talk to him, to appeal to him. **I did what was natural to me, I did it because I didn't know what else to do.** But was this true?

An overwhelming desire for the power came over him. The restlessness was driving him mad.

The wind tossed the rain against the black windows. Beyond, he heard the waves pounding the shore.

Laura looked so patient, so quietly respecting, so silent. She stood by the lamp with the Keats in her hands. She looked at the cover, and then back to him.

"Come," she said. "I have to check something. Perhaps I made a mistake."

She led the way down the hall into the master bedroom.

The little paperback book **How I Believe** was still lying on the table where she'd left it early that morning.

She opened it now and turned the brittle pages carefully.

"Yes, this is it. I wasn't mistaken. Look at the inscription."

**Beloved Felix,**
**For You!**
**We have survived this;**
**we can survive anything.**
**In Celebration,**
**Margon**
**Rome '04**

"Yes, well, Margon gave it to Felix at some point, yes," said Reuben. He didn't quite understand.

"Look at the date."

He read it aloud, "'Rome '04.' Oh, my God. He disappeared in 1992. And this, this . . . this means he is alive and . . . he's been in this house. He's been here since he disappeared."

"Apparently so, at least at some point in the last eight years, yes."

"I looked right at this and I didn't see it."

"I did too," she said. "And then it hit me. And how many other things do you think have been brought here or taken from here over the years without anyone noticing? I think he's been here. I think he left this book here. If Marrok could get into this house secretly, if he could hide himself in this house, then Felix might have often done the same thing."

Reuben paced in silence, trying to make sense of it, trying to know what, if anything, he could do.

She sat down at the table. She was paging through the little paperback.

"Are there notes?"

"Little check marks, underlining, squiggles," she answered. "Same light strokes as in the Keats. Even check marks and underlining have the stamp of a personal hand. I think he is very much alive, and you can't know who or what he is, or what he might do or want."

"But you know what Marrok said, what he accused me of."

"Reuben, the guardian was in a jealous rage," she said. "You'd had his precious Marchent. He wanted to make you pay. He thought he'd left you to die. Very likely he didn't attack by accident at all. He couldn't finish you off, no, but he thought the Chrism would likely do that. He didn't call 911 to save you. He called on account of Marchent, so her body wouldn't lie there alone and neglected until Galton or somebody else found it."

"I think you're right."

"Reuben, you are so gifted. Don't you know jealous rage when you see it? The monster's words were steeped in envy. All that about how he would never have chosen you, never given you a second glance, about how it was your fault that he turned his back on Marchent. That was envy from start to finish."

"I understand."

"You can't know anything about this man, Felix, from what the monster said. Look at it squarely. If Felix did write this letter, if he's alive now as this letter seems to indicate, he's allowed you to inherit this house. He hasn't sought to interfere by hook or by crook. Now why would he do that? And why would he send that unpleasant little creature, that strange little beast, to see to it that the owner of the house was killed, and the house lost to the probate courts again?"

"Because he's taken the only things he wanted?" Reuben offered. "The diary and the tablets? He took them right after Marchent died?"

She shook her head. "I don't believe it. There is so much more here, parchment scrolls, ancient codices, they're everywhere. So many odds and ends that Felix collected. Why, who knows what's really in the attics, or in other places in this house? There are trunks up there you haven't opened, boxes of papers. There are secret rooms in this house."

"Secret rooms?"

"Reuben, there have to be secret rooms. Look, come into the hall."

They stood at the place where the southern hall met the western hall.

"You have a rectangle of hallways here—the west, the south, the east, the north."

"Yes, but we've been in all the rooms that open off them, more or less. On the outside you have the bedrooms, and on the inside, you have linen closets and extra bathrooms. Where are the secret rooms?"

"Reuben, you are scientifically challenged. Look." She crossed the hall, and opened the first of the linen closets. "This room is scarcely ten feet deep. It's the same all the way around the inside of the rectangle."

"Right."

"Well, what's in the middle?" she asked.

"My God, you're right. That has to be a huge square space in the middle."

"Well, I searched this afternoon when you were with Jim. I went into every closet, bathroom, stairwell, and nowhere did I find a door opening to the middle of the house."

"So you think there are things here, hidden in some secret rooms, things he may still want?"

"Come. Let's try something else."

She led the way into the bedroom that had become her office. She'd moved a small desk from the wall to the windows, and her laptop was open there.

"What's the actual address of this house?"

He had to think. It was 40 Nideck Road. He'd memorized the zip when he'd been ordering equipment for the office online.

At once she typed this into the search window with the words "satellite map."

As soon as an aerial view of the coast and the forest appeared, she zoomed in on the house itself. She clicked on the house until the image got larger and then larger. There was a great square glass roof, plainly visible, surrounded and concealed by the gables that faced the four points of the compass on each side.

"Look at that," she said.

"My God, I didn't know anybody could do that!" he said. "It's not just a room, it's a huge space. And the gables completely hide the glass roof from view. Can you zoom in tighter? I want to see the details of the roof."

"It's not going any tighter," she said. "But I see what you see. Some kind of trapdoor or something on that roof."

"I've got to go upstairs, I have to check out the attics. There has to be some way to get in there."

"We've been all through them," she said. "I didn't

see any doors. But there's no telling how many times over the years that Felix or Marrok may have come here and gone into that secret part of the house through this trapdoor or some other secret entrance we have yet to find."

"That explains it," said Reuben. "Marrok was inside the house the night Marchent died. They couldn't find any evidence of anyone. But he was in that middle room or rooms."

"Look, maybe there's just more of the same in that space, you know? More shelves, bookcases, whatever."

He nodded.

"But you don't know," she said. "And as long as you don't know, there's hope that you have something to bargain with here. I mean Felix may want what's in that space; he may want his entire house. And he won't get it back simply by killing you. It will go on the market again, go to strangers. And what's he going to do then?"

"Well, he can keep sneaking in as he's done in the past."

"No, he can't. As long as the house belonged to his niece he could keep sneaking in. As long as it belonged to you, perhaps. But if the house goes to an absolute stranger, somebody who wants to turn it into a hotel or, worse yet, demolish it, well, he stands to lose everything here."

"I see your point—."

"We can't put together a complete picture," she said. "This letter just reached here. Maybe he doesn't know himself what he wants to do yet. But I doubt seriously that the man these people have been describing ever sent that sinister Marrok to put an end to our lives."

"Oh, I hope and pray you're right."

He moved to the windows. He was hot all over, anxious almost to the verge of panic. Yet he knew the change was not coming. And he did not even know whether he wanted it to come. He knew only that these physical sensations and these emotions were unendurable.

"I've got to search for a way into that space now," he said.

"Is that going to help you with what you're going through right now?"

"No," he said. He shook his head.

He took a deep breath and closed his eyes.

"Listen, Laura. We have to leave here for a little while. We have to drive."

"Where?"

"I don't know, but I'm not leaving you here alone. We have to go now."

She knew what he meant, what he was planning to do. She didn't question him.

The rain was coming down heavily as they left the house.

He drove south, picking up Highway 101 and pressing on at top speed towards the voices and the cities of the bay.

# 25

MOUNTAIN VIEW CEMETERY, Oakland: giant trees, scattered graves great and small, under the slow relentless rain. In the distance, the ghostly glitter of downtown.

A boy screaming in agony as two others tormented him with knives. Ringleader: just out of prison, wiry, naked arms covered in tattoos, T-shirt wet, transparent, body shivering, drugged up, choked with anger, savoring revenge now on the one who betrayed him, delivering up now to the gods of violence his enemy's only son.

"What?" he taunted the boy. "You think the Man Wolf will save you?"

Out of the nearby grove of oaks, Reuben appeared, closing in on the leader like a dark bestial angel in plain view of the two acolytes who turned screaming and fled.

Slash of claws, jugular ripped, figure doubling, falling, jaws closing on his shoulder, splitting the tendons, the arm loose, no time to chew this irresistible flesh.

He bounded over the fields of the dead after those who were racing in panic ever deeper into the darkness. He caught the first and ripped out half of his throat, throwing him aside as he went after the remaining tormentor, catching him in both paws and lifting him to his waiting jaws. Luscious, this pulsing feast, this dripping meat.

On a patch of blood-soaked grass lay the boy victim, nut-brown skin, black hair, curled up now like a fetus in his leather jacket, face bleeding, belly bleeding, swooning, in and out, in and out, eyes struggling to focus. Boy of twelve. Reuben bit down and picked him up by the collar of his thick jacket as a cat would pick up a kitten by the nape of its neck, and carried him easily this way as he ran along faster and faster till he came to the lights of the street. Up over the iron gates. And then he left his small charge on the corner before the darkened windows of a small café. Silence here. No late-night traffic. Streetlamps shining on empty shops. With his powerful right paw he shattered the glass of the café. The alarm shrieked. Yellow lights flashed on, garishly illuminating the wounded one on the pavement.

Reuben was gone. Back through the cemetery, he trotted, tracking the scent of those he'd slaughtered. But the kill was cold now, uninteresting. He wanted what was warm. And there were other voices in the night.

A young woman singing a low agonizing song.

He found her in the woods of the Berkeley campus, this old university landscape that, in a faraway lifetime as a human boy, he'd so loved.

Amid the towering eucalyptus trees, she'd set up a

sanctuary for her final hour—treasured book, the wine bottle, an embroidered pillow against the thick bed of fragrant leaves that curled like peelings, the small sharp kitchen knife with which she'd cut both her wrists. The blood and the consciousness oozed from her as she moaned. "Wrong, wrong!" she said under her breath. "Help me, please." She could no longer hold the wine bottle, no longer move her hands or her arms, her matted hair covering her wet face.

He hefted her over his shoulder and made for the lights of Telegraph Avenue, speeding through the dark groves of the campus, places long ago where he'd studied, argued, dreamed.

The densely packed buildings were throbbing with voices, heartbeats, the thud of drums, talk and the talk of amplified voices, the wail of a trumpet, the din of competing songs. Gently he deposited her at the open door of a busy tavern, indifferent laughter exploding inside like broken glass. As he moved upwards and away, he heard the cries of those who discovered her. "Call for help."

The voices of downtown were calling to him. Big city. Choices. Life is a garden of pain. Who shall die? Who shall live? A horror took hold of him as he moved south. **I did what seemed natural for me to do. . . . I heard the voices; the voices called me; I caught the scent of evil and I tracked it. It was as natural as breathing to do what I did.**

Liar, monster, killer, beast. **An abomination . . . this will end now.**

The sky was the color of soot when he came over the flat cluttered roof of the old gray brick hotel and down into the hatch roof of the fire stairs, slipping along the low dim hallway, silently opening the unlocked door.

Scent of Laura.

She had fallen asleep at the window, arms folded on the sill. Beyond, the leaden clouds were paling, growing shiny behind the featureless rain over a jumble of chalklike towers, freeways vibrating like bowstrings as they arched to the right and to the left. Layer after layer of cityscape between here and the great Pacific was dying to embers in the mist. Jangle and throb of the awakening streets. Garden of pain. Who will harvest all this pain? **Please, let the voices die away. No more.**

He lifted her and carried her to the bed, the white hair falling back from her face. She woke to his kisses, eyelids shuddering. What was it in her eyes as she looked up at him? **Beloved. Mine. You and me.** Her perfume flooded his senses. The voices went out as if someone had turned a dial. Tap tap came the rain against the window. In the icy light, he slowly peeled off her tight jeans, secret hair, **hair like the hair that covers me,** and folded back the flimsy blue fabric of her blouse. His tongue pressed against her neck, her breasts. Voice of the beast rattling deep in his chest. To have and to have not. Mothers' milk.

# 26

HE CAUGHT GRACE when she came in the door of the house. No one had been home when he arrived, and he'd already packed up just about all of his clothes and books and loaded them into the Porsche. He had just gone back to check the alarm.

She almost screamed. She was in her green scrubs, but she'd let her red hair down and her face was as always starkly pale against her hair with those sharp reddish eyebrows emphasizing her distress.

At once, she threw her arms around him. "Where have you been?" she demanded. He kissed her on both cheeks. She held his face with two hands. "Why haven't you called?"

"Mamma love, I'm all right," he said. "I'm up at the house in Mendocino. I need to be there now. I just stopped in to tell you that I love you, and that you mustn't worry—."

"I need you to stay here now!" she demanded. She'd dropped her voice to a whisper, which she only did when she was near hysterical. "I'm not letting you leave here."

"I'm leaving here, Mamma. I want you to know that I'm okay."

"You're not okay. Look at you. Listen to me, do you know what happened to every test they ran on you in the hospital?—everything, blood, urine, biopsies—it's all gone, gone!" She mouthed the last word, but no sound came out. "Now, you are going to stay here, Reuben, and we are going to figure out how and why this is happening. . . ."

"Impossible, Mamma."

"Reuben!" She was trembling. "I won't let you go."

"You have to, Mom," he said. "Now, look into my eyes and listen to me. Listen to your son. I am doing the best I can. Yes, I know there have been psychological changes in me since this happened. And baffling hormonal changes as well. Yes. But you must trust me, Mother, that I am handling all this in the best way that I can. Now I know you've been talking to this doctor from Paris—."

"Dr. Jaska," she said. She seemed just a little relieved that they were addressing the real questions. "Dr. Akim Jaska. The man's an endocrinologist, a specialist in this very kind of thing."

"Yes, well, I know that. And I know he's suggested a private hospital, Mother, and I know you want me to go to this place."

She didn't commit herself. In fact, she seemed a little unsure.

"Well, you've been talking about it," he said. "I know that."

"Your father's against it," she said. She was plainly

thinking out loud. "He doesn't like Jaska. He doesn't like the whole idea."

She began to cry. It was just boiling over. She couldn't help it. She dropped her voice to a whisper. "Reuben, I am frightened," she confessed.

"I know, Mom. So am I. But I want you to do what's best for me, and what's best for me is to leave me alone."

She broke away from him and backed up against the front door. "I'm not letting you go." Suddenly she bit into her lip. "Reuben, you're writing rhapsodic prose about this werewolf, this monster that attacked you—and you don't know what's really going on!"

He couldn't bear to see her like this. He moved towards her but she stiffened against the door as if she'd fight to the death before she'd let him go.

"Mom," he said softly.

"Reuben, this Man Wolf, this thing that's killing people," she stammered. "The same thing is happening to every bit of forensic evidence they recover from the creature at the scene of every crime. Now, Reuben, this is the thing that attacked you, and it's infected you with something powerful, something dangerous, something that's working in your entire system. . . ."

"What, Mother, you think I'm becoming a werewolf?" he asked.

"No, of course not," she said. "This lunatic isn't a werewolf, that's nonsense! But he's insane, dangerously, hideously insane. And you are the only person attacked by this thing that has lived. And there's something in your blood and tissues that can help them find this creature, but Reuben, we don't know what this virus is doing to you."

Ah, so this is what she actually believed was going on. Of course. It made perfect sense.

"Baby Boy, I want to take you to the hospital—not this suspect place in Sausalito, just back to San Francisco General—."

"Mamma," he said.

This was breaking his heart.

"I thought for a moment you thought I was the Man Wolf, Mamma," he said. He hated it, testing her like this, lying to her, but he couldn't stop himself. He wanted to just take her in his arms, protect her from the truth, from everything. If only she weren't Dr. Grace Golding.

"No, Reuben, I do not think you're capable of scaling brick walls and flying over rooftops, and rending people apart limb from limb."

"That's a relief," he said under his breath.

"But this creature, whoever he is, may be in the grip of a communicable madness, don't you see? Reuben, please try to follow what I'm saying. Rabies is a communicable madness, do you follow me? You've been infected by something infinitely more dangerous than rabies, and I want you to go with me to the hospital now. Jaska says there have been other cases, with the very same extraordinary details. He says there is a real possibility of a corrosive virus."

"No, Mom, I can't. I came here so you could see with your own eyes that I'm all right," he said. He was being as gentle as he could. "And now you've seen it, and I'm going. Please, Mom, move away from the door."

"All right, then stay here, in the house," she said. "No dashing off to the woods!" She threw up her hands.

"Mom, I can't."

He moved her aside, handling her so roughly that he would never forgive himself for it, and was out the door before she could stop him, down the brick steps and down the street to his car.

She stood there in the doorway, and for the first time in his life he saw her as a tiny figure, a vulnerable figure, weak and frightened and overwhelmed—his beautiful mother who could save lives every day of her life.

Within a block of the house, he was in tears himself. By the time he reached the café where Laura was waiting, he was crying too hard to see. He gave the keys to her, and went around to the passenger seat.

"It's over," he said as they headed for the freeway. "I'll never be able to be part of them again, any of them. It's over. God! What am I going to do?"

"You mean she knows."

"No. She knows things, and she can't let go of

those things. But no, she doesn't really know. And I can't tell her. I'd die before I'd tell her."

At some point, before they were even across the Golden Gate Bridge, he fell asleep.

When he woke, it was late afternoon and they had just turned off Highway 101 for the junction where they would pick up Nideck Road.

# 27

SIMON OLIVER'S E-MAIL WAS BRIEF. "Bad news which may be good news. Call me ASAP."

That had come yesterday evening.

He rang Oliver's home phone, left a message—that he was back online and at his phone. Please call.

He and Laura had supper in the conservatory, at the new marble-top table. They were in a grove of banana palms and small ficus. And the sight of the orchid trees inclining towards each other, and dripping those gorgeous pinkish-purple blossoms, filled him with happiness.

Just today, Galton had added a number of potted ferns and some white bougainvillea, and the room was surprisingly warm from the dim afternoon sun. Laura knew all about the plants, and suggested others that Reuben might love. If Reuben wanted, she could order plants for this room, and large trees. She knew where to locate very large trees. That would be wonderful, he said, the greener, the more full of flowers, the better. And she should buy the things that she wanted, the things she most loved. What she would love he would love.

Supper was a thick soup from the lamb dinner of

yesterday that Reuben had concocted, and he thought the ingredients tasted better than before.

"Tired?" Laura asked.

"No, eager to search the entire second floor until we find an entrance into that secret space."

"Maybe there is no entrance, except through a hatch in the glass roof."

"I don't think so. I think there are several entrances. Why have such a delicious secret space if you can't get in it from any number of places? There have to be panels in those linen closets, or those bathrooms, or in the gable rooms overhead."

"I think you're right," she said.

They looked at each other.

"Until we know," she said, "we won't ever know whether we're alone here, will we?"

"No, and that makes me absolutely furious," Reuben said. He was feeling protective of her, madly protective. He didn't want to scare her. He didn't say so, but he didn't want them to be even a few yards apart.

They took the fire ax with them, and a flashlight they found in the shed, and a hammer.

But they found nothing. They explored and tapped on every inner wall throughout the second floor, and the same in the attic.

They also checked the cellar. Nothing there.

Finally Reuben was tired. It was past seven o'clock now and he prayed with all his heart that the change wouldn't come, that he would be left in peace by it tonight. And yet he could not put the temptation out of his mind. He hadn't really feasted on those men last night. The hunger for it wasn't rooted in his gut, but somewhere else.

And then there were other things.

This morning, he felt that he had brought on the change simply by wishing for it, after he and Laura had made love. It had seemed more rapid, his muscles working with it rather than against it. He remembered swallowing over and over again, as if with his whole being, calling back into himself all that had been enlarged and hardened and had to dissolve.

He fastened his thoughts on the house, how to get into that secret space.

When the rain slackened he and Laura put on heavy sweatshirts and went for a walk outside the house. First thing they found were floodlights everywhere, but they couldn't find a switch to turn them on. He'd have to ask Galton. They'd been on the first night he and Galton had met.

But the lighted windows made it easy for them to see their way through the oak forest that surrounded the entire east side of the house. These were lovable trees, Reuben said, because you could climb them, look at their low inviting limbs. He wanted to come out here in the sunshine, as soon as there was sunshine, and climb from limb to limb. Laura agreed with him.

They figured the house was easily sixty feet high, maybe higher. A grove of Douglas fir grew at its northwestern corner, with trees almost as tall, it seemed, as the nearby redwoods. And then the oak forest enclosed the gravel drive along the entire east side. It was English ivy that covered so much of the walls. It had been carefully clipped around the windows. Laura told him the names of many of the other trees—the western hemlock and the tan oak, which wasn't an oak at all.

How would Reuben, as Little Reuben, ever get up on that roof without some professional help? It would be easy enough for a roofing company to get its big ladders up the front of the house, but that was just the sort of official involvement he wanted to avoid. Of course the Man Wolf could go up the rough mortared stone wall. But the Man Wolf would have to leave Laura alone, wouldn't he?

Reuben had never thought about buying a gun in his entire life, but he was thinking about it now. Laura knew how to shoot a gun, yes. But she hated guns. Her father had never kept guns. Her husband had threatened her once with a gun. She veered off that subject quickly, and went on to talk about how she would be all right with the ax if he went up to the roof, and wouldn't he hear her, just the way he had before, if she were to call for help?

The phone was ringing when they entered the house.

Reuben hurried to the library to answer it.

It was Simon Oliver.

"All right, now, don't get upset about this till I finish explaining it," he said. "I tell you, Reuben, this is one of the most unusual situations I've ever encountered, but that does not mean that things are not going very well, all things considered, and they may continue to go well if we consider carefully what we do and say."

"Simon, please, what are you talking about?" Reuben said. He sat at his desk, barely able to contain himself. Laura was building up the fire.

"Now, you know how much respect I have for Baker, Hammermill, especially Arthur Hammermill," Simon went on, "and I trust Arthur Hammermill as I would a member of my own firm."

Reuben rolled his eyes.

"The fact is, a potential heir has turned up, but you hold on while I explain. Seems Felix Nideck—this is the man who disappeared, you understand. . . ."

"Yes, I know."

"Well, this Felix Nideck had an illegitimate son, name of Felix Nideck, just like his father, and he's turned up here in San Francisco, and Reuben, just hold on now—."

Reuben was stunned.

"Simon, I have not said a word."

"Well, maybe I'm doing the worrying for you, and that of course is my job. Well, this man says he's making no claim whatsoever on the estate, I mean none, and . . . it is not at all clear that he could make a claim, not at all, the documents he's presented could easily be forgeries, and he has no 'interest,' we're told, in taking a DNA test to prove affinity—."

"Interesting," said Reuben.

"Well, it's more than interesting," said Simon. "It's suspicious. But the point is, Reuben, he's eager to meet with you here or at the offices of Baker, Hammermill, it's our call on that, and I say here, though there would be fine. Because he wants to talk to you about the house and things which his father might have left there when he disappeared."

"Really. Does he know anything about how or why Felix Nideck disappeared?"

"Nothing. He can add nothing to the investigation. That's the word from Arthur. No, nothing there at all. Hasn't heard from his father in all this time. No, that question has not been reopened at all."

"Interesting," said Reuben. "Well, how does anyone know that this man is what he says he is?"

"Family resemblance, Reuben, positively uncanny. Arthur knew Felix Nideck, and he says this man is so like him that there can be no doubt."

"Interesting."

"Now, Reuben, I've met this man myself, met him this afternoon with Arthur, and he is quite a remarkable man, quite the raconteur, really. I'd say he was a southern gentleman if I didn't know otherwise. He was born and educated in England but he doesn't have the British accent, no, not at all, I was never able to place his accent, he does have one, but he is a striking individual, and a very gracious individual, too. And he assures me, Reuben, that he is not mounting any claim on Ms. Nideck's estate, but that he only wants this meeting—to discuss his father's effects."

"And Arthur Hammermill didn't know this man existed?" asked Reuben.

"Arthur Hammermill is flabbergasted," said Simon. "You know how Baker, Hammermill has searched for Felix Nideck and for anyone who might have been connected with him in any way."

"How old is this man?"

"Oh, forty, forty-five. Let me see. Forty-five, born in 1966, London. Looks a good deal younger, actually. He has dual citizenship, apparently, British and American, lived all over the world."

"Forty-five. Hmmmm."

"Well, Reuben, I don't see why that matters. What matters here, Reuben, is that there is no will acknowledging his existence, but of course if he were to take a DNA test and establish affinity, well, he might tie up the estate at considerable expense, but it is not at all certain he would be successful—."

"He says he wants his father's personal effects?"

"Some of them, Reuben, some of them. He hasn't been too forthcoming. He wants a meeting with you. He seems quite well informed about the whole situation. He was in Paris when Marchent's unfortunate death made the news."

"I see."

"Of course, he's in a hurry. Everybody today is in a hurry. He's at the Clift Hotel here and he is asking to meet with you as soon as you can come down. Seems he hasn't very much time. He has to be somewhere. Well, I said I would do what I could."

Which means what, Reuben thought, that he means to lure me away from this house at a specific time, and for a specific time, so that he can enter it and clear out everything that belonged to Felix—and he was more than likely Felix. Oh, he was most certainly Felix, wasn't he? Why doesn't he just come here and make himself known?

"All right," Reuben said, "I'll meet with him. I can meet with him tomorrow at one p.m. You know it's a four-hour drive from here, Simon. I can call you to confirm before I get on the road."

"Oh, that's no problem, he's already indicated he'll be available all day tomorrow. He'll be pleased. He has to leave tomorrow night, it seems."

"But I insist on this, Simon. This is entirely confidential. I don't want Phil or Grace to know about this meeting. You know Mom. If I don't stop at the house while I'm down there—."

"Reuben, I don't discuss your intimate financial affairs with your mother unless you have given me your express permission to do so," said Simon.

This was not true at all.

"Reuben, your mother's very concerned about you, you know, your moving up to Mendocino and all, and not answering your e-mails or your phone."

"Okay, one o'clock, your office," said Reuben.

"Well, not so fast. Not so fast. If I could see you for about an hour before—."

"What for, Simon? You have me now on the phone."

"Well, Reuben, I have to warn you. For a potential heir to show up in a situation like this and not want some sort of monetary consideration, well, that is just not likely at all. During this meeting, I want you to rely upon me for guidance as to what you say and what you don't say, and I strongly advise you not to answer any questions as to the value of the house, or the appraisals of the house, or about the furniture, or the value of the furniture, or the value of Felix Nideck's possessions—."

"I see. I understand all that, Simon. I'll listen to the man and see what he has to say."

"That's it exactly, Reuben. You listen. Don't commit. Let him download, as the kids say today. Just listen. He has his mind set on not discussing the particulars with anyone but you, but you do not have to respond to anything that he says during this meeting."

"Got it. Tomorrow. One p.m."

"I think he's putting on the charm with Arthur Hammermill. They've been spending their evenings together. They went to the opera last night to see **Don Giovanni.** Arthur says he's the spitting image of his father. But I'll tell you, in this day and age, until the man agrees to a DNA test, no paternity claim has a chance. And the man must know that. Of course he could change his mind at any minute."

**But he won't change his mind. He can't.**

"I'll see you tomorrow, Simon. I'm sorry I was so late in returning your call."

"Oh, and by the way," said Simon. "That piece

of yours on the Man Wolf that ran this morning in the **Observer**? That was quite good. Everybody here thought so. Quite good. And this young Mr. Nideck was quite impressed with it, too."

Oh, was he? Reuben said good-bye again and hung up the phone. He was powerfully excited. This was Felix. Felix had surfaced! Felix was here.

Laura was sitting on the rug in front of the fire. She had one of those books on werewolf literature, and she'd been making notes in a small journal.

He sat down beside her, cross-legged, and laid it all out before her.

"It's Felix, of course." He stared up at the distinguished gentlemen of the picture over the fireplace. He couldn't contain his excitement. Felix alive. Felix most certainly living and breathing, Felix with the keys to the mysteries surrounding him like smoke so thick he sometimes felt he couldn't breathe. Felix who might want to destroy him, and Laura as well.

"Yes, I have the distinct feeling that you're right. Listen to this." She picked up the journal she'd been keeping. "These are the names of the distinguished gentlemen," she said. That's what they had begun to call them routinely. "Vandover, Wagner, Gorlagon, Thibault. Well, every single one of these names is connected with some werewolf story."

He was speechless.

"Let's start with Frank Vandover. Well, there's a very famous werewolf novel called **Vandover and the Brute** by a Frank Norris, published in 1914."

So it was true! He was too overwhelmed to respond.

She went on. "Take the next name, Reynolds Wagner. Well, there is an extremely famous story called 'Wagner, the Wehr-wolf,' by an author named G. W. M. Reynolds, first published in 1846."

"Go on."

"Gorlagon—he's a werewolf in a medieval story by Marie de France."

"Of course. I read that story years ago!"

"Baron Thibault—it's a combination of names from Dumas's famous story 'The Wolf-Leader.' That's 1857—first published in France."

"So it's true!" he whispered. He stood up and looked at the men gathered in the jungle. She stood by his side.

Baron was the only man who was obviously gray-haired, older, with a heavily lined but very agreeable face. His eyes were uncommonly large, pale, kindly. Reynolds Wagner might have been red-haired. Hard to tell. But he was about the same age as Felix and Margon, with narrow elegant features, and small hands. Frank Vandover appeared to be a bit younger than the others, with curly black hair and dark eyes and very pale skin. He had a well-defined Cupid's-bow mouth.

There was something in their expressions that reminded him of a famous painting, but he couldn't quite think what it was.

"Oh, and Tom Marrok?" Laura said. "Well, that is a reference to Sir Marrok, a werewolf in Sir Thomas

Malory's **Morte d'Arthur,** written in the 1400s, and you've probably read that too."

"I have," he said. His eyes were fastened on the faces of the men.

"The plots don't matter," she said. "Neither do the dates. What matters is that the names all refer to characters in werewolf literature. So it's either a clever device for members of a club. Or the names are deliberate signals to others who share the same very special gift."

"Signals," he said. "One doesn't change one's legal name just for the fun of it, to be a member of a select club."

"How many times do you think they've been forced to change their names?" she asked. "That is, how many times have they been reborn with new names? And now this man appears, Felix Nideck, who claims to be the illegitimate son of the Felix Nideck in this picture; and we know that a Felix Nideck built this house in 1880 or thereabouts."

He paced the floor slowly and then made his way back to the fire. She had settled again near the fender, with the journal still in her hand.

"You realize what this may mean," she suggested.

"That they're all part of it, of course. I'm trembling. I'm almost unable to . . . I don't know what to say. I suspected it! I suspected it almost from the beginning but it seemed so far-fetched."

"What it could mean," she said gravely, "is that

these creatures don't age, that you won't age. That they're immortal, and that you may be immortal."

"We don't know that. We can't know that. But if this is really Felix, well, he may not be aging like other men."

He thought about the bullet that didn't wound him, about the glass he'd broken which didn't cut him. He wished he had the courage to test this right now with a self-inflicted wound, but he did not.

He was dazed by the possibility that this Felix Nideck knew all the answers he was seeking.

"But why, why does he want me to come to a meeting with lawyers?" he said. "Could he want to lure me out of this house simply so he could rob it?"

"I don't believe that," she answered. "I think he wants to meet you face-to-face."

"So why doesn't he come through the front door?"

"He wants to see who you are without revealing who or what he is," she replied. "That's what I think. And he does want the tablets, the diaries, and the things that are still here. He wants them and he's being honest about it, well, honest to a point."

"Yes."

"But he may not know what's actually happened here. He may not know that Marrok is dead."

"But it's my chance, isn't it?" he asked. "To appeal to him, to somehow convey who I am and why I had to kill Marrok."

"We both killed him," she said. "We had no choice."

"I will take the full blame for having killed him," he said. "You leave that to me. But will it matter to him, why I or we did it? Will Marchent's wishes mean anything to him? Or will he see me as an abomination too?"

"I don't know, but as you said, it's your chance."

They settled down again before the fire.

They sat quietly for a long time. One of the things he devoutly loved about her was that they could sit quiet like this for the longest time. She seemed lost in her thoughts, her knees drawn up, her arms locked around them, her eyes on the fire.

He felt utterly comfortable with her, and when he thought of something happening to her, his mind went blank white with rage.

"I wish you could be at that meeting," he said. "Does that involve a risk, do you think?"

"I think you need to meet him alone," she said. "I don't know why I think that, really, but I do. I'll go with you, but I won't be in the meeting. I'll wait in a separate room."

"Oh, you have to do that. I can't leave you here alone."

After a long while, he said, "It's not coming." He was speaking of the change, of course.

"Are you certain?"

"I know it's not," he said.

He didn't feel the restlessness. He didn't feel the desire.

They didn't talk about it anymore.

Finally, Laura went up to bed early.

Reuben opened the letter again and looked over the impenetrable writing. He collected the gold watch from the mantel. **Marrok.**

At 1:00 a.m., Reuben woke Laura. He was standing by the bed in his robe, with the fire ax.

"Reuben, what in the name of God!" she whispered.

"Keep this beside you," he said. "I'm going up on the roof."

"But you can't do that."

"I'm going to try to bring the change, and if I can bring it, I'm going up. If you need me, call to me. I'll hear you. I promise you, I'm not going off into the forest. I won't leave you here."

He went outside into the oaks. The rain was quiet, irregular, and barely penetrated the canopy here. The light from the kitchen window was dim through the interlocking branches.

He put his hands up, and ran his fingers back through his hair. "Come now," he whispered. "Come."

He tensed the muscles of his abdomen and immediately the deep spasm came, sending shock waves through his chest and his limbs. He let the robe drop in the leaves. He stepped out of the slippers. "Quickly," he whispered, and the sensations rolled upwards and outwards, the power radiating from his stomach into his chest and into his loins.

He tugged at the hair as it came bursting out, smoothing it back, tossing his head, loving the weight of it, the thick protective hood of it, as it curled down to his shoulders. He felt himself rising, his limbs swelling, as the sensations themselves seemed to support him, massaging him, holding him weightless in the brightening light.

Now the night was translucent, the shadows were thinning, and the rain felt like nothing, swirling before his eyes. The forest sang, tiny creatures surrounding him, as if welcoming him.

In the kitchen window he saw Laura watching him, the light very yellow behind her, her face in shadow. But he could clearly see the glistening orbs of her eyes.

He ran towards the house, directly below where two of the gables met, and springing on the wall effortlessly, he climbed up the protruding blocks of stone, higher and higher until he reached the roof. Through the narrow little valley of slates between the gables, he made his way to the great square glass roof.

He saw now that it was set below the gable rooms, and roofed only the secret space of the second floor.

The gables showed it only blank walls as they surrounded it, as if guarding it from the world.

Dead leaves filled the deep gutters that ran along each side of it, and it gleamed like a great black pool of water beneath the light of the mist-shrouded moon.

He went on his knees to move across it. It was slippery with rainwater, and he could feel how thick the glass was, and see the iron ribs that supported it, crisscrossing beneath him, but he could not see into the room or rooms below. The glass was darkly tinted, laminated perhaps, surely tempered. In the southwest corner, he found the square hatch or trapdoor that he had only glimpsed from the satellite map. It was surprisingly large, framed in iron, fitted flush into the iron, like a large pane of the roof. And he could find no handle, or way to open it, no visible hinges, no edge to grasp. It was sealed tight.

Surely there was a way to open it, unless he'd been wrong all the time. But no. He was sure that it opened. He explored the deep gutter, digging like a dog through the leaves, but he found no handle, or lever or button to push.

What if it opened inward? What if it required weight and strength? He tested it with his paws. He figured it was about three feet square.

He climbed to his feet and stood on it, approaching the south side first and then, flexing his legs with all his strength, he jumped.

The thing flapped open, the hinges behind him, and down he went into the darkness, catching hold of the edge above him with both paws. The scents of wood and dust, of books, of mold, flooded his nostrils.

Still gripping the rim, his feet dangling, he looked around and saw the dim outlines of a giant room. He feared to be trapped in it however, but his curiosity was a lot stronger than his fear. If he could get in, he could get out. He dropped to the floor, on carpet, and the trapdoor creaked as it closed again, slowly, sealing out the sky.

This was the deepest darkness he'd ever known. The tint of the glass made the faint shine of the moon a mere blur.

He could feel a plaster wall before him, and a door, a paneled door. He felt the knob of the door, and turned it, hearing it and feeling it turn though he could scarcely see it, and he pulled it open to his right.

Creeping slowly through the door, he almost toppled and fell down a narrow steep stairs. Oh, so they had been wrong all the time that this sanctuary was accessed through the second floor. He climbed down now quickly, easily, to the first floor of the house, feeling the wall on both sides with his paws.

The door at the bottom opened inwards and he found himself in a small room he immediately recognized by its scent: linen, silver polish, candles. It was one of the pantries between the dining room and the great room. He opened the door and stepped into the wide-arched alcove that divided the two enormous rooms.

Laura came towards him out of the kitchen, through the long butler's pantry and across the darkened dining room.

"So this is the way," she said in astonishment.

"We'll need a flashlight," he said. "Even I will need a flashlight. It's quite dark."

She went into the pantry from which he'd come.

"But look, there's a light switch," she said, reaching into the stairwell. She snapped it on. At once a small bulb was illuminated at the very top of the narrow stairs.

"I see," he said. He was marveling. Could this interior sanctum be heated and wired? And how long ago had someone been here—to see to the lightbulb?

He led the way up, back to the small landing beneath the skylight.

By the weak light of the landing, they peered through an open doorway into a vast room. Books there were aplenty on shelves everywhere, covered in dust and cobwebs, but this was no simple library, not by any means.

Tables crowded the center of the room, most of them filled with scientific equipment—beakers, Bunsen burners, banks of test tubes, small boxes, stacks of glass slides, bottles, jars. One long table was entirely draped with a grayish threadbare cloth. All was encrusted with dust.

Another light switch immediately turned on the overhead bulbs, strung on iron rafters beneath the wired glass of the roof along the western side of the room.

There had once been lights everywhere but most of the sockets hung empty now.

Laura began to cough from the dust. It was a gray film on the beakers and burners, on every object they could see, even on the loose papers that lay here and there among the equipment, on pencils and pens.

"Microscopes," said Reuben. "Primitive, all of

them, antiques." He walked through the wilderness of tables. "It's old, all of it very old. Things like this haven't been used in a laboratory in decades."

Laura pointed. At the farthest end of the room from them, and from the light, stood several giant rectangular cages, rusted, seemingly ancient, like the cages for primates at a zoo. In fact, cages large and small lined the eastern wall.

Reuben felt a reflexive horror take hold of him looking at these cages. Cages for Morphenkinder? Cages for beasts? He moved slowly towards them. He opened one immense door that groaned and creaked on its hinges. Old locks, dangling from chains, were rusted too. Well, this cage might hold another Morphenkind, but it could not have held him. Or could it?

"All this," he said, "all this must be a hundred years old."

"That's perhaps the only good thing about it," Laura said. "Whatever happened here, it took place a long time ago."

"But why was it abandoned?" Reuben asked. "What caused them to give up all of this?"

His eyes moved over the bookshelves lining the northern wall.

He moved closer. "Medical journals," he said, "but they're all from the nineteenth century. Well, here's some from the early 1900s—1910, 1915, then they stop."

"Yet someone has been here," said Laura. "There's

more than one set of tracks from the door. The tracks go everywhere."

"All the same person, I think. Small tracks. A small soft shoe without a heel, a moccasin. It was Marrok. He's come and gone here, but no one else."

"How can you know?"

"Just a hunch. I think he came down through the trapdoor as I did, entered the room, and moved over there to the desk." He pointed to the northwest corner. "Look at the chair. It's been dusted, and there are a few books there, too."

"The only new things in this room."

Reuben examined them. Detective novels, classics—Raymond Chandler, Dashiell Hammett, James M. Cain.

"He camped here from time to time," said Reuben.

On the floor to the right of the chair in the shadows stood a half-full bottle of wine with a screw top. Common California vintage, but not a bad one, just one that came with a screw top.

Behind the desk was a row of leather-bound ledgers on a high shelf, with yearly dates inscribed on the spines in faded gold. Reuben slowly removed the ledger for 1912, and opened it. Sturdy, made-to-endure, parchmentlike paper still intact.

There was the enigmatic writing in ink, Felix's secret writing, waves and waves of it across page after page.

"Could this be what he wants above all?"

"It's all so old," Laura said. "What secrets could it contain? Perhaps he wants it only because it belongs to him? Or to whoever shares this language."

Laura pointed to the long table that was draped with cloth. Reuben could see the tracks in the dust leading back and forth from it to the door. There was a mess of tracks around it.

He knew what he would find. Carefully, he peeled back the cloth.

"The tablets," he whispered. "All the ancient Mesopotamian tablets. Marrok collected them and brought them here." He rolled the cloth back gingerly, unveiling rows and rows of fragments. "All preserved," Reuben said, "probably just as Felix wanted." And there were the man's diaries, a good dozen notebooks like the one that Reuben had first seen on Felix's desk, in neat stacks of four each. "Look how carefully he put these things here."

What if the secrets of this transformation went all the way back to the ancient cities of Uruk and Mari? And why should they not? **The Chrism—that's what we've called it for ages. The gift, the power—there are a hundred ancient words for it—what does it matter?**

Laura was moving along the northern and eastern walls, studying the books on those shelves. She'd come to a plain darkly stained door.

She waited for Reuben to open it. Same old brass doorknob as the others. It opened easily to reveal a door opposite with a latch. This door, too, opened with a creak.

They found themselves in one of the inside bathrooms of the north hall. The door was faced entirely with a long rectangular mirror framed in gold.

"I should have realized," Reuben said.

But there had to be some other way into the second floor at the southwest corner, he was certain. Where the first Felix Nideck had slept right after the house was built.

He found it, a door into a linen pantry, faced in bare wood and blocked by a row of shelves. It was a simple thing to remove the shelves, and they soon found themselves at the southwest end of the south hallway, right before the master bedroom door.

They made other small discoveries. A loop of heavy iron-threaded rope hung from the trapdoor, enabling one to pull it down from the inside. Old lamps throughout the big room were empty. Some of the tables were fitted with small sinks, fully plumbed with faucets and drains. There were gas pipes running beneath the tables and gas burners. The entire laboratory had been well equipped for its time.

They soon discovered that there was a door in each corner of the room, one leading into a bathroom behind a mirror quite similar to the one they'd already found, and the last one on the southeast side leading into a closet.

"I think I understand what might have happened," said Reuben. "Someone began experiments here, experiments to determine the nature of the change, the Chrism, whatever these creatures call this. If these creatures have longevity, truly great longevity, think what modern science must have meant to them after thousands of years of alchemy. They must have expected to discover great things."

"But why did they stop the experiments?"

"Could be a thousand reasons. Perhaps they relocated the laboratory somewhere else. There's only so much one can do scientifically in a house like this, isn't there? And they wanted secrecy, obviously. Or maybe they discovered that they couldn't discover anything at all."

"Why do you say that?" Laura asked. "They must have discovered something, in fact, many things."

"You think so? I think the specimens they took from themselves or others simply disintegrated before they could learn much of anything at all. Maybe that's why they turned away from the whole endeavor."

"I wouldn't have given up that easily," said Laura. "I would have sought better preservatives, better techniques. I would have studied the tissues for as long as they held together. I think they moved their headquarters someplace else. Remember what the guardian creature said about pluripotent progenitor cells. That's a sophisticated term. Most normal human beings don't know terms like that."

"Well, if that's so, then Felix wants his own personal

records, his own possessions, and those tablets—whatever those tablets mean."

"Tell me about them, please," she said. "What are they exactly?" She approached the half-draped table. She feared to touch the tiny dried clay fragments that looked as fragile as dried dough.

Reuben didn't want to touch them either, but he wished for all the world he had a bright light to shine on the tablets. He wished he could make out an order to the way in which Marrok had laid them out. Had there been an order to them on the shelves in Felix's old rooms? He couldn't remember any discernible order.

"It's cuneiform writing," he said. "Some of the earliest. I can show you examples in books or online. These were probably unearthed in Iraq, from the earliest cities ever documented in the world."

"I never realized these tablets were so tiny," she said. "I always thought of them as large, like the pages of our books."

"I'm eager to get out of here!" Reuben said suddenly. "It's suffocating me. It's grim."

"Well, I think we've done enough for now. We've learned things that are quite important. If only we knew for sure that Marrok was the only one who'd been in this room."

"I'm sure of it," said Reuben. Again, he led the way as they turned off the lights behind them and went down the stairs.

In the darkened library, they built up the fire again,

and Laura sat close, hugging herself for warmth, and Reuben sat far back against the desk, because the warmth was too much.

He felt comfortable in his lupine form, sitting there. He felt as comfortable as he ever had in his old skin. He could hear the chirping and singing of the birds outside in the oak trees, hear the prowling things of the deep brush. But he felt no urge to join these creatures, or join their savage realm, to kill or to feast.

They talked only a little, speculating that Reuben had the things that Felix wanted, and that Felix, known far and wide as a gentleman, had not seen it as his prerogative to come into the house and take these things in stealth.

"The meeting means he has good intentions," Laura said, "I'm sure of it. If he meant to raid this house he could have done it before now. If he meant to kill us, well, he could do that anytime."

"Yes, perhaps anytime," said Reuben. "Unless we can defeat him just as we defeated Marrok," he said.

"Defeating one of them is one thing. Defeating all of them is another, isn't it?"

"We don't know that they're all here in one place. We don't know that they're all even still alive."

"The letter," Laura said, "the letter belonging to Marrok. You must remember to take that with you."

He nodded. Yes, he would take the letter. He would take the watch. But he mustn't rehearse what he meant to say in this meeting.

Everything depended on Felix, what Felix said, what Felix did.

The more he thought about it, the more eager he was for the meeting, the more his hopes were now being built upon it, and the more he felt bold and even a little elated that it had come to this.

Desire was building in him now that the night was waning, not desire for the wild, but for the wild within this room.

At last, he came to her, kissing the back of her head, her neck, her shoulders. He wrapped his arms around her and felt her body melt.

"And so you will be my wild man of the forest again as we make love," she said, smiling, her eyes on the fire. He kissed her cheeks, the plumping flesh from her smile. "Will I ever make love to the smooth-faced Reuben Golding, Sunshine Boy, Baby Boy, Little Boy, Boy Wonder—of the world?"

"Hmm, now why would you want him?" he asked. "When you can have me?"

"Here's my answer to that," she said, opening her mouth to his kisses, to his tongue, to the press of his teeth.

When it was over, he carried her upstairs, which he liked to do, and set her down on the bed.

He stood at the window, because somehow it seemed appropriate to hide his face from her, as he tensed and spoke to the power, and inhaled slowly as if swallowing water from a clear stream. At once the change began.

A thousand fingers were stroking him, plucking ever so softly at every slithering hair on his head, his face, the backs of his arms.

He held up his paws, watching them in the faint light of the night sky as they changed, claws shrinking, vanishing, soft padded flesh turning back into palms.

He flexed his fingers and his toes. The light had dimmed slightly. The forest songs faded to a sweet whispering hum.

Ah, this had been a sweet accomplishment, the power serving him, at his command.

But how often could he make the change? Could it get away from him under the right provocation? Could it fail him utterly, even when he was in extreme danger? How could he know?

Tomorrow, surely, he would confront a man who knew the answers to those questions and countless others. But what exactly would happen at this meeting? What did this man want?

And even more to the point, what was the man willing to give?

# 28

SIMON OLIVER'S OFFICES were on California Street, on the sixth floor of a building with a dazzling view of the surrounding office towers, and the bright blue waters of San Francisco Bay.

Reuben, dressed in a white cashmere turtleneck sweater and his favorite Brooks Brothers double-breasted blazer, was shown into the conference room where the meeting with Felix's illegitimate son would soon take place.

It was typical of the firm, this room, with its long oval mahogany table and robust Chippendale Cupid's-bow chairs. He and Simon were seated on one flank of the table, opposite a large uninspired multicolored abstract painting that seemed no more than a glorified decoration for the wall.

Laura was in a small comfortable room nearby with coffee and the morning papers, and a television turned to the news.

Of course Simon went over and over his advice to Reuben. This could well be a fishing expedition on the part of this man, who might at any time offer a DNA test to prove his claim of paternity, and mount a full-scale legal assault on the estate.

"And I must say," said Oliver, "I've never much

cared for men who wear their hair long, but you do look pretty good with it, Reuben, all things considered. Is this bushy hair some sort of new rustic style? You must drive the young women insane."

Reuben laughed. "I don't know. I just stopped cutting it," he answered. He knew that his hair was shining clean and thoroughly groomed, so nobody had a right to complain about it. Didn't matter to him that it was getting pretty long on the back of his neck. He wished the meeting would start.

It seemed an eternity of listening to Simon's most paranoid speculations until Arthur Hammermill entered and said that Felix had just stopped at the washroom and would be right along.

Hammermill was as old as Simon Oliver, maybe seventy-five. They were both white-haired and gray-suited men, the former a little heavyset with bushy eyebrows, and the latter, a thin man who was beginning to go bald.

Hammermill was gracious to Reuben, warmly clasping his hand.

"It was so kind of you to agree to this meeting," he said with obviously carefully chosen words. He sat down opposite Simon, which left the chair directly opposite Reuben for the mysterious potential heir.

Reuben asked how they'd enjoyed the performance of **Don Giovanni,** which was an opera he truly loved. He mentioned the Joseph Losey film of it, which he'd seen many times over the years. Arthur was immediately enthusiastic about that and then volunteered how much he'd been enjoying Felix's company, and that he'd be sad when Felix left again for Europe, which was his intention, this very night. He said those last words with a pointed glance at Simon, who merely studied him gravely without a response.

At last the door opened and Felix Nideck came into the room.

If Reuben had had any lingering doubt that this was Marchent's uncle—and not his illegitimate son—that doubt was immediately dispelled.

This was the impressive man of the photograph on the library wall—the smiling man amid friends in the tropical jungle; the agreeable mentor of the family from the portrait above Marchent's desk.

The living breathing Felix Nideck, looking no older than he had twenty years ago. No son could have so perfectly embodied the form and features of the father. And there was about him an unconscious authority and subtle vivacity that marked him off from the other men in the room.

Reuben was shaken. Without moving his lips, he offered a small prayer.

The man was tall, well built, and had that kind of dark skin which is golden, and thick flowing short brown hair. He was dressed almost too exquisitely in a superbly fitted brown suit, caramel shirt, and gold-and-brown tie.

But his generous expression and easy demeanor

were the real shock. His smile was immediate, his large brown eyes filled with contagious good humor, and he extended his hand to Reuben at once. He had a naturally animated face.

Everything about the man was inviting and kind.

He sat down directly opposite as Reuben knew he would, and they were eye to eye, of the same height. He leaned forward and said,

"This is a **great** pleasure." The voice was deep, resonant, and unaffected, without a discernible accent and very warm. "Let me thank you. I'm well aware that you had no obligation whatsoever to see me, and I'm impressed, and grateful, that you've come." He gestured easily with his hands as he spoke, and they were graceful hands. There was a green jewel in his gold tie clasp, and a bit of a striped silk handkerchief, that matched the tie, just visible in his breast pocket.

Reuben was powerfully fascinated, as fascinated as he was on guard. But more than anything else, he was excited and he could feel his heart beating in his throat. If he failed to make a favorable impression on this man—but then he couldn't think of failure. All he could think was that every minute he had with the man had to count.

The man went on talking seamlessly and easily, settling back a little in the chair. He was fluid in his movements, relaxed rather than poised.

"I'm well aware that my cousin Marchent was fond of you. And you know she was so very dear to my father, his only heir."

"But you didn't actually know Marchent, did you?" said Reuben. His voice was unsteady. What was he doing? He was off to a rocky start. "What I mean is, you'd never met."

"My father had a way of making her quite real to me," the man said without missing a beat. "I'm sure our representatives have explained to you I would never presume to make a claim on the house or the land that she wanted you to have."

"Yes, they have explained," said Reuben. "That's reassuring. I'm happy to be here, to discuss anything you want."

The man's easy smile was almost dazzling. His vibrant eyes indicated a warm response to Reuben personally, but Reuben was reserving judgment on that.

How could Reuben really begin? How could he cut to the point?

"I knew Marchent briefly," Reuben said, "but I think I knew her well. She was an exceptional person—." He swallowed. "That I couldn't protect her—"

"Now, Reuben," said Simon.

"—that I couldn't protect her," Reuben went on. "Well, that's something I'll live with till my dying day."

The man nodded. There was almost a doting quality to his expression. Then he said in a soft voice, "You're a beautiful young man."

Reuben was startled. **If this guy means to kill me, he's the devil in hell.** And the man went on.

"Oh, forgive me," he said with obvious sincerity

and a little concern. "I take the license of an older man in making such a remark. I'm sorry. I am not perhaps old enough to take that license but there are times when I feel considerably older than I am. I meant only that your photographs don't do you justice. You appear conventionally beautiful in your photographs, a little remote, but in person, you're much more remarkable." He went on with a beguiling simplicity. "I see now the writer of the articles you've published in the **Observer.** Poetic, substantive, I would say."

The lawyers sat there in rigid and obviously uncomfortable silence. But Reuben was charmed, hopeful, yet cautious. **Does that mean you're not going to kill me?**—was on the tip of his tongue. **Or does all this just mean you will be talking softly and beguilingly when you try to do it like that loathsome Marrok?**

But this was Felix sitting here, Felix across a table from him. He had to get a grip.

"You want your father's personal effects," Reuben said, struggling not to stammer. "His diaries, you mean? And the tablets, the ancient cuneiform tablets—."

"Reuben," said Simon immediately, hand up to cut him off. "Let's not discuss the details of the personal effects until Mr. Nideck has made his intentions a little more clear."

"Ancient tablets?" murmured Arthur Hammermill, shifting in his chair. "What sort of ancient tablets? This is the first I've heard of ancient tablets."

"Yes, my father collected many ancient cuneiform tablets during his years in the Middle East," said the man. "And indeed, these are my primary interest, I confess, and his diaries of course. His diaries are very important to me."

"Then you can read his secret writing?" Reuben asked.

He sensed a quiver in the man's gaze.

"There's so much of the secret writing in the house," said Reuben.

"Yes, as a matter of fact, I can read the secret writing," said the man.

Reuben drew the letter to Marrok out of his pocket and pushed it across the table. "Did you perhaps write this?" he asked. "It appears to be in your father's secret hand."

The man stared at the letter with a sober expression, but the expression wasn't cold. He was clearly surprised.

He reached out and picked up the letter.

"How did you come by this, if I may ask?"

"If you wrote it, well, now it belongs to you."

"Would you tell me how you came by it?" he asked again with humble courtesy. "You'd be doing me a great service if you would let me know."

"It was left in the Inn in the town of Nideck for a man who thought of himself as something of a guardian for the house, and the things in the house," Reuben explained. "Not a very pleasant man. He never received it, by the way. I collected it after he'd disappeared."

"Disappeared?"

"Yes, he's gone, he's completely disappeared."

The man registered this in silence. Then:

"You've met this person?" Again, the eyes became soft, probing, and the voice was warmly polite.

"Oh, yes," said Reuben. "It was quite a challenging meeting." Here we go, Reuben thought. Get it all out. Go to the very edge of the cliff. "Very challenging indeed, for me and for my companion, my friend who's sharing the house with me. It was, well, you might say, a disastrous meeting, but not disastrous, as it turned out, for us."

The man appeared to weigh this carefully, with little change of expression. But clearly he was taken aback.

"Reuben, I think we had better tend to the business at hand here," Simon suggested. "We can always arrange a time in the future to discuss other matters, if we agree here—."

" 'Disastrous,' " the man repeated, ignoring Simon. The man seemed genuinely concerned. "I'm so sorry to hear it," said the man. Again, his tone was humble, gracious, and concerned.

"Well, let's just say this person, Marrok, he objected rather strongly to my presence in the house, to my relationship with Marchent Nideck; he was offended by other things as well." "Things," it was such a weak word. Why couldn't he choose another word? He looked to the man for understanding. "In fact, I'd say he was pretty angry about the way things had . . . developed. He regarded me as a bit of a blunderer. He was very angry. But he's gone, this man. Gone. He won't ever be collecting that letter."

Simon made a series of little throat-clearing noises and was about to interrupt again when Reuben gestured for patience.

The man was studying Reuben, not saying a word. Plainly, he was shocked.

"I thought that perhaps you'd written this letter to him," said Reuben. "That maybe he came at your behest."

"Perhaps we should see that letter—," said Simon.

Very carefully, the man removed the folded pages of the letter from the envelope, his finger running over the place where the envelope had been torn open.

"Yes," he said. "I wrote this letter. But I don't see how it could have prompted an unpleasant meeting. That certainly was not my intention. The message is simple, actually. I hadn't written to Marrok in ages. I told him that I'd heard of Marchent's death, and I'd be arriving soon."

This was said with such conviction and persuasion that Reuben believed it. But his heart would not stop beating in his ears and in the palms of his hands.

"Now regarding this man," said Arthur.

"Please," said Reuben. He kept his eyes on Nideck. "What was I to figure, except that you'd written to him earlier," he asked, "and that maybe his disapproval was your disapproval, that he was acting on your authority when he appeared in the house?"

"By no means," said the man softly. His eyebrows drew together in a tense little frown for a moment and then relaxed. "I assure you," he said, "whatever happened, he was not acting in my stead."

"Well, that's quite a relief," said Reuben. He realized he had begun to tremble a little, and to sweat. "Because this man, Marrok, he wasn't amenable to reason. He pushed things to a head."

The man absorbed this quietly.

Simon clasped Reuben's right wrist very hard, but Reuben ignored this.

How can I make it clearer, Reuben was thinking.

"And you say he's gone now," the man asked.

"Without a trace, as they say," Reuben answered. "Just gone." He made a gesture with his two hands to suggest the rising of smoke.

He knew this must be utterly incomprehensible to the two lawyers, but he was slamming it home. He had to.

The man was as placid and seemingly trusting as before.

"I felt under attack, you understand," said Reuben. "The woman with me was under attack. I love this woman very much. It was unfair for her to have been threatened under my roof. I did what I had to do."

Again Simon tried to protest. Arthur Hammermill was plainly stunned.

The man was the one who raised his hand for Simon to remain quiet.

"I understand," he said, looking into Reuben's eyes. "I am so sorry—so very sorry for this completely unexpected turn of events."

Suddenly, Reuben took the gold watch out of his pocket, and moved it across the table to the man. "This was left behind," he said in a small voice.

The man looked at the watch for a long moment before he reached for it and held it reverently in both hands. He looked at the face of it and then at the back. He sighed. His expression was somber for the first time, a marked departure, and perhaps even a little disappointed.

"Ah, poor reckling," he said under his breath as he looked again at the face of the watch. "Your wandering is at an end."

"What is a reckling?" asked Arthur Hammermill. He was pale with frustration and annoyance.

"A runt," said Reuben. "It's an old English word for 'runt.'"

The man's eyes flashed with pleasure as he smiled at Reuben, but he remained grieved, grieved as he turned the watch again in his hand.

"Yes, so sorry," he whispered. He put the watch in

his pocket. He took the letter carefully and slipped it inside his jacket. "Forgive me my eccentric vocabulary. I know too many languages, too many ancient books."

The lawyers were clearly flustered, exchanging glances.

Reuben forged ahead.

"Well, perhaps it's easy for one in my situation to offend others," said Reuben. He put his right hand in his lap because it was trembling. "After all, it's a magnificent house," he said. "A magnificent property, a magnificent responsibility, some might say a Chrism of sorts . . ." His face was burning.

There was a tiny shift in the man's gaze.

They regarded one another for a long moment.

The man looked as though he was about to say something momentous, but he sat silent for a while longer and then said only, "And we do not always ask for a Chrism."

"A Chrism?" Simon whispered with exasperation, and Arthur Hammermill nodded and mumbled something under his breath.

"No, quite the opposite," said Reuben. "But a man would be a fool who didn't cherish a Chrism for what it is."

The man smiled. It was a sad smile, what the world calls a philosophical smile.

"Then I haven't offended you?" Reuben asked. His voice dropped to a whisper. "That's the last thing I want to do."

"No, not at all," said the man. His voice grew softer, and eloquent with feeling. "The young are the only hope we have."

Reuben swallowed. He was now trembling all over. The sweat had broken out on his upper lip. He felt wobbly but exhilarated.

"I've never faced such challenges," said Reuben. "I think you can well imagine that. I want to face these challenges with resolve and strength."

"Obviously," said the man. "We call it fortitude, do we not?"

"Now, that's a good English word I understand," said Simon with Arthur Hammermill nodding vigorously in support.

"Thank you." Reuben blushed. "I think I fell in love with the house, I know I fell in love with Marchent. And I became enamored of Felix Nideck, with the idea of him, the explorer, the scholar—the teacher perhaps." He paused, then: "Those diaries written in that mysterious script. The house is full of treasures, and those tablets, those tiny fragile tablets. Even the name Nideck is a mystery. I found the name in an old short story. So many names in the house seem connected to old stories—Sperver, Gorlagon, even Marrok. There's a poetry and romance to that, isn't there—finding names that resonate with mysteries in lore and legend, finding names that promise revelations in a world where the questions multiply every day—."

"Reuben, please!" said Simon, raising his voice.

"You have a flair for the poetic," murmured Arthur Hammermill, rolling his eyes. "Your father would be justly proud."

Simon Oliver visibly bristled.

The man's smile was easy and again almost doting. He pressed his lips together and gave a small, almost imperceptible nod.

"I'm enthralled," said Reuben. "I've been overwhelmed. I'm glad to see you're more sanguine on the matter, because your friend was pessimistic, grim."

"Well, we can forget about him now, can't we?" the man whispered. He appeared to be marveling in his own way.

"I imagined Felix Nideck to be a fount of knowledge, maybe secret knowledge," Reuben said. "You know, someone who would know the answers to so many questions, what my father calls cosmic questions, someone who could shed some light into the darkest corners of this life."

Simon shifted uncomfortably in his chair, and so did Arthur Hammermill, as if they were signaling one another. Reuben ignored them.

The man was simply staring at him with those large compassionate eyes.

"It must be marvelous for you," said Reuben, "to read that secret writing. Just last night, I found ledgers filled with that secret writing, very old. Very old indeed."

"Did you?" asked the man gently.

"Yes, they go way back. Years back. Years before Felix Nideck can have been alive. Your ancestors must have known the secret writing. Unless of course Felix had some great secret of longevity that no one knows. One could almost believe it in that house. That house is a labyrinth. Did you know, it has secret stairways, actually, and a large secret room?"

The lawyers were both clearing their throats at the same time.

The man's face registered only quiet understanding.

"Seems there were scientists once working in that house, doctors perhaps. It's impossible to know now of course unless one can read that secret writing. Marchent tried long ago to have it decoded—."

"Did she?"

"But no one could crack it. You're in possession of a rather valuable skill."

Simon again tried to interrupt. Reuben rode over him.

"The house prompts me to imagine things," said Reuben, "that Felix Nideck is still somehow alive, that he's going to come and somehow explain things which on my own I can't grasp, may never grasp."

"Reuben, please, if you will, I think perhaps—," said Simon who actually started to rise to his feet.

"Sit down, Simon," said Reuben.

"It never entered my mind that you knew so much of Felix Nideck," said the man gently. "I didn't realize that you knew anything of him at all."

"Oh, I know many little things about him," said Reuben. "He was a lover of Hawthorne, Keats, those old European gothic stories, and he even loved theology. He was a lover of Teilhard de Chardin. I found a little book in the house, Teilhard's **How I Believe.** I should have brought it to you. I forgot to bring it. I've been treating it rather like a sacred relic. It was inscribed to Felix by one of his good friends."

The man's face underwent another subtle shift, but the openness, the generosity, remained. "Teilhard," he said. "Such a brilliant and original thinker." He dropped his voice just a little. " 'Our doubts, like our misfortunes, are the price we have to pay for the fulfillment of the universe. . . .' "

Reuben nodded. He couldn't suppress a smile.

" 'Evil is inevitable,' " Reuben quoted, " 'in the course of a creation which develops within time.' "

The man was speechless. Then very softly, with a radiant smile, he said, "Amen."

Arthur Hammermill was staring at Reuben as if Reuben had lost his mind. Reuben went on:

"Marchent painted such a vivid portrait of Felix," he said. "Everybody who knew him enriches it, deepens it. He's part of the house. It's impossible to live there and not know Felix Nideck."

"I see," said the man in the softest voice.

The lawyers were about to attempt another intervention. Reuben raised his voice slightly.

"Why did he vanish like that?" Reuben asked.

"What became of him? Why would he leave Marchent and his family the way he did?"

Arthur Hammermill immediately interrupted. "Well, all of this has been investigated," he interjected, "and actually Felix here does not have anything to add that would help us with this—."

"Of course not," said Reuben under his breath. "I was asking him to speculate, Mr. Hammermill. I just thought he might have some sterling idea."

"I don't mind discussing it," said the man. He reached over to his left and patted the back of Arthur's hand.

He looked at Reuben.

"We can't know the whole truth of it," he said. "I suspect Felix Nideck was betrayed."

"'Betrayed'?" Reuben asked. His mind shot at once to that enigmatic inscription in the Teilhard book: **We have survived this; we can survive anything.** A jumble of fragmentary memories came back to him. "'Betrayed,'" he said.

"He would never have abandoned Marchent," said the man. "He didn't trust his nephew and his nephew's wife to raise their children. It wasn't his intention to drop out of their lives as he did."

Bits and snatches of conversation were coming back. Abel Nideck had not gotten along with his uncle; something about money. What was it? Abel Nideck had come into some money, right after Felix went away.

In a low rumbling voice Arthur began whispering in the man's ear, cautioning that these were all serious questions and such, and should be discussed in another place and at another time.

The man nodded absently and dismissively. He looked again at Reuben.

"It was undoubtedly bitter for Marchent; it must have cast a shadow over her life."

"Oh, without question, it did," said Reuben. He was powerfully excited. His heart pounded like a drum, setting the pace of the conversation. "She suspected something bad had happened, not only to him but to his friends, all of his close friends."

Simon tried to interrupt.

"Sometimes it's better not to know the whole story," the man said. "Sometimes, people should be spared the whole truth."

"You think so?" said Reuben. "Maybe you're right. Maybe in Marchent's case, and in the case of Felix. How can I know? But right now, I'm a guy who is craving the truth, craving answers, craving some understanding of things, an insight, any insight, a clue—."

"These are family matters!" said Arthur Hammermill in a deep, crushing voice. "Matters in which you have no right—."

"Please, Arthur!" said the man. "It is important for me to hear these things. Please, if you will, let us continue?"

But Reuben had come to an impasse. He wanted to

leave the room, to confront this person alone some-where no matter what the danger. Why must they go through this little drama in front of Simon and Hammermill?

"Why did you want this meeting?" he demanded suddenly. He was trembling as badly as ever. His palms were wet.

The man didn't respond.

Oh, if only Laura were in this room. She'd know what to say, Reuben thought.

"Are you a man of honor?" Reuben asked.

The lawyers were beside themselves in a frenzy of mumbling that made Reuben think of kettledrums. That's just what it sounded like, kettledrums at the symphony, rumbling under the music.

"Yes," said the man. He appeared utterly genuine, sincere. "If I were not a man of honor," the man sug-gested, "I would not be here."

"Then will you give me your word of honor you're not offended by my dealings with your friend? That you mean me no harm on account of what hap-pened to him, that you'll leave me and my lady friend alone!"

"For the love of heaven!" declared Arthur Ham-mermill. "Are you accusing my client—?"

"I give it," the man said. "You undoubtedly did what you had to do." He reached across the table. But he couldn't reach Reuben's hand. "I give it," he said again, his hand still open, helplessly.

"Yes," said Reuben, struggling to find the words, "I

did what I had to do. I did what I felt driven to do. I did this—with Marrok and in other pressing matters as well."

"Yes," said the man softly. "Truly, I understand."

Reuben drew himself up in the chair. "You want Felix's possessions?" he asked. "You can have them, of course. I only moved to purchase them because I thought it was what Marchent wanted me to do, to take care of them, to see that they were protected, preserved, donated to a library, to the academy, I don't know. Come and get them. Take them. They're yours."

Both lawyers began speaking at once, Simon vigorously protesting that it was too early to reach such an agreement, that sums of money had changed hands having to do with these possessions, that some sort of new inventory was required, something a lot more detailed than had been done; Arthur Hammermill was averring in low, quasi-hostile tones that no one had ever told him that the artifacts were of museum quality, and that they would have to discuss this in detail.

"You may have the possessions," said Reuben, politely ignoring both men.

"Thank you," the man said. "I appreciate this more deeply than I can say."

Simon started shuffling his papers and making notes, and Arthur Hammermill was texting something on his BlackBerry.

"Would you allow me to visit you?" the man asked Reuben.

"Of course," said Reuben. "You could have come anytime. You know where we are. You've obviously always known. I want you to visit. I want you to come! I would love——." He was almost stammering.

The man smiled and nodded.

"I wish I could visit with you now. Unfortunately, I have to go. I haven't much time. I'm expected back in Paris. I'll call you very soon, just as soon as I can."

Reuben felt the tears threatening, tears of relief.

Suddenly the man rose to his feet, and so did Reuben.

They met at the end of the table, and the man clasped Reuben's hand.

"The young reinvent the universe," he said. "And they give the new universe to us as their gift."

"But sometimes the young make terrible mistakes. The young need the wisdom of the old."

The man smiled. "They do and they don't," he said. Then he spoke the words that Reuben had quoted from Teilhard only moments ago. " 'Evil is inevitable in the course of a creation which develops within time.' "

He left with Arthur Hammermill rushing to overtake him.

Simon was in a paroxysm. He attempted to coax Reuben back down into a chair.

"You know your mother wants you to see this doctor and frankly I think that she's got a point." He was winding up for a huge lecture and a full interrogation. This had not gone well, they had to talk about this, no, this had not gone well at all. "And you should call your mother right away."

But Reuben knew it had been a victory.

And he knew as well that there was nothing he could do to clarify things for Simon, or to mollify him, or to reassure him. So he went directly to find Laura, and to leave.

When he came on Laura in the waiting room, the man was with her, holding her right hand in both of his, talking to her in a soft intimate voice.

". . . you will never be in danger from such an intrusion again."

Laura murmured her thanks for his assurances. She was slightly dazed.

Flashing a smile at Reuben, and making a small bow, the man withdrew immediately and disappeared down a corridor of dark paneled doors.

As soon as they were alone in the elevator, Reuben asked, "What did he say to you?"

"That it had been an extraordinary pleasure to meet you," Laura said, "and that he'd been shamed by the actions of his friend, that we'd never be visited by someone like that again, that—." She broke off. She was a little shaken. "It is Felix, isn't it? This man is actually truly Felix Nideck himself."

"Without doubt," said Reuben. "Laura, I think I won the battle, if there was a battle. I think we're in the clear."

On the way to the restaurant for dinner, he recounted the entire conversation as best he could.

"He had to be telling you the truth," Laura said. "He would never have sought me out, spoken to me, if he weren't sincere." A shudder passed through her. "And perhaps he knows all the answers, the answers to everything, and he'll be willing to tell you all he knows."

"Let's hope," said Reuben. But he could hardly contain his happiness and his relief.

They hit the North Beach café well before the dinner rush, and easily scored a table by the glass doors. The rain had slacked off and a blue sky had broken through, which was wonderfully in keeping with Reuben's mood. People were sitting at the outdoor tables in spite of the cold. Columbus Avenue was busy as always. The city seemed bright and fresh, not the grim nightscape he had fled.

He was elated; he couldn't hide it. It was like the break in the rain, the sudden expanding of the blue sky.

When he thought again of Felix standing there, holding Laura's hand and talking to her, he could have cried. He was quietly proud of how attractive she had been in that moment, in her gray wool pants and sweater, sleek and groomed and shining. She'd worn her white hair tied at the nape of her neck with a ribbon as was her custom, and she'd given a beaming smile to Felix as he'd withdrawn.

Reuben looked at her lovingly now. **And you are safe. He will not let anything bad happen to you. He stopped himself to reassure you. He saw how beautiful and gentle and pure you are. You are not me. I am not you. He will not go back on his word.**

He ordered a big Italian meal, salad, minestrone soup, cannelloni, veal, French bread.

He was crunching through his salad, still going over the entire conversation to Laura, when Celeste texted: "SOS. About us."

He texted back: "Tell me."

She wrote: "Are we together or aren't we?"

"The main thing I want," he patiently tapped out with his thumbs, "is for us to remain friends."

If this was brutal, he was so sorry, so very sorry, but he had to say it. It was completely unfair to her to continue as they were.

"Does this mean you don't hate me," she wrote, "for being with Mort?"

"I'm happy you're with Mort." He meant it. He knew Mort was happy; Mort had to be. Mort had always been fascinated by Celeste. If she'd finally accepted Mort in his dusty and wrinkled genius clothes with his bushy hair and forgetful expression, well, this was terrific for both of them.

"Mort's happy too," she shot back.

"Are you happy?"

"I'm happy but I love you and I miss you and I'm worried about you and so is everybody else."

"Then you're still my friend."

"Forever."

"What's new on the Man Wolf?"

"Just what everybody knows."

"Love you. Gotta go."

He put the phone in his pocket. "That's over," he said to Laura. "She's happy; she's having an affair with my best friend."

A little bit of gladness crept into Laura's expression and she smiled.

He wanted to say that he loved her. But he didn't.

He drank his soup now as slowly as he could force himself to drink it.

Laura was actually enjoying the meal too instead of picking at it. Her face now had that steady sweet radiance he hadn't seen in her for days.

"Think about it, what it all means," he said. "We just left a man who—."

He shook his head. He couldn't talk. Tears again. He'd cried more in the presence of Laura than he had ever cried in his whole life in front of his own mother. Well, not quite. "I just want him to help me with this," he insisted. "I want him to . . ."

She reached across the table and took his hand.

"He's going to do that," she said.

He looked into her eyes.

"You'd accept the Chrism, wouldn't you?" he whispered.

She flinched, but her eyes remained fastened on him.

"You mean risk death for it?" she answered. "I don't know." She had a very grave expression on her face. "I share the power because you have the power."

That's not enough, he thought.

# 29

LAURA WAS DRIVING. With his head against the window of the Porsche Reuben slept.

They'd gone by the house before leaving San Francisco. Reuben positively knew that Simon Oliver would find some way to tell Grace or Phil that he'd been in town, and of course it turned out that he was right.

Grace had been fixing dinner, with Phil already at the dining table, and Celeste was there with Mort, standing around in the kitchen, all of them enjoying a glass of wine. A doctor friend of Grace's, a brilliant oncologist whose name Reuben could never remember, was there too, setting the table with another female doctor Reuben had never seen before. The Stan Getz–Charlie Byrd **Jazz Samba** had been playing in the background, and the entire group was obviously having a good time.

Reuben had felt an acute longing for them all, for the cozy house, for the convivial life he'd left behind, but other than that it had been perfect: too many people for an interrogation or an intervention. Everyone greeted Laura graciously, especially Celeste, who was plainly relieved that Reuben was already with someone else, though Mort seemed predictably and loyally miserable, at least when he glanced at Reuben, who just made a fist and punched Mort lightly on the arm. Rosy threw her arms around Reuben.

Grace wanted to corner him, yes, but she couldn't leave the steaks on the broiler, and the broccoli she was sautéing with garlic, and she settled for being kissed tenderly by him and the confidential whisper that he loved her.

"I wish you'd stay, of all nights, I wish you'd stay."

"Mom, we already had supper," he whispered.

"But there is someone coming tonight."

"Mom, I can't."

"Reuben, will you listen to me? I want you to meet this man, Dr. Jaska."

"This isn't the night, Mom," said Reuben and he made for the stairs.

With Rosy's help, Reuben had been able to collect the very last of his books, files, and photographs and load them into the Porsche.

Then he'd taken one last look around the pretty dining room with its many candles on the table and on the mantel, and with a kiss thrown to Grace, he'd started to head out. Phil had given him an affectionate wave.

The doorbell startled him, and he opened the door to see a tall gray-haired man there, not a very old man, really, with hard gray eyes and a square face. He had a curious but very slightly hostile expression.

At once, Grace appeared, drawing the man into

the house with one hand while she held fast to Reuben with the other.

The man didn't take his eyes off Reuben. Clearly, he hadn't expected to come face-to-face with him just yet.

A strange stillness settled over Reuben. A scent came from the man, a very faint scent that Reuben knew only too well.

"And this is Dr. Akim Jaska, Reuben. I've spoken to you about Dr. Jaska," Grace said quickly, awkwardly, uncomfortably. "Come in, Doctor. Rosy, please get the doctor his usual drink."

"Very pleasant to meet you, Dr. Jaska," said Reuben. "I wish I could stay but I can't." He glanced around anxiously for Laura. She was right behind him. She pressed his arm.

The scent was growing stronger as he looked into the man's strangely opaque eyes, and what if the scent triggered the change?

Grace was conflicted, not herself. She seemed to be watching this little exchange intently. "Good-bye, Baby Boy," she said suddenly.

"Right, love you, Mamma," said Reuben.

Laura glided out of the door in front of him.

"Have a pleasant evening, Doctor. Mamma, I'll call."

As he walked down the steps, he felt the faintest spasm in his gut. It was like a warning, the spasm. He wasn't changing. No, he must not change. And he knew he could hold fast against it, but the scent was still in his nostrils. He looked back at the house, and he listened. But all he could hear were pleasantries, and meaningless words. And the scent lingered. The scent even grew a little stronger.

"Let's get on the road," he said.

The traffic had rumbled swiftly over the Golden Gate in the heavy winter darkness, but the rain had not started.

On they traveled. And he slept.

Somehow in his thin but delicious sleep, he knew they were just nearing Santa Rosa.

And when he heard the voices, they were like an ice pick to his brain.

He sat bolt upright.

Never had he heard sharper panic, pain.

"Pull over," he shouted.

The spasms had already begun. His skin was sizzling. The scent of cruelty suffocated him—evil at its most rank.

"Into the trees," he said as they rolled into the nearby park. He was out of his clothes and sprinting through the darkness within seconds, plunging headlong through the prickling transformation as he moved up and into the trees.

Again and again, the cries ignited his blood. These were two young boys, terrified boys, being beaten, in fear of being cruelly mutilated, in fear of dying, and the seething hatred of the executioners poured out in a riff of filthy curses, sexual denunciations, grinding taunts.

They weren't in the park but in the dim long overgrown backyard just off it, behind a darkened ramshackle old house, a gang of four who'd brought the boys here for a slow ritualistic bludgeoning and bloodletting, and as Reuben closed in, he realized one of the two victims was on the edge of his last breath. Sharp scent of blood, of rage, of terror.

He couldn't save the dying boy. He knew it. But he could save the defiant one who was still fighting for his life.

With a gnashing roar he descended on the two who were driving their fists into the belly of this victim who was still resisting them, cursing them, with his whole soul. **Bullies, killers, I spit at you!**

In a boiling tangle of limbs and shrieks, Reuben's jaws champed down on the reeking head of one attacker as his right claw went for the other, snaring him by his hair. The first man, head yanked back, writhed and convulsed, as Reuben's teeth pierced his skull, the man grabbing for the bleeding victim under him, seemingly trying to draw him up as a human shield. With his right paw dragging the other attacker underfoot, Reuben crushed his head into the packed dirt of the yard. Then he clenched with delicious force on the torso of the first attacker, feasting on the scraggling flesh. The struggling victim slipped from the dying attacker's grip.

As always, there was no time to savor this repast. He ripped out the man's throat and was done with it, as the other two members of the gang came on.

With raised knives, they flung themselves at Reuben, trying to rip the hairy "costume" from him, one boy stabbing Reuben twice, three times, with his long knife, as the other sought to cut the "mask" from Reuben's head.

The blood poured out of Reuben. It poured out of his chest, and down into his eyes from the slashes to his head. He was maddened. He clawed the face off one of the men, slashing the carotid artery, and caught the other as he turned and made for the chain-link fence. In a second, the man was dead and Reuben stood still, feasting on the soft meat of his thigh before dropping him and staggering backwards, drunk with the struggle, drunk with the blood. The scent of evil was lifting, evaporating, giving way to the scents of humans swarming in the nearby dark, and the scent of death just behind him.

Lights had gone on in the surrounding houses. There was a jambling of voices—screams in the night. Lights went on in the house above the yard.

Reuben's wounds were a hot palpitating mass of pain, but he could feel them healing, feel the intense tingling above his right eye as the gash healed. In the dimness, he saw the bleeding victim crawling across the filthy trash-strewn yard towards the other—the poor boy who was already dead. The victim knelt beside his friend, shaking him, trying to revive him, and then let out the most anguished howl.

He turned to Reuben, eyes glinting in the darkness, sobbing over and over, "He's dead, they killed him, he's dead, he's dead, he's dead."

Reuben stood there silently looking down at the limp half-naked body. They couldn't have been more than sixteen, either of these boys. The grieving boy climbed to his feet. His face and clothes were covered in blood; he reached out for Reuben, actually reached out for him. Then he fell forward in a dead faint.

Only now as he lay there at Reuben's feet did Reuben see the tiny wounds oozing blood on the back of the boy's outstretched left hand. Puncture wounds! Puncture wounds in the hand, the wrist, and the lower arm. Bite marks.

Reuben was petrified.

The surrounding yards were alive with whispering, gasping spectators. The back door of the house had opened.

Sirens were approaching—again, those unfurling ribbons of sound, sharp as steel.

Reuben stepped backwards.

Flashing lights strobed the heavy damp clouds and broke around the borders of the house, luridly illuminating its hulking sagging shape against the sky, and the filth and ruin of the yard.

Reuben turned and leapt over the fence, and moved swiftly, silently, through the darkness, dropping to all fours as he cleared a mile of the woods and then another mile, spotting ahead of him the Porsche as he'd left it, under the trees. His arms flashing out before him felt like forelegs, and his speed astonished him.

Yet he had to call for the transformation.

**Leave me now, you know what I need, give me back my former shape.**

He crouched down beside the car, gasping for breath, working with the spasms, as the thick wolf-coat dropped away. His chest wounds burned, pulsed, and the hair stayed thick there, full of blood. Same over his right eye, a hank of thick wolf-hair. His claws were retracting, vanishing. With long gnarled fingers he reached for the wounds and tugged at the thick hair there which remained. His bare legs felt weak, his bare feet unsure, his hands clutching for the door of the car as he lost his balance and fell down on one knee.

Laura was beside him, steadying him, helping him into the passenger seat. The patches of hair on his chest and forehead seemed infinitely more monstrous than the full transformation, but the blood had already coagulated into a thick flaking varnish. The skin positively burned over the wounds. Ripples of dizzying pleasure encircled his head as if two hands were massaging him.

As Laura drove for the freeway, he pulled his shirt on again, and his pants. And with his left hand over the throbbing chest wounds, he felt the wolf-hair shrinking, finally falling loose. Only the soft under-fur remained. Both wolf-hair and fur were gone from his forehead.

There came the rolling darkness to drown him, take him away. He fought it, his head thumping against the window, a low moan coming from his lips.

Sirens; they were like banshees wailing, shrill, hideous. But the Porsche was moving north again, gaining the freeway, joining the thumping shuddering flow of winking, gleaming red taillights ahead, gliding from one lane to another, and finally moving at top speed.

He lay back staring at Laura. In the flashing lights, she appeared utterly calm, eyes fastened on the road.

"Reuben?" she said, not daring to take her eyes off the traffic. "Reuben, talk to me. Reuben, please."

"I'm all right, Laura," he said. He sighed. One shiver after another passed through him. His teeth were chattering. The fur was gone now from the chest wounds, and the wounds were gone too. The skin sang. The pleasure washed through him, exhausting him. The scent of death was still clinging to him, the death of the boy crumpled in the yard, scent of innocent death.

"I've done something terrible, unspeakable!" he whispered. He tried to say more but all he could hear from his own lips was another moan.

"What are you saying?" she asked. The traffic ripped and rattled ahead and behind them. They were already leaving the city of Santa Rosa.

He closed his eyes again. No pain now. Only a low fever pulsing in his face and in the palms of his hands, and in the smooth flesh where the pain had been.

"A terrible thing, Laura," he whispered, but she couldn't hear him. He saw the boy again staggering towards him, a tall broad-chested child with a pale beseeching face, a torn and bleeding face, with a mop of blond hair around it, eyes wide with horror, lips moving, saying nothing. The darkness came. And he welcomed it, the leather bucket seat cradling him, the car rocking him as they drove on.

# 30

THE LIGHTS of the big room dazzled him. The central heat pouring from the vents was too warm, the fragrances of the house dusty, close, intoxicating, even suffocating.

At once, he went into the library and made a call to the Clift Hotel in San Francisco. He had to speak to Felix. He was choked with shame. Only Felix could help him with what he had done, and ashamed as he was, as mortified and miserable, he could not rest until he had confessed this horror to Felix, that he'd bungled, that he'd passed the Chrism.

Felix was no longer there, said the clerk at the desk. Felix had checked out that afternoon. "May I ask who is calling?" He was about to hang up in despair, but identified himself in the faint hope there would be some message. There was.

"Yes, he said to tell you that he was called away. Urgent business he couldn't ignore. But that he would return as soon as he could."

No number, no address.

He sank down in the chair with his head on the desk, forehead against the green blotter. After a moment, he picked up the phone and called Simon

Oliver, leaving the desperate plea on voice mail that Oliver get in touch with Arthur Hammermill and find out if he had an emergency number for Felix Nideck. It was urgent, urgent, urgent. Simon could not imagine how urgent.

Nothing to be done; nothing to alleviate this unspeakable panic. Will this boy die? Will the Chrism kill him? Was that despicable Marrok telling the truth when he said the Chrism could kill?

He had to find Felix!

Again, he saw the boy collapsed in the dirt of that yard, his outstretched hand, and the wound.

Lord, God!

He stared at the smiling figure of Felix in the photograph. **Dear God, please help me. Don't let that poor kid die. Please. And don't let—.**

He couldn't endure this panic.

Laura was there, watching him, waiting, sensing something was dreadfully wrong.

He grabbed Laura in his arms, and ran his hands over the thick gray sweater she wore, clutching at the high neck under her chin, then ran his hands down her long pants; warm enough.

**I want to change, now, go back into the night. Now.**

Holding tight to her, he felt the wolf-coat erupt again. He let go of her only long enough to take off his clothes. The fur was insulating him from the heat of the room, his nostrils as always picking up the heady scent of the forest that pressed against the windows. Ecstasy this, these jarring volcanic waves that almost swept him off his feet.

He lifted her and went out the back door of the house into the night, the transformation now complete, and with her secure against his left shoulder he sped through the forest, bent forward, springing on his powerful thighs, until he'd left the oak wood behind and was now among the giant redwoods.

"Wrap yourself around me," he breathed into her ear, guiding her arms around his neck, and her legs around his torso. "We're going up, are you game for it?"

"Yes," she cried.

Up and up he climbed until he was in the high branches, beyond the ivy and the straggling vines, up and up, higher until the lower trees were lost, and he could see the sea now above the bluffs, the endless, sparkling sea under the ghostly white of the hidden moon, and finally he found a bed of twisted branches strong enough to hold them. He sat back, his left arm firmly locked around the branch above him, his right arm cradling her.

She was laughing under her breath, delirious with the joy of it. She kissed him all over his face where he could feel it, his eyelids, the tip of his nose, against the side of his mouth.

"Hang on tight," he cautioned her. Then he eased her just a little to the right, so that she sat on his right thigh and his right arm firmly held her. "Can you see the sea?" he asked.

"Yes," she said. "But only as utter blackness, and because I know it's there and I know what it is."

He was breathing easy against the trunk of the monstrous tree. He was listening to the chorus of the woodlands; the canopy seethed and sighed and whispered. Far to the south he could see the lights of the house winkling through the trees, as if they were so many tiny stars, snared in its many windows. Down there, way down there in the world, the house full of light, waiting for them.

She laid her head on his chest.

For the longest time, they remained that way, together, up there, and he looked out at the sea and saw nothing at all but the shimmering water and the inky sky above it and the faintest stars. The clouds gathered and broke over the moon, sustaining that illusion that the moon was again and again burning its way through the clouds. The damp salty wind whispered and blew in the tall trees around them.

Just for a moment, he sensed danger. Or was it merely the presence of some other creature near them? He wasn't sure, but he was certain that he could not communicate this sudden alarm to Laura. She was totally dependent on him here. Quietly he listened.

Maybe it was only the inevitable rustling of the canopy, and possibly some fleet little beast he didn't know wending its way nearby. The vesper bats were at these heights, the flying squirrels, the chickadee and the chipmunk could spend their lives in these upper branches. But why would such little things have awakened his protective spirit? Whatever it was, it was gone, and he thought to himself that it was because he had her here, her heart beating against his heart, that he had felt such a vague alarm at all.

All was well around them.

He thought of the boy. He was in agony.

Unspeakable, all this.

He begged the forest to hold him close, to protect him from the merciless sharpness of his own conscience. A long time ago in his short life, the voice of conscience had been the voice of Grace, Phil, Jim, and Celeste. But that was no longer the way it was at all. And now his own conscience sank the knife into his soul.

**Heal this, if you can with all your secret boiling power! Morphenkind, what have you done to that boy? Will he survive only to become what you are?**

At last, he couldn't stand these thoughts anymore. The sublime peace of these leafy heights was paling in the heat of his misery. He had to move, and he began to climb from tree to tree, with her arms and legs once more locked to him. They moved on in a great arc through the woods, and slowly back to the edge of the redwood forest. As always, she weighed nothing; she was fragrant and sweet as if he carried bundles of flowers close to him for their luscious scent. His tongue sought out her neck, her cheek, his growls turned to low moans serenading her.

She locked her arms and legs even tighter around him again, and he descended into the warmer closer air of the lower forest.

Her hands felt icy. Even he could feel this, feel the iciness as if it was smoke coming from her hands.

He walked slowly through the great generous gray-barked oaks, carrying her, stopping here and there so they could kiss, so he could move his left paw under her sweater and feel the hot silky naked flesh there, so moist, so bare, so redolent of citrus and blossoms he couldn't name and the stark searing scent of her living flesh. He lifted her up and suckled her breasts as she sighed.

Once inside the house, he laid her down on the great long dining room table. He held her icy hands between his paws, his warm paws, weren't they warm? The room was dark. The house creaked and sighed against the pummeling of the ocean wind. Light fell languidly through the alcove from the great room.

For a long moment he looked at her, lying there waiting for him, her hair loose and snagged with bits of aromatic leaf or petal, her eyes large and drowsy yet fixed on him.

Then he gave the match to the oak wood that was built up in the fireplace. The kindling crackled, exploded, and the flames leapt. The eerie light danced on the coffered ceiling. It danced in the high lacquer of the tabletop.

She began to remove her clothes, but he begged

her with a quiet gesture to stop. Then he took them off of her, rolling back the sweater and pulling it gently away, and pulling loose the pants and throwing them aside. She kicked off her shoes.

The sight of her naked on the bare table maddened him wondrously. He ran the soft side of his paws under her naked feet. He caressed her naked calves. "Don't let me hurt you," he whispered in that low voice, so familiar to him now, now so much a part of him. "Tell me if I hurt you."

"You never hurt me," she whispered. "You can't hurt me."

"Tender throat, tender belly," he growled, licking her with his long tongue, soft under-paws lifting her breasts. **Get thee behind me, tragedy.** Kneeling over her, he lifted her and impaled her gently on his sex and the room went dim around him, the fire roaring and crackling in his ears, his mind filled with nothing but her, till it was no mind at all.

Afterwards, he picked her up and carried her up the stairs and down the hollow hallway—such a long walk in the secretive dark—to the warmer air of their bedroom. Perfume; candles. It was so very dim here, so very silent.

He laid her down on the bed, a shadow against the pale whiteness of the sheets, and sat beside her. Without fanfare he closed his eyes and brought the change. A little fire burst inside his chest; the air itself seemed to lift the wolf-coat, soften it, dissolve it. The orgasmic waves rocked him violently but quickly. Then the fur began to melt away, his skin drew breath, and he looked down again at his hands, his familiar hands.

"I did a terrible thing tonight," he said.

"What was it?" She clasped his arm and pressed it gently.

"I injured that boy, that boy I was trying to save. I think I passed the Chrism."

She said nothing. Her shadowy face was a picture of understanding and compassion, and what a marvel that was, because he expected neither from anyone. Hoping for something is not the same as expecting it.

"And what if he dies?" he asked with a sigh. "What if I've shed innocent blood? Or what if the best of all possible outcomes is that he becomes what I am?"

# 31

THE STORY EXPLODED on the morning news, not because the Man Wolf had had the temerity to go to the northern city of Santa Rosa and shred four vicious killers, but because the surviving victim was already famous.

As the juvenile victim of a near-fatal attack, his identity was protected, but by 5:00 a.m. he had called the press from his hospital bed, and given his version of the story out to several reporters.

His name was Stuart McIntyre, a sixteen-year-old high school graduate who six months before had made international headlines by insisting on taking a male date to his senior prom at Blessed Sacrament Catholic Academy in Santa Rosa. The school had not only said no to Stuart's request, but stripped him of the title of valedictorian, thereby denying him the right to make the key speech on graduation night, and Stuart had taken his case to the media, granting interviews by phone and e-mail to anybody and everybody who was interested.

This had not been the first gay activist cause of which Stuart was a champion. But his greatest claim to fame before the prom crisis had been his success as a high school actor, persuading Blessed Sacrament to put on a full-scale production of **Cyrano de Bergerac,** just so that he could ably play the lead in it, which he had, to good reviews.

As soon as Reuben saw Stuart on the news he recognized him. Stuart had a square face, a sprinkling of freckles across his broad nose and cheeks, and a huge mop of unruly blond hair that suggested a halo. His eyes were blue and his habitual smile was a bit mischievous. It was actually a grin. His was a likable and at times pretty face. The camera loved him.

Reuben had just begun reporting for the **Observer** when Stuart became a local celebrity, and Reuben had never paid much attention to the story, except to be amused that this plucky kid thought he could convince a Catholic high school to let him take his boyfriend to the prom.

The "boyfriend," Antonio Lopez, had been the unfortunate kid murdered last night by the four gay bashers, who had, by the way, expressed their intent, to the boys and to others, to mutilate both victims postmortem.

By noon, the story was huge, again, not only because the seeming "invincible" Man Wolf had intervened, saving Stuart's life, but because the person behind the gay bashing was rumored to be Stuart's stepfather, a golf instructor named Herman Buckler. Two of the killers had been brothers-in-law of the dead boy, Antonio, and other members of their family spilled the story fingering the stepfather as the man who had masterminded the attack to get rid of his stepson.

Stuart also told police that his stepfather had set up the attack, and that the young men who had tried to kill him had told him as much.

There was more. Stuart's mother, a bottle-blond named Buffy Longstreet, had been a teen actress in a short-lived sitcom for a few years, and Stuart's father had been a computer tech genius who made a killing in Silicon Valley before the dot-com crash, leaving Stuart well off and the mother moderately comfortable when he died of an infection in Salvador da Bahia while on a dream trip to the Amazon. The stepfather's crime had been for the money all right and because he devoutly hated Stuart. He was denying everything, and threatened to sue Stuart.

Stuart was now a student at the University of San Francisco, living alone in his own Haight-Ashbury apartment three blocks from the school, and had been back in Santa Rosa for a visit with his boyfriend, Antonio, at the time of the gay bashing. Stuart's whole goal in life, or so he repeatedly told the press, was to become a lawyer and work for human rights. He was a frequent guest on radio talk shows by call-in, and he was the first survivor of a Man Wolf encounter willing to talk to the press directly since Susan Larson had spoken to Reuben at the offices of the **San Francisco Observer.**

Reuben was processing all this as rapidly as he could when he was interrupted by two officers from the Mendocino sheriff's department who wanted again to talk to him about the Man Wolf, and whether or not he had remembered anything more about that terrible night when Marchent had died. Did he know the Man Wolf had struck in Santa Rosa?

The interview was brief because Reuben actually didn't remember "anything more" about that terrible night. And both officers really wanted to express their fury that people were not getting to the bottom of this Man Wolf thing by catching this maniac before he took a chunk out of an innocent person.

Five minutes after they had left, Reuben was interrupted again by a phone call on his cell from Stuart.

"You know who I am," came the energetic voice through the phone. "Well, listen, I just got off the phone with your editor, Billie Kale, and I read the piece you did on that woman, the first person to ever really see the Man Wolf. I wanna talk to you. I really do. If you're the least bit interested, please come to Santa Rosa. They won't let me out of here right now. And look, if you're not into this, okay, but I need to know now because I want to call someone else if you're not, all right? So yes or no, what do you think? Otherwise I'm calling your editor back, she said this was a long shot—."

"Stop. Tell me exactly where you are. I am coming."

"Oh, my God, I thought I was talking to your machine. It's you? Cool. I'm at St. Mark's Hospital in Santa Rosa. And hurry because they're threatening to shut me down."

By the time Reuben got there, Stuart had started to run a fever and Reuben wasn't permitted to see him.

Reuben decided to wait, no matter whether it was a couple of hours or a couple of days, and finally, about two o'clock, he did get in to see the boy. By that time, Reuben had texted Grace twice urging her to get in touch with the Santa Rosa doctors and "share" whatever protocol she'd used with Reuben, just in case the kid had been scratched or bitten, who knew?

Grace was reluctant to take that initiative. She texted back: "Nobody said anything about the kid being bitten."

But the kid had been bitten.

When Reuben walked in, Stuart was propped up on a mound of pillows and had two different packages of IV fluids pumping into his veins. There were bandages on his face and on his left hand and arm, and probably more bandages under his hospital gown, but he was making a "miraculous" recovery. He was drinking a chocolate milk shake, and grinning. The freckles and the big laughing eyes made Reuben think of Huck Finn and Tom Sawyer.

"I got bitten!" Stuart said, holding up his bandaged left hand, with the tubes dangling from it. "I'm going to turn into a werewolf." He broke into seemingly uncontrollable laughter.

Pain meds, Reuben thought.

Stuart's mother, Buffy Longstreet, a fatally cute blond who had the same plump freckled cheeks as her son and a tiny upturned plastic surgery nose, was sitting in the corner with her arms folded staring at her son with a combination of fascination and horror.

"Seriously, let me tell you right now," declared Stuart, "if this guy is wearing a costume, which nobody sane has the slightest doubt of, it's a primo number. I mean this is the costume to end all costumes, and the guy has got to be on PCP, because there's no other drug that can give a guy that kind of strength. I mean this guy rushes in where angels fear to tread. You wouldn't believe this guy in action.

"Myself, I am not ruling out that this is some unknown species of animal. But I'll tell you my pet theory, no pun intended."

"Which is what?" asked Reuben, but in truth this was the type of interview where the reporter does not have to ask any questions.

"Okay," said Stuart, jabbing a thumb in the direction of his own chest, "this is what I personally think is happening with this guy. I think he's a normal human being to whom something horrible happened. I mean, forget the werewolf crap, it's getting old, it's going nowhere, and we've seen the mugs and the T-shirts. What I mean is, this guy got some kind of infection or disease—like acromegalyia-something-or-other—and it changed him into this monster. Now, my father went to the Amazon which was his big dream, I mean, all-time huge dream to go to the Amazon, go down the river, walk in the jungle, whatever, and he got an infection that within one week destroyed his pancreas and his kidneys. He died in a Brazilian hospital."

"That's horrible," murmured Reuben.

"Oh, yeah, right, it was. But this, this creature has had something like that happen to him. The hair, the bone growths—."

"What bone growths?" asked Reuben.

"He's got huge bony hands, bony feet, bony forehead, you know. There are diseases that produce this kind of growth, and in his case he's covered with shaggy hair on top of it. He's isolated like the Phantom of the Opera, like the Elephant Man, like a freak in a carnival, like Claude Rains in **The Invisible Man,** and he's out of his mind. And this guy has feelings! I mean intense feelings. You should have seen him standing there looking at Antonio. I mean he was just staring and staring at Antonio. And he put his own hands up, like this, oops, almost pulled out the IV, shit—."

"It's okay. You didn't."

"He put his hands up to his head like this, like the sight of Antonio lying there dead—."

"Stuart, stop!" screamed his mother. Her tiny little body squirmed in the chair. "You're just going on and on and on!"

"No, no, no, Mom, I am talking to a reporter. This is an interview. If this guy did not want to hear about Antonio and what happened, he wouldn't be here. Mom, can you get me another milk shake? Please, please?"

"Gaaaarrrrr!" said his mother and rushed out of the room on her spike heels. Beautiful body, without question.

"Now," said Stuart, "we can really talk, can't we? I mean she's driving me crazy. My stepfather beats the hell out of her and she blames it on me. Me. I'm the one to blame for his slashing her entire closet full of clothes with a box cutter, me!"

"What else do you remember about the attack?" Reuben asked. It was inconceivable that this ruddy, bright-eyed boy could die from the Chrism or from anything.

"Strong, unbelievably strong," Stuart replied. "And these guys stabbed him too. I saw that! Saw that! I mean they really stabbed him. He didn't even flinch, man. He just tore them apart. I mean tore them apart. I mean we are talking gross, man. I mean we're talking cannibalism here. They're not letting witnesses talk to the press, but they can't stop me. I know my rights under the Constitution. I cannot be stopped from talking to the press."

"Right. What else?" asked Reuben.

Stuart shook his head. Suddenly his eyes watered and he turned into a six-year-old right before Reuben's eyes and started sobbing.

"I'm so sorry they killed your friend," said Reuben.

But the boy was inconsolable.

Reuben stood by the bed with his arm around him for fifteen minutes.

"You know what I'm really afraid of?" the boy asked.

"What?"

"They're going to get this guy, the Man Wolf, and

really hurt him. They'll shoot him up with a machine gun, they'll club him like a baby seal. I don't know. They'll really hurt him. He's not a human being to them. He's an animal. They'll pump him full of lead the way they did Bonnie and Clyde. I mean they were human beings, yes, but they pumped them full of bullets like they were animals."

"Right."

"And they'll never know what went on in the guy's mind. They'll never know who he really is or was or why he does what he does."

"Does your hand hurt?"

"No. But I wouldn't know if it was on fire. I have so much Valium and Vicodin in me right now that—."

"Gotcha. Been there. Okay. What else do you want to tell me?"

For half an hour, they talked about Antonio and his macho in-law cousins and how much they'd hated him because he was gay, and hated Stuart, whom they blamed for Antonio "becoming" gay; they talked about his stepfather Herman Buckler who paid the guys who'd kidnapped Antonio and Stuart, and wanted to kill and mutilate them both; they talked about Santa Rosa, about Blessed Sacrament High School, and they talked about what it means to be a really really great criminal lawyer, like Clarence Darrow, who was Stuart's hero, and he would take the cases of the marginalized, the neglected, the despised.

Stuart started crying again. "Must be the drugs," he said. He crumpled up again like a little child.

His mom came in with the chocolate milk shake.

"You're going to get sick, drinking this!" she said with a vengeance, slamming it down on the bedside tray.

When the nurse appeared, she discovered that Stuart had a temperature again and said Reuben had to go. Yes, she said, they were giving him the rabies treatment, of course, and a cocktail of antibiotics that ought to take care of anything contagious from this wolf being. But Reuben had to go now.

"The 'wolf being,'" said Stuart, "that really has a nice ring. Hey, will you come back, or do you pretty much have your whole story?"

"I'd like to come back tomorrow, and see how you are," said Reuben. He gave Stuart his cards, with the Mendocino address and number written on the back. He wrote all his numbers down for Stuart in his hardcover copy of **Game of Thrones.**

On the way out, Reuben left his card at the nurses' station. If there is any change, please call, he asked. If he thought about this kid actually dying, he would break down right then and there.

He caught the attending physician, Dr. Angie Cutler, right outside the elevator and urged her to contact Grace in San Francisco, since he'd been through all this with his mother handling the case. He tried to be as tactful about this as he could, but he was inwardly convinced by now that his mother's treatment of him probably helped him to survive. Dr. Cutler was a lot more responsive than he'd expected. She was younger than Grace, knew Grace, and respected her. She was kind of sweet. Reuben gave her his card. "Call me anytime about this," he said, murmuring something about what he himself had experienced.

"I know all about you," said Dr. Cutler with an inviting smile. "I'm glad you came to see that boy. He's crawling the walls in there. But he does have marvelous recuperative powers; it's a miracle. If you had seen the bruises on him when they brought him in."

On the way down in the elevator, he called Grace and urged her please to connect with the doctor. The kid had been bitten. It was true.

His mother was silent for a moment. Then she said in a strained voice,

"Reuben, if I were to tell this doctor the things I observed in your case, I'm not sure I'd have much cred with her at all."

"I know that, Mom, I understand. I know," he said. "But there just could be some really important things you could share with her, you know, about the antibiotics you used, the rabies treatment, whatever you did in my case that might help this boy."

"Reuben, I can't really call the boy's doctor out of the blue. The only person who's been the least interested in what I actually observed in your case was this Dr. Jaska, and you wouldn't give him the time of day."

"Yeah, Mom, I realize. But I'm talking now about the kid getting treatment for the bite, that's all."

A chill came over him.

He was walking out of the hospital now to the car, and the rain had started up again.

"Mom, I'm sorry I didn't stay and talk to Dr. Jaska. I know you wanted me to. And maybe if it will make you feel better, I can talk to the man soon."

**And if I had stayed, well, then by the time I'd passed Santa Rosa, Stuart McIntyre would have been dead.**

There was such a long silence that he feared he'd lost the connection, but then Grace spoke up again, and she sounded like somebody else with Grace's voice.

"Reuben, why have you gone up to Mendocino County? What's really the matter with you?"

How could he respond?

"Mamma, not now, please. I've been here all day. If you could just call the doctor, just volunteer, you know, that you handled a case like this one—."

"Well, listen. You have to take the final rabies shot tomorrow. You know that, right?"

"I completely forgot."

"Well, Reuben, I've left messages for you every day for a week. It's twenty-eight days tomorrow and you have to have the final shot. Does this beautiful young woman, Laura, have a phone? Does she answer it? Could I perhaps be leaving messages with her?"

"I'm going to get better at all this, I swear."

"Okay, listen to me. We were going to send the nurse up there with the shot, but if you like, I can contact this doctor in Santa Rosa and arrange for her to give it to you tomorrow morning, when you visit this boy. I could strike up a conversation with her, and if there is anything I know that would be of use to her, anything that I'm willing to share, that is, well, let's just see what develops."

"Mom, that would be perfect. You are my peach of a mother. But does this mean it's actually been twenty-eight days since that night?"

It seemed a century had passed; his life had been so completely altered. And it had only been twenty-eight days.

"Yes, Reuben, that's when my beloved son, Reuben Golding, disappeared and you took his place."

"Mamma, I adore you. I will somehow in time answer all questions and solve all problems and bring harmony back to the world we share."

She laughed. "Now that does sound like my Baby Boy."

She rang off.

He was standing beside the car.

A strange feeling came over him, unpleasant but not terrible. He imagined a future, in a flash, in which he was sitting with his mother in front of the fire in the great room at Nideck Point and he was telling her everything. He imagined their speaking to one another in intimate tones, and that he shared this thing with her, and she welcomed it, and enfolded him with her expertise, her knowledge, her unique intuition.

There was no Dr. Akim Jaska in this little world, or anybody else. Just him and Grace. Grace knew, Grace understood, Grace would help him grasp what was happening to him, Grace would be there.

But that was impossible, rather like imagining angels over his bed in the dark at night, guarding him, with wings that arched to the rafters.

And when he imagined his mother in this tête-à-tête, she took on a sinister coloration that terrified him. There was a malevolent gleam in her eye in his mind, and her face was half in shadow.

He shuddered.

That could never be.

This was a secret thing, and could be shared perhaps with Felix Nideck, and always, and forever, as long as that might be, with Laura. But not with anyone else . . . except perhaps that chipper, bright-eyed boy with the freckles and the grin who was upstairs now healing miraculously. Time to go home, home to Laura, home to Nideck Point. Never had it seemed so like a refuge.

He found Laura in the kitchen making a large salad. She said one of the things she did when she was worried was make a large salad.

She'd rinsed and dried the romaine lettuce with paper towels. She had a large square wooden bowl rubbed with oil and with freshly cut garlic. The smell of the garlic was tantalizing.

Now she broke the lettuce into crisp bite-sized

pieces, and she tossed the pieces in olive oil till they were glistening. There was quite a pile of these bits of lettuce, glistening.

She gave the wooden spoons to Reuben and asked him to toss the lettuce slowly. Then she put the finely chopped green onions in and the herbs, taking out pinches of each herb—oregano, thyme, basil—and rubbing each pinch between her hands as she sprinkled it over the salad. The herbs clung perfectly to the glistening leaves. Then she added the wine vinegar and Reuben tossed more and then she served up this salad with sliced avocados and thin sliced tomatoes, and soft warm French bread from the oven, and they ate it together.

The sparkling water in the crystal glasses looked like champagne.

"Feel better?" he asked. He'd eaten the largest plate of salad he'd ever been served in his life.

She said yes. She was eating daintily, looking now and then at her freshly polished silver fork. She said she'd never seen silver like this old silver, so heavily and deeply carved.

He stared out the window at the oaks.

"What's wrong?" she asked.

"What isn't?" he asked. "Want to know something terrible? I've lost track completely of how many people I've killed. I have to get a pen and paper and make a count. I don't know how many nights it's been either, I mean how many nights I've been changing. I have to make a count of that. And I have to write, write in a secret diary, all the little things I've been noticing."

Strange thoughts were running through his mind. He knew he couldn't continue this way. It was virtually impossible. He wondered what it would be like to be in a foreign land, a lawless land where there was evil to hunt in hills and valleys, where no one kept track of the number you killed or how many nights you did it. He thought of vast cities like Cairo and Bangkok and Bogotá, and of vast countries with endless tracts of land and forest.

After a while, he said:

"That boy. Stuart. I think he's going to make it. I mean he's not going to die. Whatever else will happen I don't know. I can't know. If only I could talk to Felix. I'm putting too much hope on talking to Felix."

"He'll come back," she said.

"I want to remain here tonight. I want to stay indoors. I don't want the change to come. Or if it does, I want to be alone with it in the forest, the way I was in Muir Woods that night when I met you."

"I understand," she said. "And you're afraid, afraid that you can't control it. I mean that you won't stay here alone with it."

"I never even tried," he said. "That's shameful. I have to try. And I have to go back down to Santa Rosa in the morning."

It was already getting dark. The last rays of the

western sun had vanished from the forest and the deep dark blue shadows were broadening and thickening. The rain came, light, shimmering beyond the panes.

After a while, he went into the library and called the Santa Rosa hospital. The nurse said Stuart was running a high fever, but was otherwise "holding his own."

He had a text from Grace. The final rabies shot had been set up with Dr. Angie Cutler, Stuart's doctor, for tomorrow morning at ten o'clock.

The night had closed in around the house.

He stared at the large photograph of the gentlemen on the wall—at Felix, at Margon Sperver, at all of them, gathered there against the tropical forest. Were they all beasts like him? Did they all gather to hunt together, to exchange secrets? Or was Felix actually the only one?

**I suspect Felix Nideck was betrayed.**

What could that have meant? That Abel Nideck had somehow plotted his uncle's demise, even somehow collected money for it, and kept this knowledge from his devoted daughter Marchent?

Vainly, Reuben searched the Internet for the living Felix Nideck, but could find nothing. But what if, in returning to Paris, Felix had reentered another identity, at which Reuben couldn't even guess?

The evening news said that Stuart's stepfather had been released on bail. Taciturn police admitted to reporters that he was "a person of interest," not a suspect in the case. Stuart's mother was protesting that her husband was innocent.

The Man Wolf had been spotted in Walnut Creek and Sacramento. People reported seeing him in Los Angeles. And a woman in Fresno claimed to have taken his picture. A couple in San Diego claimed to have been rescued by the Man Wolf from an attempted assault, though they did not get a clear look at anyone involved. Police were investigating a number of sightings in the vicinity of Lake Tahoe.

The California attorney general had convened a special task force to deal with the Man Wolf, and a commission of scientists had been formed to study all forensic evidence.

Crime had not slacked off due to the Man Wolf. No, the authorities were not willing to say that at all; but the police said that it had. The streets of Northern California were relatively quiet just now.

"He could be anywhere," said a cop in Mill Valley.

Reuben went to the computer and tapped out his story on Stuart McIntyre for the **Observer,** again leaning heavily on Stuart's own rich descriptions of what had happened in the attack. He included Stuart's theories as to the mysterious illness of the monster; and as in the past he closed with heavy editorial emphasis on the impossible moral problem posed by the Man Wolf—that he was judge, jury, and executioner of those he massacred and that society could not embrace him as a superhero.

We cannot admire his brute intervention, or his savage cruelty. He is the enemy of all we hold sacred, and therefore he is our personal enemy, not our friend. That he has again rescued an innocent victim from almost certain annihilation is, tragically, incidental. He cannot be thanked for this any more than an erupting volcano or an earthquake can be thanked for whatever good may follow in its wake. Speculation as to his personality, his ambitions, or even his motives must remain just that, speculation, and nothing more. We celebrate what we can—that Stuart McIntyre is alive and safe.

It was not an original piece or an inspired piece, but it was solid. And what drove it was the personality of Stuart, the seemingly invincible freckle-faced teen star of **Cyrano de Bergerac** who had survived a near-fatal gay bashing to talk to reporters personally from his hospital bed. Reuben only noted the "bite" in passing, because Stuart had only noted it in passing. No one was attaching significance to the fact that Reuben himself had been bitten. The drama of the bite was not playing out in the public eye.

Reuben and Laura went upstairs, got into the high-backed bed, and cuddled together watching a beautiful French film, Cocteau's **Beauty and the Beast,** and Reuben's eyes grew heavy with sleep. It disturbed him actually to see the Beast talking so eloquently in French to Beauty. The Beast wore velvet clothes and fine lace shirts, and had glistening eyes. Beauty was fair and gentle like Laura.

He began to dream, and in his dream he was running in full wolf-coat through an endless field of blowing grass, his forelegs bounding effortlessly before him. And beyond lay the forest, the great dark never-ending forest. There were cities mixed up in the forest, glass towers rising as high as the Douglas fir and the giant sequoia, buildings festooned with ivy and trailing vines, and the great oaks swarming over many-storied houses with peaked roofs and smoking chimneys. All the world had become the forest of trees and towers. **Ah, this is paradise,** he sang as he climbed higher and higher.

He wanted to wake and tell Laura about the dream, but he'd lose the dream if he woke, if he stirred at all, because the dream was as fragile as mist and yet utterly real to him. Night came, and the towers were covered in glowing lights, sparkling and winking amid the dark trunks of the trees and the immense branches.

"Paradise," he whispered.

He opened his eyes. She was leaning on her elbow looking down at him. The ghostly light from the television illuminated her face, her moist lips. Why would she want him the way he was now, just a young man, a very young man, with hands as delicate as his mother's?

But she did. She began to kiss him roughly, her fingers closing on his left nipple, shocking him with immediate desire. She was playing with his skin as he'd played with hers. Her oval-tipped fingernails scratched playfully at his face, fingers finding his teeth, pinching a little at his lips. Her weight felt good to him, the tickle of her hair falling down. It felt good, naked flesh against naked flesh, and this soft moist slippery flesh, yes, against his flesh, yes. **I love you, Laura.**

He awoke just as the sun was rising.

This was the tenth night since the transformation had first happened, and this was the first night that he had not experienced the change. He was relieved, but he felt curiously unsettled, that he had missed something of vital importance, that he had been expected somewhere and he had failed to appear, that he was not being true to something inside him that felt like, but was not, conscience.

# 32

SEVEN NIGHTS PASSED before Reuben got in to see Stuart again.

Reuben was able to get his own final rabies shot from Dr. Cutler as agreed, but Dr. Cutler just couldn't let anyone near Stuart until the fever was under control, among other things. She was in contact with Grace, and very grateful to Reuben for that connection.

If Grace had not been attending the boy from then on, even coming up to Santa Rosa to see him personally and confer with Reuben personally, Reuben would have gone mad from the suspense. Dr. Cutler took his calls, and was more than friendly, but she wasn't going to chat freely. She did let slip that Stuart was experiencing a remarkable growth spurt and she couldn't quite figure it out. Of course the boy was only sixteen. The epiphyseal plates hadn't closed yet, but still, she'd never seen anyone physically grow the way this boy was growing. And the growth spurt was affecting his hair too.

Reuben was frantic to see him, but absolutely nothing he said could change Dr. Cutler's mind.

Grace was infinitely more forthcoming as long as not a single word of what she confided saw print.

Reuben swore absolute confidentiality. **I just want him to be all right, to live, to survive, to be as if none of this happened to him.**

Feverish, at times incoherent, Stuart was not only surviving but thriving, Grace said, exhibiting all the same symptoms Reuben had exhibited, bruises vanishing, ribs completely healed, skin glistening with health, and the boy's body experiencing the baffling growth spurt, as Dr. Cutler had described.

"It's all happening faster with him," Grace said. "Much faster. But then he's so damned young. Just a few years makes such a remarkable difference."

Stuart had broken out in a terrible rash from the antibiotics and then the rash had simply vanished. Not to worry, Grace said. The fever and delirium were frightening but there was no infection and the boy came out of it for hours every day, long enough to demand to see people, to threaten to break out of the window if he didn't get his cell phone and computer, and to fight with his mother who wanted him to exonerate his stepfather completely. He claimed to be hearing voices, to know things about what was going on in buildings surrounding the hospital, to be agitated, eager to get out of bed, uncooperative. He was afraid of his stepfather, afraid of him hurting his mother. Invariably the staff sedated him.

"She's an awful woman, this mother," Grace confided. "She's jealous of her son. She blames him for the stepfather's rages. She treats him like a pesky little brother who's ruining her life with her new boyfriend. And the boy doesn't get how childish she really is, and it makes me sick."

"I remember her," Reuben murmured.

But Grace was as adamant as everyone else that Reuben couldn't see Stuart. No visitors were allowed just now. It was all they could do to hold off the sheriff and the police, and the attorney general's office. So how could she make an exception for Reuben?

"They upset him with their questions," she said.

Reuben understood.

They came to Nideck Point four times during the week, pressing for information, as Reuben sat patiently on the couch by the big fireplace explaining again and again that he had seen nothing of "the beast" that attacked him. Over and over again, he led them to the hallway where the attack had taken place. He showed them the windows that had been bashed out. They seemed satisfied. Then they came back twenty-four hours later.

He hated it, struggling to sound sincere, helpless in the face of their curiosity, eager to please, when inwardly he was trembling. They were honest enough, but they were a nuisance.

The press was camped on the Santa Rosa hospital door. A fan club had sprung up among Stuart's old high school friends, and they picketed daily demanding that the murderer be brought to justice. Two radical nuns joined the group. They told the world that the San Francisco Man Wolf cared more about cruelty to gay youth than the people of California.

In the early evenings, Reuben, in his hoodie and glasses, faithfully wandered the pavements outside the hospital, circling the block, listening, pondering, brooding. He could have sworn once that he saw Stuart at the window. Could Stuart hear him? He whispered that he was there, that he wasn't leaving Stuart alone, that he was waiting.

"This kid is in no danger of death," Grace averred. "You can forget that. But I have to get to the root of these symptoms. I have to figure out what this syndrome signifies. And this is becoming a consuming passion."

Yeah, and a dangerous one too, thought Reuben, but he cared more than anything else that Stuart live, and he trusted Grace to care more about that than anything else.

Meantime there had been a falling-out between Grace and the mysterious Dr. Jaska, though Grace obviously didn't want to tell Reuben why. Suffice it to say the doctor was making suggestions Grace didn't like.

"Reuben, the guy believes in things, unusual things," Grace said. "It's a veritable obsession. There are other red flags. If he contacts you, cut him off."

"Will do," said Reuben.

But Jaska was buzzing around Stuart and engaging his mother in long conversations as to the boy's mysterious encounter with the Man Wolf, and Grace was leery of it. He was suggesting that mysterious hospital in Sausalito that had no documentation and was licensed only as a private rehabilitation center.

"He's not getting anywhere for one good reason," said Grace. "That woman doesn't give a damn."

Reuben was frantic with worry. He drove south and sought out Stuart's mother at her sprawling modern redwood-and-glass palace east of Santa Rosa on Plum Ranch Road.

Yes, she remembered him from the hospital, he was the handsome one. Come on in. No, she wasn't worried about Stuart. Seems like he had more doctors than she knew what to do with. Some weirdo from Russia, a Dr. Jaska, wanted to see him but Dr. Golding and Dr. Cutler said no. This Dr. Jaska thought he should go into some kind of sanitarium, but she couldn't figure why.

Sometime during the interview, which wasn't much of an interview, the stepfather, Herman Buckler, sauntered in. He was a short, wiry man with exaggerated features and dark eyes. He had crew-cut platinum hair and a dark tan. He didn't want his wife talking to reporters. In fact, he was furious. Reuben eyed him coldly. He was picking up the scent of malice clearly, much more clearly than he'd picked it up from Dr. Jaska, and he remained in the man's presence as long as he could, though he was being ordered ever more violently to leave, just so he could study the guy.

The guy was poisoned with resentment and rage.

He'd had enough of Stuart turning his life upside down. His wife was terrified of him, doing everything she could to placate him, apologizing for what had happened, and asking Reuben to go ahead and go.

The spasms were churning in Reuben. And it was daylight, the first time they'd ever come to him in daylight except for a very mild visitation when he'd seen Dr. Jaska. He kept his eyes on the man even as he walked out of the big glass and redwood house.

For a long time, he sat in the Porsche, looking at the surrounding forest and hills, just letting the spasms wane. The sky was blue overhead. This had the beauty of the wine country here, this lovely sunny weather. What a great place for Stuart to have grown up.

The change hadn't really threatened. Could Reuben bring it about in daylight? He wasn't sure. Not at all. But he was sure that Herman Buckler was capable of trying to kill his stepson, Stuart. And the wife knew it but she didn't know it. In the midst of all this she was involved in a choice between her husband and her son.

As for the nights, Reuben felt certain that he now had the Wolf Gift entirely under his control.

For the first three nights after he last saw Stuart, he held off the change altogether, and gratifying as this was, it soon resulted in a kind of agony. It was like fasting, when one finds out how much more food and drink are than mere sustenance.

After that, when the change came, he confined

himself to the woods near Nideck Point, hunting, roaming, discovering the creeks of his property, and climbing the tallest of the old-growth trees to heights not attempted in the past. There was a bear hibernating in his little forest, some sixty feet up an old fire-scarred tree; and a big cat, most likely the male cub of the mother he'd killed, was roaming Reuben's part of the woods as well. There were deer he did not want to slay. But the sleek plump furry squirrel, wood rat, beaver, shrew, shrew mole—he fed on them all, and on cold, surprisingly tender reptiles—salamanders, garter snakes, frogs. Fishing in the creek was heavenly, his giant paws soon capable of snaring any sleek darting prey he chose. High up in the canopy, he could snatch the hapless scrub jays and wrens right out of the air, and devour them feathers and all while their little hearts still pumped vainly against their tiny narrow breasts. He feasted on the woodpecker and on junco and an endless supply of thrushes.

The utter "rightness" of devouring what one killed fascinated him, as did the desire to kill in the first place. He longed to wake the hibernating bear. He wanted to know if he could best it.

Far to the north where the forest grew as thick as it did on his own land, he caught the scent of the bull elk and longed for it, but didn't go after it. He dreamed of fields of sheep, of scattering them with a roar, and chasing down the biggest to rip into its woolly neck with his fangs, and gorge himself on the hot breathing mutton.

But he wanted to remain unseen, unnoticed in his own territory, and was never too far away from Laura, in her bower of white lace and flannel in the big master bed, whom he would awaken on his return with beast paws and beast kisses.

But was it enough, these blissful nights in the enchanted woodland that was his own? It was the pale shadow of the raucous urban wilderness that lay to the south, beckoning with its promises of thousands of mingled voices. **Garden of Pain, I need you.** What were the songs of beasts to the cries of sentient souls? How long could he keep this up?

In a way, the days were easier, even with the police coming and going.

He studied all the werewolf literature, the books, the "reports" of man wolf sightings the world over, from the Yeti of Tibet to the Bigfoot of California. He combed the records of the world for mentions of the distinguished gentlemen over the mantel and found nothing.

He learned the house in all its different ways, thinking all the while that it might well be turned over to Felix in the days to come, but for now it was his, and he would continue to love it and know it. He searched now and then for yet undiscovered rooms and doors and so did Laura.

A band of local Nideck people came to the door. Nina, the little high school girl he'd met on his very first night here with Marchent, was used to hiking the forest behind the house, and Galton had warned them away. In tears, she explained what it meant to the locals to roam the property.

Laura invited the hikers in for tea, and a compromise was worked out. Anyone could hike the paths by day, but no camping at night. Reuben agreed to it.

Later on, Laura confessed that she knew what it meant to those people to be able to hike these woods, she really did. And sometimes she wished there were more of them around. There were times when she felt so utterly alone here.

"I've never been afraid anywhere ever in my life," she said, "least of all in the California forests. But I could have sworn yesterday there was somebody out there in the trees, somebody watching."

"Probably one of those hikers," said Reuben with a shrug.

She shook her head. "Not like that," she said. "But you're probably right. And I have to get used to it here. It's as safe as Mill Valley."

They agreed it might well have been one of the reporters.

He didn't like her being worried by anything. He was confident he would hear and scent anyone of malevolent intent. But she couldn't. And he resolved not to leave her alone unless it was absolutely necessary.

He moved heaven and earth to have a big mechanical gate installed on the private road that led to the property, just to stop the vehicles of the reporters who were now revisiting the site of the original Man Wolf attack in light of Stuart's growing fame. Of course the reporters and cameramen came on up the road on foot, but at least they couldn't drive to the front doors.

Galton said over and over the story would die down like it had before, not to worry. He had a small crew coming and going to renovate the bedrooms on the front of the house, with new wiring, fresh paint, and all the appropriate electrical and cable connections.

This is what it means to live in such a house, Reuben thought, or what it would mean for a while. The quiet would come again. And so might Felix.

Laura took the conservatory in hand and made of it a splendid paradise, with giant weeping ficus encircling the smaller orange and lemon trees, while she brought flowering vines of all sorts—honeysuckle, jasmine, morning glory—to climb the iron-ribbed walls with the aid of delicate trellises. There were potted rose trees now with picture-perfect blooms. And the orchid trees were fully recovered from their long journey and heavy with spectacular blossoms. Laura slipped small virtual-sunlight lamps into nooks and crannies to supplement the pale northern sun. And a handsome Victorian white enameled woodstove was found to take the chill out of the room and provide a warmth the plants would welcome, as well as Reuben and Laura dining every night before the fountain on the white marble table.

Halfway into the week, Reuben astonished himself. He did not know quite why he did what he did.

But he found a small secondhand computer shop in Petaluma that did not have video camera surveillance and, dressing in his hoodie and sunglasses, he purchased there two laptop Apple computers for cash.

He was angry with Felix for vanishing without a word. He was sick with worry about Stuart. He was ravenous for the succulent evil of the southern cities.

And so he created an e-mail account under the name Vera Lupus exclusively for one of these computers, and wrote on it a long letter from the Man Wolf to the **San Francisco Observer.**

This letter was a great sprawling uncontrolled document and it was really an angry appeal to Felix Nideck to please come back and help him!

All he had to do to send it anonymously was drive into any city, park somewhere near a hotel or motel, beyond camera reach, and hook up to its Wi-Fi network, and hit SEND.

No way could the e-mail be traced back to him or to anyone.

But he didn't send the letter. It was too full of pleading and rage and admissions of not knowing what he was doing. It was too full of self-pity that "there was no wise guardian of secrets" to guide him. It was his own fault, wasn't it, that Stuart's life was at risk? How could he blame Felix for this? One moment he wanted absolution and understanding. The next he was wanting to hit Felix.

He held on to the Man Wolf's letter. He hid the

computer in the old steamer trunk in the cellar. And he waited.

There were long dark times when he thought, If that boy dies, I will kill myself. But Laura cautioned him that he could not leave her, or leave himself, or leave the mystery—that if he meant to do something so brutal and terrible to himself, then he might as well give himself over to his mother and to the authorities. And when he thought of what that might mean to Felix, well, he backed off from all such ideas entirely.

"Wait for Felix," she said. "Keep that in your mind. When you become like this, think: I will not do anything until Felix comes. Promise me."

Jim called more than once, but Reuben could not bear the thought of telling him about Stuart. He got off the phone as quickly as possible.

As for Laura, she was battling her own demons. Every morning, she went down the long steep perilous trail to the beach and walked for hours near the cold banging surf. (Reuben found the path just about impossible. And the ocean wind turned him into a block of mean-spirited uncooperative ice.)

And for hours as well she walked in the woods, with or without Reuben, determined to conquer her new fear. Once, from the beach, she saw someone high on the cliffs, but that was to be expected.

Reuben was on edge whenever she went out, listening with the inner ear of the wolf to the world that surrounded her.

It crossed his mind more than once that there could be some other Morphenkind out there, some vagrant being of which Felix knew nothing, but he had no real evidence of such a thing. And he trusted that had it been possible, Felix would have warned him. Maybe he was romanticizing Felix. Maybe he had to romanticize him.

Laura brought back tender little sword ferns for the conservatory and nursed them in specially prepared pots, and collected beautiful rocks and pebbles for the basin of the fountain. She found interesting fossils in the gravel driveway beneath the kitchen windows. Then she pitched herself into work on the house, restoring the historic William Morris wallpaper in the old bedrooms, or directing the workmen who were repainting the crown molding and other woodwork. She ordered curtains and draperies, and began an inventory of the china and silver.

She also found a magnificent Fazioli grand piano for the music room.

She began to document the Nideck forest with her camera. By her calculation there were some seventy-five old-growth redwoods on Reuben's land. She estimated their height at over two hundred fifty feet; there were Douglas firs that were almost as high, and countless young redwoods, western hemlock, and Sitka spruce.

She taught Reuben the names of all the trees, how to recognize the California bay tree, and the maple, and how to tell the fir from the redwood, and how to recognize a host of other plants and ferns.

In the evenings, she read Teilhard de Chardin, just as Reuben did. And other works of theology and philosophy, and sometimes poetry. She confessed that she did not believe in God. But she believed in the world, and she understood Teilhard's love of the world and faith in the world. She wished she could believe in a personal God, a loving God who understood all this, but she didn't.

One night she burst into tears as they talked of these things. She asked Reuben to bring about the change, and to take her out and up into the forest canopy again. He did. For hours, they roamed the upper branches. She was fearless of the heights, and gloved and dressed in tight-fitting black campers' clothes that kept her insulated against the wind, and likely invisible in the dark to any prying eyes, as Reuben was. She cried against his chest, inconsolably. She said she would risk dying to have the Wolf Gift, there was no doubt of it. When Felix comes, if Felix has the answers, if Felix can somehow direct, if Felix knows how . . . they speculated for hours. Finally when she was drowsy and calm, he carried her down to the forest floor, and brought her to the creek where he so often fed alone. She bathed her face in the icy water. They sat among the moss-covered rocks as he told her all the things he could hear, about the bear that slept not far off, about the deer moving in the dark enfolding shadows.

Finally, he brought her home and once again they made love in the dining room before a raging fire in the old grim medieval black fireplace.

In the main, she was not unhappy. Far from it.

The western-facing bedroom chosen for her office had been refurnished with a glass-top desk, several attractive wooden filing cabinets, and a large easy chair with an ottoman for reading, the beautiful old antique furniture relegated to the cellar.

Marchent's old room no one touched. Someone, likely the law firm, had packed up all Marchent's personal things before Reuben had ever come back to the house, and now it was a lovely spacious bedroom done in pink chintz and white ruffled curtains, with a white marble fireplace.

The study and adjoining bedroom that had belonged to Felix, which completed the western row of rooms at the northwestern end of the hall, remained a sanctum.

Laura and Reuben cooked all meals together, and did the errands together. Galton handled almost all the real time-consuming problems of the property.

Laura had done a lot of thinking, true, she admitted, about how she could easily accept the brutality of the Man Wolf's attacks. She did not know the answer. She was deeply in love with Reuben, she said. She'd never leave him. That wasn't even conceivable to her.

But yes, she thought about it, thought about it night and day, the drive we have for revenge against those who are cruel to us, and the cruelty of revenge and what it does to those who give themselves over to it.

True, she wished he could hunt the forest forever, that he would never again go to the mysterious voices that called him. But she could not explain away the fact that the voices did call, and every day the press elaborated in more detail the spectacular "fallout" of the Man Wolf's "intervention."

The beneficiaries of his savagery captured the imagination of the press as much as the criminal victims. The old woman of Buena Vista Hill, having suffered excruciating torture before the Man Wolf burst into her window, was now mentally recovered from her ordeal and granting interviews. She said boldly on camera that the Man Wolf should be caught alive, not shot down like a beast, and that she would devote her fortune to supporting him and protecting him if he were captured. Susan Larson, the Man Wolf's first "contact" in North Beach, also lobbied hard for his "safe" capture. To Larson, he was "The Gentling Wolf," because of the way that he had touched her and comforted her. Meanwhile Man Wolf fan clubs formed online and on YouTube, and at least one famous rock star had written "A Ballad of the Man Wolf," and other songs would shortly follow. There was a Man Wolf Facebook page, and a Man Wolf poetry contest on YouTube. And a whole variety of Man Wolf T-shirts had appeared.

Near the end of the week, Simon Oliver called to say that the title company had all documents on

Nideck Point ready for signature. Reuben agreed, but secretly he had misgivings.

What about Felix? This was Felix, the real Felix. Didn't this house belong to him?

"Nothing can be done about this question now," said Laura. "I think you should go to the title company, sign the papers, and let them file the title. Remember, there is no legal way for Felix to acquire this house. He won't and can't take a DNA test to prove anything, either affinity to Marchent, or that he is the man himself. He'd have to buy the house from you. For now, this place is yours."

The visit to the title company was brief. It was unusual to clear title in this amount of time, they told Reuben, but this house had been owned by only one family down through the years, which had made it easy. Reuben signed where they told him to sign.

Nideck Point was now legally his. Property taxes were paid in advance through the end of the following year. Insurance was in place.

He drove Laura south to get her Jeep and the bulk of her possessions, which amounted to so few boxes that he was kind of amazed. Half of them were filled with flannel nightgowns.

Finally Grace called with the news that Stuart might be visited the following Tuesday. He'd not had a temperature for two days, and the rash and the nausea were gone. So were all signs of injury. And the boy's height and weight had increased.

"Like I told you, it's all happened so much faster,"

she said. "He's not so manic now. But the moodiness has begun."

Frankly, she wanted Reuben to see him. She wanted Reuben to talk to him. The boy wanted to go home, and that meant San Francisco. His mother wouldn't have him in the Santa Rosa house, she was afraid of the stepfather, and Grace didn't trust him on his own.

"Yes, it's a hell of a lot easier for me to look after him down here," said Grace, "in San Francisco. But this kid is acting too weird, just too weird. Of course he's clever as they come. He knows better than to say anything more about hearing voices. Reuben, it's playing out like it did with you, exactly. The lab results. Well, we make a little progress and then the specimens disintegrate! We haven't solved that problem. And he's not the same boy he was when I first talked to him. I want you to see him."

He sensed that they were able to talk about all this much more easily now that it involved Stuart. They were speaking as if there was no silence between them, no secret, no mystery, as if all the mystery had to do with Stuart.

That was all right.

Reuben said he would see Stuart anytime that he could. He'd be there early Tuesday morning.

Finally Grace asked: would he and Laura be willing if she, and Jim, and Phil came to dinner?

Reuben was overjoyed. He could control the Wolf Gift now. He had no fear of it. This was what he so wanted!

He and Laura spent all day Monday preparing for a feast in the august dining room.

They dug out linen for the table, great cloths trimmed in old lace, dinner-sized napkins embossed with the initial **N,** and heaps of old graven silver. They ordered flowers for the main rooms, and specialty desserts from the nearest bakery.

Grace and Phil were completely taken with the house, but it was Phil who fell in love with it, just as Reuben had anticipated. Phil stopped responding to questions or remarks and roamed off by himself, humming under his breath, running his hands over paneling and doorjambs, and the varnish of the piano, and the crinkled leaves of the weeping ficus, and the leather-bound books of the library. He put on his thick glasses to examine the carved figures of the hunters' boards and the medieval fireplace. Phil looked like he belonged to the place in his disheveled tweed with his long unkempt gray hair.

They had to pull him down from the second-story rooms finally because everyone was starving. But Phil was whispering to the house, communing with it, and paid absolutely no attention to Grace when she began to talk about the obvious expense of it.

Reuben was thrilled by this. He kept hugging Phil. Phil was in a dream world with the house. He murmured under his breath, "I'd live here in a second." And now and then he beamed proudly, lovingly, at Reuben.

"Son, this is your destiny," he said.

Grace said such houses were obsolete, ought to be converted into institutions, museums, or hospitals. She looked especially beautiful to Reuben, with her red hair natural around her face, her lips only slightly rouged, and her sharp intense features expressive as always. Her black silk pantsuit looked new; she had put on her pearls for the occasion. But she was tired, worn, and watching him intently no matter who was doing the talking.

Jim came to the defense of the place, pointing out Reuben had never been a terribly expensive kid. He'd traveled on a shoestring, used to tiny hotel rooms and coach fares, and attended a state university and not an Ivy League college. The most extravagant thing he'd ever done was ask for a Porsche when he graduated and he was still driving the same car two years later. He'd never gone into the principal of any of his trusts until now, and had lived for years on half his income. Yes, the house was expensive, but they didn't heat the whole thing every day, did they?

And how long was Reuben expected to live with his parents anyhow? Yes, the house cost. But what would it cost to buy a new condo or refurbished Victorian in San Francisco? And what would Grandfather Spangler have thought of all this, the gift of a property of this value? He would have approved the maintenance in the blink of an eye! He'd been a real estate developer, hadn't he? Someday this whole place would sell for a fortune, so would everybody please leave Reuben alone!

Grace accepted all this with a casual nod. What Jim didn't say was that he, Jim, had turned his trust funds back over to the family when he'd joined the priesthood, and so shouldn't his opinion count for something?

Jim had dropped out of medical school to be a priest, and his education in Rome had cost little in comparison. The family had made a hefty donation to the Church when he was ordained, but the bulk of his inheritance was now at the disposal of Reuben.

Reuben didn't care what the hell any of them said. He kept his counsel about Felix, and Felix's possible moral claim to the house naturally. His heart broke when he thought of losing the house, but it was the least of his worries. What would Felix think when he found out about Stuart?

What would Stuart think when he found out about Stuart?

But maybe nothing would happen. Hadn't Marrok indicated that sometimes nothing happened? Oh, faint hope.

What Reuben loved was that they were here, his family, that their voices were filling the big shadowy dining room, that his father was happy and not bored, and it felt good, oh, so good, to be near them.

The meal was a great success—roast filet, fresh vegetables, pasta, and one of Laura's enormous simple and herb-laden salads.

Laura got into a discussion with Jim about Teilhard de Chardin, and Reuben understood less than half of what they were saying. What he saw however was how much they enjoyed the conversation. Phil was smiling at Laura in a particularly delighted way. When Phil talked about the poetry of Gerard Manley Hopkins, Laura listened with rapt focus. Grace started another conversation, of course, but Reuben had long ago grown used to listening to their two separate conversations simultaneously. The fact was Laura liked his father. And his mother.

Grace asked what good theology ever did anybody, or poetry for that matter.

Laura remarked that science was dependent upon poetry, that all scientific description was metaphoric.

Only when the conversation turned to Dr. Akim Jaska did things turn unpleasant. Grace didn't want to discuss the man, but Phil went into a fury.

"That doctor wanted to have you legally committed," he said to Reuben.

"Well, that was the end of the matter, wasn't it?" said Grace. "Because nobody, I mean nobody, was going to even remotely consider such a thing."

"Legally committed?" Laura asked.

"Yes, to this phony-baloney rehab center of his in Sausalito," said Phil. "I knew the guy was a fraud from the moment I met him. I practically threw him down the front steps. Coming at us with those papers."

"Papers?" Reuben asked.

"He is most certainly not a fraud," said Grace, and it suddenly became a screaming match between Phil and Grace, until Jim intervened to declare that yes, the doctor was obviously brilliant and extremely knowledgeable in his field, but something wasn't on the level there, not with this attempt at commitment.

"Well, you can forget him," said Grace. "That was the end of it, Reuben. We just weren't on the same page, Dr. Jaska and I. Not at all unfortunately." But she insisted in a rolling murmur that he'd been one of the most brilliant doctors she'd ever met. Too bad he was a bit of a lunatic himself on the subject of werewolves.

Phil was snorting, throwing down his napkin, picking it up, and throwing it down again, and saying the guy was a Rasputin.

"He had some theory," said Jim, "about mutational changes and mutational beings. But the man's credentials just aren't what they should be, and Mother realized this soon enough."

"Not soon enough for me," said Phil. "He tried to cover his record with some cock-and-bull story about the fall of the Soviet Union and the loss of all his most valuable research. Nonsense!"

Reuben got up, put on some soothing piano music by Erik Satie, and when he sat down again, Laura was talking softly about the forest and how they must all come when the rains finally stopped and spend a weekend hiking the trails behind the house.

Jim managed to get Reuben alone, for a brisk walk after dark in the woods.

"Is it true," he demanded, "this kid was bitten?"

Reuben went silent and then broke down, confessing everything. He was sure now that Stuart wasn't going to die from the Chrism, but that Stuart was going to become exactly what he was. This sent Jim into a paroxysm.

He actually knelt down on the ground, bowed his head, and prayed. Reuben talked on and on about his meeting with Felix and how he felt that Felix knew the answers.

"What are you hoping for?" demanded Jim. "That this man can make these brutal attacks entirely morally acceptable to you!"

"I'm hoping what all sentient beings hope . . . that somehow I'm part of something larger than myself, in which I play a role, an actual role that is somehow intended and meaningful." He tugged at Jim's arm. "Will you please get up off the ground, Father Golding, before somebody sees you?"

They walked a little deeper into the woods, but close enough to the house to see the bright lights of the windows. Reuben stopped. He listened. He was hearing things, all manner of things. He tried to explain it to Jim. In the dimness, he could not make out the expression on Jim's face.

"But is a human being meant to hear those things?" Jim asked.

"If he isn't, then why am I hearing them?"

"Things happen," Jim said. "There are mutations, developments that the world includes but never embraces, things that have to be repudiated and rejected."

Reuben sighed.

He glanced upwards, longing for the fuller clarity of night vision that came with the wolf-coat. He wanted to see stars above, to be reminded that this earth was no more than an ember in the blaze of never-ending galaxies, a thought that always, somehow, comforted him. Strange that it did not do this for others. The vastness of the universe brought him closer to faith in a God.

The wind moved through the branches over him. Something jarred him, a series of sounds that seemed out of cadence with the night. Was he seeing something up there in the dark, something moving? The darkness was too thick. But at once the chills rose all over him. He felt the hair standing on end on his arms. **Someone out there, up there.**

The inevitable convulsion came. But he suppressed it. He forced it back. He shivered deliberately banishing the chills. No. He could not see anything there. Yet his imagination filled in the nightscape. **Beings up there in the dark, more than one, more than two.**

"What is it? What's wrong?" asked Jim.

"Nothing," he lied.

Then the wind came hard through the trees, gusting, doubling its fist, and the woods sang as if with one voice.

"Just nothing."

At nine o'clock, the family took off with the prospect of not reaching San Francisco before one in the morning. Grace was coming back to Santa Rosa tomorrow afternoon to argue further in person that Stuart stay in the hospital. Grace was afraid of something.

"Do you know any more now about this whole syndrome?" Reuben asked.

"No," she said. "Nothing else at all."

"Would you be absolutely straight with me on something?"

"Of course."

"Dr. Jaska—."

"Reuben, I sent the guy packing. He'll never come near me again."

"What about Stuart?"

"He has absolutely no way to get to Stuart. I've warned Dr. Cutler in no uncertain terms. Now this is strictly confidential, but I'm going to tell you. Dr. Cutler's trying to get custody of Stuart, or at least some kind of power of attorney with regard to his medical decisions. He can't go home and he shouldn't be alone in San Francisco in his Haight-Ashbury apartment either. Look, forget I told you this."

"Right, Mamma."

She looked at him almost despairingly.

They'd done a lot of talking about Stuart, but not about him.

When had his mother ever given up on anything? Surgeons never give up. Surgeons always believe that something can be done. That's their nature.

This is what all of these things have done to my

mother, Reuben thought. His mother stood on the front step staring up at the house, at the dark trees gathered to the east of it, her eyes haunted, unhappy. She looked back to Reuben, and there came that warm affectionate smile on which so much of his well-being depended, but only for an instant.

"Mom, I'm so glad you came up here this evening," he said. He put his arms around her. "I can't tell you."

"Yeah, I'm glad we came too," she said. She held him close, looking into his eyes. "You are all right, aren't you, Baby Boy?"

"Yes, Mom, I'm just worried about Stuart."

Reuben promised to call her in the morning as soon as he'd been to the hospital.

# 33

A WILD BOAR HAD COME into his woods—a lone male. He heard the boar about two in the morning. He was reading, fighting the change. Then came the scent and the sound of the male, hunting on its own, the family left behind somewhere in a makeshift den of broken branches and leaves.

How his senses told him these things he could not quite grasp. He stripped, heart pounding, spasms rolling, and entered the forest in full wolf-coat— taking to the heights and then plummeting to the forest floor to track the thing on foot as it was on foot, gaining on it, and at last bringing it down, powerful hairy brute, fangs chomping deep into its back, and finally into its throat.

This was a feast, all right, a feast he'd been hungering for. He took his time, feasting on the boar's belly, and other soft innards, and devouring the dripping heart. The great white tusks gleamed in the dimness. What a fierce thing it had been. He glutted himself with the juicy and fragrant flesh.

A sleepiness came over him as he devoured more and more, chewing the meat now more slowly, draining the blood juice out of it, and feeling an immense satisfying warmth throughout his chest and stomach and even his limbs.

This was heaven, the soundless rain all around him, the scents of the fallen leaves rising, the boar's scent intoxicating him, the flesh more than he could possibly consume.

A scream shocked him. It was Laura, screaming for him in the darkness.

He raced towards the sound of her voice.

She stood in the clearing behind the house, in the glare of the yellow floodlights. She was calling and calling, and then she bent her knees and let out another scream.

He bounded out of the forest towards her.

"Reuben, it's Dr. Cutler," she cried. "She can't reach your mother. Stuart's broken out of the hospital, broken out of the second-story window, and disappeared!"

So it had happened. It had happened to Stuart in half the time. And the change was on Stuart and Stuart was alone.

"My clothes, the big clothes," he said. "And clothes for the boy. Put them in the Jeep and drive south. I'll find you around the hospital or wherever I can."

He took off for the forest, determined to follow it all the way to Santa Rosa, heedless of whether he had to cross busy roads or freeways, or grasslands—soon certain that he was traveling infinitely faster towards Stuart than he might in any other way—praying to the gods of the forest, or the God of his heart, to please help him reach the boy before anyone else might.

By the highways of the world, the distance was about ninety miles.

But there was no accounting for the way that he traveled, taking to the canopy of the forest when he could or racing by foot when he had to, traversing any fence, road, or obstacle in his path.

Only one thought governed him, and that was to find Stuart, and the abandon he knew in the name of that cause was sublime. His senses had never been so acute, his muscles as powerful, or his direction so certain.

The forest never failed him, though at times he smashed branches in his path, leapt huge distances, and crashed noisily through the underbrush or risked exposure as he bounded over open fields.

The voices of the populated south rose to meet him, the mingled scents of humankind deepening the spell of the woodland, and at last he knew he was now traveling through the parklands of forested yards of the city, the wolf-mind and the human-mind scanning for Stuart, for the sounds of Stuart or the scent of Stuart, or for whatever voices had called Stuart to wherever he'd gone.

It was futile to hope that Stuart had not been seduced by the scent of evil, as Reuben had been seduced by it, or that his newfound strength hadn't carried him into realms where he might be discovered, even caught.

The night was alive with sirens, with crackling radio voices, with the pulse of the sweet city of Santa Rosa awakened to the shocking news of violence.

Bewildered, maddened, Reuben circled the hospital, then moved east. He caught the scent of terror, the scent of pleading, and desperation, a voice rising over the inevitable tide of petty prayers and garden-variety complaint.

Further to the east he bounded, when his instincts as well as his all-too-human brain told him: head for the boy's home because where else can he go? Head for Plum Ranch Road.

Naked and alone in this peopled woods, he'll hover there, frightened, seeking to make a lair of a basement or an attic known to him in that redwood mansion where he wasn't welcome, the place that used to be his home. But as Reuben came within sight of the police cars and their swirling lights, of the big rumbling fire trucks and the ambulances, he caught the cacophony of those gathered on the knoll, and the stench of death.

The woman sobbing was Stuart's mother. The dead man on the stretcher Herman Buckler, and the men fanning out to search the surrounding trees were goaded by the thrill of the hunt. The Man Wolf. There was a mixture of hysteria and glee amongst those gathered on foot for the spectacle.

Dogs barked. Dogs howled.

The boom of a gun echoed over the hillside. And there came the fierce blast of a bullhorn demanding caution. "Do not shoot. Report your position. Do not shoot."

Searchlights swept the trees, the grassland, the scattered rooftops—revealing cars in unlighted driveways, windows just flashing into life.

He could not get any closer. He was in greater danger now than he'd ever known.

But the night was dark, the rain thick and steady, and only he could see the terrain of twisted tree limbs that stretched before him as he circled and circled the blinking, crackling center of activity that was the family home.

He went as high as he could in the scrub oaks, lay still, paws over his eyes, making himself into darkness when the lights sought him out.

Ambulances were leaving the house. The cries of the mother were soft, broken, fading in the distance. Police cars crawled the dark roads in all directions. Porch lights and yard lights were snapped on, laying bare swimming pools and smooth shimmering lawns.

More vehicles were converging on the knoll.

He had to move out, make his circle wider again. And suddenly the obvious thought came to him: signal. The boy can hear what they cannot hear. In a low growing voice, he called Stuart's name. "I'm searching for you," came his muffled, guttural words. "Stuart, come to me." The syllables rolled out of him, deep, throbbing, elongated so that for human ears they might sink beneath the rumble of tires and engines, the grind of domestic machines. "Stuart, come to me.

Trust in me. I'm here to find you. Stuart, I am your brother. Come to me."

It seemed the backyard dogs were answering him, barking ever more fiercely, yelping, wailing, howling, and in that increasing din, he raised his own voice.

Slowly he moved eastward, out of the orbit of the search, certain the boy would have been clever enough to do the same. To the west lay the dense neighborhoods of Santa Rosa. To the east the forest.

"Stuart. Come to me."

At last, through the snarled web of branches before him, he saw the flicker of living eyes.

He pitched forward towards those glittering eyes, again sounding the name "Stuart!" like a deep-throated bell in the blackness.

And he heard the boy crying, "For the love of God, help me!"

His right arm flew out and caught the Boy Wolf around the shoulders, shocked to see he was as large as Reuben, and certainly as powerful, as they moved together rapidly through the high thick oak boughs.

Over yards of forest they ran. Finally, in a deep valley of unbroken darkness, they stopped. Reuben for the first time knew the heat of exhaustion in the wolf-coat, and lay back against the trunk of a tree, panting, and thirsting and scanning for the scent of water. The Boy Wolf lingered right beside him as if afraid to move away even an inch.

The eyes were blue, large, peering from a wolf-face of dark brown hair like his own. The Boy Wolf's ruff was streaked with white. In silence he gazed at Reuben, asking nothing, demanding nothing, trusting completely.

"I'm going to get you away from here," Reuben said, his voice pitched so deep a human being might not have understood it, as though he knew instinctively what the boy would hear that no one else could hear.

The response came in the same dark low rumbling timbre. "I'm with you." Just the faint catch of human pain in that, of human angst. Do animals know how to cry—that is, really cry? What animal breaks into sobs or into laughter?

They moved swiftly down a hillside and into a dark gulley, coming together in the bracken, till Reuben held the Boy Wolf close to him again.

"This is safe." He breathed the words into the boy's ear. "We wait."

How completely natural the Boy Wolf felt to him, these immense hairy shoulders, the soft silken wolf-coat of his arms, the voluminous mane that was glinting now in the pellucid light of the veiled moon. Indeed the light of the moon seemed to slip into the clouds and spread out in them, and then slide into a billion tiny splinters of rain.

Reuben opened his mouth, and let the rain hit his parched tongue. Again, he scanned for the scent of water, collected water, and found it in a small natural pool formed some yards away in the hollowed-out roots of a rotting tree. He scrambled on his paws and knees towards it and drank greedily, lapping the delicious sweet water as fast as he could. Then he sat back and let Stuart do the same.

There were only the smallest safest sounds around them in the dark.

The sky was slowly lightening.

"What happens now?" asked Stuart desperately.

"In an hour or less, you'll change back."

"Out here? In this place?"

"We have help coming. Depend on me. Let me listen now, let me see if I can pick up the scent or the sound of the person who's coming. This may take time."

For the first time in all his life, Reuben really didn't want to see the sun rise.

He lay back against the old rotted tree and listened, urging the boy again to be silent with the firm grip of his paw.

He knew where she was!

Not close, no, but he had caught her scent and her voice. **Oh, Laura, you are so clever.** She was singing that song he'd been singing the night they met:

"'Tis the gift to be simple . . . 'Tis the gift to be free . . .'"

"Follow me," he said to Stuart and he headed back towards the search parties, yes, and the probing lights, yes, but towards Laura, gaining speed as she gained speed, gradually closing in until he saw the pale streak of road she was traveling.

They raced along the border of the road together,

finally pulling up beside her, and then Reuben dropped down on the hood of the Jeep, his paws clutching at the driver's window and the windshield, and she brought the car to a sharp halt.

Stuart stood paralyzed. Reuben had to force him into the backseat.

"Hunker down," he said. To Laura he said, "Drive for home."

The Jeep rattled as it took off. Laura told the boy there were blankets back there, and he should cover up as best he could.

Reuben commanded himself to change. He lay back exhausted in the passenger seat, letting the waves of transformation pass through him. And never had it been so hard to give up the wolf-coat, to give up the power, to give up the smell of the dangerous woodland.

The sky was suddenly marbled with smoke and silver, the rain drenching the dark green fields on either side of them, and he felt that he might fall into a deep sleep. But there was no time for that. He pulled on his polo shirt and his flannel pants, his loafers, and rubbed his face with the palms of his hands. His skin didn't want to let it all go. His skin was singing. He felt he was still running through the woods. It was like when you get off a bicycle after an all-day ride, and you walk and you feel like you're pedaling and still going up and down, up and down.

He turned and looked into the backseat of the car. The Boy Wolf lay there, a coarse army blanket pulled up over him, his large blue eyes peering up at Reuben, from the sleek shining brown hair of his wolf-face.

"You!" the Boy Wolf said. "It's you!"

"Yes. I'm the one who did it to you," Reuben said. "I'm the one who passed the Chrism to you. I didn't mean to. I meant to kill the men who were trying to kill you. But I did it."

The eyes continued to fasten on him.

"I killed my stepfather," said Stuart, his voice deep and rough and vibrant. "He was beating my mother, dragging her through the rooms by her hair. He said he would kill her if she didn't sign the papers to commit me. She was saying no, no, no. Her hair was full of blood. I killed him. I tore him apart."

"Figures," said Reuben. "Did you identify yourself to your mother?"

"God, no!"

The Jeep bumped and jogged along the freeway, swerving to pass a car, and then gained speed again as it sailed into the left lane.

"Where can I go? Where can I hide?"

"You leave that to me."

They were still speeding along Highway 101 north under the heavy iron sky when Stuart began to change.

It took perhaps five minutes. Reuben timed it. Not even that much.

The boy shuddered, and bowed his head, elbows on his naked knees. His long blond curly hair covered his face. He was gasping in syllables but the syllables didn't add up to words. Finally, he managed to say:

"I thought I wouldn't change back. I thought I would be that way forever."

"No, not the way it is," said Reuben calmly.

He helped Stuart put on one of the knit shirts that Laura had brought for him. The boy managed the jeans and the running shoes on his own.

He was bigger all over than Reuben was, with a broader chest and obviously longer legs. He had powerful muscular arms. But the clothes were okay. He sat back staring at Reuben. It was the boy face again, with freckles and the big alert eyes, though not the familiar grin.

"Well, you're one splendid boy wolf, I'll tell you that," Reuben said.

Silence.

"You're going to be all right with us, Stuart," said Laura. She never took her eyes off the road.

The boy was too stupefied and exhausted to answer. He kept staring at Reuben as though it was a miracle that Reuben looked like a perfectly ordinary man.

# 34

His eyes snapped open. By the digital clock it was just after 4:00 p.m. The blinds were drawn. He'd been sound asleep for hours. There were voices outside the house, voices in front and in back, voices on the sides.

He sat up.

Laura was nowhere around. He could see the landline blinking. He could hear it ringing far off somewhere in the house, perhaps in the kitchen or even in the library. On the night table, his iPhone throbbed.

The TV screen flickered and flared in silence, the news crawl recycling the news he'd been watching when he went to sleep: Santa Rosa Panic Over Man Wolf.

He'd watched as much as he could before he'd passed out.

There was a statewide search for Stuart McIntyre, who'd disappeared from St. Mark's Hospital during the night. His stepfather had been murdered by the Man Wolf at 3:15 a.m. His mother had been hospitalized. Sightings of the Man Wolf were coming in from all over Northern California.

People were panicking up and down the coast. It was not fear of the Man Wolf, so much as it was utter confusion, helplessness, frustration. Why couldn't the police solve the mystery of the werewolf avenger? He saw clips now from a governor's news conference, flashes of the attorney general, the redwood-and-glass house in Santa Rosa on its knoll.

Voices out there, around the house. Scent of any number of human beings, moving along the western side of the property and the east.

He got out of bed, naked, barefoot, and crept to the front window, cracking the drapery just a tiny bit, letting in the dull afternoon light. He could see the police cars down there, three of them. No. One was a sheriff's car. The other two were highway patrol. There was an ambulance there, too. Why an ambulance?

There came a booming knock on the front door. Then another. He narrowed his eyes because it helped him to hear. They were moving around the sides of the house, yes, both sides, and hovering at the back door.

Was the back door locked? Was the alarm on?

Where was Laura? He caught Laura's scent. She was in the house, moving closer.

He pulled on his pants and crept into the hallway. He could hear Stuart's breathing. Looking into the front bedroom beside his own, he saw Stuart across the bed, dead asleep as Reuben had been only moments ago.

He and Stuart had both given in to sleep because they had no choice. He'd tried to eat a little but hadn't been able to. Stuart had devoured a porter-house steak. But both of them had been glassy-eyed, slurry- voiced, weak.

Stuart had said he was almost sure that his step-father had shot him twice. But there were no bullet wounds.

Then they'd both headed for the beds and gone out, Reuben like a light pinched out in the darkness. Just gone.

He listened. Another car was coming up the road.

Suddenly, he heard the soft slap of Laura's bare feet on the stairs. She emerged out of the shadows and came towards him, slipping into his arms.

"This is the second time they've been here," she whispered. "The alarm's armed. If they break a window or push in a door, the sirens will blast us from all four corners of the house."

He nodded. She was trembling. Her face was white.

"Your e-mail's filled with messages, not just from your mother, but from your brother and your father, and from Celeste. From Billie. Something very bad is going down."

"Did they see you through the windows?" he asked.

"No. The drapes are still drawn from last night."

They were calling his name down there, "Mr. Golding, Mr. Golding!" Hammering on the door in the back as they had hammered on the door in front.

The wind sighed and threw the rain gently against the windows.

He took a few steps down the stairs.

He remembered that crash that had awakened him the night Marchent had been killed. We're living in a palace of glass, he thought, but how in the world can they justify breaking in here?

He glanced back at Stuart. Still barefoot, stripped to his shorts and shirt, sleeping like a baby.

Galton had just pulled up. He could hear Galton calling out to the sheriff.

He went back into the bedroom and drew near to the south-facing window again.

"Well, I don't know where they are. You can see the same as I can that both cars are here. I don't know what to tell you. Maybe they're sleeping in. They didn't come rolling up the road till early this morning. You mind telling me what all this is about?"

The sheriff wasn't saying, and neither were the highway patrolmen, and the paramedics from the ambulance were standing back with their arms folded looking up at the house.

"Well, why don't I give you a call later on when they wake up?" asked Galton. "Well, yeah, I do know the code, but I have no authorization to let anybody in. Listen . . ."

Whispers. "All right, all right. We'll just wait then."

**Wait for what?**

"Wake up Stuart," he told Laura. "Get him into the secret room. Fast."

He dressed hurriedly putting on his blue blazer,

and combing his hair. He wanted to look like the picture of respectability whatever happened.

He glanced at his cell phone: text from Jim.

"Landed. On our way."

What in the world could that mean?

He could hear Stuart protesting in a drunken-sounding voice, but Laura was guiding him firmly into the linen closet and through the secret door.

He checked it behind them. Perfectly smooth wall. He put the shelves back in place against it, and hefted two loads of towels onto the shelves. And then he shut the door.

He crept down to the first floor, and made his way along the hallway towards the darkened front room. The only light came from the conservatory doors. Milky, dim. The rain teemed lightly on the glass dome. A gray mist sealed the glass walls.

Someone was trying the outside knobs one by one of the conservatory's western French doors.

Another car had pulled up outside, and it sounded as though a truck had come with it. He didn't want to disturb the draperies, even a little. Quietly, he listened. A woman's voice this time. And then Galton—talking loudly into his phone.

". . . just better get up here right now, Jerry, I mean this is happening here right now at the Nideck place and I don't see any warrant here, and if somebody is going to break into the Nideck house without a warrant, well, I'm telling you, you ought to get up here right now."

Silently moving to the desk, he stared at the stream of e-mail subject lines crawling down the screen.

"SOS," said Celeste over and over again. Billie's e-mails said, "Warning." Phil's e-mail "On the way." The last one from Grace read: "Flying up with Simon now." That had been sent two hours ago.

So that's what Jim meant. They'd landed at the Sonoma County Airport, most likely, and were driving the rest of the way.

And just how long would that take? he wondered.

More cars were arriving out front.

Billie's last e-mail had been an hour ago: "Tip off; they're coming to put you away."

He was furious, yet calculating. What could have triggered this? Had someone seen them early this morning with Stuart in the car? Surely Galton wouldn't have breathed a word to anyone, but how on such a slender bit of evidence could a campaign like this have ever gained steam?

Ambulance. Why was there an ambulance? Had Dr. Cutler gotten custody of Stuart and was she coming to take him to the nuthouse or to jail? That was Dr. Cutler's voice out there, wasn't it? And the voice of another woman, a woman speaking with a distinct foreign accent.

He moved out of the library and over the soft Oriental carpets of the great room and stood just inside the door.

The woman with the foreign accent, possibly Russian, was explaining that she had had experience in these things before, and if the officers all cooperated this would go completely smoothly. Things like this usually did. There came a man's voice underscoring hers with long ominous syllables of the same general meaning. **This was Jaska.** He could smell Jaska, and he could pick up the scent of the woman. **Liar.** A deep unwholesome malice.

Reuben felt the spasms beginning; he rested his right hand against his abdomen. He could feel the heat. "Not yet," he whispered. "Not yet." The prickly icy feeling was traveling all over the backs of his arms and up his neck. "Not yet."

It was getting dark already. Sunset would be in a few minutes, and on a wet overcast day like this it would be full dark very soon.

There must have been fifteen men out there now. And more cars were coming up the road. A car was pulling up right opposite the door.

He could make it to the hidden room, no question of that, but what if Galton knew about the hidden room and always had? And if Galton didn't, if nobody did, how long could the three of them hide inside?

Outside, Dr. Cutler was arguing with the Russian doctor. She did not want Stuart committed. She didn't even know for certain that Stuart was here, but the Russian doctor said she knew, that she'd been tipped off, that Stuart was most certainly here.

Suddenly his mother's voice cut through the argument, and he could hear the low rumbling voice of

Simon Oliver under her voice. . . . "Writ of habeas corpus if you so much as attempt to take my son anywhere against his will!"

Never had he been so happy to hear that voice. Phil and Jim were murmuring together right on the other side of the door, calculating the peace officers to be around twenty in number, trying to figure a plan of what to do.

A noise within the house startled him.

The spasms grew stronger. He could feel his pores opening, every hair follicle tingling. With all his will he held back.

The noise was coming from the hallway; it sounded for all the world like someone coming up those bare wooden cellar steps. He heard the creak that he knew to be that door.

Slowly out of the shadows a tall figure materialized before him, and another figure stood to his left. Against the light of the conservatory he could not make out the faces.

"How did you get into my house!" Reuben demanded. He walked boldly towards them, his stomach churning, his skin on fire. "Unless you have a warrant to be in this house, get out."

"Down, little wolf," came the soft voice of one of the two figures.

The other who stood nearest the hallway snapped on the light.

It was Felix, and the man beside him was Margon Sperver. Margon Sperver had spoken those words.

Reuben all but cried out in shock.

Both men were dressed in heavy tweed jackets and boots. The scent of rain and earth came from their clothes and their boots; they were windblown and ruddy from the cold.

A wash of relief weakened Reuben. He gasped. Then he put his hands up to make a steeple before his face.

Felix stepped forward out of the light of the hallway. "I want you to let them in," he said.

"But there's so much you don't know!" Reuben confessed. "There's this boy here, Stuart—."

"I know," said Felix comfortingly. "I know everything." His face softened with a protective smile. He clamped a firm hand on Reuben's shoulder. "I am going upstairs to get Stuart now, and bring him down here. Now you light the fires. Turn on the lamps. And as soon as Stuart is ready for them, I want you to let them in."

Margon was already attending to these things, turning on one lamp after another. And the room was springing to life out of the gloom.

Reuben didn't think twice about obeying. He felt the spasms loosening, and the sweat flooding his chest under his shirt.

He quickly lighted the oak fire.

Margon moved as if he knew the place. Soon fires were going in the library, and the dining room and the conservatory as well.

Margon's hair was long, as it had been in the picture, only tied back with a leather thong. There were leather patches on the elbows of his jacket, and his boots looked ancient, heavily creased and crazed over the toes. His face was weathered, but youthful. He appeared to be a man of forty at most.

Finishing with the lamps of the conservatory, he drew up beside Reuben and looked into his eyes. There was an arresting warmth emanating from him, the same kind of warmth Reuben had sensed from Felix when first they met. And there was a hint of good humor in Margon as well.

"We've been waiting for this for a long time," said Margon. His voice was easy, smooth. "I wish we could have made all this easier for you. But that wasn't possible."

"What do you mean?"

"You'll understand all in time. Now, listen, as soon as Stuart gets here, I want you to step out under the arch, and welcome the doctors inside, and ask that the lawmen remain where they are for the time being. Offer to talk. Do you think you can do that?"

"Yes," said Reuben.

The argument outside was going fast and furious. Grace's voice rang out over the imbroglio. "Not valid, not valid. You paid for this! Either produce the paramedic who signed it or it's not valid—."

Something quickened in Margon's face. He reached out and placed his hands on Reuben's shoulders.

"You have it in check?" he asked. There was no hint of judgment, only the simple question.

"Yes," said Reuben. "I can keep it down."

"Good," he said.

"But I don't know about Stuart."

"If he starts to change, we'll get him out of sight," he explained. "It is important that he be here. You leave matters to us."

Stuart appeared, suitably dressed now in polo shirt and jeans. He was clearly alarmed and looked to Reuben silently but desperately. Laura, too, was now dressed in her usual sweater and slacks and took her place resolutely by Reuben's side.

Felix motioned for Margon to draw back, and the two moved closer to the dining room, signaling to Reuben to go ahead.

He snapped on the switch for the outside lights, turned off the burglar alarm, and opened the door.

It was a sea of wet angry people in glistening rain-coats with glistening umbrellas, and a good many more enforcement personnel than he had realized. At once the female Russian doctor—middle-aged, thick-bodied, with a short tight cap of gray hair—advanced, beckoning for Jaska and her squadron of supporters to follow, but Grace barred her way.

Phil came up the steps and slipped into the house, with Jim right behind him.

"If you would all please listen," said Reuben. He raised his hands for patience and quiet. "I understand how cold it is out here, and I'm sorry I've kept you waiting."

Grace was backing up the steps with Simon Oliver and trying to keep the Russian doctors at bay. The scent of malice rose decisively from the two Russians, and Jaska's cold eyes fixed Reuben harshly, as if they were beams that could somehow paralyze a victim as he pushed relentlessly closer.

The female doctor was powerfully excited by the sight of Reuben, eyeing him arrogantly with small milky-blue eyes.

"Doctors, please," said Reuben. Grace was now at his elbow. "Do come in, and you too, Dr. Cutler—." (He hoped and prayed Felix and Margon knew what they were doing, that they were the beings he believed them to be, but suddenly it seemed a slender and fantastical faith!) "We need to talk inside, you and I." He went on. "And Galton, I'm so sorry to have brought you out in this weather. Galton, maybe you could rustle up some coffee for all these people. You know the kitchen here as well as anybody else. I think we have enough cups for the whole party—."

Beside him, Laura motioned to Galton and said she'd meet him at the back door.

Galton was amazed, but immediately nodded and started taking orders for sugar and cream.

Grace pushed into the room behind Reuben.

But the two Russian doctors remained on the steps, in spite of the pelting rain. Then the woman said something under her breath and in Russian to Jaska, and Jaska turned and told the men and women peace officers to please be ready, to draw close to the house.

The men were none too sure about following his orders, obviously. And a great many hung back, though a few in uniforms Reuben didn't recognize came forward and even tried to follow Jaska inside.

"You may come in, Doctor," said Reuben. "But the men must remain outside."

Suddenly the sheriff came forward, very much objecting, and Reuben, saying nothing, allowed him into the great room as well.

He shut the door, and faced them—the sheriff, the family, Simon Oliver, the girlish and pretty Dr. Cutler, and the two formidable Russians who appraised him with eyes of stone.

Dr. Cutler suddenly let out a cry. She'd picked Stuart out of the shadows by the fireplace and rushed to him with her arms out.

"I'm all right, Doctor—," Stuart said. He put his big ungainly arms around her immediately. "I'm sorry, I'm just so sorry. I don't know what happened to me last night, I just somehow had to get out of there, and I broke the window—."

His words were drowned out as the female Russian doctor and Grace began to shout at each other, the Russian woman insisting, "This does not have to be difficult, if your son and this boy will simply come!"

There was something grindingly presumptuous and vicious in her tone. Reek of malice.

Simon, looking very wet and very worn out in his

usual gray suit, but more than anything outraged and militant, grabbed Reuben's arm and said, "The fifty-one-fifties are bogus. They had these papers signed by paramedics who aren't even here! How can we verify these signatures, or that these people even know you two boys?"

Reuben only vaguely knew what a "fifty-one-fifty" was, but he could tell it was a legal paper of commitment.

"Now you can see perfectly well that there is nothing wrong or violent about this young man, both of you," Simon continued in a quaking voice, "and I warn you, if you dare to attempt to take him or that boy there out of this house by force—."

With a steely firmness, the Russian doctor turned and introduced herself to Reuben. "Dr. Darya Klopov," she said in a thick accent, with a slight raise of her white eyebrows, her eyes narrowing as she extended her small naked hand. Her smile was a grimace baring perfect porcelain teeth. The scent of deep resentment came from her, absolute insolence. "I ask only that you trust me, young man, that you trust my knowledge of these extraordinary experiences that you've had to endure."

"Yes, yes," said Dr. Jaska. Another grotesque smile that was not a smile, and another thick accent. "And absolutely no one has to be harmed in this situation, where, you see, we have so many armed men." His lips drew back menacingly from his teeth as he said the words "armed men." He turned anxiously to the

door as he gestured, seemingly on the verge of opening it and inviting the "armed men" in.

Grace flew at the doctor with a volley of legal
threats.

Jim, in his full black suit and Roman collar, had
taken up a position directly beside Reuben, and now
Phil came round and stood with him as well. Phil,
looking professorial with his disheveled gray hair and
rumpled shirt and crooked tie, was shaking his head,
murmuring, "No, no, this is not going to happen.
Absolutely not."

Reuben could hear Stuart pouring out his heart
to Dr. Cutler. "Let me just stay here with Reuben.
Reuben's my friend. If I can just stay here, Dr. Cutler,
please, please, please."

**What do I do now?**

"You see," said Dr. Klopov unctuously, "this is a
signed order entrusting you to our care."

"And have you ever even laid eyes on the paramedic who signed this order?" demanded Grace.
"They bought these two pieces of paper. They do not
understand. They will not get away with this."

"I can't come with you," Reuben said to the doctor.

Jaska turned and opened the door on the icy wind.
He called out to the men.

The sheriff at once protested. "I'll take care of that,
Doctor. You just leave those men outside." He immediately stepped up to the door. "You stay where you
are!" he called out. A mild-mannered gray-haired
man in his late sixties, he was plainly out of sorts

with the whole predicament. He turned to Reuben now and appeared to rather theatrically take a good look at him. "If somebody could just explain to me in plain English why either of these two boys should be committed against their will, I would welcome that explanation because I don't see the problem here, I really just don't——."

"Of course you don't see it!" fired back Dr. Klopov, pacing in her thick black high heels, as though she needed the sound of them thonking on the oak parquet. "You have no sense of the volatile nature of the illness we're dealing with, or our knowledge of these dangerous cases——."

Simon Oliver raised his voice. "Sheriff, you should take those men and go home."

The door was still open. The voices outside were getting louder. The scent of coffee wafted on the wind. Galton's voice was mingled with the others, and from what Reuben could see, Laura was out there too in the rain serving the coffee in mugs from a large tray.

**And where the hell are Felix and Margon? And what the hell do they expect me to do?**

"All right!" declared Reuben. Again, he held up his hands. "I'm not going anywhere." He closed the front door. "Sheriff, the last time I saw a paramedic was over a month ago. I don't know who signed this paper. I picked up Stuart last night because the kid was lost and frightened. That's Stuart's doctor right there, Dr. Cutler. Granted, I should have called somebody, notified somebody last night, but Stuart's fine."

With ugly patronizing facial expressions the doctors were shaking their heads, and pursing their lips, as though this was out of the question. "No, no, no," said Dr. Jaska. "You are most certainly coming, young man. We have gone to great trouble and expense to see to your care, and you will come. Will you come peacefully or must we—."

He stopped dead, his face going blank.

Beside him, Dr. Klopov turned pale with shock.

Reuben turned around.

Margon and Felix had come back into the room. They stood to the right side of the great fireplace, and beside them stood yet another of the distinguished gentlemen from the photograph, the gray-haired older-appearing Baron Thibault, the man with the very large eyes and deeply wrinkled face.

The men moved naturally and almost casually closer, as Grace stepped back and out of the way.

"It's been a long time, hasn't it, Doctors," said Baron Thibault in a deep well-assured baritone. "What has it been, exactly, would you say? Almost ten years?"

Dr. Klopov was inching backwards towards the door, and Jaska, who stood beside it, reached out, groping, for the knob.

"Oh, surely you're not leaving," Margon said. The voice was pleasant, polite. "But you've only just arrived, and as you said, Dr. Jaska, you've gone to so much trouble and expense."

"You know these men?" Grace asked Margon.

She gestured to the doctors. "You know what this is about?"

"Stay out of it, Grace," said Phil.

Margon acknowledged both of them with small nods and an agreeable enough smile.

The doctors were petrified, and in a silent rage. The reek of evil was so seductive. The spasms were churning again in Reuben.

Felix merely watched, his face impassive and faintly sad.

Suddenly a riff of cries broke out beyond the door.

Jaska jumped back. And Klopov too was startled but recovered herself, firing a fierce malevolent look at Margon.

Something immense and heavy thundered against the door. Reuben saw it actually shuddering as the doctors scrambled to get clear of it, and the sheriff let out a shout.

People on the other side were screaming, men and women alike.

The door burst inward, falling off its screeching hinges, and was slammed violently to his left.

Reuben's heart was in his throat.

It was a man wolf, emerging from the swirling rain as if from nothingness, a great seven-foot monster in full dark brown wolf-coat with blazing gray eyes, shining white fangs, and a deep gargling roar breaking from its throat.

The spasms made a fist inside of Reuben. He felt

the blood drain from his face. At the same time he felt a wave of nausea and his knees went weak.

The man wolf's great paws reached out for Dr. Klopov and caught her by her arms, lifting her off her feet.

"You will not, you will not!" she bellowed, squirming, feet thrashing, struggling to make her own groping fingers into claws, as the beast raised her up into the full glare of the outside lights.

Everyone in the room was in motion, Reuben himself stumbling backwards, and Dr. Cutler shrieking over and over again as if she couldn't stop herself, and Jim scrambling to his mother's side.

The men and women outside were in total panic, yelling, fighting with one another. Shots rang out and then came the inevitable, "Don't shoot, don't shoot."

"Rush it, take it alive!" roared Dr. Jaska, grabbing at the petrified sheriff. "Capture it, you fool!"

Reuben watched utterly astonished as the man wolf sank its gobbling fangs into the doctor's throat, the blood spurting and pouring down over her rumpled clothes. Her arms went dead like broken branches. Dr. Jaska gave the loudest and most terrible wail. "Kill it, kill it!" he was now screaming, and the sheriff was struggling to get his gun out of the holster.

Shots came again from the screaming crowd on the outside.

Undeterred the beast closed its powerful jaws on the woman's flopping head and tore it loose from her neck, snapping ribbons of rubbery bloody skin. Then swinging the head back and forth wildly, the beast sent the head flying out into the night.

The mangled bloody body of the doctor, it dropped to the steps—lunging into the room and knocking the sheriff flat on his back, as it caught the fleeing Dr. Jaska in the doors of the conservatory.

Crashing into the potted trees and flowers, the two figures merged as the doctor let loose a desperate boiling tirade in Russian before the man wolf ripped his head off as he had done to the woman doctor and threw the head back into the great room where it rolled across the floor before the open door.

The sheriff was struggling to get up and almost fell on the head, and then got his gun out and couldn't get control of his right arm to aim.

The towering man wolf strode past him, pale eyes staring forward, dragging the headless broken body of Jaska by one hook of a claw.

Reuben stared aghast at its powerful hairy legs, the way it moved on the balls of its feet, heels high, knees flexed. He had felt all this, but never beheld it.

The monster dropped the body. With one great leap it vaulted through the assembly, pounding past Grace and Jim as it raced across the great room and into the library where it burst through the drapery and glass of the eastern window and vanished into the night. The shattered glass clattered down with the brass drapery rod and the crumpling fabric and the glittering rain swept in.

Reuben stood stock-still.

The spasms were running rampant inside him. But his skin was like an icy armor containing him.

He saw around him utter pandemonium—Dr. Cutler in hysterics being held by the desperate stammering Stuart, his mother climbing up from her knees and staring after the monster, and Jim down on his knees with his hands over his face, praying with his eyes shut.

Phil rushed to the aid of his wife. And Laura, who appeared now in the open door, and standing well to one side of the doctor's dead body, stared at Reuben and Reuben stared at her. He reached out to welcome her into his arms.

Simon Oliver had fallen into a chair, and clutching at his chest, his face flushed and wet, was struggling to get back to his feet.

Only the three men—Felix, Margon, and Thibault—had not moved. Now Thibault collected himself and went to assist the sheriff. The sheriff took his arm gratefully and rushed past Laura and Reuben, shouting commands to his men.

The sirens of the patrol cars were now slicing up the night with their shrill pulsing wails.

Felix stood quite still, looking to his right at the severed head of Dr. Jaska that lay on its side, as heads apparently tend to do, staring blankly at nothing. And Margon went to put his arms round Dr. Cutler and assure her in the most tender voice that "the creature" had apparently fled. Dr. Cutler was plainly nauseated and about to be really sick.

The patrolmen were fanning out into the woods. More sirens were cutting up the night. Those hideous strobing lights were flashing across the great room, in one garish turn after another, and the crumpled body of Dr. Klopov lay on the top step, a sack of bloody clothes in the falling rain.

Men stumbled over it as they came into the house, guns raised.

Stuart's face was utterly expressionless and white.

Poor Stuart. Reuben stood there, holding Laura in his arms. He was trembling. Stuart had seen what this monster could do twice, had he not? Reuben had never even seen it once. Never once seen the great hairy beast pick up a human being as if it were a weightless mannequin and decapitate it as though pulling a fat chunk of overripe fruit off a crackling stem. The sheriff burst back into the room, face wet and shining, with a highway patrolman beside him. "Nobody leaves this place, nobody leaves, nobody leaves!" he yelled. "Until we get a statement from everybody."

Grace, white-faced, shaking, her eyes grotesquely wide and glassy with tears, was being stroked and comforted by Phil, who spoke to her in a soft confidential voice. Felix also stood beside her, and Thibault drew close to Reuben and Laura.

Grace looked at her son.

Reuben looked at her.

He looked at Stuart. Stuart stood helpless by the fireplace merely looking at Reuben, his face now remarkably calm and with a dreamy remote perplexity.

Reuben watched Margon and Felix conferring with the sheriff, but he didn't hear the words they spoke.

Then Grace did something Reuben had never seen before, or ever thought he would see. She passed out cold, slipping like a greased sack out of Phil's arms, and hit the floor with a thud.

# 35

It was the strangest party that Reuben had ever seen in all his life. And it was a party.

The forensics teams were long gone, including men from San Francisco, Mendocino County, and the FBI.

So were most of the paramedics as they were needed elsewhere and had been questioned first.

Simon Oliver had been taken to the local emergency room, after suffering all the symptoms of heart failure which might have been only a panic attack.

The house was filled with the scent of the rain and the aroma of coffee, lemon tea, and red wine.

All the comfort cookies had been taken out of the pantry and piled upon trays. Dried salamis had been sliced and set out with crackers and mustard. The wife of one of the local sheriff's deputies had come with platters of fresh sliced pumpkin bread.

At the breakfast table and in the kitchen, and in the dining room, people were gathered in little knots mulling over what had happened, giving their statements to the sheriff, the highway patrol, and the men from the attorney general's office who'd been sent from Fort Bragg.

Galton and his cousins had done their best to

board up the library window at least halfway, draping it with heavy plastic; and after an hour of hard work had managed to rehang the front door on serviceable hinges with a new dead-bolt lock.

Now they sipped coffee, chatted, milled around with everyone else.

Fires blazed in the big fireplaces. All the lamps had been lighted, from ornate wall sconces to old electric lights on corner tables or chests which Reuben had never even noticed before.

And the young armed patrolmen and paramedics moved through the rooms like singles at any party, eyeing one another and the "more important" guests who clung together in small cliques.

Dr. Cutler hunkered down deep in the big old couch by the great room fireplace, a blanket around her shoulders, shivering not from the cold but from the experience, explaining to the investigators, "Well, surely it was some species for which we have no present scientific label or definition; either that or a truly monstrous mutation, a victim of a combination of rampant bone development and hair growth. Why, the floorboards were shaking under the thing. It must have weighed three hundred pounds."

Grace, Phil, and Jim were gathered at the great dining table in the oddly cheerful light of the medieval fireplace, talking to Felix who explained amicably that Jaska and Klopov had been connected for years with unorthodox experiments and clandestine research, funded for decades by the Soviet government, and later by questionable private patrons for dubious ends.

"They were heavy into the occult, as I understood it," said Felix, "always insinuating that the Soviets knew secrets about the world of lore and legend that others had foolishly dismissed."

Grace studied Felix sympathetically as he went on.

"You mean they were interested in this thing, this man wolf, for private medicinal research?" asked Phil.

Jim's face was solemn, remote, his eyes moving over Felix gently and unobtrusively as Felix spoke.

"Does it surprise you?" asked Felix. "There are scientists out there treating billionaire clients with unorthodox youth serums, human growth hormone, stem cells, sheep glands, cloned skin and bone, and cosmetic transplants of which the rest of us only dream. Who knows what they know, or where their research has led them? Of course they wanted to get their hands on the Man Wolf. Perhaps there are sub rosa laboratories under American auspices with the same aims."

Grace murmured wearily that there would always be scientists and doctors who dreamed of being morally free to do exactly as they pleased.

"Yes," said Felix, "and when I heard from Arthur Hammermill that Jaska had been pestering Reuben's family, well, I thought to myself perhaps we can be of some assistance."

"And you'd met them in Paris—," said Phil.

"I knew them," said Felix. "I suspected their methods. I suspected the lengths to which they might go to achieve their ends. I suspect the police will discover their Sausalito Rehabilitation Center was a front, that they had a plane waiting to take Stuart and Reuben out of the country."

"And all this to determine why the boys were exhibiting these symptoms, whatever they are, these strange changes—," said Phil.

"Because they'd been bitten by this thing," said Grace. She sat back, shaking her head. "To see whether the saliva of the Man Wolf had imparted some element that could be isolated from the victims' blood."

"Precisely," said Felix.

"Well, they would have been extremely disappointed," said Grace. "Because we ourselves have researched the matter from every conceivable angle."

"Oh, but you don't know what scientists like that have at their disposal," said Phil. "You've never really been a research scientist. You're a surgeon. Those two were Frankensteinian fanatics."

Jim looked past the others at Reuben, his eyes tired, grieved, faintly afraid.

Jim had gone with Simon Oliver to the emergency room, and had returned only an hour ago, reporting that Simon was all right and on his way back to the city by special ambulance. He would be fine.

"Well, there is one thing we all know, isn't there?" asked Grace. "Whether we are surgeons, priests, or poets, right Phil? We've seen this monster with our own eyes."

"Doesn't matter," said Phil. "It's like a ghost. You see it yourself, you believe it. But nobody else will believe it. You'll see. They'll sneer at us just like they're sneering at everybody else who's seen it. The witnesses could fill Candlestick Park and it wouldn't make any difference at all."

"That's true," said Jim softly, speaking to no one in particular.

"And what did you learn from this," asked Felix, looking intently at Grace, "that you didn't know before?"

"That it is real," said Grace with a shrug. "That it's no criminal in a costume, or matter of a collective hallucination. It's a freak of nature, to use the old phrase, a human being who's suffered a monstrous deformity. It will all eventually be explained."

"Perhaps you're right," said Felix.

"But what if it's an unknown species?" asked Phil. "Something that simply has not been discovered yet?"

"Nonsense," said Grace. "That's impossible in today's world. Oh, I mean maybe it could happen in New Guinea but not here. It's a one-off. It's suffered some hideous calamity or it's a freak since birth."

"Hmmm, I don't know," said Phil. "Exactly what accident or illness or congenital deformity could account for that thing? Nothing I ever heard of, but you're the doctor, Grace."

"It will all be explained," she said. She wasn't adamant or arguing, really. She was merely convinced. "They'll catch the thing. They have to. There's no safe corner of the modern world for such a thing. They'll get to the bottom of what he is and how he became what he is, and that will be the end of it. In the meantime, the world can run rampant with the idea of the Man Wolf as if he were a template for a new form of hero, when, sadly, he's no more than an aberration. Eventually, they'll autopsy him, eviscerate him, stuff him, and mount him. He'll end up in the Smithsonian in a glass case. And we'll tell our grandchildren that we once glimpsed him with our own eyes, during his brief and brilliant glory days, and he'll be sentimentalized as a tragic figure—rather like the Elephant Man, in the end."

Jim said not a word.

Reuben wandered out to the kitchen where the sheriff stood with his thirteenth cup of coffee, talking to Galton about the werewolf legends around "these parts" that hadn't been heard in many a year.

"Now, there was an old lady up here, a crazy lady, years ago, in this house. I remember my grandmother talking about it. She sent word down to the mayor in Nideck, that there were werewolves in these woods—."

"I don't know what you're talking about," said Galton. "I'm older than you and I never heard any such thing—."

"—claimed the Nideck family were werewolves. I meant she went screaming crazy up here, insisting—."

"Oh, your grandmother made that up."

And so forth and so on.

Stuart had disappeared with Margon Sperver. And Baron Thibault was assisting Laura as she arranged the last of the Fig Newtons and coconut macaroons on a pretty flowered china plate. The kitchen smelled strongly now of fresh-cut apples and cinnamon tea. Laura looked emotionally threadbare but she obviously liked Thibault enormously and they'd been conversing all evening in low voices as the party rolled on. Thibault was saying to her, "But all morality is of necessity shaped by context. I'm not talking relativism, no. To ignore the context of a decision is in fact immoral."

"Then how exactly do we define immutable truths?" Laura asked. "I do see exactly what you're saying but I lack the skills to define how we construct moral decisions when context is continually shifting—."

"By recognizing," said Thibault, "the conditions under which every moral decision is made."

Some people were leaving.

The official interviews were winding down.

The sheriff reported that the search for the Man Wolf around Nideck had been abandoned. And he was just getting word that Jaska and Klopov had both been wanted by Interpol for questioning in a number of open cases in Germany and France.

Someone had gotten a clear and unmistakable series of shots of the Man Wolf south of San Jose. "Looks like the real thing to me," said the sheriff checking his iPhone. "That's the same devil all right. Take a look. And how could the critter have gotten that far that quick?"

The forensics teams had called to say that the crime scenes could be released.

Finally, the party began to break up.

The family had a plane waiting for them at the nearby airport. Reuben walked with his mother to the door.

"These friends of the Nidecks', they've been invaluable," she conceded. "I like that Felix very much. I thought Arthur Hammermill was in love or something when he went on and on about the man, but I understand now. I do."

She kissed Reuben tenderly on both cheeks.

"You'll bring Stuart in to see Dr. Cutler for his shots."

"Absolutely, Mom. Stuart's my little brother from now on."

His mother looked at him for a long moment.

"Try not to think about all the unanswered questions, Mom," said Reuben. "You taught me once that we have to live with unanswered questions all our lives."

She was surprised. "You think I'm worried, Reuben?" she asked. "You don't know what this night has done for me. Oh, it's been ghastly, yes. It was the Day from Hell and the Night from Hell. But someday I'll have to tell you all about my worries, what they actually were." She shook her head sadly. "You know, medicine can confound the most rational of human beings. We doctors witness the inexplicable and the miraculous every day. You wouldn't believe how relieved I am now about a lot of things." She hesitated, but then said only, "A surgeon can be as superstitious as anybody else."

They walked in silence to the waiting van.

He embraced Jim warmly, and promised to call soon. "I know the burden you're carrying," Reuben whispered to him. "I know what I've put you through."

"And now you have a houseful of these creatures?" Jim asked in a hushed confidential voice. "What are you doing, Reuben? Where are you going? Is there any turning back? Well, they've snookered everybody, haven't they? And what now?" Immediately he was sorry, terribly sorry. He hugged Reuben again.

"This gives me time and space," said Reuben.

"I know. It takes the heat off you and that kid. I understand that. I don't want anyone to hurt you, Reuben. I can't bear the thought of them catching you, hurting you. I just don't know what to do for you, myself."

A few of the law enforcement people were still taking photographs and the sheriff reminded them: "No publishing of private photos on Facebook and I mean it!"

It seemed an eternity as they took their leave, Dr.

Cutler the absolute last, who wanted so to check on Stuart, but realized that the boy shouldn't be awakened after what he'd been through.

Stuart's mother would be in the hospital for another few days. Yes, he would help Stuart to get to see his mother. He would handle it. Not to worry.

Phil gave him a rough hug. "One of these days I'm going to appear on your doorstep," he said, "with a suitcase under my arm."

"That would be wonderful, Dad," he said. "Dad, there's a little house over there, down over the rise, with a view of the sea. It needs a lot of repair, but somehow I see you in there, hammering away on your old typewriter."

"Son, don't push it. I might show up here and never leave." He shook his head, one of his favorite little gestures. He shook his head negatively at least fifteen times a day. "Be the best thing that ever happened to your mother, if I did," he said. "You just whistle when you're ready for me to come."

Reuben kissed him on his rough unshaven face and helped him into the van.

At last they were gone, all of them, and he wandered back through the drizzling rain into the house and bolted the door.

# 36

THEY WERE in the dining room. There were candles burning on the hunters' boards, and on the table, in heavy engraved candlesticks. Thibault was feeding the fire again.

And across the table, Felix sat with his arms around Laura who was crying softly, her lips pressed to the back of her left hand. Her hair was loosened now and down around her face in that ethereal white veil that Reuben loved, full of flickering and reflected light.

Reuben bristled in his heart at the sight of this powerful and enthralling man holding her, and as if Felix sensed this, Felix drew back now, stood up, and gestured for him to take the chair at Laura's side.

He went round to face Reuben across the table, seating himself beside Thibault, and they were quiet for a moment in the vast dreamy and warm room.

The candle flames played softly on their faces. The smell of beeswax was sweet.

Laura had stopped crying. Her left arm locked around Reuben and she laid her head against his chest. He enfolded her with his right arm, kissing the top of her head and cradling her face with his left hand.

"I am so sorry, so sorry for all of it," he whispered.

"Oh, not for you to say," she said. "Not your doing, any of it. I'm here because I want to be here. I'm sorry for such tears."

What had brought on these particular words, Reuben wondered. They seemed related to a long conversation that he had missed.

He forced himself to look up at Felix, ashamed suddenly of his jealousy, heart breaking that he was now alone with Felix, that Felix and Thibault were under this roof with him and with Laura and that they were at last alone. How many times had he dreamt of such a moment? How many times had he prayed for it? And now it had come, and there was no impediment. The night's horrors were behind them. The night's horrors had been climactic, and were done.

Immediately Felix's cheerful and affectionate expression melted his soul. Thibault, with his large heavy-lidded eyes, looked thoughtful and kind, gray hair tousled, the soft folds of his face framing an expression that was gentle, wise.

"We couldn't tell you what we were doing," he said. "We had to draw them out, Klopov and Jaska. With Jaska it was simple. He was dogging your mother, dogging Stuart. But Klopov only surfaced at the very close."

"I thought as much," said Reuben. "It was clear Jaska deferred to her. I could sense it. So she was behind it all."

"Oh, she was the last of the governing committee that took us prisoner twenty years ago," said Felix.

"The very last, and Jaska her eager apprentice. It took a little provocation bringing her into it, but never mind that now. We couldn't warn you, we couldn't reassure you. And you do realize that not the slightest suspicion will ever attach to you or Stuart now for the Man Wolf's attacks."

"Yes, that was brilliant," said Reuben.

"But you were never in the slightest danger," said Thibault. "And if I may say so, you behaved superbly, rather like you did with Marrok. We never dreamed that Marrok would approach you. We didn't account for that at all."

"But how long have you been watching exactly?" asked Reuben.

"Well, in a way, since the beginning," said Felix. "Since I picked up the **Herald Examiner** in Paris and saw Marchent's death splashed across the front page. As soon as the 'San Francisco Man Wolf' made his debut, I was on a plane."

"Then you never left the country after our meeting at the law offices," said Reuben.

"No. We've been close to you ever since. Thibault arrived within hours; then Margon had to cross the Atlantic, and then Vandover and Gorlagon, too. But I've been in this house unbeknownst to you. You were quite clever in finding the Inner Sanctum, as we used to call it. But you did not discover the entrance in the cellar. The old obsolete furnace is a hollow aluminum dummy. I'll show you later. Grasp the right side of the lower portion of it, bring it towards you, and you will open a door to which it is attached. There is a sanctuary of rooms there, all electrically lighted and heated, and then a stairs down to a narrow tunnel which runs to the west, opening just above the huge rocks at the base of the cliff at the end of the beach."

"I know the place," said Laura. "At least I think I do." She picked up one of the old lace-trimmed linen napkins that lay in a little fan-shaped display near her, near to a plate of fruit and candies, and she dabbed at her eyes with this, and then clenched it tightly in her hand. "I found it on my walks. I couldn't quite get over those slippery rocks. But I bet I saw the place."

"Very likely you did," said Felix, "and it is very dangerous there, and the tide often pours into the tunnel, flooding it for a hundred yards or more. Best for Morphenkinder and their like, who can swim and climb like dragons."

"And you've been down there in the cement rooms behind the cellar," said Reuben.

"Yes, most of the time, or in the nearby woods. Of course we followed you into Santa Rosa to see Stuart. We knew at once what had happened. We followed you when you went in search of him. If you hadn't rescued him, we would have intervened. But you were handling things beautifully, as we suspected you would."

"The man wolf," said Laura, "who broke into the house tonight, this is one of the men in the library picture?"

"It was Sergei," said Thibault with a smile in his

deep flowing baritone voice. "We vied for the privilege, but Sergei was adamant. And Frank Vandover is with Sergei now, of course. Dr. Klopov held us prisoner for ten years. Klopov murdered one of us. This night provided considerable satisfaction for us all."

"They'll be back tomorrow," said Felix. "What they are doing right now is establishing a path south for the Man Wolf. They'll arrange an unimpeachable sighting in Mexico before morning. When they return, I'm hoping you'll receive them, that we can all, with your permission, sleep under this roof."

"This is your house," said Reuben. "Think of me as a custodian."

"No, dear boy," said Felix, saying it exactly the way Marchent had so often said it, "it's your house. Most definitely it is your house. But we will accept your invitation."

"Absolutely," said Reuben, "for now and forever and whenever and wherever you like."

"I'll take my old rooms, if you don't mind," said Felix, "and Margon has always been comfortable in one of the smaller rooms along the north side facing the woods. We will put Thibault in one of the southern rooms, just next to Stuart, if this is agreeable to you, and Frank and Sergei will sleep on the northeast end in those corner rooms above the oaks."

"I'll go see to things," said Laura, who started to get up.

"My darling, you mustn't," said Felix. "Please, do sit down. I know for a fact that everything is as comfortable as it ever was. Older, perhaps a little musty, but entirely comfortable. And I want you here, close to us. Surely you want to know what happened, too."

Reuben nodded and murmured his assent to that, holding Laura close again.

"I must say, Reuben," said Felix, "with a house of this size you must have a trusted servant or two, or this young woman completely out of her own generosity will become a drudge."

"Absolutely," said Reuben. He blushed. He didn't want to think he'd been exploiting Laura, forcing her into any domestic role. He wanted to protest, but now was not the time for it.

He had a dream in his heart that these men would never leave.

He did not know how to bring them back to the subject of Dr. Klopov. But Laura did it for him.

"Was it in the Soviet Union that Klopov held you captive?" she asked.

"It began that way," said Felix. "We were betrayed into her hands in Paris. It was quite a maneuver. Of course she had help from a very dear member of my own family and his wife."

"Marchent's parents," said Reuben.

"Correct," said Felix. His voice was even, without rancor or judgment. "It's a long story. Suffice it to say we were sold to Klopov and her cohorts by my nephew, Abel, for a fantastic sum. We were lured to Paris, with a promise of archaeological secrets discovered by a Dr. Philippe Durrell who was supposed to be working on a dig in the Middle East on behalf of the Louvre." He sighed, then went on:

"This Durrell, he was a genius of a conversationalist, and dazzled us over the phone. We converged on Paris, accepting his invitation for accommodations in a small hotel on the Left Bank."

"The trap had to be sprung in a very crowded city, you see," said Thibault, clearing his throat, his voice deep as always, and his words coming with a little more emotional resonance. "We had to be where our senses would be overwhelmed with sounds and scents so that we wouldn't detect the people who were closing in. We were narcotized individually except for Sergei, who managed to escape, and never after gave up the search for us." He glanced at Felix who gestured for him to go on.

"Almost immediately Durrell and Klopov's team lost their government funding. We were smuggled out of Russia to a grim and ill-equipped concrete prison-laboratory near Belgrade, where the battle of wits and endurance began." He shook his head as he remembered. "Philippe Durrell was brilliant without doubt."

"They were all brilliant," said Felix. "Klopov, Jaska, all of them. They believed in us completely. They knew things about our history that astonished us, and they had immense scientific knowledge in areas where more conventional scientists refuse to speculate."

"Yes, my mother was confused by that brilliance,"

said Reuben. "But she became suspicious of Jaska early on."

"Your mother's a remarkable woman," said Felix. "She seems utterly unconscious of her own physical beauty—oblivious as if she were a disembodied mind."

Reuben laughed. "She wants to be taken seriously," he said in a small voice.

"Well, yes," said Thibault, interrupting gently. "She would have found Philippe Durrell even more seductive. Philippe had immense respect for us, and for what we might willingly or unwillingly reveal. When we refused to manifest in the wolf state, he resolved to wait. When we confided nothing, he engaged us in long conversations and bided his time."

"He was intrigued as to what we knew," Felix offered gently. "By what we'd seen of this world."

Reuben was fascinated as to what this might mean. Thibault continued:

"He treated us as delicate specimens to be pampered as well as studied. Klopov was impatient and condescending and finally brutal—the kind of monster who pulls apart a butterfly the better to know how its wings work." He paused as though he did not like to remember the details now. "She was hell-bent on provoking the change in us, and when occasionally we did change, in the beginning, we learned quickly enough that we could not escape, that the bars were too strong and the numbers too overwhelming, and we then refused to manifest at all." He stopped.

Felix waited, then picked up the thread.

"Now the Chrism cannot be extracted from us by force," he explained, glancing from Laura to Reuben and back again to Laura. "It cannot be withdrawn with a hypodermic or a sponge biopsy from the tissue in our mouths. The crucial cells become inert and then disintegrate within seconds. I discovered this long ago in my own stumbling fashion in the early centuries of science, and only confirmed it in the secret laboratory in this house. The ancients knew this from trial and error. We were not the first Morphenkinder ever imprisoned by those who wanted the Chrism."

Reuben shuddered inwardly. Weeks ago, though it seemed like years, when he'd first gone to Confession to Jim, all of these possibilities—imprisonment, coercion—had come full blown into his mind.

"But to return to the moment," said Felix, "one cannot inject the serum into another. That simply will not work." He became a little more passionate as he continued.

"A critical combination of elements must be present to deliver an effective dose of the Chrism, which is why the bite of Morphenkinder more often than not produces no effect on victims at all. Now we understood full well what those elements were, and that we cannot be forced to give the Chrism, even if the change is induced, and the hand or arm of a victim is thrust into our very mouths."

"But that in itself is rather difficult to accomplish,"

Thibault interjected with a little laugh. "Shall we say that with any such attempt, casualties are high. If one is manipulated into changing, it is quite easy to rip the arm off any proffered laboratory specimen, or decapitate a man before he can get out of range. End of experiment right there."

"I understand," said Reuben, "of course. I can imagine it. In fact, I've thought it over. Oh, I mean, I can't imagine what you suffered, what you endured. But I can well imagine how this might play out."

"Imagine years of being isolated," said Felix, "subjected to freezing holding cells and days and nights of pitch darkness, of being starved and bullied and threatened, of being systematically tormented by insinuations that your companions are dead. Oh, some night I'll tell you the whole story if you want to hear it. But let's cut to the point. We refused to manifest, or to cooperate in any way. Drugs couldn't make us manifest. Neither could physical torture. We had long ago schooled ourselves to sink deep into an altered state of consciousness to defeat such efforts. Klopov became royally sick of it, and sick of Philippe's long discourses on the mystery of the Morphenkinder and the great philosophical truths that we undoubtedly knew."

He glanced at Thibault and waited for him to take up the tale.

Thibault nodded, with a faint resigned gesture of his right hand. "Klopov had Reynolds Wagner, our beloved companion and fellow prisoner, bound to an operating table and she and her team started to dissect him alive."

"My God!" Reuben whispered.

"We were forced to witness, via video cameras from our cells, what took place," said Thibault. "We could recount the story to you blow by blow. It is enough to say Reynolds couldn't endure the agony. He changed because he could not prevent it, becoming a ravening wolf, blind with rage. He managed to kill three of the doctors and almost killed Dr. Klopov before she and others disabled him with bullets to the brain. Even then he would not stop attacking. He was blind, on his knees. But he brought down one of the laboratory assistants. Klopov quite literally decapitated Reynolds with bullets, firing again and again at his throat until there was no more throat—or neck. She severed his spinal cord. Then Reynolds fell over dead." He paused, his eyes closing and his eyebrows coming together in a small frown.

"She'd been threatening us with death daily," said Felix. "Gloating as to the wealth of forensic discoveries she'd reap from our autopsies, if only Durrell had allowed her to proceed."

"I can imagine what happened."

"Oh yes," said Felix. "You've seen it." He sat back, his eyebrows raised, staring at the table. "As you know from your experience with Marrok, Wagner's remains disintegrated before her very eyes."

"She and her team made frantic efforts to stop the disintegration," said Thibault. "But they could do nothing. That's when they found out that dead we were worth nothing. And around that time Vandover tried to take his own life, or so it seemed to them, and they resolved to wear us down through Durrell's methods again. Durrell ever after hated Klopov, but he could not do without her, or have her removed. She and Jaska together were too much for him. With the other doctors lost, Jaska became even more important. We survived as best we could."

"For ten years this went on," said Reuben in amazement. It was all too real to him, this horror. He could vividly imagine being enclosed in a sterile cell.

"Yes," said Felix. "We did everything we could to trick them into allowing us access to one another, but they were far too clever for that.

"Finally a crisis in Belgrade forced them to move. Sergei had discovered us. He put pressure. And then in their haste they made their fatal mistake. They brought us together, without heavily narcotizing us, for transport in one van."

"They thought we were quite thoroughly demoralized by that time," said Thibault, "that we were far weaker than we were."

"We worked the change simultaneously with one another," said Felix, "which is relatively simple for us to do. We broke the bonds and slaughtered the entire crew, including Durrell and all the other doctors, except, that is, for Klopov and her assistant Jaska who managed to escape. We burned the laboratory to the ground."

Both men went quiet for a moment, as though lost in their reminiscence. Then Thibault, with a dreamy faraway look in his eyes, smiled. "Well, we escaped into Belgrade where Sergei had everything waiting for us. We thought we'd take care of Klopov and Jaska in a matter of days."

"And it didn't happen," Laura affirmed.

"No, it didn't," said Thibault. "We were never able to locate them again. I suspect they used other names. But when a doctor's credentials depend upon the birth name, well, he or she is likely to return to it, for obvious advantages." His smile became faintly bitter. "And that is what inevitably happened. Of course the pair has found new backing, and we must eventually worry about that backing, but not just now."

He cleared his throat and went on.

"Then came the news from America that Felix's beloved Marchent had been murdered by her own brothers and a Morphenkind had dispatched the killers in the age-old way of the beast."

For a long time they were silent.

"I was certain I would be united with Marchent someday," Felix said in a small defeated voice. "I was so foolish, not to have contacted her, not to have simply come home." He looked off, and then at the table in front of him, as though intrigued by the satin finish of the wood. But he was not seeing that at all. "I had come here often enough when she was traveling. And once or twice spied on her from the woods. You see—." He broke off.

"You didn't want to tell her who had betrayed you," suggested Laura.

"No, I didn't," said Felix. His voice was low, tentative. "And I didn't want to tell her that I had paid them both—her father and mother—in kind. How would she have ever understood unless I'd revealed **everything** to her, and that I did not want to do."

A silence fell over them all.

"When the news broke about the attacks in San Francisco . . . ," Felix started, then his voice just trailed away.

"You knew that Marrok had passed the Chrism," Laura suggested. "And you suspected that the good doctors would be unable to resist."

Felix nodded.

Another interval of silence fell. The only sounds were the rain pattering on the windowsills, and the fire spitting and crackling in the huge grate.

"Would you have come here," Reuben asked, "if there had been no question of Klopov or Jaska?"

"Yes," said Felix. "Most definitely yes. I would not have left you to face this alone. I wanted to come on account of Marchent. I wanted the things I'd left in the house. But I wanted to know you. I wanted to discover who you really were. I wasn't going to abandon you to all this. We never do that. That's why I arranged that awkward meeting at the lawyers' offices.

"And if I'd been unreachable for any reason, Thibault would have come to seek you out. Or Vandover or Sergei. As it was, we were together when the news broke. We knew it was Marrok. We knew that the assaults in San Francisco had been carried out by you."

"Then whenever the Chrism's passed, you go to help that individual?" asked Reuben.

"My dear boy," said Felix. "It does not happen all that often, really, and seldom in such a spectacular way."

They were both looking fondly at Reuben now, and the old warmth came back into Felix's face.

"So you were never angry," asked Reuben, "that I put the Man Wolf in the public eye."

Felix laughed under his breath, and so did Thibault, as they exchanged glances.

"Were we angry?" he asked Thibault with a sly smile, nudging him with his elbow. "What do you think?"

Thibault shook his head.

Reuben couldn't figure out what this actually meant, only that it did seem the very opposite of anger, and that was more than he had a right to ask.

"Well, I was not so very delighted with it," said Felix, "but I would not say I was ever angry, no."

"There's so much we can tell you," said Thibault, affectionately. "So many things we can explain—to you, and to Stuart, and to Laura."

**And to Laura.**

Felix looked at the dark window with its glittering

sheet of sliding rain. His eyes moved over the elaborate ceiling with its varnished crisscross beams and those panels of painted sky with their gold stars.

And I know what he is feeling, thought Reuben, and he loves this house, loves it as he did when he built it, for surely he did build it, and he needs it, needs to come home to it now.

"And it would take years of nights such as this," Felix said, dreamily, "to tell you all we have to tell."

"I think it's enough for now, for this first night, this remarkable night," said Thibault. "But remember, you were never in danger as we waited to play our hand."

"I understand that completely," said Reuben. There was more he wanted to say, especially now. So much more. But he was almost too dazzled to form words.

His many questions seemed insignificant as a vision of knowledge took form in his mind, vast, well beyond the arithmetical strictures of language, a great organic yet limitless vision that dissolved words. It was something infinitely more like music, expanding and rolling like the symphonic triumphs of Brahms. His heart was beating quietly to the mounting rhythm of his expectations, and a light was slowing breaking in on him, heated, incandescent, like the Shechinah, or the inevitable light of every dawn.

In his mind, he was back in the high forest canopy, a man wolf resting in the branches, seeing the stars again above him, and wondering once more if the great longing he felt was somehow a form of prayer.

Why was that so important to him? Was that the only species of redemption he understood?

"It's Margon who will counsel you," said Thibault. "It's always best that Margon do the counseling. He is the very oldest of us all."

It sent a thrill through Reuben. And Margon, "the very oldest," was with the Boy Wolf right now. How different all this would be for Stuart who was so energetic and inquisitive by nature, how remarkably different from what it had been for Reuben stumbling from one discovery to another on his unlighted path.

"I'm tired now," said Felix, "and the sight of so much blood earlier has played upon my inveterate hunger."

"Oh, give it a rest!" said Thibault in a mock-scolding voice.

"You were born old," said Felix, gently nudging Thibault with his elbow again.

"Perhaps I was," said Thibault. "And it's not a bad thing. I'll take the offer of any bed in this house."

"I need the forest," said Felix. He looked at Laura. "My darling," he said, "would you allow me to take your young man away for just a little while, should he want to come?"

"Of course, go," she said earnestly. She clasped Reuben's hand. "And what about Stuart?"

"They're close," said Thibault. "I think Margon is deliberately exhausting him for his own good."

"There are reporters out there," said Reuben. "I can hear them. I'm sure you can too."

"And so can Margon," said Felix gently. "They'll come through the tunnel or over the roof into the sanctum. You need not worry. You know that. You need not ever worry. We will never be seen."

Laura was on her feet and in Reuben's arms. He felt the intense heat of her breasts against his shirtfront, his chest. He pressed his face against her tender neck.

Reuben didn't have to tell her what this meant to him, to go out there into the divine leafy darkness with Felix, to go deep into the very heart of the night at Felix's side.

"You come back to me soon," she whispered.

Thibault had come round to take her arm, to escort her, as it were, as if this had been a formal dinner in an earlier time, and they left the room together, Laura vaguely enchanted and Thibault doting as they disappeared into the hall.

Reuben looked at Felix.

Felix was again smiling at him, his face serene and full of compassion and a simple, effortless, and shining goodwill.

# 37

THEY WENT DOWN through the cellar. All one had to do was swing back the heavy door to which the furnace was affixed above a concrete base that was in fact a hollow plastered box, and they were walking through a nest of cluttered dimly lighted rooms, beneath dusty electric bulbs and past heaps of trunks and old garments, and hulking pieces of furniture, and past other doors.

Down the stairs they went, and at last entered the broad earthen tunnel beamed and supported like a coal mine, a faint silvery light sparkling on the rich veins of clay in the damp walls.

Round one turn and another they walked until far ahead of them, there broke the metallic light of the wet sky.

The tunnel went straight to the roaring sea.

Felix, fully clothed, began to run. He ran faster and faster and then leapt forward with his arms out, his clothes breaking from him, his shoes flying away as in midair his arms turned to great wolfen forelegs and his hands to great furred claws. On and on he galloped, gliding through the narrow opening out of sight.

Reuben gasped in astonishment. Then, trusting

himself utterly to the example, he too began to run. Faster and faster he ran, the spasms rolling inside him, seemingly lifting him as he too leapt forward, his clothes ripping and releasing him, his limbs elongating, the wolf-coat erupting from the top of his head to his toes.

When he hit the ground again, he was Morphenkind, pounding towards the roar of the surf, the roar of the wind, the welcoming light of the night sky.

He cleared the opening effortlessly, rushing through the icy frothing waves.

Above on the perilous and jagged rocks, the man wolf who was Felix waited for him and then they scaled the impossible cliff together, digging into earth and vine and root, and romping into the dank fragrant refuge of the trees.

Where Felix led, he followed, running as he had run south to Santa Rosa to find Stuart, with that rippling power, as they went north beyond the woods of Nideck Point, farther and farther into cathedral groves of redwoods that dwarfed them in the journey, like the lost monoliths of another world.

Boar, wildcat, bear—he caught the scents, and the hunger rose in him, the imperative to kill, to feast. The wind carried the scent of fields, of flower, of earth baked by sun and soaked with rain. On and on they ran, until there came on the wind the scent he'd never truly relished before: the bull elk.

The bull elk knew it was being pursued. Its heart thundered inside it. It ran with majestic speed and grace, dashing ever faster ahead of them until they both caught it, descending on its broad back, closing their jaws on either side of its mighty arched neck.

Down went the immense animal, its thin graceful legs twitching, its mighty heart pumping, its great gentle dark eye staring unquestioningly at the broken fragments of starry sky above.

Woe to you, all living things that appeal to such a heaven for help.

Reuben pulled loose the long dripping strips of meat as if he'd never known restraint in all his life. He crunched the gristle and bones, snapping the bones, grinding them, sucking at the marrow, swallowing all.

They nuzzled into the soft underdown of the belly—oh, this was always the sweetest with either man or beast—and tore at the richly flavorful rubbery guts, lapping with quick pink tongues at the thickening blood.

And so they feasted together in the soundless rain.

Afterwards, they lay at the base of the tree together, motionless, Felix obviously listening, waiting.

Who could have told the difference between them, beasts of the same size and color as they were? It resided in the eyes.

Critters sang of the fresh kill, the carrion. Slithering through the underbrush an army of tiny mouths moved towards it, the bloody carcass shivering as they assaulted it, as if in being devoured it had taken on a new life.

Out of the deep shadows came the coyotes, huge,

hulking, gray, lethal-looking as wolves with their pointed ears and snouts.

Felix appeared to watch, a great silent hairy man being with patient but glittering eyes.

He crept forward now on all fours and Reuben followed.

The coyotes yelped, danced back, snapped at him, and he at them, taunting them with his right paw, laughing under his breath, growling, allowing them to move in again, and teasing them again and then watching them as they tore at the broken body of the elk.

He made himself so still they grew bolder, drawing closer to him, then shying violently at the sound of his laugh.

Suddenly he sprang, pinioning the largest with his paws, and clamped its wolflike head in his jaws.

He shook the dying animal and tossed it to Reuben. The other coyotes had fled in a chorus of cries and yelps.

And they feasted again.

It was almost dawn when they descended the cliff, clutching, sliding, and scampering over the slick rocks to the entrance of the cave. How small it seemed, near invisible, this seam in the thick rocks, a broken narrow cavity hung with gleaming moss and foaming with the lapping tide.

They walked together through the cave, and Felix changed back into the man without ever breaking his stride. Reuben found he could do it too. He felt his feet shrinking, his calves contracting with every step.

They dressed together in the murky light, the clothes soiled and torn, but all they had, and Felix threw his arm around Reuben, his fingers stealing affectionately through Reuben's hair and then clasping the back of his neck.

"Little brother," he said.

These were the first and only words he had spoken since they went out together.

And they went up into the welcome warmth of the house and to their separate rooms.

Laura stood at the bedroom window, staring out at the steel-blue dawn.

# 38

THE DINING ROOM ONCE AGAIN.

The fire was built high and roaring under the black medieval mantel, and the candles flickered and smoked down the length of the table, amid platters of roast lamb fragrant with garlic and rosemary, glazed duckling, steaming broccoli, Italian squash, heaps of unpeeled potatoes, artichoke hearts tossed with oil, and roasted onions, freshly sliced bananas and melon, and hot freshly baked bread.

The wine was red in the delicate stem glasses, the salad glistening in the big wooden bowls, sharp sweetness of the mint jelly as delicious as the aroma of the succulent meats, and sweet butter smeared on the hot rolls.

The company came and went from the kitchen, all hands helping with the feast—even Stuart who had laid out the old linen napkins at every place and straightened the silver, marveling at the size of the old knives and forks. Felix set the bowls of sugared cinnamon-almond rice on the table. Thibault brought the platter of bright orange yams.

Margon sat at the head of the table, his long thick brown hair loose to his shoulders, his burgundy-colored shirt open casually at the neck. His back was to the eastern windows and the not-uncommon sight of a reporter or two out there prowling in the tangled oaks.

The early afternoon light was white but very bright through the thick, twisted web of gray branches.

All were seated finally, and Margon called for a moment of thanks, and bowed his head.

"Margon the Godless, thanks the gods," whispered Felix with a wink to Reuben who was once again opposite him, and Laura who sat beside him smiling, but Felix closed his eyes and so did all of them.

"Say what you will to the force that governs the universe," said Margon. "Perhaps we'll call it into being, and it will yet love us as we love it."

Again, the silence, the sweet incessant patter of the rain slowly washing the world clean and nourishing it, and the logs sputtering and spitting as the flames danced against the darkened bricks, and a soft distant music emanating from the kitchen—Erik Leslie Satie again, the piano, **Gymnopédie No.1.**

Oh, that humankind could make such music, thought Reuben, on this tiny cinder whirling in a tiny solar system lost in a tiny galaxy hurtling through endless space. Maybe the Maker of all this will hear this music as a form of prayer. Love us, love us as we love You.

Stuart, seated between Felix and Thibault on the other side of the table, in a white T-shirt and jeans, began to cry. He crumpled, his face hidden in his enormous hand, his large shoulders heaving silently, and then he went still, his eyes closed, and puckered, tears spurting as if from a little child.

His curling blond hair was tied back, away from the bones of his large face, and with his short broad nose and the ever-visible sprinkling of freckles, he looked as he so often did like a large little boy.

Laura bit her lip and fought tears watching him. Reuben squeezed her hand.

And a grief took hold of Reuben, but it was mingled entirely with the happiness that he felt. This house, so full of life, life that embraced all that had happened to him, all that had frightened him and at times almost defeated him, well almost—this life was straight from his wordless dreams.

Margon looked up, the moment of silent prayer ended, taking in all those seated with his eyes.

The party came alive. Platters were passed, more wine poured, butter slopped on hot steaming slices of bread and light flaking rolls, the scent of garlic rising from the tumbling, sliding spoonfuls of salad, and great forkfuls of meat slapped onto the old flowered china plates.

"So what am I to offer you?" said Margon as if they'd been talking all the while, instead of attending to a thousand unimportant yet essential things. "What am I to give you to help you with this journey that you've begun?"

He took a deep gulp of the sparkling water that stood beside the empty glass for the wine he didn't drink.

He took a heaping portion of the hot broccoli and green squash, and even more of the artichoke hearts, and tore off a hunk from a hot buttered roll.

"The basic things you must know are these. The change is irreversible. Once the Chrism has taken hold, you are Morphenkinder, as we call it now, and that can never be undone."

Stuart woke from his tears just as quickly as he'd given into them. He was eating such enormous chunks of lamb that Reuben feared he might choke, blue eyes flashing at Margon as Margon went on.

Margon's voice was as agreeable and almost humble as it had been the night before. He was a man of persuasion and subtle power, his light golden brown face very plastic and expressive, black eyes rimmed in thick black lashes that gave a drama and an intensity to his expressions that seemed more fierce than his words.

"Never in all my existence," he continued, gesturing unconsciously with the silver fork, "have I known someone who truly wanted it reversed, but there are those who rush headlong into perdition as the result of it, driven insane by the lust for the hunt, and scorning every other aspect of life until they are destroyed by the weapons of those who hunt them down. But you needn't worry about this. You are not,

any of you"—his eyes took in Laura as he said this—
"of the sort to be so foolish or such spendthrifts with
the gifts of fate."

Stuart started to ask something but Margon gestured for silence.

"Allow me to continue," he cautioned. He went on:

"The Chrism is almost always passed by accident.
And it can only be passed by us when we are in the
wolfen state. However, my mind, my limited mind,
my mortal mind, is haunted by a grim legion of those
to whom I refused it and I restrain myself no more.
When one is worthy, and one asks, I give the Chrism.
I ask only an ardent and informed desire. But this
you—Reuben and Stuart—must not seek to do—
offer the Chrism, that is. The responsibility's far too
great. You must leave such fateful choices to me, to
Felix, to Thibault, even to Frank and Sergei who will
be joining us soon."

Reuben nodded. Now was not the time to press
him on Laura, but did it even need to be done? There
had not been the slightest suggestion that Laura was
not already one of them, and this, in Reuben's mind,
had to mean one thing. Yet he did not know and it
tortured him. He did not know.

"Now the Chrism can prove fatal to the infected
one," said Margon, "but this happens very seldom
and usually only with the very feeble or the very
young, or those who are so severely bitten or otherwise injured that the Chrism can't overtake the injury
and the loss of blood. What I know I know from

happenstance. It can kill, but in the main it does not—."

"But Marrok said that it could," said Reuben, "and it almost invariably did."

"Forget Marrok," said Margon. "Forget what others might have told Marrok to try to curb his desire to fill the world with Morphenkinder like himself. We will say our own Requiem when we dance in the woods soon, together; enough on Marrok for now. Now Marrok knows or does not know because no one knows. And we can't know which it is."

He stopped long enough for a bite of the duck, and another chunk of the buttered roll.

"Now when the Chrism is given to young men or women your age, there's no danger," he said, "and when it's given with the deep bite, injecting the Chrism directly into the bloodstream at many points, well, it acts as it did with you, in about seven to fourteen days. The moon has nothing to do with it. Such legends have a different origin and nothing to do with us. But it's undeniable that in the first few years the change comes only after nightfall, and it is extremely difficult to induce in the light of day. But you can, after a while, if you are very determined, induce it anytime that you like. Your goal should be complete mastery of it. Because if you do not have that, you will never be in charge of it. It will be in charge of you."

Reuben nodded, murmuring that he had found

that out in the most painful and fearful and personal way. "But I thought it was the voices that made me change," he said. "I thought that the voices triggered it and had to trigger it—."

"We'll come to the voices," said Margon.

"But why do we hear the voices?" asked Stuart. "Why do we hear the voices of people in pain and who are suffering and who need us? My God, I was going crazy in the hospital. It was like hearing souls in hell begging for mercy—."

"We'll come to that," said Margon. He looked at Reuben.

"Of course you worked out how to control it as best you could," said Margon, "and you did well. You did extremely well. You're a new generation and you have a strength we never saw in the past. You come to the Chrism with a health and vigor that was only occasional for centuries, in fact, exceptional. And when this is combined with intellect, the Morphenkind is nothing short of superb."

"Oh, don't flatter them both too much," Thibault mumbled in his familiar baritone. "They're exuberant enough."

"I want to be perfect!" shouted Stuart, jabbing his thumb at his chest.

"Well, if you would be perfect as I see perfect," said Margon, "then evaluate all the gifts you possess, not merely the Morphengift. Think about the threads of your human life and what they mean to you." He turned to Reuben. "Now you are a poet, Reuben, a writer, a potential chronicler of your time. This is a treasure, is it not?" Without waiting for a response, he continued, "Last night, before I took this young one into the woods, I talked at length with your father. He is the parent who has given you your greatest talents, not your brilliant mother whom you so devoutly adore. It's the man in the shadows behind you who has endowed you with the love of language that shapes the very way you perceive the world."

"I don't doubt it," said Reuben. "I failed my mother. I couldn't be a doctor. Neither could my brother, Jim."

"Ah, your brother, Jim," said Margon. "Now that is an enigma—a priest who longs with all his heart to believe in God, but does not."

"Not so rare at all," said Reuben, "if you ask me."

"But to knowingly give one's life to a God who might never answer?" asked Margon.

"What God has ever answered anyone?" asked Reuben. He fixed on Margon and waited.

"Need I point out that thousands have claimed to hear his voice?"

"Ah but do they really hear it?"

"How are any of us to know?" asked Margon.

"Oh, come now!" said Felix, speaking up for the first time. He put down his knife and fork and scowled at Margon. "You're going to hedge on religion now with these boy wolves? You're going to soft-pedal your own nihilism? Why?"

"Oh, forgive me," said Margon sarcastically, "for acknowledging the abundant evidence that human-kind from the beginning of recorded history has claimed to have heard the voices of its gods, that con-versions are generally quite emotional and real to the convert."

"Very well," said Felix with a little genial gesture. "You go on, Teacher. I need to hear these things once again myself."

"I don't know if I can bear it," said Thibault sono-rously with a little mocking smile.

Margon laughed under his breath, eyes sparkling as he looked at Thibault. "It was a dark day when you joined this company," he said, but this was entirely in a convivial spirit. "Always so bitterly amused, always so droll. I hear that droning bass voice in my sleep."

Thibault enjoyed this.

"Your point's clear," said Felix. "Reuben's a writer. Perhaps the first Morphenkind who has ever been a writer—."

"Oh, nonsense, am I the only one with a memory for unpleasant things?" asked Thibault.

"It's not the chronicle of the Morphenkinder I want to reveal here," said Margon. "I am saying this." He looked pointedly at Stuart, who was reaching again for the potatoes. "You are creatures of body and soul, wolfen and human, and balance is indispensable to survival. One can kill the gifts one is given, any of them and all of them, if one is determined to do so, and pride is the parent of destruction; pride eats the mind and the heart and the soul alive."

Reuben nodded vigorously. He took a deep drink of the red wine. "But surely you'll agree," said Reuben, "that human experience pales in comparison to the wolf experience, that every single aspect of the wolf experience is more intense." He hesitated. Morphenkinder, Morphengift—these were beautiful words.

But he remembered the words he had chosen for this himself when he was entirely alone: the Wolf Gift.

Yes, it was a gift.

"We don't exist at maximum intensity all the time, do we?" Margon replied. "We sleep, we doze, we meditate—we discover ourselves in our passions and our disasters, but also in our slumber, and in our dreams."

Reuben conceded that.

"This music you're playing for us, this piano music by Satie. This is not Beethoven's Ninth, is it?" Margon asked.

No, and it's not Brahms's Second Symphony either, Reuben thought, remembering his musings of last night.

"So how many nights is the change going to just

come over me," asked Stuart, "whether I want it or not?"

"Try really fighting it," said Thibault. "You might be surprised."

"It's too soon for you to resist it," said Margon. "It will come on you every night for perhaps fourteen days. Now, with Reuben he learned to control it after what?—the tenth? But only because he had yielded to it so completely before."

"Yes. That's probably so," said Thibault.

"But it's always been a fortnight in my experience," said Felix. "After that, the power is infinitely more controllable. For many, seven nights in any one month is enough to maintain vigor and sanity. Of course, you can learn to keep it down indefinitely. There is often a discernible personal rhythm to it, an individual cycle; but these responses vary greatly, and of course the voices of those in need of protection— the voices can provoke us anytime. But in the beginning, you need that fortnight because the Chrism is still working on your cells."

"Ah, the cells, the cells," said Reuben. "What were those words that Marrok used?" He turned to Laura.

"The pluripotent progenitor cells," said Laura. "He said that the Chrism worked on these cells and triggered the mutation."

"Well, of course," said Stuart.

"Or so we theorize," said Felix, "with the feeble insights we have today." He took a deep drink of his wine, and sat back. "We reason that those are the only cells which can be responsible for the changes that take place in us—that all humankind has the potential to be Morphenkinder—but that's based on what we now know of human chemistry, which is more than we knew twenty years ago, or twenty years before that, and so forth and so on."

"Nobody has yet clearly defined what happens," said Thibault. "In the early days of modern science, we attempted to grasp things with the new critical vocabulary at our disposal. We had such high hopes. We outfitted laboratories, hired scientists under clever ruses. We thought we'd finally learn all there was to know about ourselves. We learned so little! What we know is what you've observed in yourselves."

"It involves glands, hormones, surely," said Reuben.

"Indisputably," said Felix, "but why and how?"

"Well, how did it start?" Stuart asked. He smacked the table with his hand. "Has it always been with us, I mean with human beings? Margon, where did all this begin?"

"There are answers to those questions . . . ," said Margon under his breath. He was reticent, obviously.

"Who was the very first Morphenkind ever?" asked Stuart. "Come on, you must have a Genesis myth. You have to tell us these things. Cells, glands, chemicals—that's one thing. But what's the history of this? What's the tale?"

Silence. Felix and Thibault were waiting for Margon to answer.

Margon was considering. He appeared troubled, and for a moment lost in his thoughts.

"The ancient history isn't all that inspiring," said Margon. "What's important now is that you learn how to use these gifts."

There was a pause and very gently Laura spoke up. "Does the hunger increase over time—the desire to hunt and feast?"

"Not really," said Margon. "It's always inside us. We feel partial, diminished, spiritually starved if we don't give in to it, but I would say that is there from the beginning. Indeed, one can get sick of it, and withdraw for long periods, ignoring the voices." He stopped.

"And your strength, does this increase?" Laura asked.

"Skill increases, of course," said Margon, "and wisdom. Ideally that increases as well. We have bodies that renew themselves constantly. But our hearing, our vision, our physical abilities—these do not increase."

He looked at Reuben as though inviting his questions now. He hadn't done this before.

"The voices," said Reuben. "Can we talk now about the voices?"

He'd tried to be patient, but this seemed the moment surely to cut to the point.

"Why do we hear the voices?" he asked. "I mean I understand our sensitive hearing, it's part of the transformation, but why do the voices of people who need us bring on the change? And why would stem cells in our bodies transform us into something that can track the scent of malice and cruelty—it's the scent of evil, isn't it—and we're driven to seek to wipe it out?"

He put down his napkin. He looked intently at Margon.

"This is for me the central mystery," Reuben continued. "It's the moral mystery for me. Man into monster, all right, it's not magic. It's science and it's science we don't know. I can accept that. But why do I smell fear and suffering? Why am I impelled to go to it? Every time I've killed, it's been a consummately evil perpetrator. I've never erred." He looked from Margon to Felix and to Thibault. "Surely it's the same for you."

"It is," said Thibault. "But it's chemical. It's in our physical nature. We smell evil and we are driven almost madly to attack it, destroy it. We cannot distinguish between an innocent victim and ourselves. They are one and the same to us. What the victim suffers we suffer."

"Is this God-given?" asked Stuart. "Are you going to tell me that?"

"I'm telling you just the opposite," said Thibault. "These are finely developed biological traits, rooted in the elusive chemistry of our glands and our brains."

"Why is it that particular way?" asked Reuben. "Why aren't we chemically driven to track the innocent and devour them? They're sweet enough."

Margon smiled. "Don't try it," he said. "You'll fail."

"Oh, I know. This is what undid Marrok. He couldn't bring himself merely to do away with Laura. He had to ask forgiveness of her, launching into a long confession as to why she had to die."

Margon nodded.

"How old was Marrok?" asked Reuben. "How much experience had he had? Shouldn't he have been able to defeat us both?"

Margon nodded. "Marrok wanted to do away with himself," he said. "Marrok was weary, careless—the shell of the being he'd once been."

"Doesn't surprise me," said Laura. "He challenged us to destroy him. At first, I thought he was trying to confuse us, frighten us to death, so to speak. Then I realized he simply couldn't do what he wanted unless we fought back."

"That's exactly right," said Reuben. "And then when we fought back, he wasn't able to overmaster us. Certainly he must have, on some level, known that this would be the case."

"You are going to tell me, aren't you," asked Stuart, "who this person was, this Marrok?"

"The story of Marrok is finished," said Margon. "For reasons of his own he wanted to destroy Reuben. He'd passed the Chrism through carelessness and convinced himself that he had to eliminate the evidence of his mistake."

"Just as I passed it to you," murmured Reuben.

"Ah, but you're very young," said Thibault. "Marrok was old."

"And so my life opens up in flaming colors," said Stuart exuberantly. "And with the blare of trumpets!"

Margon laughed indulgently with a knowing glance at Felix.

"But truly, why do we seek to protect the victims of evil, to prevent them from being murdered or raped?" Reuben asked.

"Little wolf," said Margon, "you want a splendid answer, don't you? A moral answer, as you say. I wish I had one for you. I fear it was a matter of evolution like everything else."

"This evolved in Morphenkinder?" asked Reuben.

"No," said Margon. He shook his head. "It evolved in the species from which the power came to us. And they were not **Homo sapiens sapiens** as we are. They were something entirely different, rather like **Homo ergaster** or **Homo erectus.** Do you know those terms?"

"Yes, I know them," said Stuart. "And that's exactly what I suspected. It was an isolated species, thriving somewhere in an out-of-the-way pocket of the world, right? Like **Homo floresiensis**—the hobbit species in Indonesia—a humanoid offshoot different from everything else we know."

"What is the hobbit species?" asked Reuben.

"Little people, no more than three feet tall," said Laura, "skeletons just found a few years ago, evolved completely separately from **Homo sapiens sapiens.**"

"Oh, I remember this," said Reuben, "yes."

"Tell us, tell us about this species," said Stuart insistently.

Felix appeared uneasy and was about to try to quiet him when Margon gestured that it was all right.

Margon apparently had hoped to avoid this part of the story. He was thoughtful, then agreed to go on.

"First we clear the board," he said gesturing to the table. "I need a moment in my thoughts."

# 39

THE PLATTERS of the feast were relegated to the kitchen island counter, a spread that would sustain the house all evening long.

Once again, the entire company worked swiftly, quietly, replenishing the water, the wine, setting down carafes of hot coffee, and green tea.

The fresh-baked pies were brought into the dining room, apple, cherry, peach. The soft white French cheeses, plates of candies, fruits.

Margon took his place again at the head of the table. He appeared to have misgivings, but one glance at Stuart's eager face and Reuben's patient but inquisitive expression appeared to confirm for him that he had to go on.

"Yes," said Margon, "there was such a species, an isolated and dying species of primates who were not what we are and they did exist on an isolated island, yes, thousands of years ago off the African coast."

"And this power came from them?" asked Stuart.

"Yes," said Margon, "through a very foolish man—or a wise man depending on one's point of view—who sought to breed with them, and to acquire the power they had—to change from cooperative ape man to ravening wolf man when threatened."

"And the man bred with them," Stuart said.

"No. That was not successful," said Margon. "He acquired the power by being severely and repeatedly bitten, but only after he'd been prepared by imbibing the fluids of the species—the urine, the blood—in whatever quantities he could acquire for two years. He had also invited playful bites from the tribe whenever he could. They had befriended him, and he was an outcast from his people—exiled from the only real city in the whole world."

His voice had darkened as he said those words.

A silence fell over them all. They were all looking at Margon, who stared at the water in his glass. The expression on his face was deeply perplexing to Reuben, and obviously maddened Stuart, but Reuben sensed there was more to this remembering, this retelling, than simple weariness or distaste. Something troubled Margon about the telling of the tale.

"But how long ago was this?" Stuart asked. "What do you mean, the only real city in the world?" He was wildly stimulated, and obviously thrilled, his smile broadening as he repeated the words.

"Stuart, please . . . ," Reuben pleaded. "Let Margon tell it in his own way."

After a long moment, Laura spoke up.

"You're talking of yourself, aren't you?" she said.

Margon nodded.

"Is it difficult to remember?" asked Reuben respectfully. He couldn't fathom this man's facial expressions. He appeared at once remote and then vital, at once totally absent from all around him and then again completely, openly engaged. But what was to be expected?

It was wondrous and shocking to contemplate, that this was an immortal man. And it was no more than Reuben had long suspected. Only the length of time shocked him. But the secret, that these beings were immortal? It felt like something revealed to him in his own blood by the Chrism. Something he couldn't quite absorb yet could never forget. But even before the Chrism ever entered his veins, in his very first encounter with the photograph of the distinguished gentlemen in the library, he had sensed that an otherworldly knowledge bound the men together.

Stuart's eyes were locked on Margon, scanning his face, his form, his hand that rested on the table—just feasting on all the little details of the man.

And what do they tell you? Reuben wondered. That so little has changed with us in thousands of years, that one so old can walk down the street in any city and go unnoticed really except for his unusual poise perhaps and the subtle, wise expression on his face? He was an imposing man, but why? He was commanding, but why? He was forthcoming and yet somehow utterly unyielding.

"Tell us what happened," said Stuart as gently as he could. "Why were you exiled? What did you do?"

"Refuse to worship the gods," said Margon, his words coming in a half murmur as he stared forward. "Refuse to sacrifice in the Temple to deities carved out of stone. Refuse to recite hymns to the monotonous beat of drums about the marriage of gods and goddesses who never existed and which never took place. Refuse to tell the people that if they did not worship, if they did not sacrifice, if they did not break their backs in the fields and digging the canals that watered them, that the gods would bring the cosmos to an end. Margon the Godless refused to tell lies."

He raised his voice just a little. "No, I do not have trouble remembering," he said. "But some deep emotional and visceral faith in the act of recounting it has long been lost."

"Why didn't they just execute you?" Stuart asked.

"They couldn't," Margon said in a small voice, looking at him. "I was their divine king."

Stuart was delighted with the answer. He couldn't conceal his excitement.

This is so simple, Reuben was thinking. Stuart keeps asking all the questions to which I want the answers, and to which Laura probably wants answers. And the questions are indeed driving the flow of revelation, so why complain?

He could feel the hot oppressive sun of the Iraqi desert suddenly. He saw the dusty trenches of the archaeological dig on which he'd worked. He saw those tablets, those ancient cuneiform tablets, those precious fragments laid out on the table in the secret room.

He was so excited by this little bit of intelligence that he might have gone off, perplexed, pondering for a long time. It was like reading a wonderful sentence in a book, and not being able to continue because so many possibilities were crowding his mind.

Margon picked up the water, and tasted it, then drank it. And carefully he set it down again, staring at it as if fascinated by its bubbles, the play of light in the leaded-crystal glass.

He did not touch the bits of fruit on the small plate in front of him. But he drank the coffee, drank it while it was still smoking. And reached suddenly for the silver carafe.

Reuben filled the cup for him. Cupbearer for a king.

Felix and Thibault were gazing calmly at Margon. And Laura had turned in her chair, the better to see him, arms folded, comfortable as she waited.

Stuart was the only one who couldn't wait.

"What city was it?" Stuart asked. "Come on, Margon, tell me!"

Felix gestured for him to be quiet, with a severe reprimanding look.

"Ah, it's only natural for him to want to know," said Margon. "Remember, there have been those who weren't curious at all, who wanted to know nothing of the past, and how did that serve them? Maybe it would have been better for them if they had had a history, an ancestry, even if it was nothing more than descriptive. Maybe we need this."

"I need it," whispered Stuart. "I need to hear everything."

"I'm not sure," said Margon gently, "that you've really heard what I have said so far."

That's just it, thought Reuben, the very difficulty. How to hear that the man sitting here has been alive continuously since the beginning of recorded time? How do you hear that?

"Well, I will not be the chronicler of the Morphenkinder just now," said Margon, "and not ever perhaps. But I will tell you some things. It's enough for you to know I was deposed, exiled. I wouldn't claim to be the divine son of the fictive god who'd built the canals and the temples—venerable forerunner to Enlil, Enki, Marduk, Amun Ra. I sought for answers within ourselves. And believe me, this point of view was not so radical as you might think. It was common. But to express the point of view was not common at all."

"This was Uruk, wasn't it?" Stuart asked breathlessly.

"Far older than Uruk," Margon shot back. "Far older than Eridu, Larsa, Jericho—any city you might name. The sands have never yielded the remains of my city. Perhaps they never will. I myself don't know what happened to it, or my descendants, or what its full legacy proved to be for the cities springing up around it. I don't know what happened to its trading outposts. Its trading posts trafficked in a way of life as well as in livestock and slaves and goods. Yet I don't know what became of them, of that particular way of life. I was no conscious chronicler or witness of the events that unfolded in those times. Surely you understand. You must understand. Do you look thousands of years into the future? Do you measure what's happening to you now by what may matter a thousand years hence? I was stumbling and lurching, groping and from time to time drowning, as any man might." His voice was now heated and running smoothly. "I had no view of myself as positioned by fate or happenstance at the birthplace of a continuity that would endure for millennia. How could I? I underestimated every single force that impinged on my existence. It couldn't have been otherwise. It's a mere accident that I survived. That's why I don't like to talk of it. Talk is suspect. When we talk about our lives, long or short, brief and tragic or enduring beyond comprehension, we impose a continuity on them, and that continuity is a lie. I despise what is a lie!"

When he paused this time, no one spoke. Even Stuart was still.

"It's enough to say I was deposed and exiled," said Margon. "My brother was behind it." He made a little gesture of disgust. "And why not? Truth is a risky proposition. It's the nature of mediocre human beings to believe that lies are necessary, that they serve a purpose, that truth is subversive, that candor is dangerous, that the very scaffold of communal life is supported by lies—."

Again he stopped.

He smiled suddenly at Stuart.

"That's why you want the truth from me, isn't it?

Because people have taught you all your short life that lies are as vital to you as the air you breathe and you are hurtling full tilt into a life dependent upon the truth."

"Yes," said Stuart gravely. "That's it, exactly." He hesitated, then said, "I'm a gay boy. I've been taught ever since I can remember that there were excellent reasons for me to lie about it to everybody I knew."

"I understand," said Margon. "The architects of any society depend upon lies."

"So tell me what really happened."

"Doesn't matter, all that about gods and goddesses or exiled princes," said Margon. "But let's go back to the narrative in which we both want to find a bit of salvageable truth."

Stuart nodded.

"Fortunately for Margon the Godless, no one was going to shed the blood of the heretic king. Margon the Godless was put outside the walls, and left to go his way like a desert drifter, with a skin of water and a staff. It is enough to say I found myself in Africa, traveling down through Egypt, and along the coast and then to this strange island where a peaceful and much despised people lived.

"They were hardly what one would call human beings. No one in those days would have thought them human. But they were a human race, a species of human, and a cohesive tribe. They took me in, fed me, clothed me insofar as they wore clothes. They looked rather more like apes than men and women. But they had language, they knew and exchanged expressions of love.

"And when they told me their enemy, shore people, were coming, when they described the shore people to me, I thought we would all die.

"They themselves lived in complete harmony with one another. But the shore people were people like me. They were **Homo sapiens sapiens**—fierce, armed with throwing spears and crude stone axes, and ravenous to destroy a contemptible enemy for sheer sport."

Stuart nodded.

"Well, I thought it was over as I said. The simple apelike creatures could never mount a defense against such a sophisticated and vicious invader. There was no time for me to teach them how to protect themselves.

"Well, I was wrong.

" 'You go and hide,' they said to me. 'We will know when their boats are coming.' Then dancing wildly in circles as the shore people landed, they brought on the transformation. The elongated limbs, the fangs, the abundant wolfen hair—all you've seen yourselves, all you boys have experienced for yourselves. The tribe—male and female alike—were transformed into such monsters right before my eyes.

"They became a pack of howling, snarling dogs. I had never seen such a thing. They overwhelmed the enemy, driving the attackers into the ocean, devouring them, even demolishing their boats with their teeth and their claws, stalking every fugitive and consuming every morsel of enemy flesh.

"Then they reverted back to who they were before—apelike, peaceful, simple. They told me not to fear. They knew the enemy by his evil scent. They caught it on the wind before the boats ever appeared. They would never do such things as I had seen except to an enemy. It was the power given them by the gods long ago to defend themselves against others so evil that they would break the peace of their world for no reason at all.

"I lived with them for two years. I wanted that power. As I said, I drank their urine, their blood, their tears, whatever they would give to me. I didn't care. I slept with their women. I took the semen of their men. I bought their precious secretions and their blood with bits of wisdom, cunning advice, clever little inventions of which they'd never dreamed, solutions to problems they couldn't solve.

"Now there was one other case, an obvious one, for which the change could be induced: to punish a lawbreaker, usually a homicide—the most despised traitor to the peace.

"Again, they knew the criminal by his scent, and they'd surround him, dancing themselves into a frenzy until the change was fully upon them and they would devour the guilty man. To the best of my knowledge, they were never wrong in their judgment, and I saw more than one accused outlaw vindicated.

They never abused the power at all. It seemed relatively simple to them. They could not shed innocent blood; their gods had given them the power only to eradicate evil, and they had no doubts on the matter, and they thought it very amusing that I should want the power or think that I could induce it in myself.

"Yet whenever the change was upon them, I did whatever I could to elicit small bites from them, which they thought was powerfully funny and a little indecent, but they were in awe of me, so they gave in."

He closed his eyes for a moment and pressed his fingers to the bridge of his nose, then opened his eyes again and stared forward as though lost.

"Were they mortal?" Laura asked. "Could they die?"

"Yes, indeed, they were mortal," said Margon. "They were. They died all the time from simple things which my palace physicians could have easily cured. An abscessed tooth that could have been pulled, a broken leg improperly set and then infected. Yes, they were mortal. And they held me to be the most magical of persons because I could cure certain ailments and certain injuries, and that gave me great power in their eyes."

He paused again.

Thibault, who had teasingly complained earlier of not wanting to hear Margon was listening now, fascinated, as if he'd never heard this part of Margon's story before.

"Why did they turn on you?" he asked. "You've never said."

"Oh same old story," said Margon. "I'd learned enough of their rudimentary language after two years to tell them I did not believe in their gods. Remember I was very young at the time, perhaps three years older than Stuart is now. I wanted the power. The power did not come from the gods. I thought I should say so. In those days, I always told the truth." He laughed under his breath. "Understand, theirs was no complex religion like that of the cities of fertile plains. It was no great system of temples and taxes and bloody altars. But they had their gods. And I thought I should tell them, as a matter of fact, that there were no gods at all.

"Now they had always been kind to me, and loved to learn the clever things that I could teach. They'd laughed at me for wanting their power, as I said, or more truly for thinking that I could acquire it. You cannot get what the gods will not give, they said. And the gods had given the power to them, not to others—like me.

"But now, when they came to understand the full extent of my denial of their gods, and the full heretical dimension of my insistence that I could acquire the power, they pronounced me a lawbreaker of the worst sort, and set a time for me to die.

"Such killing rituals always took place at dusk. Understand, they could easily transform into wolf people in the daytime if an enemy approached; but for executions they always waited until dusk.

"And so as darkness fell, they lighted their torches

and formed a great circle, forcing me into the middle of it, and they began to dance to bring about the change.

"It wasn't easy for them. They were not all a party to it. Some stood back. I had saved the lives of many of them, healed their sick children. I could see it there and then, the great disinclination in these crude beings to harm an innocent. Indeed, I am not sure what scent they caught from me at that time, and I'll never know.

"But I know what scent I caught from them—a hideous, acrid scent, a scent of malice threatening my very life, when they came down on me like wolves.

"Now if they'd torn me apart as they did the other enemies and lawbreakers, that would have been the end of the story. And my journey through time would have ended like that of any mortal man. But they did not. Something restrained them, some lingering respect or fascination, or distrust of themselves.

"And it is conceivable that from the playful bites I'd extracted, and from the fluids I'd imbibed, I had some great glandular immunity working in me, some powerful fount of healing that allowed me to survive their attack.

"Whatever the case, I suffered bites all over and I crawled on my belly towards the jungle to die. This was the worst torture I'd ever endured. I was angry— enraged that my life was ending in this fashion. And they were dancing back and forth all around me, on either side of me, and behind me. They were shifting back into their regular shape, and cursing me, then struggling into the wolfen form again, because I was not dead. But they could not bring themselves, obviously, to finish me off.

"And then I changed.

"Before their eyes, I changed.

"Maddened by the sounds and scents of their hatred for me, it was I who changed and attacked them."

His eyes grew wide peering into something that only he could see. They all sat silent waiting. There came over Reuben a strong sense of Morgon's demeanor, the way that he maintained an unspoken supremacy though not a single inveterate gesture of his was imposing and his voice was, even at its most heated, rolling steadily beneath the governance of a deeply private and disciplined man.

"They were no match for me at all," he said with a shrug. "They had been like yapping puppies with milk teeth. I was a seething wolfen monster with a human being's resolve and wounded pride. They didn't have emotions like that! Nothing was so necessary to them, ever in all their lives, as killing them was then to me."

Reuben smiled. This so beautifully touched on the lethal edge of the human species that he marveled.

"Something far more deadly than either of us had ever beheld had now been born," said Margon. "The man wolf, the werewolf, the wolf man—what we are."

Again, he paused. He seemed to be struggling with something he wanted to express but could not.

"There's so much about it I do not understand," he confessed. "But I know this and it's what all people know now, that every particle of life explodes from mutation, from the accidental combining of elements on every level, that accident is the indispensable nuclear power of the universe, that nothing advances without it, without a reckless and random blundering, whether it is seeds ripped from a dying flower by the wind, or pollen carried on the tiny feet of winged insects or blind fish tunneling into caverns of the deep to consume life forms undreamt of by those on the surface of the planet above. Accident, accident, and so it was with them and with me: a blunder, a stumbling—and what you call a man wolf was born. What we called the Morphenkinder were born."

He stopped and drank some more of the coffee, and once again Reuben filled his cup.

Stuart was enthralled. But the old impatience was cooking again in him. He couldn't help himself.

"There's a virtue," Felix said, "to listening to a reluctant storyteller. You know that he is in fact diving deep for the salvageable truth."

"I know this," said Stuart, struggling. "I'm sorry, I know it. I know it. I'm just—. I want so much to—."

"You want to embrace what you see before you," said Felix. "I realize. We all realize."

Margon was drifting. Maybe he was listening to the unobtrusive music, the isolated and methodical piano notes that rose and fell, rose and fell, as the Satie went on.

"And you managed to escape the island?" asked Laura. Her voice wasn't tentative so much as it was respectful.

"I didn't escape," Margon said. "They could draw but one conclusion from what they'd witnessed. Their gods had willed it, and Margon the Godless was none other than the father of their gods."

"They made you their ruler," said Stuart.

"They made him their god," said Thibault. "That's the irony. Margon the Godless became their god."

Felix sighed. "Your inescapable destiny," he said.

"Is it?" asked Margon.

"And you will not be king amongst us, will you?" Felix said, almost confidentially as if the others weren't there.

"Thank God for that," Thibault whispered with a secretive smile. "But really, I've never heard you tell the story in quite this way."

Margon burst out laughing, not loudly but in a very natural way. Yet he picked up the thread.

"I was their ruler for years," he conceded with a long sigh. "Their god, their king, their headman, whatever one wants to call it—I lived in utter harmony with them, and when the inevitable invaders came, I led the defense. I smelled evil as they smelled evil. I had to destroy it as they had to destroy it. The scent of the enemy evoked the change in me as it evoked the change in them. And so did the presence of evil in our midst.

"But I suffered a craving to punish that they did not suffer. I longed for the scent of the attacker and they never really did. I would have sought out the attacker in his own land for the thrill of destroying him, so irresistible to me was that scent, and the thrill of annihilating that supposed evil, that supposed cruelty, that threat. In sum, I would have produced aggression towards myself in order to declare it to be evil and destroy it."

"Of course," said Stuart.

"It was the king's temptation," said Margon. "Perhaps it's always the king's temptation. I knew it. I, the first **Homo sapiens sapiens** who'd ever experienced the change.

"And so it is with us now. We can fly from the voices. We can come here to this great majestic forest and hope to save ourselves from the savagery within us but eventually we are tortured by our abstinence and we go to seek out the very evil we loathe."

"I follow you," said Stuart, nodding his head.

Reuben also nodded.

"So true," said Felix.

"And eventually we will seek it out," said Margon. "And in the meantime, we will hunt the forest because we can't resist what the forest offers, can't resist the simplicity of the slaughter that involves only brute inevitability rather than innocent blood."

"Did they induce the change in order to hunt?" asked Reuben. His head was teeming. He could taste the blood of the elk in his mouth, the elk, the soft-eyed beast who was not itself a killer, but food for killers. The brute inevitability, yes. The elk was not evil, had never been evil, had never carried the scent of evil, no.

"No," said Margon, "they did not. They hunted game without the change. But I was not the same as they were. And when the forest or the jungles called me, when the hunt called to me, I went into the change. I loved it. And these people marveled at it. They saw it as the god's prerogative, but they never followed suit. They could not."

"And this was another surprise of the mutation," said Laura.

"Exactly," said Margon. "I was not what they were. I was something new." He paused and then went on with the story.

"Oh, I discovered many things in those months and years.

"I didn't catch on at first that I couldn't die. I'd seen that the tribesmen were nearly invulnerable in battle. Stab wounds, spear wounds, they almost always survived anything they were subjected to as long as the change was on them. And of course I shared this strange, inexplicable vigor. But I healed much more quickly from any wound sustained either during the wolf state or the man state, and I did not realize what this could mean.

"I left them without ever realizing that I would roam this earth for centuries to come.

"But there's one more thing I must tell you about what happened to me on that island," he said. He looked intently at Reuben. "And someday perhaps you will share this with your brother, when he is suffering acutely from his dark night of the soul. I have seldom if ever told anyone this small thing, which I want to reveal now."

Felix and Thibault were watching him as though they were mightily intrigued and couldn't guess what he meant to say.

"There was a holy man on the island," he said, "what we call now a shaman, a mystic of sorts who imbibed the few plants there that could intoxicate and induce madness and trance. I paid little attention to him. He didn't hurt anybody and he spent most of his existence in a blissful stupor and scratching signs and symbols understood only by him into the dirt or the sand of the beach. He was actually quite beautiful in a ghastly sort of way. He never challenged me and I never questioned him on his supposed mystical knowledge. And of course, I believed in nothing, and held that I'd acquired the power, as I saw it, on my own.

"But when I prepared to leave the island, when I had passed on the scepter so to speak to another, and was ready to embark for the mainland, this shaman came down to the beach and called out to me before the assembled tribe.

"Now this was a time of ceremonial well-wishing and even tears. And so for this strange being to appear, crazed by his revolting potions and talking in riddles, well, it was not something any of us wanted to see.

"But he came on, and when he had the attention of everyone present, he pointed his finger at me and he said the gods would punish me for the theft of the power that had been given to 'the people,' and not to me.

"I was no god, he told the others.

"He cried out: 'Margon the Godless One, you cannot die. The gods have decided it. You cannot die. There will come a time when you'll beg for death but it will be denied to you. And wherever you go and whatever you do, you will not die. You will be a monster among your own kind. The power will torment you. It will give you no rest. This is because you have taken into yourself the power which the gods intended for us alone.'

"The tribe was very agitated, outraged, confused. Some wanted to beat him and chase him back to his hut and his drunken stupors. Others were merely afraid.

"'The gods have told me these things,' he said. 'They are laughing at you, Margon. And they will always be laughing at you, wherever you go or whatever you do.'

"I myself was shaken, though why I didn't fully grasp. I bowed to him, thanked him for his oracle, firmly resolved that he ought to be pitied, and prepared to leave. For many a year after that, I never so much as thought of him.

"But then came the time when I did begin to think of him. And not a year goes by that I have not remembered him and every word that he spoke."

He paused again, and he sighed. "Well over a hundred years later I returned to that island, to see how my people, as I called them, had fared. They had been wiped out to the last one. **Homo sapiens sapiens** ruled the island. And only the legend of the feral people survived."

He looked at Reuben and then at Stuart and finally to Laura, letting his gaze linger on Laura.

"Now, let me put it to you," he said. "What is there to be learned from such a story, may I ask?"

No one spoke up, not even Stuart, who was merely studying Margon, with his elbow on the table and his right fingers curled under his lip.

"Well, obviously," said Laura, "that the power had evolved in them in response to their enemies, over how many thousands of years no one could say. It was a survival mechanism that was gradually enhanced."

"Yes," said Margon.

She went on.

"And catching the scent of the enemy was part of it and became the trigger mechanism for the change."

"Yes."

"But clearly," she continued, "they never used it for simple hunting or feasting, because they were more intimately connected with the animals of the jungle."

"Yes, perhaps."

"But you," she said, "a human being, **Homo sapiens sapiens,** you suffered the divide from the wild beasts that we all suffer, and you did want to slay them, and though they were neither innocent nor guilty, neither good nor evil, they were fair game, just what the expression means, fair game, and you hunted them in your new form."

Stuart interjected: "And so the power took a new evolutionary turn in you. Well, that means it must have taken other evolutionary turns in you, and in others since. We're talking thousands of years, are we not? We're talking many changes."

"I would say so," said Margon. "Understand one thing more. At the time I had no sense of these things of which you're speaking, no sense of an evolutionary continuum. So I could not conceive of this new power, this wolfen power, as anything but depravity, a sinking, a loss of soul, a contamination with a lower and bestial drive."

"Yet you'd wanted it," said Stuart.

"Yes, always, I wanted it. I very much wanted it, and loathed myself for the wanting of it," said Margon, "and only afterwards, only as time passed, as my understanding deepened, did I come to think that something magnificent might lie in this great potential to become the unbeatable monster while still retaining my cunning, my intellect, my human soul as it were."

"So you believe in the soul?" Stuart said. "You

didn't believe in the gods, but you believed in the soul."

"I believed in the uniqueness and the superiority of humankind. I was not a man who thought animals had anything to teach. I didn't know there was a universe—not in the way we use the word now. I thought this earth was all that there was. Think for a moment of what that truly means—that we, the people of that time, truly thought this earth was all there was. Any spirit realm above or beneath was a mere antechamber. That's how small our imagined cosmos was. I know you know this, but think about it. Think about what it must have felt like to us.

"Whatever the case, I wanted the ability in order to possess a marvelous weapon, a powerful extension of myself. If my brother ever came after me, I wanted the ability to turn into a beast and rip him apart. Of course that was hardly the only thing I wanted. I wanted to see and feel as the wolfen beast and bring back to my human state whatever I'd learned. Yet it was a selfish and greedy thing that I sought it, and obtained it, and afterwards I was a suffering man, resorting most often to the beast in defeat, and rarely ever in joy."

"I see," said Laura. "And when did you begin to see it differently?"

"What makes you think I ever did?"

"Oh, I know you did, and that you do," she said. "You see it now as a Chrism. Why else would you use the word, even if you didn't originate it? You see it now as a great synthesizing power, uniting not the higher and the lower, but two ways of being."

"Yes, I did come to that. I admit it. I did. Slowly, I did come to that. I woke from the self-loathing and the guilt and I came to see it as instructive and even at times magnificent. I didn't need the wisdom of Darwin to know by then that we are all one great family, we creatures of the earth. I'd come to sense it, the communion of all living things. I needed no principles of evolution to open my eyes to it. And I did hope and dream of a lineage of immortals, creatures like us who, possessing the power of human and beast, would see the world as human beings themselves could not see it. I conceived a dream of witnesses, a tribe of witnesses, a tribe of Morphenkinder, drawing from the beast and the human a transcendent power, as it were, to have compassion and regard for all forms of life, rooted in their own hybrid nature. I conceived of these witnesses as set apart, incorruptible, unaccountable, but on the side of the good, the merciful, the protective."

He held her gaze, but he'd stopped speaking.

"And you don't believe that now," she ventured. "You don't believe in the magnificence of it, or that there should be this tribe of witnesses?"

He seemed on the verge of answering but then did not. His eyes moved back and forth on the empty space before him. Finally he said in a small voice.

"All creatures born in this world want immortality," he said. "But why should a tribe of immortal witnesses be Morphenkinder, part human, part beast?"

"You just said it yourself," said Laura. "They should draw from the two states a transcendent power, and have compassion for all forms of life—."

"But is that true of us?" Margon asked. "Do we truly draw on both states for a transcendent power to feel compassion? I don't know that we do. I don't know that our immortality is anything other than incidental, as much of an evolutionary accident as consciousness itself."

Felix appeared deeply affected by what Margon was saying, and eager to interrupt.

"Don't go on with this now," he pleaded gently. "You're traveling into your darkest memories, darkest disappointments. This is not the time or the place."

Margon appeared to agree.

"I want others to have the dream," he said, looking again to Laura, and then at Stuart and Reuben. "I want there to be such a dream of transcendent witnesses. But I don't know if I believe in it, or ever really, truly, did."

He seemed personally hurt by his own confession. Suddenly and obviously broken. Felix was visibly protective and concerned. Thibault appeared fearful, and faintly sad.

"I believe it," said Felix gently, but not reprovingly. "I believe in the tribe of witnesses. I always have. Where we go, what we do—it's not written. But I believe we are to survive as the tribe of those who have the Chrism."

"I don't know," Margon responded, "that our witness will ever matter, or that our synthesis of powers will ever have other witnesses—."

"I understand," said Felix, "and I accept that. I take my place among the hybrids, those who continue, those who see the spiritual world and the brutal world in a unique way, those who look to both as a source of truth."

"Ah, that's it, of course," said Margon. "We always come back to that—that both the brutal world and the spiritual world are sources of truth, that the truth resides in the viscera of all those who struggle as well as in the souls of those who would transcend the struggle."

The viscera of all those who struggle. Reuben drifted, caught again in that chapel of the forest canopy gazing up at the stars. And in the viscera is the pulse of God.

"Yes, we do always come back to that," said Felix. "Is there a maker hopelessly beyond this world we know of cells and breath, or is He holding all this within Himself?"

Margon shook his head, glancing sadly at Felix, and then he looked away.

The expression on Stuart's face was beautiful to behold. He had something of what he had wanted, and he was no longer asking anything. He was gazing off, clearly mounting up and up through all the lofty thoughts that were being inspired in him, keeping company now with possibilities that hadn't occurred to him before.

And Laura was engrossed, and turning inwards. Maybe she too had what she wanted.

And if only I could describe what I see now, Reuben thought, that my soul is opening, that my soul is breathing and I am penetrating ever deeper into the mystery, the mystery that includes the viscera . . . but it was more than he could express.

Something immense had been attempted. And now it seemed all backed off from the peak that had been conquered.

"And you, Margon," Laura asked, in the same respecting but probing manner. "Can you die, as Marrok died? Or Reynolds Wagner?"

"Yes. I am sure that I can. I have no reason to believe I am in any way different from any other of the tribe. But I don't know. I don't know if there are in the universe gods who cursed me for stealing this elemental power, and cursed those to whom I've passed it with my teeth. I don't know. What does it explain, any of it? We are all an enigma. And that will be our only truth—as long as we know only how and when . . . and not the why of anything."

"You don't believe in such a curse, surely," said Felix reprovingly. "Why do you say these things now? And that is hardly our only truth, by the way, that we are an enigma. You know that too."

"Oh, perhaps he does believe these things," said Thibault, "more than he's ever cared to admit."

"A curse, it's a metaphor," said Reuben. "It's the way we describe our worst unhappiness. I was brought up to believe the entire creation was cursed—fallen, depraved, damned until Divine Providence saved it, that is, from the curse imposed on the entire creation by Divine Providence Itself."

"Amen," said Laura. "Where did you go from there?" she asked. "Who was the first one to whom you ever gave the Chrism?"

"Oh, it was an accident," he said, "as it so very often is. And little did I realize it would provide me with my first true companion for the years to come. And I'll tell you the best reason there is to make another Morphenkind. It's because he or she will teach you something that all your years of struggle have not taught you, and can't teach you. He or she will give you a new truth of which you never dreamed. Margon the Godless meets God in each new generation."

"Amen, I understand," she whispered, smiling.

Margon looked at Reuben. "I can't give you the moral insight that you so badly need," he said.

"Perhaps you're wrong," said Reuben. "Perhaps you already have. Perhaps you misunderstood what I wanted."

"And Stuart," said Margon, "what's happening in your mind now?"

"Oh, the most wonderful things," said Stuart, shaking his head and smiling. "Because if we can have such a great purpose, to synthesize, to bring together in ourselves a new truth, well, then, all the pain, the confusion, the regret, the shame . . ."

"The shame?" asked Laura.

Stuart erupted in laughter. "Yes, the shame!" he said. "You have no idea. Of course, the shame."

"I understand," said Reuben. "There is shame in the Wolf Gift. There has to be."

"In those early generations there was only shame," said Margon, "and sullen obdurate refusal to give up the power."

"I can see it," said Reuben.

"But this is a resplendent universe in which we live now," said Margon softly, with wonder. "And in this universe we treasure all forms of energy and creative process."

This thrilled Reuben.

Margon put up his hands. He shook his head.

"And we must now address the question none of you has asked," said Margon.

"Which is what?" asked Stuart.

"Why is it that no scent alerts us to the presence of one another?"

"Oh, right," whispered Stuart in amazement. "And there is no scent, not even the faintest—not from you, not from Reuben, not from Sergei when he was the Man Wolf!"

"Why?" asked Reuben. Why, indeed? In the struggle with Marrok, there had never been the scent of evil or malice. And when Sergei had destroyed the doctors before his very eyes, there had been no scent to the monster.

"It's because you are neither good nor evil," suggested Laura. "You are neither beast nor human."

Margon, having elicited the answer he wanted, merely nodded. "Another part of the mystery," he said simply.

"But we should pick up the pure scent of any Morphenkind just as we pick up the scent of humans or animals out there," Reuben protested.

"But we do not," said Thibault.

"That's a crippling disability," said Stuart. He looked at Reuben. "It's why you had such a time finding me when I was lost."

"Yes," said Reuben. "But I did find you—and there must have been innumerable small signals— the sound of your crying, I heard that."

Margon offered nothing further. He sat quiet in his own thoughts as Stuart and Reuben went over it. Reuben had picked up no scent from Felix in the law offices, or in this house when Felix and Margon had first appeared. No, no scent.

And this was a disability, Stuart was right. Because they would never know whether another Morphenkind was approaching.

"There must be more to it," said Reuben.

"Enough," Margon said. "I have told you enough for now."

"But you've only begun," cried Stuart. "Reuben, join me in this. You know you want the answers.

Margon. How did you first pass the Chrism? What happened?"

"Well, now, perhaps you'll learn those things from the person to whom I passed it," said Margon with a mischievous smile.

"And who would that be?" Stuart turned to Felix and then to Thibault. Felix merely regarded him with one eyebrow raised, and Thibault laughed under his breath.

"Think on what you've learned so far," said Felix.

"I do, I will," vowed Stuart. He looked at Reuben, and Reuben nodded in assent. And why couldn't Stuart realize, Reuben thought, that this was only one of many conversations, conversations without end in which answers would flow to questions yet unimagined?

"That we're as old as humankind," said Felix. "That's what you know now, all three of you. That we're a mystery just as all humankind is a mystery. That we are part of the cycle of this world, and how and why we must discover on our own."

"Yes," said Margon. "There are many of us on this earth and there have been at times many, many more. Immortality as we use this word is a grant of immunity from old age and illness; but not from violent annihilation. And so we live with mortality as do all others under the sun."

"How many others are there?" asked Stuart. "Oh, don't look at me like that," he shot at Reuben. "You want to know these things, you know you do."

"I do," Reuben admitted. "When Margon wants us to know. Look, there's an inevitability to the way this story unfolds."

"I don't know how many others there are," said Margon with a little shrug. "How could I know? How could Felix or Thibault know? I do know this. The danger we face in today's world is not from other Morphenkinder. It's from men and women of science like Klopov and Jaska. And the greatest difficulties we face in day-to-day survival have to do with the advances in science—that we cannot now pass ourselves off as our own descendants to a world that requires DNA evidence of parentage or affinity. And that we must more than ever be clever as to where and how we hunt."

"Can you father a child?" Laura asked.

"Yes," said Margon, "but only with a female Morphenkind."

She gasped. Reuben felt a sudden shock. Why had he been so certain he could not get Laura with child? And it was true. He could not. But this new little revelation was stunning.

"Then the female Morphenkind can bear, obviously," said Laura.

"Yes," said Margon. "And the offspring are Morphenkinder always, with very occasional exceptions. And sometimes . . . well, sometimes a litter. But I must say that fertile couplings are extremely rare."

"A litter!" Laura whispered.

Margon nodded.

"This is why female Morphenkinder often form their own packs," said Felix, "and men tend to club together. Well, it's one of the reasons, anyway."

"But in all fairness," said Thibault, "tell them it seldom happens. I haven't known five born Morphenkinder in all my years."

"And what are these creatures like?" asked Stuart.

"The change manifests in early adolescence," said Margon, "and they are in all other respects very much like us. When they reach physical maturity, they cease to age, just as we have ceased to age. If you give the Chrism to a young child, you will see the same thing happen: the change will come with early adolescence. The child will mature, and then become fixed."

"So I'm likely to keep growing for a while yet," said Stuart.

"You will," said Margon with a sarcastic smile and a roll of his eyes. Felix and Thibault also laughed.

"Yes, it would be very considerate and gentlemanly of you if you were to stop growing," said Felix. "I find it disconcerting looking up into your big baby blue eyes."

Stuart was obviously exultant.

"You'll mature," said Margon, "and then you will not age."

Laura sighed. "One couldn't hope for anything much better than that."

"No, I don't suppose so," said Reuben, but it was only just hitting him, the obvious truth that he would never father normal human children, that if he fathered a child, that child would likely be what he was now.

"And this matter of others out there," said Felix. "In time these boys should come to know what we know about them, don't you think?"

"What," asked Margon, "that they're secretive, often unfriendly? That they seldom if ever let themselves be seen by other Morphenkinder? What more is there to say?" He opened his hands.

"Well, there's a great deal more to say and you know it," Felix said softly.

Margon ignored him. "We are all too like wolves. We travel in packs. What do we care about another pack as long as it doesn't come into our forest or our fields?"

"Then they're no threat to us basically," said Stuart. "That's what you're saying. There are no wars for territory or anything like that? No one seeks to gain power over the rest?"

"I told you," said Margon, "the worst threat to you is from human beings."

Stuart was pondering. "We can't shed innocent blood," he volunteered. "So how could we fight each other for power? But has there never been a Morphenkind who went rogue, or started slaughtering the innocent, who went mad perhaps?"

Margon considered for a long moment. "Strange things have happened," he conceded, "but not that."

"Are you contemplating being the first rogue?" asked Thibault with a deep mocking drawl to his words. "A juvenile delinquent Morphenkind, so to speak?"

"No," said Stuart. "I just wanna know."

Margon only shook his head.

"The need to annihilate evil can be a curse," Thibault said.

"Well, then why couldn't we breed a race of Morphenkinder who would annihilate every bit of evil?" Stuart asked.

"Oh, the young and their dreams," said Thibault.

"And what is our definition of evil?" asked Margon. "What have we come to settle for, we Morphenkinder? People we recognize as our own are under assault, isn't that it? But what is the actual root of evil, may I ask?"

"I don't know what the root of it is," said Felix. "But I know that evil comes into the world anew every time a child is born."

"Amen," said Margon.

Thibault spoke up, looking directly at Laura, "As we were discussing last night," he said, "evil is a matter of context. That is unavoidable. I am no relativist. I believe in the objective and true existence of good and of evil. But context is inevitable when a fallible human being speaks of evil. This we all must accept."

"I think we argue over the words we use," said Laura. "Not much else."

"But wait, you're saying the scent of evil for each of us is contextual?" Reuben asked. "That is what you're saying, isn't it?"

"It has to be," said Laura.

"No, that really is not quite it," said Margon, but then he seemed frustrated. He looked to Felix who seemed reluctant as well to continue with this same train of thought.

There're many things they are not saying, Reuben thought. They cannot say it all. Not now. He had a strong sense suddenly of how very much they were not explaining, but he knew better than to ask.

"The Chrism—the question of individual variation, strength," asked Stuart. "How does this work?"

"There are huge differences in receptivity and in development," said Felix, "and in the end result. But we don't always know why. There are certainly very strong Morphenkinder and very weak Morphenkinder, but again, we do not know why. A born Morphenkind can be quite impressive, or a shrinking and timid individual, not at all receptive to his or her fate. But then it's the same with those who are bitten, unless they ask for the Chrism, of course."

Margon drew himself up and gestured emphatically with his hands, palms down, as if to say he was bringing this to a close.

"What's important now is for you to remain here," he said, "both of you, and Laura of course as well. For you to live here with us now, with Felix, with Thibault, and with the others of our small and select company when you meet them, which you soon will. What's important is that you learn to control the transformation, and to resist the voices when you must. And above all, for now, to withdraw from the world until all chatter about the notorious California Man Wolf finally dies away."

Stuart nodded. "I understand that, I accept that. I want to be here. I'll do anything you say! But there's so much more."

"This will be harder than you think," said Margon. "You've tasted the voices. You will grow restless and miserable when you don't hear them. You'll want to seek them out."

"But we are with you now, all three of you," said Felix. "We came together a long time ago. We chose our last names in the modern age, as you guessed, from the werewolf literature of earlier decades. And we did this, not to signal our identity or common bond to anyone else, but for those names to serve as markers for ourselves and those few friends outside of our group who knew who we were. Names become a problem for people who don't die. Just as does property and inheritance, and the matter of legality within a nation. We sought a simple and somewhat poetic solution to one of those problems with our names. And we continue to seek solutions to the other problems by a variety of means.

"But what I mean to say is, we are a group, and we are now opening our group to you."

Stuart, Reuben, and Laura all nodded and expressed their warm acceptance. Stuart was beginning to cry. He could hardly remain seated. Finally he got up and began to pace right in back of his chair.

"This is your house and your land, Felix," said Reuben.

"Our house and our land," said Felix graciously, with that warm beaming smile.

Margon rose to his feet.

"Your lives, little wolves, have just begun."

The meeting was at an end. All were scattering.

But there was one burning matter which Reuben could not leave unresolved.

There was something he had to know, and he had to know it now.

He followed Felix, to whom he felt closest, into the library and caught up with him as he was lighting the fire.

"What is it, little brother?" asked Felix. "You look troubled. I thought the meeting went well."

"But Laura," Reuben whispered. "What about Laura? Will you give the Chrism to Laura? Must I ask you, or ask Margon or—."

"She's worthy," said Felix. "That was decided immediately. I didn't know there was the slightest doubt. She knows this. There have been no secrets kept from Laura. When she's ready, she has but to ask."

Reuben's heart had started to skip. He couldn't meet Felix's gaze. He felt Felix clasp his shoulder. He felt the strong fingers on his arm.

"And if she wants it," asked Reuben, "you will do it? You?"

"Yes. If she wants it. Margon or I. We will."

Why was this so painful? Wasn't this exactly what he'd wanted to know?

He saw her again in his mind's eye, as he'd first seen her that night on the edge of Muir Woods, when he'd come singing into the grassy clearing behind her house, and she had appeared to him, as if out of nowhere, standing on the back porch of her little house, in her long white flannel gown.

"I must be the most selfish man in all creation," he whispered.

"No, you're not," said Felix. "But it is her decision."

"I don't understand myself," he said.

"I understand you," said Felix.

Moments passed.

Felix struck the long fireplace match and ignited the kindling. There came that familiar roar as the kindling caught and the flames danced up the bricks.

Felix stood there patiently, waiting. Then he said softly, "You are such remarkable children. I envy you your brand-new world. I don't know that I would have the courage for it if you were not here with me."

# 40

IT WAS THE FORTNIGHT of many things.

Margon drove Stuart down to pick up his car in Santa Rosa, an old Jaguar convertible that had once belonged to his father. And they visited Stuart's mother who was in a psychiatric facility but "bored to death" and "sick of all the crummy magazines" and ready to get a whole new wardrobe to help her cope. Her agent had called from Hollywood to say she was hot again. Well, that was an overstatement. But they had work for her if she could get herself on a plane. Maybe she'd go shopping on Rodeo Drive.

Grace, anointed as the most articulate and significant of the witnesses to the Man Wolf's latest attack in Mendocino County, made the rounds of the talk shows, convincing the world in reasonable terms of her theory that this unfortunate creature was the victim of a congenital condition or a subsequent illness that had left it physically deformed and mentally challenged, but that it would soon blunder into the hands of authorities and get the confinement and treatment which it required.

Over and over again the investigators from the attorney general's office, and from the FBI, and from the San Francisco Police Department came back to interview Stuart and Reuben, as they had been the mysterious focus of more than one Man Wolf attack.

This was difficult for Stuart and for Reuben, as neither was a skilled liar, but they soon learned the trick of minimal answers, murmurs, and mumbles as they went the distance and were finally left alone.

Reuben wrote a long comprehensive piece for the **San Francisco Observer** which essentially synthesized his earlier pieces, spiked with his own vivid descriptions of the Man Wolf attack, "the first" he'd seen with his own eyes. His conclusions were predictable. It was no superhero, and the adulation and fan worship should come to an end. Yet it had left us with many questions. Why had it been so easy for so many to embrace a creature so uncompromisingly cruel? Was the Man Wolf a throwback to a time when we had all been cruel and happy to be so?

Meanwhile the beast had made one last spectacular appearance deep in Mexico, slaying a murderer in Acapulco, and passed for the moment into oblivion.

Frank Vandover, tall, black-haired, with very fair skin and his handsome Cupid's-bow mouth, had returned with the Nordic giant Sergei Gorlagon— filling the house with quasi-humorous tales as to how they had baited police and witnesses alike in their journey south. Frank was certainly the most contemporary of the distinguished gentlemen, a wisecracking American with a Hollywood sheen, and a penchant for teasing Reuben mercilessly about his early exploits and tousling Stuart's hair. He called them the Wonder Puppies, and would have baited them into a race in the forest if Margon had not laid down the law.

Sergei was a brilliant scholar, with white hair, bushy white eyebrows, and clever, amused blue eyes. He had a voice somewhat like Thibault's, deep and resonant, and even a bit crackling. And he went into a delightful tirade about the brilliant and prophetic Teilhard de Chardin with Laura and Reuben, having a love of abstract theology and philosophy that surpassed theirs.

It was impossible to guess the age of any of these men, really, Reuben felt; and it was clearly not polite to ask. "How long have you been roaming the planet?" just did not seem an acceptable question, especially from what Frank persisted in calling a pup or a cub.

Any number of times, over lunch or dinner, or whilst gathered just for talking at the breakfast room table, two or more of these men would lapse into another tongue, apparently forgetting themselves, and it was always exciting to Reuben to hear those rapid confidential riffs that Reuben couldn't relate to any language he'd ever heard.

Margon and Felix frequently spoke a different tongue when they were alone. He'd overheard them without meaning to. And he had been tempted to ask if they all shared a common language, but that seemed—like asking their ages, or places of birth, or asking about the secret writing in Felix's diaries and letters—to be intrusive, something that was not done.

Stuart and Reuben both wanted to know who had introduced the term "Morphenkinder," or "Morphengift," and what other terms there had been, or might be now. But they figured this information and a great deal more would come in time.

People broke into sometime pairs. Reuben spent most of his time either with Laura or with Felix. And Laura loved Felix as well. Stuart adored Margon and never wanted to be separated from him. In fact, Stuart seemed to have fallen in love with Margon. Frank often went off with Sergei. And only Thibault seemed a genuine loner, or a man equally at home with any of the group. There developed a sympathy between Thibault and Laura. They all adored Laura, but Thibault enjoyed her company especially, and went walking in the woods with her, or on errands, or sometimes watched a film with her in the afternoons.

Reuben's entire family, as well as Celeste and Mort Keller, and Dr. Cutler, came north for Thanksgiving, joining Reuben, Laura, Stuart, and the distinguished gentlemen, and it was the greatest party the house had seen so far, and the most inescapable proof of the truth of Margon's maxim, that one must live in both worlds—the world of the human and the world of the beast—if one was to survive.

Frank surprised Reuben and his family by playing

the piano with spectacular skill after dinner, making a run at the Satie compositions that Reuben so loved and moving on into Chopin and other romantic compositions of his own.

Even Jim, who had been morose and withdrawn all evening, was drawn into conversation with Frank. And finally Jim played a composition he had written long ago, before the seminary, to accompany a poem by Rilke.

This was a painful moment for Reuben, sitting there in the music room on the small gilded music chair, listening to Jim lose himself in that brief, dark, melancholy melody, so like Satie, meditative, slow, and eloquent of pain.

Only Reuben knew what Jim knew. And Jim alone of all the guests and the family knew who the distinguished gentlemen were and what had happened to Stuart, and what had become of Reuben.

They did not talk, Reuben and Jim, all during that Thanksgiving Day or evening. There was just that moment in the candle-lighted music room when Jim had played that mournful music. And Reuben felt the shame of having done a terrible cruelty to Jim with his secrets and did not know what to do. There would come a time in the future when he would again meet with Jim to discuss all that had happened. But this was something he couldn't face right now. It was something he did not want right now.

Grace was relaxed with the company, but something was not the same between Reuben and his mother. She no longer struggled to understand what was happening to him, no, and seemed to have found a place in her own orderly mind for the phenomenon she'd been obsessed with for so long. But there was a shadow between her and Reuben. With all his might, he sought to pierce that thin darkness, to draw her close again as she'd been before; and perhaps to all the world, this effort appeared successful. But it was not. His mother sensed something, if only a decisive change in her son, and there lived in her bright, sparkling world now a nameless dread she couldn't confide to anyone.

Celeste and Mort Keller had a marvelous time, Celeste lecturing Reuben unendingly on the inadvisability of anyone his age "recollecting in tranquillity," and Mort and Reuben wandered in the oak forest talking of books and poets they both loved so much. Mort left the latest draft of his dissertation for Reuben to read.

After the holiday, the piano was moved into the great room, where there was an excellent spot for it near the doors to the conservatory, and the music room became a screening room, soon furnished with comfortable white leather couches and chairs so that the entire company could enjoy films and television together when they chose.

Reuben began to write a book. But it was not an

autobiography, or a novel. It was something quite pure and had to do with his own observations, his own deep suspicions that the highest truths a person could discover were rooted in the natural world.

Meantime the old dilapidated two-story cottage on the lower cliff beneath the point—the guest-house Reuben had seen with Marchent on their walk together—was being completely restored for Phil. Felix wrote the check for this and told Galton to spare no expense. Galton was in total awe of Felix because of the extent to which he resembled his late father, and Galton seemed fired with a new zeal to please the masters of Nideck Point.

Felix also introduced himself in the town of Nideck as the son of the late Felix Nideck, and invested in the Inn so that it did not have to be sold. He bought up the shops for the asking prices, planning to offer bargain rents to new merchants. It was important, he explained to Reuben, that the family exert some beneficent influence over the town. There was land around the town that could be subdivided and developed. Felix had thoughts on all of this.

Reuben was eager, dazzled. Felix surprised and delighted him by pointing out that his grandfather Spangler (Grace's father) had been famous during the last century for planned communities of amazing vision and scope, and they visited the websites together to study them. Who owned the land around Nideck? Felix owned the land under another name. Not to worry.

Reuben went to dinner with Felix at the house of the mayor of Nideck. On the Internet they soon found a quilt merchant eager to open up shop on the main street, together with a used book dealer, and a woman who sold antique dolls and toys out of her home.

"Hardly the beginnings of a metropolis," Felix confessed. "But it's an excellent start. The town needs some sort of small library, doesn't it? And a theater. How far from here must we go to see a new film?"

Meanwhile, as the Man Wolf receded rapidly into myth, the sale of Man Wolf T-shirts, mugs, and paraphernalia increased exponentially. There were Man Wolf tours operating in San Francisco, and Man Wolf costumes for sale. Of course a local tour company wanted to bring busloads to Nideck Point, but Reuben flatly refused and for the first time the south boundary of the property was being fenced.

Reuben wrote two long pieces for Billie on the lore of the werewolf throughout history, and on the iconic engravings of werewolves that he most liked, and some of the free circulating Man Wolf art that was easy to find and difficult to avoid.

Every night Reuben hunted the forests with Felix. They went farther and farther north into Humboldt County, hunting the fierce wild boar with its razor tusks, and on another occasion chasing down a powerful cat, bigger than the female Reuben had so handily killed on his own. Reuben did not like to hunt the herd animals, or the free-roaming deer and elk—because they weren't killers—though Felix reminded him that they often died by terribly violent and painful means.

Margon and Stuart went with them twice. Stuart was a lusty, blustering hunter, ravenous for any experience, and wanted to hunt the surf off the cliffs if only Margon would allow, but Margon would not. Margon seemed infatuated with Stuart, and gradually their conversations involved more questions from Margon about the world of today than Stuart had ever asked about the past or anything else.

Margon moved his room from the back of the house to the front, obviously to be closer to Stuart, and the two could be heard talking and arguing late into the night. They had periodic squabbles over clothing, Stuart taking Margon to purchase jeans and polo shirts, and Margon insisting that Stuart buy a three-piece suit and several dress shirts with French cuffs. But most of the time they were plainly and exuberantly happy.

Servants arrived from Europe, including a solemn quiet French-speaking man who had been Margon's valet, and a cheerful and uncomplaining old woman from England who cooked, cleaned, and baked bread. Thibault hinted that more would be coming.

Even before Thanksgiving, Reuben was hearing casual talk of a private airport above Fort Bragg that the others were using for short flights to distant hunting grounds. He was blazing with curiosity and so was Stuart. Stuart spent his days deep in study of werewolf lore, world history, evolution, civil and criminal law, human anatomy and endocrinology, archaeology, and foreign film.

Frequently the distinguished gentlemen disappeared into the Inner Sanctum, as they called it, to work with the ancient tablets which they were putting in some kind of order, and which they were not eager, for obvious reasons, to move again.

Felix spent much time trying to put his own galleries and libraries in reasonable order. And could often be found in the gabled attic over the master bedroom, reading in the very place where Reuben had found the little book of theology by Teilhard de Chardin.

Thanksgiving night, after the family left, Laura went south to spend a few days alone in her little house on the edge of Muir Woods. Reuben begged to go with her but she insisted that this was a trip she had to make alone. She wanted to visit the cemetery where her father and mother, her sister, and her daughter were buried. And when she came back, she said, she'd know what the future held for her. And so would Reuben.

He found this damned near unbearable. He was tempted more than once to drive south just to spy on Laura. But he knew that Laura needed this time. He did not so much as call her.

Finally, the distinguished gentlemen gathered up the cubs, and took them by plane for a hunt in the Mexican city of Juárez, just across the border from El Paso, Texas.

This was to be a hybrid hunt, according to Margon, and that meant clothing had to be worn—the predictable hooded sweatshirts and loose raincoats, baggy pants and loafers that would accommodate their transformed bodies.

Stuart and Reuben were both powerfully excited.

It was thrilling beyond their sharpest dreams— the hollow stripped-down cargo plane landing at the secret airstrip, the black SUVs tunneling through the jet-black night, and then the trip over the rooftops when the company spread out like cats in the dark, lured by the scent of the suffering girls and women held captive in a brothel-slave barracks from which they'd soon be smuggled into the United States under threat of torture and death.

They cut the power to the barracks before they invaded it, and quickly locked the women away for their own safety.

Reuben had never dreamed of such carnage, such abandon, such a massacre in the low concrete building, its escape routes latched from the outside, and its vicious male inmates scrambling like rats in the wet slippery corridors and dead-end rooms—to escape the remorseless sharp-toothed enemy that descended on them.

The building shook with the roars of the Morphenkinder, the shrieks and bellowing of dying men, and the screams of terrified women huddled in their filthy dormitory.

At last the stench of evil had died out; in remote corners of the compound, Morphenkinder still feasted, chomping on the remains. Stuart, the great shaggy Boy Wolf, in his long open coat, stood dazed staring at the bodies scattered around him. And the women had ceased their wailing.

Now it was time for them all to slip away—for the women to be freed in the blackness to stumble towards the light never knowing the identity of the hulking hooded giants who had avenged them. And the sure-footed hunters were gone, vaulting over the rooftops once more, their paws and garments stained with blood, their mouths smeared with it, their stomachs full.

They dozed like a litter, piled on one another in the hold of the plane. Somewhere over the Pacific they dropped their bloody garments into the sea, and emerged into the chill windy night of Mendocino County in the fresh rags they'd taken for their return—still bleary-eyed, glutted, and at peace, or so it seemed, silent on the short ride to Nideck Point as the rain, the familiar, relentless California rain, beat upon the windshield.

"Now that was hunting!" said Stuart, staggering in a half sleep towards the back door. And throwing back his head he let out a wolfen howl that echoed off the stone walls of the house, the others dissolving into soft laughter.

"Soon," said Margon, "we hunt the jungles of Colombia."

Reuben dreamed, as he dragged his exhausted limbs up the stairs, that Laura would be there waiting for him, but she was not. Only her fragrance was there in the soft down comforter and pillows. He took one of her flannel nightgowns from the closet, and held it in his arms, resolving to dream of her.

Hours later, he awoke to the miracle of the blue sky over the Pacific and the miracle of the dark blue water glittering and dancing under the sun.

Showering and dressing quickly, he went out to walk in the bright and glorious light, marveling at the common spectacle of snow-white clouds moving beyond the gables of the house which rose above him as severe and strong as battlements.

One had to live on this bleak and chilly coast to understand the full miracle of a clear day when the marine mists were simply gone as if their wintry reign had finally ended.

It seemed a lifetime ago that he had come to this very terrace with Marchent Nideck, and he had looked up at this house and asked of it that it give him the darkness, the depth, he so needed. Be the minor-key music in my life, he had said to it, and he had felt certain the house answered him, promising revelations of which he could not dream.

He walked across the windswept flags, straight into the brisk and fresh ocean wind, until he stood at the old broken balustrade that separated the terrace from the edge of the cliff, and that narrow perilous path that led down to the ribbon of beach below with its forlorn rocks and bleached driftwood.

The sound of the surf swallowed him whole. He felt weightless, and as if the wind would support him if he let himself go, with arms out towards the sky.

To the right of him rose the dark green tree-shrouded bluffs that sheltered the redwood forest. And to the south the twisted Monterey cypress and scrub oak that the wind had turned into tortured sculpture.

A tragic happiness took hold of him, a deep recognition that he loved what he was, loved it, loved the mad hunt in the filthy corridors of the brothel in Juárez, loved the mad sprinting through the clean forest north, loved the feel of the victim in his teeth, or the beast struggling so desperately and vainly to get away from him.

But there was a deep awareness in him that this was only the beginning. He felt young, powerful, and safe from a reckoning. He felt he had time to discover how and why he was wrong, and why he must change or give up the Wolf Gift that had extinguished so many other passions in him.

Heaven and hell wait for the young. Heaven and hell hover beyond the ocean before us and the sky spreading above us.

So the sun shines in the Garden of Pain. In the Garden of Discovery.

He saw the face of his brother on Thanksgiving night, saw Jim's sad weary eyes, and his heart broke, as if his brother were more important than God himself, or God himself was speaking through Jim as he might speak through anyone put in our inevitable or accidental path, anyone who threatened to call us back to ourselves, who looked at us with eyes that reflected a heart as broken as our own, as fragile, as disappointed.

The wind was icing him now all over. His ears were cold and the fingers with which he covered his face were so cold he could scarce move them. And yet it felt so good, so lovely, lovely as it felt to feel nothing like this at all when the wolf garb protected him.

He turned and looked back again at the house, at the high ivy-covered walls, and the smoke from the chimneys winding skyward—to be snatched by the wind, to be dissolved into invisibility.

**Dear God, help me. Do not forget me on this tiny cinder lost in a galaxy that is lost—a heart no bigger than a speck of dust beating, beating against death, against meaninglessness, against guilt, against sorrow.**

He did lean into the wind; he did let it hold him there, and keep him from falling into space, keep him from tumbling down over the balustrade and cliff, down and down and down towards the rocky surf.

He took a deep breath, and the tears came into his

eyes, and he felt them blasted off his cheeks by this same wind that was supporting him.

"Lord, forgive me my blasphemous soul," he whispered, his voice breaking. "But I thank You with all my heart for the gift of life, for all the blessings You have rained down upon me, for the miracle of life in all its forms—and Lord, I thank You for the Wolf Gift!"

*The End*

August 2011
Palm Desert,
California

# LIKE WHAT YOU'VE READ?

If you enjoyed this large print edition of
**THE WOLF GIFT,**
here are two of Anne Rice's latest
bestsellers also available in large print.

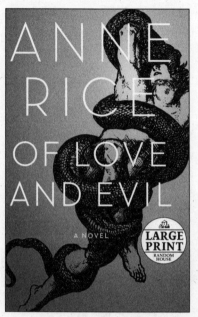

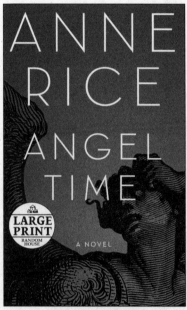

**OF LOVE AND EVIL**
(paperback)
978-0-7393-7790-1
($25.00/28.95C)

**ANGEL TIME**
(paperback)
978-0-7393-7735-2
($26.00/$32.00C)

Large print books are available wherever books
are sold and at many local libraries.